A BRIDE FOR THE RUNAWAY GROOM

BY
SCARLET WILSON

Published in Great Britain 2015
by Mills & Boon, an imprint of Harlequin (UK) Limited,
Eton House, 18-24 Paradise Road, Richmond, Surrey, TW9 1SR

© 2015 Scarlet Wilson

ISBN: 978-0-263-25133-3

23-0515

Printed and bound in Spain
by CPI, Barcelona

Scarlet Wilson writes romances and medical romances for Mills & Boon. She lives on the west coast of Scotland with her fiancé and their two sons. She loves to hear from readers and can be reached via her website, scarlet-wilson.com.

For two gorgeous brides who are now two fabulous mummies, Carissa Hyndman and Hayley Dickson.

And to my fellow authors
Jessica Gilmore and Sophie Pembroke
for making this such fun!

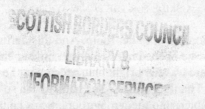
CHAPTER ONE

SOMETHING WASN'T RIGHT.

No, scratch that. Something was very, very wrong.

Everything should be perfect. Her sister's wedding yesterday had been beautiful. A picture-perfect day with a bride and groom that truly loved each other. It was a joy to be a part of a day like that.

But, by midnight, the days of jet lag that she'd been ignoring had finally caught up with her and she'd staggered to bed and collapsed in a heap, catching up on some much-needed sleep.

Her new brother-in-law, Seb, had a house to die for. Hawksley Castle, a home part Norman, part Tudor and part Georgian. The room she was in was sumptuous and spacious with the most comfortable bed in the world.

At least it would be—if she were in that bed alone.

She could hear breathing, heavy breathing, sometimes accompanied with a tiny noise resembling a snore.

Right now, she was afraid to move.

She hadn't drunk much at all yesterday—only two glasses of wine. Because of the jet lag they'd hit hard. But not so hard she'd invited someone into her bed.

She'd attended her sister's wedding alone. No plus-one for Rose.

There had been no flirtations, no alluring glances and

no invitations back to her room. And this definitely was *her* room. She opened her eyes just a little to check.

Yes, there was her bright blue suitcase in the corner of the room. Thank goodness. She hadn't been so tired that she'd stumbled into the wrong room. Seb's house was so big it might have happened.

But it hadn't.

So, who was heavy breathing in her bed?

She didn't want to move. Didn't want to alert the intruder to the fact that she was awake. She could feel the dip in the bed at her back. Turning around and coming face-to-face with a perfect stranger wasn't in her plans.

She needed to think about this carefully.

She edged her leg towards the side of the bed. Stealth mode. Then, cringed. No satin negligee. No pyjamas. Just the underwear she'd had on under her bridesmaid dress that was lying in a crumpled heap at the bottom of the bed. Brilliant. Just brilliant.

Her painted toenails mocked her. As did her obligatory fake tan. Vulnerable. That was how she felt. And Rose Huntingdon-Cross didn't take kindly to anyone who made her feel like that.

Just then the stranger moved. A hand slid over her skin around her hip and settled on her stomach. She stifled a yelp as her breath caught in her throat. Something resembling a comfortable moan came from behind her as the stranger decided to cuddle in closer. The sensation of an unidentified warm body next to hers was more than she could take.

She slid her legs and body as silently as possible out of the bed. The only thing close to hand that could resemble a weapon was a large pink vase. Her heart was thudding against her chest. How dared someone creep into bed with her and grope her?

She held her breath as her feet came into contact with the soft carpet and she automatically grasped the vase in both hands.

She spun around to face the intruder. In other circumstances, this would be comical. But, right now, it felt anything but comical. She was practically naked and a strange man had crept into bed beside her. How dared he?

Who on earth was he? She didn't recognise him at all. But the wedding of an earl and a celebrity couple's daughter was full of people she couldn't even take a guess at. Undoubtedly he was some hanger-on.

If her rational head were in place she would grab her clothes and run from the room, getting someone to come and help with the intruder.

But Rose hated being thought of as a shrinking violet. For once, she wanted to sort things for herself.

She padded around to the other side of the bed in her bare feet, hoisting the vase above her head just as the stranger gave a little contented moan.

It was all she needed to give her a burst of unforgiving adrenaline. The initial fear rapidly turned to anger and she brought the vase down without a second thought. 'Who do you think you are? What are you doing in my bed? How dare you touch me?' she screamed.

The vase shattered into a million pieces. The guy's eyes shot open and in one movement he was on his feet—fists raised and swaying.

He blinked for a few seconds—big, bright blue eyes with a darker rim that didn't look the least bit predatory, but a whole lot shell-shocked—then dropped his fists and clutched his head.

'Violet, what on earth are you doing? Are you crazy?' He groaned and swayed again, one of his hands reaching out to grab the wall—leaving a bloodstained mark on the expensive wallpaper.

She couldn't breathe. Her heart was thudding against her chest and her stomach was doing crazy flip-flops. 'What do you mean, *Violet*? I'm not Violet.'

This just wasn't possible. Okay, Violet was her identical twin. They didn't usually look so similar, but a few years stateside and not seeing each other on a daily basis meant she'd shown up with an identical hairstyle to her sister.

This clown actually thought he was in bed with her sister? What kind of a fool did that?

He was still shaking his head. It was almost as if his vision hadn't quite come into focus. 'But of course you're Violet,' he said.

'No. I'm not. And stop dripping blood on the carpet!'

They both stared down at the probably priceless carpet that had two large blood drips, and the remnants of the vase at his feet and across the bed.

He grabbed his shirt from the chair next to the bed and pressed it to his head. It was the first time she'd even noticed his clothes—discarded in the same manner as her yellow and white bridesmaid dress.

His eyes seemed to come into focus and he stepped forward, reaching one hand out to her shoulder. He squinted. 'Darn it. You're not Violet, are you? You haven't got her mole on your shoulder.'

His finger came into contact with her skin and she jumped back. One part of her knew that this 'intruder' wasn't any danger to her. But another part of her was still mad about being mistaken for her twin and being felt up by her twin's boyfriend. How on earth could this be explained? This guy was obviously another one of Violet's losers.

Violet burst through the door. 'What's going on? Rose,

are you okay?' Her eyes darted from one to the other. The guy, in his wrinkled boxer shorts and shirt pressed to his forehead, and Rose, in her bridesmaid underwear. The broken vase seemed to completely pass her by.

She wrinkled her nose in disgust and shook her head. 'Will? My sister? Oh, tell me you didn't?'

They didn't sound like words of jealousy—just words of pure exasperation.

She threw her hands in the air and spun around, muttering under her breath. 'Runaway groom my sister and I'll kill you.'

Rose was feeling decidedly exposed. The only thing she could find to hold in front of herself was her crumpled bridesmaid dress.

Whoever he was, he obviously wasn't Violet's boyfriend—not with that kind of reaction. But did that make things better or worse? She'd still been groped by an absolute stranger.

He wobbled again and sagged down into the chair strewn with his clothes, arching one eyebrow at her. 'So, crazy twin. Do you assault every man you meet?'

'Only every man who climbs into my bed uninvited and cops a feel!'

'Well, lucky them.' He sounded oh, so unimpressed. Then he frowned. 'Did I touch you? I'm sorry. I was sleeping. I didn't even realise I'd done that.'

The blood was starting to soak through his shirt. She cringed. Maybe the vase had been a bit over the top. And at least she'd got some kind of apology.

She stepped forward and took the shirt from his hand. 'Here, let me.' She pressed down firmly on his forehead.

'Youch! Take it easy.'

She shook her head. 'The forehead's a very vascular

area. It bleeds easily and needs a bit of pressure to get the bleeding to stop.'

'How on earth would you know that?'

'Friends with children who seem to bang their foreheads against every piece of furniture I own.'

He gave her half a smile. It was the first time she really noticed how handsome he was. There were no flabby abs here. Just a whole load of nicely defined muscles. With those killer blue eyes and thick dark hair he was probably quite a hit with the ladies.

A prickle flooded over her skin. In the cold light of day this guy seemed vaguely familiar.

'How do you know Violet?' she asked.

He winced as she pressed a little harder. 'She's my best friend.'

Rose sucked in a deep breath. Things were starting to fall into place for her. Because she'd been working in New York she hadn't met Violet's best friend for the last few years. But she had heard a lot about him.

She pulled her hand back from his forehead. Now she understood what Violet had said. '*You're* the Runaway Groom?' She was so shocked she dropped her dress.

A single dark red drop of blood snaked down his forehead as he looked at her in disgust.

'I hate that nickname.'

The Runaway Groom. No wonder he looked vaguely familiar. He'd been on the front page of just about every newspaper in the world. Self-made millionaire Will Carter had been famously engaged three—or was it four?—times. He'd even made it down the aisle once before turning on his heel and bolting.

The press should hate him. But they didn't. They loved him and ate it up every time he fell in love and got engaged again. Because Will was handsome. Will was charming. And Will was sitting semi-naked in front of her.

She was trying so hard not to look at the abs and the scattering of dark hair that seemed to lead the eye in one direction.

She gave herself a mental shake just as a heavy drop of blood slid past his eye and down the side of his face. She leaned over to catch it with the shirt, just as he lifted his hand to try and brush it away.

The contact of their skin sent a tingle straight up her arm, making her heart rate do a strange pitter-patter. All the little hairs on her arms stood on end and she automatically sucked in her stomach.

'Look, I'm sorry about your head. But I woke up and there was a strange man in bed with me—then you touched me and I was frightened.' And she hated saying those words out loud but since she'd caused bodily harm to her sister's best friend it seemed warranted. She raised her eyebrows. 'You're lucky it was only a vase.'

His gaze was still on her. 'So you're Rose?' It wasn't really a question—more an observation and it was obvious from his expression that a million thoughts were currently spinning through his brain. What on earth had Violet told him about her?

He looked at the fragments beneath his feet and gave a half-smile. A cute little dimple appeared in one cheek. 'Oh, you're definitely not going to be Seb's favourite sister-in-law. At a rough guess that's over two hundred years old.'

A sick feeling passed over her. Defence was her automatic position. 'Who puts a two-hundred-year-old vase in a guest bedroom? He must be out of his mind.'

He shrugged. 'Your sister obviously doesn't think so. She just married him.'

Daisy, Rose's youngest sister, was still floating happily along on cloud two hundred and nine. And Seb seemed a really sweet guy. Just as well since she'd told her sisters just before the wedding that two were about to become three. The first baby in the family for more than twenty years. Rose couldn't wait to meet her niece or nephew, and she was doing her best to ignore the vaguest flicker of jealousy she'd felt when Daisy had told her.

She frowned. How much did a two-hundred-year-old vase cost anyway? She lifted the shirt again and winced. 'Hmm.'

His eyebrows shot up. 'What's "hmm"?'

'*Hmm* means it's deeper than it originally looked and I think you might need stitches. Maybe I can get you a packet of frozen peas from the kitchen?' She paused and looked around. 'Do you even know where the kitchen is in here?' Even as she said the words she almost laughed out loud. Seb's kitchen would probably spontaneously combust if someone even said the words 'frozen peas' in it. Daisy really had moved into a whole different world here.

He shook his head and placed his hand over hers. His hand was nice and warm, whereas hers was cold and clammy. Another thing to annoy her. He wasn't nearly as worked up as she was. This was all just another day in the life of the Runaway Groom. How often did he wake up next to a strange woman?

'What were you playing at anyway? You might be Violet's best friend but why on earth would you be climbing into bed with my sister? It's obvious from Violet's reaction that there's nothing going on between you. What on earth were you doing?'

Will gestured his head towards her suitcase. 'If I'm going to need stitches why don't you get dressed? You'll need to take me to the hospital.'

He hadn't answered her question. Did he think she hadn't noticed? Of course she had.

And the assumption that she'd take him to the hospital made her skin bristle.

All of a sudden she was conscious of her distinct lack of clothes. She slid her hand out from under his and moved over to her suitcase, cursing herself when she remembered he'd just had a big view of her backside.

Still, if he sometimes bunked in with Violet, then he was used to being around her sister in a semi-naked state. She glanced backwards. He didn't seem to have even noticed. Was she relieved or mad? She couldn't work it out. Apart from a few freckles, moles and little scars—one of which he'd already noted—she and her sister were virtually identical. Maybe that was why he wasn't looking? He'd seen it all before.

She grabbed a summer dress from her case and pulled it over her head. A little rumpled and yesterday's underwear still in place. Not the best scenario. But she didn't fancy fishing through her smalls to find a new set while he sat and watched in his jersey boxer shorts that left nothing to the imagination.

'Don't you have a bride in waiting that can take you to hospital?'

He scowled at her. 'Not even funny, Rose. You work in PR, don't you? Surely you know better than to believe everything you read in the papers?'

His words were dripping with sarcasm. The nerve she'd apparently just touched ran deep.

She folded her arms across her chest. 'But I thought most of the time you sold those stories and worked them in your favour.'

'What made you think that?' he snapped.

'Oh, I don't know. The ten-page photo spreads in *Ex-*

clusive magazine. How many of them have you featured in now?'

He gritted his teeth together. '*Not* my idea.'

It was good to see him uncomfortable. Waking up with a strange guy in your bed was horribly intimidating. To say nothing of the discomfort and embarrassment. What if she snored—or made strange noises in her sleep?

And he still hadn't answered the question about sleeping with her sister. What exactly was the deal? His eyes were still fixed furiously on her and the blood was soaking through his shirt. She decided to give him a little leeway.

She gestured towards him. 'What about you? You can't wear that shirt. Where are your clothes?'

He wrinkled his nose. 'I'm not sure. I ran in here at the last minute yesterday. I think my bag might be in Violet's room.'

'Violet's room?' She said it bluntly, hoping he'd take the hint and decide he should go there. But if he did, he ignored it.

'Yeah, would you mind running along and grabbing something for me?' He had that smile on his face. The one that was usually plastered all over the front page of a magazine, or on his face when he was charming some reporter. It was almost as if someone had flicked a little switch and he'd just fallen into his default position. His voice and smile washed over her like a warm summer's day. Boy, this guy was good. But she was determined not to fall for his charms.

'I will. But only because I've probably scarred you for life. I'm not Violet. I'm not your best friend—or your bed buddy. Once I've taken you to the hospital, we're done. Are we clear?'

His Mediterranean-sea-blue eyes lost all their warmth.

'Crystal.' He waited until she'd reached the door before he added, 'And you're right. You're not Violet.'

He watched her retreating back as she stomped out of the door. His head was definitely muggy and he wasn't quite sure if it was from the alcohol last night or the head injury this morning.

Part of him felt guilty, part of him felt enraged and part of him was cringing.

Last night was a bit of a blur. He'd just made it to the wedding on time and hadn't eaten a thing beforehand. His charity commitments were hectic and he was anxious not to let people down, which meant he'd been pulling on his tie and jacket in the sprawling car park at Hawksley Castle. A business call had come in just as dinner had arrived so he'd missed most of that, too. Then the party had truly started. And Violet had mentioned something about staying in her room as she'd fluttered past in her yellow and white bridesmaid dress.

A bridesmaid dress he'd definitely seen on the floor as he'd stumbled into the room. She'd been sleeping peacefully with her back to him and he hadn't even thought to wake her. Actually, he knew better. If he'd shaken Violet awake to let her know he was there she would have killed him with her bare hands.

Maybe the sisters had more in common than he thought?

It was strange. He'd never once considered Violet in a romantic sense. They'd clicked as friends from the start. Good friends. Nothing more. Nothing less.

He trusted her. Which was a lot more than he could say of some people. She gave it to him straight. There was no flirting, nothing ambiguous. Just plenty of laughs, plenty of support and plenty of ear bashing.

But Violet's identical twin… Well, she was a whole different story.

It didn't matter they looked so similar it was scary. They were two totally different people. No wonder they got annoyed when people mixed them up. And you couldn't get much more of a blunder than the one he'd just made.

But it wasn't the blunder that was fixating in his head. It was that little missing mole on her left shoulder. The memory of her skin beneath the palm of his hand. And the site of her tanned skin and rounded backside when she'd turned to get dressed. They seemed to have imprinted on his brain. Every time he squeezed his eyes shut, that was the picture he saw inside his head.

He stood up and walked over to the en suite bathroom. He grimaced when he saw his face. It was hardly a spectacular sight. His shirt—worn once—was ruined. Not that he couldn't afford to buy another one. But he'd picked this one up especially for the wedding. Even millionaires didn't like waste.

He stuck his head back out of the bathroom door. Maybe he should put his trousers back on? Meeting someone for the first time dressed only in jersey boxers was a bit much—even for him. But every time he lifted his hand from his forehead the blood started gushing again. Struggling into a crumpled pair of trousers one-handed was more than he could think about.

He couldn't help but smile. He knew Violet well. Her sister Rose? He didn't know her at all. This was their first meeting. And she obviously wasn't bowled over by him.

Will wasn't used to that. Women normally loved him. And he normally loved women. This was a whole new experience for him.

There was more to Rose Huntingdon-Cross than met the eye. And he'd already seen more than his fair share.

He could even forgive the Runaway Groom comments. Violet said her sister was a PR genius and she'd handled the whole publicity for their father's upcoming tour and charity concert.

Maybe he should get to know Rose a little better?

Rose strode down the hall. She could feel the fury building in her chest. The audacity of the guy. Who did he think he was?

She pushed open the door of her sister's room. 'Violet? What on earth is going on? Why would the Runaway Groom be in bed with me—and think I was you? Why would you be in bed with that guy? And why would there be touching?'

Violet was leaning back on her bed drinking tea, eating chocolate and reading a celebrity magazine. She lifted her eyebrows at her sister and started laughing. 'You didn't hook up with Will?'

'No! I didn't hook up with Will! I woke up and he was lying next to me. He thought I was you!'

Violet folded her arms across her chest and looked highly amused. 'He doesn't like the Runaway Groom tag.'

Rose rolled her eyes. 'So I gathered.'

Violet grinned. 'Will copped a feel?'

Rose shivered and waved her hand. 'Don't even bring that up.'

Violet shrugged and continued to drink her tea. 'So, it was a simple mistake. I'd say send him back along the corridor, but…' she paused and raised her eyebrows, giving Rose that oh, so knowing smile '…I'm thinking this looks a whole lot more interesting than that.'

'What's that supposed to mean?' Rose was getting mad now. Neither Violet nor Will was really giving anything away about their relationship and she couldn't understand why it irked her so much.

'Violet, come and take your plaything back. I don't have time for this. I've got a hundred things to sort out for Dad's tour. Another set of wedding rings to make for a couple who are getting married in two weeks. And a runaway groom who needs his head stitched. Be a good sister and take him to the hospital for me?'

Violet shook her head and jumped off the bed. 'Not a chance, dear sister. You caused the injury. You can try and make it up to Will. He can be very good company, I'll have you know.'

She gave Rose a little nod of approval. 'By the way, Daisy and Seb's wedding rings? Probably the nicest I've ever seen. That's what you should be doing. You're wasting your talent running Dad's tours for him.'

Rose sighed and sat down on the edge of the bed. A little surge of pride rushed through her chest. Violet's opinion mattered to her. 'Making those rings was the best thing I've ever done, Vi. I know I've made lots of different pieces for people before. But making something for your sister?' She smiled and gave her head a little shake. 'And watching the person she loves with her whole heart give it to her and knowing that she'll wear it for a lifetime? You just can't beat that.'

A flicker of something passed over Violet's face. Not annoyance. Not frustration. Just…something.

'I'll make your wedding jewellery for you, too,' she added quickly.

Violet let out a laugh. 'I'll need to find a groom first. In fact, we both do. Our baby sister's gone and beat us to it.'

Rose leaned backwards on the bed, propping herself up with her elbows. 'I know.' She lifted one hand up. 'And she's done it in such style. Do we really need to call her

Lady Holgate now, or Countess? Because I can tell you right now—' she shook her head '—it's never, *ever* going to happen.'

The two of them laughed out loud and collapsed back onto the bed. 'Daisy Waisy it stays.'

Rose turned her head to look at her sister, leaning over and picking up a strand of her blonde hair. 'You know, Vi, we almost look like twins,' she said sarcastically. 'We'll have to do something about these hairdos.'

Violet sighed. 'I know. I couldn't believe it when I saw you the other day. Maybe I'll go back to curls.'

'Don't you dare. That frizzy perm was the worst thing I've ever seen.'

Violet laughed and shook her head. 'Oh, no, the worst thing *I've* ever seen was you kissing Cal Ellerslie at that party years ago.'

Rose's shoulders started shaking with laughter and she shuddered. 'Oh, yuck, don't remind me. I still feel sick at the thought of that. He was all tongue. The guy had no idea what he was doing.'

She turned on her side and rested her head on her hand. 'Is there anyone you've been kissing lately?'

Violet sighed again. 'You're joking. There are absolutely no decent men around.'

'What about Will—your runaway groom?' She was prying and she knew it. But she couldn't help but ask the question out loud. Violet had been talking about Will for months. Maybe Rose just hadn't been paying enough attention.

But Violet's eyes widened. 'Are you joking—Will?' She let out a snort. 'No way. I mean, I love him to bits—just not like that. Never like that. I trust Will. Completely. I've been in his company lots of times, sometimes even raging drunk. He's a gentleman through and through. He's the kind of guy that sees you home, puts you to bed and stays with you until morning.' She wrinkled her nose. 'In fact, I've done the same for him. We're good company for each other.' She smiled. 'And every time he gets engaged, I get to buy a new wedding outfit with matching shoes and bag. What more could a girl want? Even if they never get an airing.'

Rose rolled her eyes. She knew better than most that Violet couldn't care less about wedding outfits, shoes and handbags. She was much more down-to-earth than most celebrities. They all were. 'Yeah, right.'

But Violet had drifted off. Her eyes were fixed on the ornately decorated ceiling, carved with cherubs. 'There's just no spark between us, Posey. None. Not even a little zing, a little tingle.' She turned her head to face her sister on the bed. 'You know what I mean?'

Oh, boy, did she. She'd felt that little tingle shoot up her arm like an electric shock. She blinked. Her sister was looking at her with her identical big blue eyes. They were unyielding. Their bond was strong. She'd always been able to see inside Rose's head—even when Rose didn't want her to.

Rose shifted uncomfortably on the bed. But Violet blinked. For once, she was lost in her own little world. 'I mean, there's got to be someone out there.' She regained her focus. 'For both of us,' she added quickly.

Rose smiled. It was the first time she'd ever seen her sister actually contemplate a future partner. Maybe the fact their younger sister, Daisy, had beat them both up the aisle and was going to be a mother had made their biological clocks start to tick. It was an interesting concept. And one she wasn't quite sure she was ready to explore.

Coming back to England had been hard enough. Visiting in the last three years had been painful. Everything seemed to be a reminder of that dreadful night a few years ago. The one that was imprinted on her brain like a painful branding.

But sisters were sisters. She couldn't really stay away too long. She still spoke to, Skyped or emailed her sisters every day. Not even an ocean—or a tragic death—could come between them.

But now her father's tour was coming back to Britain. It was big news for the band. A relaunch after a few quiet years—with only an annual charity concert—followed by a brand-new album. And she had to be here, in England, to deal with the last few PR issues. Her quietly building wedding jewellery business would have to be pushed to the side for a few months. She needed time to focus on the final details of the tour.

The last thing she needed was any distractions. And that was exactly what the Runaway Groom was—a distraction. Even if he did make her arm tingle.

Rose rolled off the bed. She hated that little feeling at the pit of her stomach. The one that had given a little flutter when her sister had assured her there was nothing between her and Will.

Nothing at all. Funny how those words were so strangely satisfying.

CHAPTER TWO

THE FROZEN PEAS were a godsend. It appeared that Hawksley Castle did have some—even though Rose had doubted. The lump on his head wasn't quite so big and, as long as he kept them pressed to his head, the bleeding stopped.

He'd managed to struggle into the T-shirt and jeans that Rose had brought from his bag in Violet's room. But instead of leaving him alone to get dressed, she'd leaned against the wall with her arms folded.

'What, no privacy?'

'From the guy who was in my bed? You lost the privacy privilege a while ago, mister. Anyway, hurry up. I've got things to do today.'

'Really? I would have thought after your sister's wedding you might want to chill out a bit.'

She crossed the room as he slid his feet into his training shoes. 'I'd like to have time to chill out, but I don't. I've got the final touches to make to my dad's tour, then I need to finish some jewellery for another bride.'

He looked up. 'Ready. Do you know where the nearest hospital is?'

She nodded. 'I know this area well. Let's go.'

They walked down the corridor and out of the front doors of Hawksley Castle. She opened the door of a pale blue Rolls-Royce and nodded at him to get in the other side.

Will couldn't hide the smile on his face as he slid into the cream leather seat. 'Didn't take you for this kind of car,' he said in amusement.

She started the engine and frowned at him. 'What kind of car did you think I'd drive?'

'Something sporty. Something small. Probably something red.' He looked thoughtful for a second. 'Probably one of those new-style Minis.' He wasn't revealing that his identical Rolls-Royce was parked a few cars down in the car park.

She pulled out of the car park and down the sweeping mile-long driveway. 'This is my dad's. You forget, I've been in New York for the last three years. There isn't much point in me having a car here right now, so I just borrow one when I'm home.'

'And he lets you?' Rick Cross's car collection was legendary. 'How many does he actually have?'

She laughed. And it was the first genuine laugh he'd heard from her. It was beautiful. Light and frivolous. Two things that Rose didn't really emanate. 'You mean, how many does Mum think he has—or how many does he *actually* have?'

Now Will started laughing. 'Really? How does he manage that? Where on earth can he hide cars from her?'

She shrugged. 'He's a master. We've got more than one home. You'll have seen the garages at Huntingdon Hall. There are eighteen cars there. Four in New York. Three in Mustique. And—' she glanced over her shoulder as if to check if someone was there '—another twelve at an unspecified location in London.'

'Another twelve? You've got to be joking.'

'I never joke about my father.' She shrugged. 'What can I say? It's his money. He can spend it how he likes. Same with my mother. They have beautiful homes, there might even have been the odd nip and tuck here and there, and to the outside world they seem like a pretty frivolous couple.'

He could hear the edge in her voice. Just as he'd heard the same tone in Violet's voice on a few occasions. He'd met Rick and Sherry. They seemed like regular, nice folks. Polite, well-mannered, and they obviously loved their daughters.

'So, what's the problem?'

Her head whipped around. 'Who said there was a problem?'

'You did. Just now.'

'I did not.'

He sighed. 'You and Violet are more alike than you think. She does that, too—starts talking about your parents and then starts to say strange things.'

'She does?' Her voice was a little squeaky and her knuckles turned white on the steering wheel. It was nothing to do with her driving. And nothing to do with the car.

The Rolls-Royce was eating up the country roads with ease. It should be a pleasant enough drive. But Rose looked tense.

'You must deal with the press all the time. Why does it annoy you when they describe your parents as frivolous?'

'Because they're not really. Not at heart. Yes, they spend money. But they also give a lot away. Lots of celebrities do. My mum and dad both support lots of charities.'

He nodded. 'Yeah, I remember. I've seen her in the magazines and doing TV interviews.'

'That's what you see. What you don't see is all the work they don't let the public know about. My dad does a lot of work for one of the Alzheimer's charities. He doesn't tell anyone about it. My mum works on a helpline for children. She sometimes does a twelve-hour shift and then goes out to do her other charity work.'

'That sounds great. So, why are you annoyed?' He couldn't understand why either of the sisters would be unhappy about their mum and dad doing good work.

'Because they are so insistent that no one finds out. Sometimes I think they're working themselves into the ground. To the world they seem quite frivolous. But they're not like that in person.'

'I don't get it. Why the big secret? What's the big deal?' His arm was beginning to ache from holding it against his head. He might be a millionaire himself, but even he didn't want to risk bleeding all over the inside of Rick's precious car.

Rose turned the car onto a main road, following signs toward the hospital. 'Because they don't want people to know. My uncle—my dad's brother—has Alzheimer's. He developed it really early. It's in my dad's family and he says it's private. He doesn't want people knowing that part of his life and invading my uncle's privacy. Mum's the same. She says the calls from the kids are all confidential. If people knew she worked there, the phone line would probably get a whole host of crank calls that would jam the lines.'

He nodded. 'I get it. Then, the kids that needed to, couldn't get through.'

She pulled into the hospital car park. 'Exactly.'

'So, your parents do something good.' He waited while she pulled into a parking space. 'I can relate to that.'

'You can?' She seemed surprised.

'Yeah. I do a lot of work for one of the homeless charities. But it doesn't get a lot of good publicity. It's something I need to think about.' He gave her a smile. 'Maybe you could give me some advice? You do PR for your father? Maybe you could tell me what I should be doing to raise the profile of the charity.'

She gave the slightest shake of her head. 'Sorry, Will, but this is it for me. I've got a hundred and one things to do in the next few weeks. I don't even know how long I'll be staying. Once your head is stitched I need to get back to work.'

He climbed out of the car, still pressing the now unfrozen peas to his head. Rose was intriguing him. He could use someone to give him PR advice. Someone who knew how to try and spin the press. Maybe he should try and persuade her?

The woman behind the desk didn't even blink when he appeared at the desk. 'Name?'

'Will Carter.'

She lifted her eyebrows and gave a half-smile. 'Oh, it's you. Did one of those brides finally give you the smack you deserved?'

He couldn't help but smile. 'No. I'm all out of brides at the moment—have been for a little while.' He glanced towards Rose, who was looking distinctly uncomfortable. 'It was just a friend who did this.'

A nurse walked towards them and the receptionist handed her a card. 'Will Carter, the Runaway Groom. Head injury.' She rolled her eyes. 'What a surprise.'

The nurse gave a little grin and nodded her head. 'This way.'

'Come on.' He followed the nurse down the corridor and gestured to Rose to follow them.

Her footsteps faltered. It was obvious she didn't really want to come along. But Will had just been hit by a brainwave. And a perfect way to make it work.

'I'll just sit in the waiting room,' she said quickly. She'd no wish to see Will Carter getting his head stitched. Even the thought of it made her feel a bit queasy.

'No, you won't.' His voice was smooth as silk. 'I want you with me.'

The nurse's eyebrows rose just a little as she pulled back the cubicle curtains. 'Climb up on the trolley, Mr Carter, and I'll go and get some supplies to clean your wound.'

She disappeared for a second while Rose stood shifting self-consciously on her feet, not quite sure where to put herself.

'What's wrong, Rose? Don't like hospitals?'

'What? No, I don't mind them. I just would have preferred to sit in the waiting room.'

He lifted the peas from his head. 'Don't you want to see the damage you've done?'

Her face paled. 'But I didn't mean to. I mean, you know that. And what did you expect? You climbed into bed with a perfect stranger.'

The nurse cleared her throat loudly as she wheeled the dressing trolley into the cubicle.

Rose felt the colour flood into her cheeks. Twenty-seven years old and she was feeling around five. 'I didn't mean… I mean, nothing happened…' She was stumbling over her words, her brain so full of embarrassment that she couldn't make sense to herself, let alone to anyone else.

The nurse waved her hand as she walked to the sink and started scrubbing her hands. 'Everything's confidential here. My lips are sealed.'

'But there's nothing to—'

Will was laughing. He leaned over and grabbed her hand. 'Leave it, Rose. You're just making things worse.' As he relaxed back against the trolley, his hand tugged her a little closer. There was a gleam of amusement in his eyes. Mr Charming wasn't flustered at all and it irked her.

'I kind of like seeing you like this.' Even his voice sounded amused. She'd never wanted out of somewhere so badly. She could practically hear the waiting room calling her name.

'Seeing me like what?' she snapped. The nurse had finished washing her hands and was opening a sterile pack and some equipment on the dressing trolley. She couldn't wipe the smile from her face.

Will's dimple appeared. 'You know—babbling. Violet doesn't get like this at all. It's quite nice to see you flapping around.'

'I'm not flapping around. This is all your fault anyway—and you know it.'

The nurse lifted the peas from Will's head and deposited them in the bin. 'Youch,' she said, pulling a head lamp a little closer. 'It looks as though you might have a tiny fragment in your wound. What caused your injury?'

'She did.'

'A vase.'

Their voices came out in unison. Rose was horrified. He'd just told the nurse this was her fault. The nurse's eyes flickered from one to the other. Thank goodness she was bound by confidentiality, otherwise this would appear all over the national press.

But she was the ultimate professional. She picked up some swabs and dipped them in the solution on the dressing trolley, along with a pair of tweezers. 'Brace yourself, Mr Carter. This is going to sting a bit. I'm going to give this a clean, then try and pry out the little piece of vase that is embedded in your wound. Five or six stitches should close this up fine.'

'Five or six?' Rose was beginning to feel light-headed. 'Can't you just use that glue stuff?'

The nurse shook her head. 'Not for this kind of wound. It's very deep. Stitches will give the best result—and hopefully the least amount of scarring.' She pulled up some liq-

uid into a syringe. 'I'm just going to give you an injection
to numb the area before we start.' Her experience showed.
The injection was finished in a few seconds. 'It will tingle
for a bit,' she warned. Her gaze shot from one to the other.
'I'm obliged to ask, but I take it from your tone this was
an accidental injury?'

Rose felt her cheeks flame. 'Absolutely.' She couldn't
get the words out quickly enough.

Will was watching Rose with those dark blue-rimmed
eyes. She saw a flicker of something behind his eyes. He
looked at the nurse with a remarkable amount of sincerity. 'Rose wouldn't normally hurt a fly. There's nothing to
worry about. So, you said I'll definitely have a scar, then?'

'Yes.' She nodded as she cleaned the wound. 'Think of
yourself as Harry Potter.' She gave a little laugh. 'I hear
he gets all the girls.'

Was it hot in here? Or had she just forgotten to put de-
odorant on this morning? It was getting uncomfortably
warm. She pulled her dress away from her body for a few
seconds to let the air circulate.

Will was still watching her as he continued his conversation with the nurse. 'Will it be a bad scar?'

Rose shifted on her feet. Boy, he was laying it on thick.
Stop talking about the scar. Guilt was flooding through
her. She'd just scarred a man for life. And it seemed as if
he'd talk about it for ever.

The nurse bent forward with her tweezers, then pulled
back. 'Here it is!' She dropped the microscopic piece of
vase on the dressing trolley. How on earth had she even
seen it?

She gave Will's head a final clean, then picked up the
stitching kit. 'This won't take long. I'll give you some instructions for the next few days.' She glanced towards
Rose. 'When the vase hit you—were you knocked out?'

'No,' he said quickly. 'I was sleeping and, believe me, once the vase hit I was wide awake.'

Rose rolled her eyes and looked away. He was making a meal of this. It was clear the nurse was lapping up his Mr Charming act. And it was making her more than a little uncomfortable.

Because, like it or not, it was hard not to get pulled in. One look from those big eyes, along with the killer smile and dimple, was enough to make the average woman's knees turn to mush.

No wonder this guy got so much good press. Why on earth would he think he needed any help?

She fixed her eyes on the floor as the nurse started expertly stitching the wound. Will Carter, Runaway Groom would now have a scar above his left eyebrow. A scar that *she'd* caused. It was definitely making her feel a bit sick.

The stitches were over in a matter of minutes and then the nurse handed Will a set of head injury instructions. 'You shouldn't be on your own for the next twenty-four hours.' She gave Rose a smile. 'I'm assuming that won't be a problem?'

'What? You mean me? No. No, I can't. Will? I'm sure there must be someone who can keep you company for the next twenty-four hours.' A wave of panic was coming over her.

But Will shook his head, then lifted his hand towards his head. 'Ouch.'

The nurse moved forward again and looked back to Rose. 'This is why he really needs someone to be around him. There can be after-effects with a head injury. If you can't supervise he'll need to be admitted to hospital. Are you sure you can't help?'

Her tone was serious. It was obvious she was apportioning the blame at Rose's door. The words were stuck in her throat. And as the guilt swamped her she couldn't think of a single good reason to say no.

Will leaned forward a little. The tiniest movement. The nurse had her back to him with her hand on her hip. Will's face appeared through the gap at her elbow and he pointed to his head. 'Scarred for life,' he mouthed before giving her a wink.

The cheeky ratbag. He was trying to blackmail her. And she hated to admit it—but it was working.

'Fine.' She snatched the instructions from the nurse's hand. 'Anything else?'

The nurse switched on her automatic smile. 'Not at all.' She turned to Will. 'Pleasure to meet you, Mr Carter. Pay special attention to the instructions and—' she glanced at Rose '—I wish you well for the future.' She wheeled her dressing trolley out of the cubicle.

Rose was fuming. Half of her thought this was all his own fault, and half of her was wondering if the millionaire would sue her for personal damages. She'd heard of these things before. What if Will couldn't sell his next wedding to *Exclusive* magazine because of his scar?

What if he sold the story of how he got his scar instead? She groaned and leaned back against the wall.

'Rose, are you going to pass out? Sorry, I didn't think you were squeamish.'

She opened her eyes to face his broad chest. He'd made a miraculous recovery and was standing in front of her with his hand on her arm to steady her.

The irony wasn't lost on her. *She* was supposed to be looking after *him*—not the other way about.

He'd told her he needed help with publicity. Maybe she'd unwittingly played into his hands? Her brain started to spin.

Her head sagged back and hit against the cold hospital

wall. Her eyes sprang back open and he was staring right at her again.

How many women had he charmed with those blue eyes? And that killer dimple…

His arm slid around her shoulders. 'It's hot in here. Maybe you'll feel better if we get some fresh air.'

His body seemed to automatically steer hers along. Her feet walking in concordance with his, along the hospital corridor and back out to the car park. Her first reaction was to shake off his unwanted arm.

But something weird was happening. Her body seemed to enjoy being next to his. She seemed to fit well under his shoulder. In her simple sundress the touch of his arm across her shoulders was sending little currents to places that had been dormant for a while.

Twenty-four hours. That was how long she would have to be in his company.

Panic was starting to flood through her, pushing aside all the other confusing thoughts. This guy could charm the birds from the trees. She'd thought she'd be immune. But her body impulses were telling her differently.

As soon as the fresh air hit she wriggled free from under his arm. 'I'm fine.' She walked across the car park and jiggled her keys in her hand.

'We need to have some ground rules.'

He leaned against the Rolls-Royce. She could almost hear her father scream in her ear.

'What exactly might they be?' One eyebrow was raised. He probably couldn't raise the other. That part of his forehead would still be anaesthetised. Darn it. The guilty feelings were sneaking their way back in.

'I think when we get back to Hawksley Castle we should ask Violet to stay with you. After all, she knows you best. She'll know if you do anything out of character—like grope strange women.' She couldn't help but throw it in there. She waved the instructions at him. 'You know, anything that might mean you need to go back to hospital.' Now she was saying the words out loud they made perfect sense.

He waved his finger at her. 'Oh, no, you don't.'

'Don't what?'

'Try and get out of this.' He pointed to his forehead. 'You did this to me, Rose. It's your job to hang around to make sure I'm okay.'

He was so smooth. A mixture of treacle and syrup.

'Oh, stop it, Will. I'm not your typical girl. I'm not going to fall at your feet and expect a ring. And if you keep going the way you are I'll hit you again with the next vase I find. I've got things to do. I can't hang around Hawksley Castle.'

He smiled and opened the car door. 'Who said we were spending the next twenty-four hours at Hawksley Castle?'

She started as he climbed in. She pulled open the car door and slid in. 'What on earth do you mean? Of course we're going back to Hawksley Castle.'

He shook his head. 'I think both of us have overstayed our welcome. You've damaged one of Seb's precious heirlooms and I've probably put immovable stains on an ancient carpet and wall. I suggest we regroup and go somewhere else.'

She started the engine. 'Like where?'

'Like Gideon Hall.'

Gideon Hall. Will Carter's millionaire mansion. At least at Hawksley Castle she'd be surrounded by family and friends. There was safety in numbers. Being alone with Will Carter wasn't something she wanted to risk.

'Oh, no. I need to work, Will.'

'I can give you access to a phone and computer. What else do you need?'

'My jewellery equipment, my soldering iron, my casting machine. My yellow, white and rose gold. My precious stones. Do you have any of those at Gideon Hall?'

The confident grin fell from his face. 'You're serious about making the jewellery?'

His question annoyed her. 'Of course I am. Working for my dad is the day job. Working to make wedding jewellery? That's the job I actually want to do. I spend most of my nights working on jewellery for upcoming weddings. I have an order to make wedding rings for a bride and groom. I can't afford to take any time off.'

It was nice to see his unwavering confidence start to fail. It seemed Mr Charming hadn't thought of everything.

She sighed. 'If need be, we can collect our things from Seb's, then go back to my parents' place. If you've hung around with Violet long enough you must be familiar with it.'

He settled back in the chair. 'Do you have your equipment at your parents' house?'

She nodded. 'I have one set in New York, and one set here.'

'That's fine. We can move it to my house in the next hour. I'll get someone to help us.'

He pulled his phone from his pocket and started dialling. 'What? No. What on earth is wrong with you? I've said I'll hang around you for the next twenty-four hours. Isn't that enough?'

He turned to face her. 'Actually, no, it's not. I've got a meeting later on today with a potential investor for the homeless charity. It's taken for ever to set up and I don't want to miss it.'

'Can't you just change the venue?'

Will let out a long, slow puff of air and named a footballer her father had had a spat with a few months ago. 'How would your dad feel about him being in his house?'

She gulped. 'Wow. No. He'd probably blow a gasket. He hates the guy.' She frowned. 'Are you sure he's the right kind of guy to help your charity?' She was racking her brains. Her dad was a good judge of character. He could spot a fake at twenty paces and didn't hesitate to tell them. She was sure there was a good reason he didn't like this footballer—she just couldn't remember what it was.

Will still couldn't frown properly. It was kind of cute. 'I've no idea. I've never met him before. But he's well known and popular with sports fans. It's not so much about the money. It's the publicity I need help with. We need to get the homeless agenda on people's radars. They need to understand the reason people end up on the streets. It's not just because they're drunks, or drug addicts or can't hold down a job.'

She turned back into the grounds of Hawksley Castle. 'You're really serious about this, aren't you?'

'Of course I am. Why would you think I'm not?'

She bit her lip. 'What's in it for you? Why is a homeless charity your thing?'

It took him a few seconds to answer. 'I had a friend at university who ended up on the streets. I didn't know. He didn't ask anyone for help because he didn't want anyone to know the kind of trouble he was in. I found out later when someone tried to rob him and stabbed him in the process. The police found my details amongst his things.'

She pulled the car to a halt and turned to face him. 'Was he dead?'

Will shook his head. It was the first time she'd really seen complete sincerity on his face. No charm, no dimple, no killer smile. In a way, it made him all the more handsome even though she tried to push that thought from her brain.

'No. But Arral needed help. And there's a lot more people out there who need help, too.'

'So, you really want good PR to raise awareness and you think this footballer will give you it?'

He folded his arms across his chest. 'Is that scepticism I hear in your voice, Rose?'

She gave him a smile as she opened the door and took the key from the ignition. 'I just don't know if he's your best choice.'

Will climbed out next to her. 'Neither do I, but, right now, he's my only option. How long will it take you to grab your stuff?'

She shrugged. 'My clothes? Five minutes. What about my equipment?'

'I'll arrange for someone to go your parents' and pick it up. Do you want to drop by first?'

She nodded. 'It won't take long. Let me get my clothes and I'll meet you back here.'

Will was true to his word. There was a man with a van waiting outside her parents' house when they arrived. She took him around to her workshop and collected the things she'd need to start work later that night.

As she was collecting a few other items her father appeared. 'Oh, hi, Dad. I didn't expect you to be back yet. I thought you'd still be at Hawksley Castle.'

He smiled. 'Your mother and I came back an hour ago. We had a few things we wanted to discuss.'

Her mother appeared at her father's side, his arm slipping around her waist and resting on her hip. Sherry Huntingdon still had her model-girl looks and figure even though she was in her fifties.

Rose's father's face was a little more lived-in. Rock and roll did that to you. His hair was still longer than normal—he still loved the shaggy rock-star look.

Rose's stomach started to do little flip-flops. Her father's words were a bit ominous. He had a tendency to spring things on her. And it looked as if nothing was about to change.

Rick crossed the room and put his hand out towards Will. 'Will, aren't you hanging around with the wrong daughter?' There was an amused tone in his voice. 'And what happened to your head? Did one of those brides finally get you?' He threw back his head and let out a hearty laugh.

Rose cringed. How many times was Will going to hear those words?

But Will seemed unperturbed. 'Ask Rose—she was the one that socked me with a vase.'

'She what?' Rose's mother seemed shocked.

Rose waved her hand quickly. 'It was a misunderstanding. That's all. What did you come back to talk about, Dad?' She wanted to distract them before they asked too many questions.

Her mother and father turned and smiled at each other. There it was. That sappy look that they got sometimes. In a way it was nice. Still romantic. It was obvious to the world that they still loved each other.

It was just a tad embarrassing when it was your parents.

'Your mother and I have made a decision.'

'What kind of decision?' She had a bad feeling about this.

Both of them couldn't stop smiling and it was making her toes curl. She just knew this was going to be something big.

'After all the preparations for Daisy's wedding—and

the fact everything went so beautifully—your mother and I have decided to renew our wedding vows.'

'You have?' It was so not what she expected to hear.

Her mother put her hand on her father's chest. She was in that far-off place she went to when ideas started to float around her head. 'You know we never had a big wedding.' She turned to acknowledge Will. 'We ran away to Vegas and got married after only knowing each other for a week-end. I never really had the fancy dress, flowers or meal like Daisy had. So, we've decided to do it all again.'

Rick shrugged and smiled at Will. 'It might seem hasty, but believe me—' he smiled at his wife '—when you know, you just know.'

A thousand little centipedes had started to crawl over Rose's skin. She had a horrid feeling she knew exactly where this was going.

'It's a lovely idea. When were you thinking? Next year—after the tour is over?'

'Oh, no.' Rose's mother laughed. 'In a few weeks.'

'A few weeks!' She couldn't help but raise her voice. Will shot her a look, obviously trying to calm her. But he had no idea what was coming next. Rose did.

Sherry stepped forward. 'What's the problem? We have the perfect venue.' She spun around. 'Here. We just need a marquee for the grounds. And a caterer. And some flow-ers. And some dresses.' She turned to Rick and laughed. 'And a band!'

Rick stepped forward. 'It shouldn't be a problem. You can arrange all that in a few weeks, can't you, Rose? You do everything so perfectly. And you're just so organised. We couldn't possibly trust anyone else with something so important.' Her father stepped over and gave her a hug and dropped a kiss on her cheek. It was clear he was floating on the same love-swept cloud that her mother was.

'Me?' Her voice came out in a squeak as Will's eyes widened in shock.

Oh, now he understood. This was what she got for doing such a good job. She was the official PA for her father's band and her mother's career. With all the tour preparations she barely had time to sleep right now. But she loved her parents dearly so she let them think it was all effortless. Her parents had been so strong and so supportive when she'd needed them—even though she secretly felt she'd disappointed them. Their love and support was the only thing that had got her through. All she wanted to do was make them proud. If they were trusting her with something like this? It made her anxious to please them, to let them be confident in her choices, even if this was the last thing she needed.

Her father's voice was steady. 'You know just how hard your mother's been working recently. And what with planning Daisy's wedding, she's just exhausted. If you could do all this it would be a whole weight off our minds.'

The dopey smiles on her parents' faces were enough to melt her heart—even though it was fluttering frantically in her chest and her brain was going into overdrive.

Will seemed to pick up on her overwhelming sense of panic. He stepped forward. 'What a fantastic idea. But these things normally take a while to plan—don't you want to wait a while and get everything just right?'

It was a valiant attempt. But Rose knew exactly how this would go. Once her parents got an idea in their heads there was no changing their minds.

Rick gave a wave of his hand. 'Nonsense. It didn't take long to sort out Daisy's wedding, did it?' He gave Rose *that* look. The one he always did when she knew he meant business. Rick Cross had invented the word *determined*.

'I'm not sure, Dad. There's a lot to do, what with the tour and the charity concert and everything.'

His hand rested on her arm and he glanced in his wife's direction. 'Now, Rose. Let's give your mother the wedding she always deserved.'

The truth was he wasn't picking up her cues. He was too busy concentrating on the rapt expression on his wife's face. Anxiety was building in her stomach. If she could do this, maybe she could repay her parents for everything they'd done for her. When she'd been splashed over the press when her friend had died she couldn't have asked for better advocates or supporters. Family was everything.

She started to murmur out loud. 'But I know nothing about weddings. Receptions, marquees, dinners, dresses…'

Her mother smiled. 'Oh, honey. Leave the dress to me. I'm going to get the one I always wanted.' Her gaze locked with Rick's and it was clear they were lost in their own little world.

Rick waved his hand. 'Ask Daisy. She knows all about it.' He let out a little laugh. 'Or ask your friend. He's had his fair share of organising weddings.'

Her parents turned and drifted back out of the room, lost in conversation with each other. That was it. Decision made. And *everything* left to Rose.

Rose turned to face Will. Her tongue was stuck to the roof of her mouth. She'd kill for a cosmopolitan right now. Her mouth was so dry she couldn't even begin to form words. She'd been blindsided. By her parents.

Will was looking just as pale.

She lifted her hands. 'I… I…' But the words wouldn't come out. The only sound that did come out was a sob. All this work. Organising a wedding in a few weeks might be okay for some people. But some people weren't Rick Cross and Sherry Huntingdon. They'd have a spectacular guest list—who'd all come with their list of demands. Where on earth would she find the kind of caterer she'd need at short notice? Her parents were very picky about food.

And what was worse—already she wanted it to be perfect for them.

Her heart was thudding in her chest. The more she thought, the more she panicked. Her chest was tight. The air couldn't get in. It couldn't circulate. Tears sprang to her eyes.

Will stepped straight in front of her. 'Rose? Sit down. You're a terrible colour.' He pulled a chair over and pushed her down onto it, kneeling beside her. 'In fact, no. Put your head between your legs.'

The inside of his palm connected with the back of her head and pushed down. She didn't even have time to object.

The thudding started to slow. She wasn't quite so panicky. After a few seconds she finally managed to pull in a breath.

This was a nightmare. A big nightmare. She didn't have enough hours in the day to do what her parents wanted. But how on earth could she say no?

She lifted her head a little and a tear snaked down her cheek. She wiped it away quickly.

Will looked worried. 'There must be someone else who can organise this for them? What about your sisters? They can help? Or can't you hire someone?'

'To organise my own parents' renewal of vows? How, exactly, would that look?' She waved her hand. 'And Daisy might just have done it all but she's off on her honeymoon to Italy for the next two weeks. Violet knows as much about weddings as I do.' Her voice cracked as their gazes collided.

And something in her head went *ping*.

'Will, you have to help me.'

A furrow creased his brow. The anaesthetic had finally started to wear off. 'But isn't it supposed to be the other way? I wanted you to give me some advice about PR for my homeless charity.'

She straightened her shoulders and drew in a deep breath. Things were starting to clear in her head. She wasn't dumb. Only an hour ago Will Carter hadn't been above trying to blackmail her. Head injury or not—it was time for her to use the same tactics.

'Dad was right. You have the perfect skill set to help me out here. Help *us* out.'

Realisation started to dawn on him and he shook his head. 'Oh, no. Your dad wasn't being serious.' It was his turn to start to look panicked.

She smiled. This was starting to feel good. 'Oh, I think he was.'

She placed her hands on her hips as she stood up. Will was still kneeling by her chair. It was the first time she'd been head and shoulders above him. There was something empowering about this. She held out her hand towards him. This might be the only way out of this mess.

'Will Carter? If you want my help, then I want yours.' She could feel herself start to gain momentum.

'You can't be serious.'

'Oh, but I am. I help you and you help me.'

He stood up. 'Do what exactly?'

There was something good about the way he mirrored the same panicked expression she'd had a few minutes earlier.

She stretched her hand a little further. 'I help you with your PR. You help me with this crazy wedding renewal.'

He shook his head. 'I think you've got this all wrong. I only ever made it to one wedding. The rest never got anything like that far. Sure, I helped with some of the planning but that doesn't make me an expert. The label in the press—Runaway Groom—it doesn't really mean that. I've never even been a groom.' He was blustering, trying anything to get out of this. 'I don't even like weddings!' was his last try.

She pressed her lips together to stop herself from laughing out loud. She liked seeing him floundering around. Will Carter liked to be in control. Liked to be charming. She could almost feel the weight lift from her shoulders. This might even be the tiniest bit fun.

She smiled at him. 'Will Carter? I think you're about to be my new best friend.'

The Runaway Groom was starting to look a whole lot more interesting.

CHAPTER THREE

WILL WAS STARTING to freak.

What had started as a bit of flirting and curiosity was turning into something closely related to the things he normally fled from.

It didn't matter that this was someone else's wedding. Weddings were the *last* thing he wanted to get involved in.

Except, he'd said that before. Four times exactly.

And he always meant it. Right up until he met the next girl—the next love of his life—and things went spectacularly. The romance, the love, the inevitable engagement, the press and then the plans started.

Everything always started swimmingly. Beautiful, fairy-tale venues. Wonderful menus. Great bands.

Then, things started to get uncomfortable. Fights about meaningless crap. Colours, ties or cravats, kilts or suits. Sisters and mothers-in-law interfering in he didn't even know what.

Arguments about wedding vows, dresses—spectacular scenes about dresses having to be ordered eighteen months in advance and not arriving in time. Ridiculous costs for 'favours'—things that no one even cared about and everyone left lying on the dinner tables anyway.

Tantrums over cakes. Tantrums over cars.

And love dying somewhere along the process. But it

wasn't the wedding process that really did it for him. It was that feeling of *for ever*. That idea of being with one person for the rest of your life. Whenever his bride-to-be had started talking about wedding vows Will always felt an overwhelming sense of panic. And all of a sudden he wasn't so sure.

It didn't help that he knew his friend Arral's wife had walked out and left Arral when he'd lost his job. It had all contributed to Arral sinking into depression and ending up homeless. For better or worse. Someone to grow old with. The theory was great. But what if when the chips were down his potential bride-to-be decided she didn't want for ever any more?

He didn't really understand why, but as the wedding date drew nearer Will always had a massive case of cold feet. Actually, it wasn't cold feet. More like being encompassed by the iceberg that had sunk the *Titanic*.

The trouble with being a nice guy was that it was hard to realise when exactly to back out. Once, he'd got right to the main event, but had backed out in spectacular fashion, earning him the nickname the Runaway Groom.

Even now he winced and closed his eyes. His bride-to-be had sensed his doubts and made veiled threats about what she might do if he didn't turn up.

So, he'd turned up. And made sure when he left she was surrounded by family and friends—even if all the family and friends were about to do him a permanent injury.

Violet had a theory on all this. She said that he hadn't met the right girl yet. Once he had? Everything would fall into place. Everything would click and he wouldn't have any of these doubts and fears. But what did Violet know about all this?

'I'm not the guy for this,' he said quickly.

Rose seemed capable. From what Violet had told him

Rose ran her life like clockwork. She never missed a deadline and made sure all those around her never missed one, too. He would only get in the way of someone like that.

Rose was standing in front of him. Her pale blue eyes fixed on his. 'Oh, yes, you are.' There was an edge to her voice. A determination he hadn't heard before.

But he recognised the trait. She was obviously her father's daughter.

'Oh, no, I'm not.'

Rose folded her arms across her chest. It was very unfortunate. All it did was emphasise her breasts in her pale yellow sundress. He could hardly tear his eyes away.

'Will Carter, you are not going to leave me in this mess.'

It felt as if the room were crowding around him. The walls, slowly but surely pushing forward. Sort of the way he normally felt when he knew he had to run from a wedding. None of this was his making. None of this was his responsibility.

'This isn't anything to do with me, Rose. It's bad enough that you cracked me over the head and scarred me for life with some vase. Now, you're trying to force me to help with your parents' wedding plans. This is nothing to do with me. Nothing at all. I'm far too busy for this. I've got a hundred other things to do to get publicity for my homeless charity. That's where I need to focus my efforts right now. Not on some celebrity wedding.' He flicked his hand, and she narrowed her gaze.

She was mad. And not just a little.

'Don't you give me any of your crap.' She poked her finger into his chest. 'You slunk your way into my bed uninvited. You've forced me to be around you for the next twenty-four hours when I should be working. I'm good at my job, Will. I manage my commitments. But this? On top of everything else I've got to do? I know nothing about weddings. Nothing. Ask me to design the jewellery—fine. Ask me to do anything else? I don't have a clue.' She poked his chest again. 'Which is where you come in.'

She lifted her chin and gave him a smug smile. 'You want publicity for your homeless charity? Oh, I can get you publicity. I can get you publicity in ways you might never even have imagined. But it comes at a price.'

Boy, she could look fierce when she wanted to. He wondered whatever happened to any guy that crossed her. He could barely begin to imagine.

'Weddings give me cold sweats,' he said quickly.

'Weddings have you running for the hills,' she countered.

There was no way she was going to back down. He was beginning to regret virtually blackmailing her into coming back to his house for twenty-four hours. Somehow him doing the blackmailing didn't seem quite so bad as her doing it back.

That would teach him.

But something happened. Rose seemed to change tack. A smile appeared on her face and she reached over and rubbed his arm. 'This one won't require you to break out in a cold sweat, Will. You're safe. This is someone else's wedding you're organising—not your own.' The smile stayed fixed on her face. He had a sneaking suspicion she was used to getting her own way.

But something was burning away underneath. It didn't matter that the face was identical to his best friend's. The personality and actions were totally different. She even smelled different. And her scent was currently winding its way around his senses. Something fruity. Something raspberry.

She flicked her blonde hair over her shoulder and he got another waft. Shampoo. It must be her shampoo. Rose

Huntingdon-Cross was a knockout. And he was in danger of being bitten by her quirky charm. Her words had already captured his attention but the image in front of him and that enticing scent were in danger of doing much more.

He tried to focus. He needed PR for the homeless charity, he needed the rest of the world to understand why people ended up that way and help put in place things to prevent it.

'What exactly do you mean? Forget about the wedding stuff. Tell me about your PR ideas.'

She wagged her finger at him. 'Oh, no. Not yet. You have to earn the privilege of my PR expertise. You help me, and I'll help you.'

What mattered more to him? Giving some crazy recommendations for caterers or wedding cars—or raising the profile of the charity he supported? There was no question. Of course he could do this. It couldn't possibly take that long. Rose looked like the kind of girl who could make a decision quickly. With wedding planning that was half the battle. Maybe this wouldn't be as bad as he thought?

She was biting her lip now, obviously worried he wouldn't agree. Biting a pink, perfectly formed lip. Perfectly formed for kissing. It was the thing that finally tipped him. Rose looked vulnerable. And he was a sucker for damsels in distress. It had got him into a whole lot of trouble in the past and probably would in the future.

His impulses got the better of him. He reached forward and grabbed her hand. 'Right, you've got a deal. Now, let's go before your parents appear again and give you something else to do.'

'You'll help me? Really?' He could almost hear her sigh of relief. 'Fabulous!' She was practically skipping alongside him as they crossed the room.

What on earth was he getting into?

* * *

Her brain was spinning. The guys from Will's place had packed up her gear in their van. She'd run after her parents and tried to get them to answer a few basic questions—like a date. But that had been fruitless. Apparently everything was up to her. They just wanted to decide on the guests.

The journey in the car to Will's place had been brief while she'd scribbled frantic notes in her handy black planner. She didn't go anywhere without that baby. He'd spent most of his time on the phone talking business. Then they'd turned down a country road that seemed to go on and on for ever.

Then, all of a sudden they were driving alongside a dark blue lake with an island in the middle, all sitting in front of a huge country house. The driver pulled up outside and she turned to him as he pushed his phone back into his pocket.

'You own a lake? And an island?' Her jaw was practically bouncing off her knees. Rose had been lucky. She'd had a privileged background. She was used to country mansions and houses costing millions. Seb's castle had just about topped everything. But this place?

Wow. The house might not be so big. But the amount of land was enormous. Will Carter was sitting on a gold mine.

'You like?' He was smiling at her amazed expression as she climbed out of the car.

The wind had picked up a little and was making her dress flap around her. She stepped around the car and walked towards the lake. There was a wooden jetty with two expensive boats sitting next to it.

She shook her head. 'Violet never mentioned a lake, or an island.' She thought she knew her sister well. This was definitely the kind of thing she would normally mention.

Will walked up behind her, blocking the wind. Her first thought was relief. Her next was how close he was standing. The soft cotton of his T-shirt was brushing against her shoulder blades.

In any other set of circumstances she would step away. But for the first time in a long time, she didn't feel like that. She was comfortable around Will. They might have got off to a bad start but there was something safe about him. It didn't help that the driver had just magically disappeared.

And it was easier to think safe than sexy. Because that was the other thought circulating around in her brain.

Will Carter was more than a little handsome. He was tongue-hanging-out, drip-your-food-down-your-dress handsome.

'Violet was never that interested in the lake or the island. She wouldn't even let me take her over in the boat.' His deep voice, right next to her ear, made her start.

'Oh, sorry. Did I give you a fright?' His arm slid naturally to her hip, to stop her from swaying. And she didn't mind it there. She naturally turned her head towards his and gave her full attention to the dark blue rim around his paler blue eyes. It was unusual. It was almost mesmerising.

'No,' she murmured, giving the slightest shake of her head.

This was freaking her out. She could feel her heart miss a few beats as she made the association. Last time she'd paid this much attention to a man had been over three years ago.

Three years ago and a party. A party where she'd left her friend to her own devices—because she'd been distracted by that man. Her friend had made some bad decisions that night and paid the ultimate price. And Rose had spent the last three years in New York to get away from the fallout.

She'd still spoken to her sisters every day and had been back in England every year for their father's annual rock concert, but she just hadn't stayed for long. It was easier to avoid the same circle of friends and their whispers if you weren't there to notice them.

But things were changing. It was looking as though a move back to England was on the cards. The European tour would need her close at hand. It would be just as easy to do the rest of her work here as in New York. The annual rock concert was due to take place soon and as long as she had equipment she could make her wedding jewellery anywhere.

'Rose?'

Will reached over and slid his hand in hers. 'Come on, I'll take you over to the island.'

He gave her hand a little tug. Oh, no. There was a warm feeling racing up her arm, making her heart rate do strange things. Pitter-pattering and electric shock kind of things.

She was trying to be cool. She was trying so hard to be cool. But his touch brought a natural smile to her face. She couldn't stop the little edges of her mouth turning upwards. 'Sure,' she said as he pulled her towards the boat.

It was one of two moored on a little wooden jetty and it certainly wasn't your old-fashioned rowing boat. It was white and sleek with a small compact engine on the back.

He jumped down and held out his hand towards her as the boat wobbled on the rippling surface of the water.

She leaned forward and hesitated a little. The step to the boat was a little broader than normal; chances were she would have to pull up her dress to make it across.

But it was almost as if Will read her mind. He reached forward with his long arms, circled her waist and lifted her across. He did it so quickly she didn't even have time to think. Her feet touched the base of the boat as the momentum made it sway a little more.

'Sorry.' He smiled. 'Forgot about your dress. Don't want

to get a glimpse of anything I shouldn't.' He had that twinkle in his eye again—knowing full well he'd more or less glimpsed the full package this morning. *As had she.*

She sat down on one of the comfortable leather seats in the boat and shook her head. 'My grandmother would love you—but you're just full of it, aren't you? I often wondered if Mr Charming might be a journalist's daydream. I always wondered how you managed to stay on the good side of the media. But you're just every mother's dream, aren't you?'

He started the engine and laughed. 'I think I can name at least four mothers who don't like me that much at all.'

The boat moved easily across the peaceful lake. It really was perfect. A few swans were gathered at the other side and a few ducks squawked from the edges amongst the reeds.

Rose couldn't help but shake her head. 'I don't get it. I just don't. You must have known you didn't want to marry those girls. Why on earth would you leave it to the last minute? Who does that?'

He sat down next to her as he steered the boat. He wasn't as defensive as before. Maybe because they'd been around each other a bit longer. He'd seen the fix her parents had just left her with.

He sighed as the boat chugged across the water. 'I know. It's awful. And I don't mean to—I never do. And, to be fair, I've had bad press. I've only *actually* done it on the day once. It's just much more fun for the press to label me the Runaway Groom on every occasion. My problem is I always start to have doubts. Doubts that you can't say out loud without hurting the person you're with. The would-she-still-love-me-if-I'm-bankrupt? kind of doubts. Then, you start planning the wedding and the lovely woman you've fallen in love with is replaced by a raging, seething perfectionist.'

Rose laughed. 'What's wrong with that? Doesn't every bride want her day to be perfect? And don't most people have a few doubts in the lead-up to a wedding?'

But Will looked sad. 'But why does it all have to be about the details? Shouldn't it just be about two people in love getting married? Why does the wedding planning always turn into "this wedding has to be better than such and such's wedding"? I hate that.'

The words sent a little chill over her skin. He was right. More than he could ever know. She couldn't believe that the man the press called the Runaway Groom actually felt the same way she did.

'Why do you have doubts?' she asked quickly.

He paused and shrugged his shoulders. 'I'm not always sure. What I can tell you is that I don't regret calling off any of my weddings. I just regret the one time of being an actual runaway groom. At least two of my exes have since agreed that we should never have got married. They've met their perfect person and are happy now.'

Rose gave a sad kind of smile. 'Not every wedding is a disaster. Some couples are meant to be together. Daisy's wedding was fast, but she did plan everything she wanted. I might have been in New York but she emailed every day.' The island was getting closer, giving little hints of what lay beneath the copse of trees. She gave a little shudder. 'I'm not a fan of big weddings. I like small things. And I like the idea of two people, alone, agreeing to spend the rest of their lives together. Let's face it. That's what it's all about.' She smiled at Will. 'Just as well I'm not the bride. If it was a big, flamboyant wedding maybe I would steal your thunder and be the Runaway Bride?'

He leaned back a little in the boat as they neared the island's jetty. 'Really? A woman that wants a quiet wedding? Even after all the splendour of Daisy's?' He raised his eyebrows in disbelief. 'You don't want a little of that for yourself?'

'Absolutely not.' Her answer was definite.

He paused for a second. 'It really wasn't about the weddings. It was about the relationships. Once the initial happy buzz of being engaged vanished I started trying to picture myself growing old with that person. And no matter how hard I tried, I could never see it. I realised I didn't love them the way I should. The way a husband should love a wife—like your mum and dad.' He was gazing off onto the island and he suddenly realised what he'd said. Will Carter had probably revealed much more than he wanted to. He gave a little start and tried to change the subject quickly. 'Anyway, I don't believe you. I bet you want the big wedding just like every other girl.'

He stood up as the boat bumped the jetty and tied the mooring line securely. He jumped onto the wooden platform and she held out her hand to his. But Will seemed to think they'd set a precedent. He reached both arms down and caught her around the waist, lifting her up alongside him.

Her feet connected with the wooden structure but his hands didn't move from her waist. She was facing his chest, his head just above hers. Her hands lifted naturally to rest on his muscled biceps. The only noise was the quacking ducks and rippling water. She'd seen a little glimpse of the real Will Carter. Not the one in the media. Not Mr Charming. And she actually liked it. She would never admit it to anyone but he intrigued her. She smiled. 'No, I don't want any of that. What's more, I bet I could outrun you, Will Carter.' Her voice was quiet, almost a whisper. It was just the two of them. And their position was so close it seemed almost intimate. She could feel his fingers spread a little on her waist—as if he were expanding his grip to stop her getting away.

The perfect smile appeared, quickly followed by his dimple. It was all she could do not to reach out and touch it. 'The Runaway Bride and the Runaway Groom? We could be quite a pair.' He left his words hanging in the air. Leaving them both to contemplate them.

Her breath was caught in her throat. Never. She was too young. Too stupid. She had too many plans. There was no room for someone like Will Carter in her life right now. Especially when she found it so hard to trust her instincts. Her stomach flipped over. He was joking. They both were. But she couldn't help but feel a little surge of confidence that he'd even suggested it.

She stepped back, breathing deeply and breaking the intimate atmosphere between them. 'What's on this island anyway?'

Something flitted across his eyes. Disappointment? She felt a tiny surge of annoyance. She'd no intention of being his next passing fling. He'd already admitted he fell in love too easily. Rose didn't have that problem. She'd never fallen in love at all.

Ever the gentleman, he gestured with his hand to the path ahead leading through some trees. She walked ahead of him and looked around. The thick, dark trees were deceiving. They were hiding more than she could ever have imagined.

Her hand came up to her mouth as they stepped out from the path to a red-brick stone church with a huge stained-glass window.

'A hidden church? You have got to be joking.'

'No.' He walked over and swung open the thick wooden door, flicking a switch. The sun was shining down through the dark copse of trees. The church was tiny, the window almost taking up one whole wall. Only around twenty people could fit in here along the four benches on each side of the aisle.

The late afternoon sun was streaming through the window, sending a beautiful array of colours lighting up the white walls. There was a dark wooden altar table at the front. Nothing else.

'This place is amazing. You own a church?'

He nodded. 'There's an equally tiny cottage behind the church. Both were ruins when I bought the place. I had the church rebuilt and the stained-glass window put in. The cottage was just refurbished.'

She spun around in the rainbow of lights. 'I love this place. What was it originally?'

'No one really knows for sure. I think it was some kind of retreat. There used to be a monastery on these grounds right up until the dissolution of the monasteries in the fifteen-hundreds. This is the only thing that was left.'

Rose took a deep breath and walked over and touched the white wall. 'Think of all the history here. Think of all the things that could have happened between these four walls over the centuries.' She walked over and gently touched one of the pieces of stained red glass as she swept her eyes over the scene in the window. 'What is this? Was there something like this already here?'

'It's inspired by Troyes Cathedral in France. They have some of the oldest medieval stained-glass windows. This is two of the prophets, Moses and David.' He seemed genuinely interested in what he was telling her. It was obvious a lot of thought—and a lot of expense—had gone into the restoration work.

'You should get a grant of approval to do wedding ceremonies here.'

He shook his head. 'What? And have the bride fall out

of the boat on the way over? This lake might look pretty, but, I can assure you, it's dark and murky at the bottom.'

She laughed and stepped closer. 'Words from a man that sounds like he fell in.'

'I did. I came out like a creature from the black lagoon.'

She held out her hands. 'So what do you use this place for?' She finally felt as if she was getting to know Will a little better. He might be Mr Charming for the press but he was also a nice guy. He was easier to be around than she'd first experienced. Violet wasn't known for her poor judgement. She should have trusted her sister.

He waved her forward. 'Come and I'll show you.'

They walked outside and behind the church to a white-washed cottage with black paint around the windows and a black door. He pushed it open and showed her inside.

It was tiny, but spectacular. Almost every part was in view. An open modern kitchen at one end, a sitting area in the middle and a platform with a king-sized bed. There was even a smoky glass bricked wall, which hid the wash-hand basin and toilet, but the roll-top bath was placed in front of one of the two windows.

'You bathe at the window!' Rose's mouth dropped open.

Will grinned. 'It's all private. If someone is staying here, the island is all theirs. No one else can set foot on the place. Total privacy. People like that.'

It was just the way he said the words. They were happy, nonchalant. But as they left his mouth she tried to picture who would want to get away from everything. There was no obvious TV, no phone and she doubted there would be an Internet signal.

'Who comes here, Will? Do you hire it out?'

He shook his head. 'Never. This place is for friends. For people who need a little time, a little space.'

She tilted her head to the side. She'd heard of places

like this. One of the members of her dad's band had taken himself off to a mountain retreat a few years ago after numerous visits to rehab clinics. She sucked in a breath. Was this the kind of place she should have gone three years ago after her friend had died from the drug overdose?

This place was a sanctuary. A private hideaway from the world outside. It was perfect.

'Like your friend who was homeless?'

He was fighting an internal battle that played out on his tightly composed features. He gave a brief nod.

'I love it,' she whispered. 'I hope the people that come here find what they need.'

Will's hands appeared at her waist. She hadn't even realised he'd moved close to her. He exhaled sharply and she could feel his muscles relax behind her. 'That's so nice to hear you say. And it's why I don't bring people here—don't advertise the fact there's anything on this island.'

He was trusting her. He was trusting her not to say anything to the world outside. Something inside her chest fluttered.

All of a sudden she had a real awareness of the big bed on the platform behind her. It looked sumptuous. It looked inviting. They were here alone, on an island that no one else could reach. They wouldn't be disturbed.

'You don't bring people here?'

He shook his head. 'Never.' His voice was low, husky. It was sending blood racing through her veins.

Her head was swimming. She was crazy. She'd just met this guy. He might be her sister's best friend but she hardly knew him at all. Trouble was, everything she did know she liked.

Her hands rested on the warm skin of his muscled arms again, feeling the tickle of tiny hairs under the palms of her hands.

'Then why me?' Her throat felt scratchy. She was almost afraid to breathe.

Before she knew what she was doing she lifted one hand and touched his rumpled, slightly too long hair. With his dimple and killer blue eyes all he needed was a white coat and he could easily replace that actor from the lastest TV hospital show.

His head tilted slightly towards her hand as she ran her fingers through his hair, holding her breath. What on earth was she doing?

Her mouth was dry and she had a strong urge for some of the leftover wine from her sister's wedding. Last night she'd just been too exhausted to have even more than two glasses.

Will didn't seem to object to her touch. He responded instantly, stepping forward and firming his gentle grip on her waist. His face was only inches from hers. She could feel his breath on her cheek. She could see the tiny, almost invisible freckles on the bridge of his nose, the tiny lines around his eyes. Her mouth was wet and she ran her tongue across her lips. They tingled. All the pores of her skin lifted up in a soft carpet of goosebumps, each hair on her body standing up and tingling at the roots. She'd never experienced anything like this before.

He didn't bring people here—but he'd brought her. What did that mean? She had absolutely no idea.

'I thought you might like it. Might appreciate it the way others wouldn't. I was right.'

Her head was telling her to back away, to break their gaze and step out of his hold. Her brain was befuddled. She'd learned not to trust her instincts. She'd learned to question everything. But Will moved forward, the hard planes of his chest and abdomen pressing against her breasts, his hands sliding downward and tilting her pelvis towards his.

His words were like a drug. As an independent woman Rose had never craved a man's approval before. But suddenly Will Carter liking her, respecting her, seemed like the most important thing on earth.

This was it. Enough. It was time to step away. This man had led enough women on a merry dance. She wasn't about to be the next.

But her body wasn't listening to her brain.

Neither of them had spoken for the last few seconds. Any minute now he'd step away and she'd feel like a fool. She was sleep deprived—that was what was wrong.

Even though she'd gone to bed at midnight and slept soundly until this morning she was still on New York time. It was making her do strange things. It was making her act in ways that she wouldn't normally.

Will blinked. His gaze was hypnotic. She couldn't pull herself away. She didn't want to—no matter what her brain said.

'I don't just like it,' she whispered. 'I love it.' It was true. This place felt safe. Felt private. Like a complete and utter haven where two people could suspend disbelief and do anything they wanted.

She moistened her lips as his gaze lowered to her mouth.

He reached up a finger and brushed a strand of hair away from her face. His touch like butterfly wings on her skin. She bit her swollen lips. As he moved forward his scent enveloped her. Pure and utter pheromones. She couldn't get enough of them.

It was her last thought as Will Carter's lips came into contact with hers.

CHAPTER FOUR

FOR A FEW seconds he was lost. Lost in the smell of her. Lost in the taste of her. And lost in the surge of hormones that were rushing around his body.

He was engulfed in the wave of restless energy floating through the air between them, colliding like seismic waves. Someplace, somewhere the Richter scale was measuring the magnitude between them.

It was great. *She* was great. His hands skirted over her curves, his fingers brushing against her silky skin. A groan escaped from the back of his throat as every body part acted accordingly.

Then, from out of nowhere, a voice echoed in his head. *Runaway groom my sister and I'll kill you.*

It brought him back to his senses, back to reality. Violet would kill him. There was no doubt.

He stepped back, leaving Rose's lips mid-kiss and her eyes still shut. She was frozen for the tiniest of seconds in that position before her startled eyes opened.

He was trying to catch his ragged breath. Trying not to still taste her on his lips.

Their gazes collided and he saw a million things flash through her eyes. Confusion. Embarrassment. Lust.

He lifted his hands and shook his head. 'Rose, I'm so sorry. I should never have done that. I just…I just…'

He couldn't find the words—probably because his brain was completely scrambled. He walked over to the edge of the bed and sat down, running his fingers through his hair. The same motion that she'd been doing only seconds earlier.

Bad idea. Very bad idea. She looked even more confused now. He threw up his hands. 'It's this place. Here, and the church.' She still hadn't said a word. But the expression on her face was killing him. Violet really would kill him if her sister told her about this.

'I never meant for this to happen. I didn't plan it.'

'Obviously.' It was her first word and it was as cold as ice. The beautiful ambient temperature had just dropped by about twenty degrees.

'No. That's not what I mean. You're beautiful. You're more than beautiful. And your smell. And your curves. I just…'

The initial glare disappeared and the corners of her mouth started to turn upwards. His babbling must be amusing her. But he couldn't help it. He always got like this when he'd blundered. Why say three words when you could say twenty?

She stepped forward so that the fabric of her dress was almost touching his nose. It was swaying gently. He was trying not to think what was underneath. Or about the feel of her skin.

She sighed. 'Will, do I make you nervous?' He couldn't miss the hint of amusement in her voice.

He looked up. She was close, oh, so close. Her scent was there again.

'Yes…I mean no. Well, maybe.'

She folded her arms across her chest. 'How about we just file this away somewhere? You're Violet's best friend and…' she raised her eyebrows '…you have just about the worst reputation on the planet. I'm never going to get involved with a guy like you.'

'You're not?' He couldn't help it. Defence was the instant reaction to her words. What was so wrong with him anyway? Okay, he might have been engaged a few times but he was a good guy. Really, he was.

She was definitely smiling now. He should be relieved. He should be thankful. So why was he feeling a little insulted?

'No. I'm definitely not.' She turned and walked over to the window. 'Why don't we just chalk this up to a moment of madness? I need you to help me with the wedding stuff. You need me to help with your publicity. We can do this, can't we? We can spend the next few weeks around each other and forget that this ever happened.'

It wasn't a question. It was a statement of fact. She was right. He knew she was right. But Will had never had problems getting a woman before. Rose telling him outright *no* was a bit of a revelation for him.

He stood up and touched his head. She was trying to brush this off. The easiest thing in the world to do was let her. 'Why don't we just pin it down to my head injury?' He was teasing her. Hinting that she'd caused the whole thing.

But Rose was far too quick for him. She laughed. 'Are you trying to make out I've taken advantage of the person I'm supposed to be looking after? What does that make me?'

'A ruthless businesswoman.'

She smiled. She seemed to like that, then something flitted across her eyes and she glanced at her watch. 'Will? Weren't you supposed to have a business meeting this afternoon?'

Recognition flooded through him. 'Oh, no. What time is it? Darn it.'

She shook her head and opened the door. 'We've got five minutes. We can make it in that time, can't we?'

'Let's run.' He grabbed her hand as he jogged past and pulled the door closed behind them. It only took a minute to run along the path to the boat and he started the engine quickly. Rose didn't wait to be helped into the boat. She lifted her skirt up, giving him a complete flash of her bronzed legs as she jumped over the gap between the jetty and the boat. The boat rocked furiously as she landed and he grabbed her around the waist and pushed her into one of the seats.

The boat crossed the water in a few minutes. This meeting was important. He had to make it on time. But his eyes kept skimming across to Rose. Her blonde hair was streaking behind her in the wind and her yellow dress outlined her curves again.

He groaned. How on earth was he going to manage the next few weeks?

The football player was every bit as sleazy as she remembered. He'd practically sneered once Will had introduced her and he'd clicked about who her father was. But Rose couldn't have cared less. She'd work to do.

Her jewellery equipment had arrived and with the help of two of Will's staff she'd set it up quickly and spent a few hours putting the finishing touches to the two wedding rings.

'Rose, are you in here?'

She looked up from giving the rings a final polish. Will crossed the room in a few steps, smiling as usual. 'I see you managed to get things set up. How's it going?'

She held up the rings encased in their black velvet boxes. 'I've just finished. The courier will be here to pick them up in the next hour. What do you think?'

He bent forward and moved her Anglepoise light to get a better look at the intricate mix of rose and yellow gold for the bride's ring, and solid white gold for the groom's. She could see the flicker of surprise on his face.

'Rose, these are beautiful. You made these from scratch? Yourself? How on earth did you know where to start?'

She sighed and leaned back. 'Did you think I was pretending to make jewellery?'

He shook his head, obviously realising his mistake. 'No, I didn't mean it like that, it's just…' Then he stopped. And smiled. And sat down next to her.

'How do you do that to me?'

She couldn't help but grin. She knew exactly what was coming but she put on her most innocent expression. 'Do what, exactly?'

He shrugged his shoulders. 'Make me start babbling like some teenage boy. I always seem to say the wrong thing around you, then can't find the words to straighten things out.'

She raised her eyebrows. 'I thought you said I didn't make you nervous.'

He frowned. 'Well, you don't. But then—you do.' He flung up his hands. 'See, I don't know.'

She laughed. 'How did your business meeting go with El Creepo?'

His mouth fell open and his shoulders started shaking. 'El Creepo? That's what you're calling him?'

She nodded sombrely and folded her arms. 'I think it suits him.'

'I think you might be right.' He ran his fingers through his hair, carefully avoiding his stitched forehead. Guilt surged through her again. It had to be sore, but he hadn't complained at all. 'But at the moment he's the best bet I've got. You're right. There's just something about him I can't put my finger on. But if it's the only way to raise publicity then what choice do I have?'

Sitting in such close proximity to Will, she could see the tiny lines around his eyes and on his forehead. He was genuinely worried about this. He was genuinely trying to do some good. How far would he go?

She bit her lip. 'I might have some alternative ideas about that.'

'For the publicity?'

'Yes.' She rubbed her hands on her dress. It was warm in this room. Her soldering equipment gave out a lot of heat, which only made it worse. And she couldn't wait to actually hit the shower and change her clothes.

'Tell me more.'

She shook her head. 'Not yet, and you still have to hold your side of the bargain.' She stood up. 'I want to get changed and have a shower but I don't have any of my things.'

He looked a little sheepish. 'Actually you do. Violet sent your bright blue case over. I take it you'll have everything you need in there? Why don't you freshen up and we can have some dinner?'

Violet had sent her case over? Just like that? Just wait until she spoke to her sister. She'd better not be trying to matchmake.

She gave a little nod of her head just as Will's eyes twinkled and his smile broadened to reveal his dimples. Darn it. Those were the last things she needed to see right now.

'Now, I'm only showing you to a room in my house if you promise not to cause any damage.'

He was waiting for her at the door. 'Do you keep any ancient vases in your rooms?' she quipped.

'Not in yours,' he countered.

'Any unidentified men crawling into bed with perfect strangers?'

His gaze met hers. 'Only if requested.'

Her breath caught in her throat as her skin prickled involuntarily. Oh, boy, he was good. She had to keep remembering just how many times this guy had been attached. Still, dinner at Gideon Hall might actually be quite nice. Rose was as nosey as the next person and always liked to see around beautiful homes.

Will led her up the large curved staircase and along a corridor. Everything was sparkling. Everything was clean. Everything was cream.

He swung open the door of one room and she stepped inside. Finally, a tiny bit of colour. Pale yellow to complement the cream. It was gorgeous. She couldn't help but walk straight across to touch the ornate curtains. Curtains and soft furnishings had always been her weakness. It was like something from one of those classy house magazines. An enormous bed with soft bedding and cushions that just invited you to dive in, pale yellow wallpaper with tiny flowers, a pale yellow carpet and light-coloured furniture all leading to large windows looking over the gardens.

'These are beautiful. The whole place is beautiful.' She smiled wickedly. 'Which one of your brides-to-be helped you decorate?'

'Actually, some of it I chose myself. Others, I had some help from professionals.' He straightened a little more and his chest puffed out. He was obviously pleased with the backhanded compliment.

'Really?' She was surprised. She'd just imagined that he'd waved his hand and asked someone else to sort all this out for him.

'Yes, really. Why does that seem strange?'

'It just does, that's all.'

'It's strange that a guy is interested in how his home looks?'

She paused. When he said it out loud it didn't seem so strange. She just couldn't imagine Will Carter sitting with a dozen sample books and picking wallpaper and soft furnishings.

She walked over and stuck her head into the white bathroom with pale yellow towels. Everything matching perfectly. 'Okay, maybe not.'

He gave a little nod. As if he was pleased he'd won the argument. 'How about I leave you to freshen up and we meet downstairs later for dinner?' He hesitated. 'Is there anything you don't like? Any allergies?'

She shook her head. 'I'll let you into a secret. I'm a simple girl. Chicken is my favourite no matter what you do to it.'

He looked relieved. 'I can definitely do chicken.' He glanced towards the window again. 'How do you feel about sitting outside? We could have dinner on the patio overlooking the gardens and the lake.'

Her insides gave a little flutter. This was starting to sound a lot more like a date than a business meeting. And even though it was wrong—even though she'd already told Will he would never be for her—it was still flattering.

The last few years had been hard. She wasn't the party girl she'd been before. She'd been used to flirting and high-speed dating. As soon as she'd bored of one guy, she'd moved on to the next—none of them serious.

But everything had changed after Autumn's death. They'd been friends for a few years and had liked socialising together. When Rose had left the party with the man of the moment she'd assumed Autumn was fine, too. An assumption that was completely wrong. She'd been foolish. And partly to blame. Even though Rose had never dabbled with drugs herself she'd known that Autumn did so on occasion. But Autumn was independent and strong-willed. Telling her not to do something was practically impossible. But the guilt Rose felt was still overwhelming. If she'd been there, she would have noticed Autumn was unwell. Her friend wouldn't have been found slumped in a corner and not breathing. She could have called an ambulance and intervened.

Instead a few hours later she'd heard her dad's scratchy voice on the phone demanding to know where she was and if she was okay. Rose had known straight away something was wrong. Her parents were very liberal and once the girls had reached the age of twenty-one they could pretty much do what they wanted. By the grand old age of twenty-four she should have known so much better. She'd never forgotten the look on his face as she'd pulled up in a taxi outside Huntingdon Hall. He'd been standing in the doorway watching for her while her mother was sitting inside waiting to tell her the news.

Drug deaths were always good media fodder. And Rose had found herself the unwitting angle for every story.

Pop star's daughter at drug party.

Wild child Rose Huntingdon-Cross's friend dies of drug overdose.

After the funeral she hadn't been able to get out of the country quick enough. Dealing with PR was the last thing she'd wanted to do. But it went hand in hand with the job for her dad's band. She'd learned who to talk to, who to ignore and who to threaten to sue. All valuable skills in this life.

Skills she was going to exploit to help Will Carter get what he wanted. She only hoped he'd listen to reason when she explained what she wanted to do. She smiled at him. 'Dinner outside would be lovely. Thanks. Give me an hour to get changed.'

He gave a little nod of his head and walked out, closing

the door behind him. Leaving Rose staring out over the lake towards the island. She ran her hands up and down her arms. There was something about that place. Something magical. Something mystical. And there was no way she was ever setting foot there again with Will Carter.

Violet's sister. Violet's sister. He muttered the words under his breath all along the length of the corridor. If he kept reminding himself that he'd put the relationship with his best friend at risk if he ventured too near, he might actually convince himself.

He had to do something, because right now his head was full of *that kiss*.

The softness of her hair, the silkiness of her skin, the taste of her lips. Enough.

He had to stop this. Violet had warned him, and she almost knew him better than he knew himself. She knew he fell head over heels with the next beautiful woman to come along—suitable or not. And Rose was definitely *not* suitable.

But Rose wasn't like any of the others. He'd never felt compelled to take any of his fiancées to the island—none of them had ever shown much interest.

And none of them had ever had the same expression in their eyes that Rose had when he'd shown her into her room. It wasn't anything to do with wealth or prosperity; it was to do with making a house a home. Rose appreciated that. And he appreciated her because of it.

He walked down the wide staircase and into the kitchen where Judy, his housekeeper and chef all rolled into one, was waiting. 'What'll it be?' She smiled.

'Chicken. Do whatever you like with it, as long as it's chicken.'

She nodded. 'Well, that's easy. Do you want some dessert, too?'

Darn it. He hadn't even thought to ask. But Judy was used to him.

'How about some fresh fruit pavlova? I made some earlier for that grump of a football player but he didn't want any.'

Will gave a sigh of relief. 'Perfect.' He took a quick look around the kitchen. As usual everything was gleaming. The staff who worked here really took their jobs seriously. He was lucky to have them.

Judy started pulling ingredients from the huge fridge. 'So, who is our guest, then? Anybody I should know?'

He shook his head quickly. 'It's nobody. It's just Violet's sister.'

Judy looked interested. 'Rose? I've heard Violet talk about her a lot but I've never met her before. Are they alike?'

He paused, not quite sure how to answer. Violet had never made the blood race back through his veins as Rose had. 'They look alike, but they're totally different people,' he said quickly. It seemed the simplest enough answer.

Judy gave a little nod of her head as she started slicing vegetables on a wooden board. 'I'll look forward to meeting her, then. Dinner will be ready in about forty minutes. Just give me a shout when you're ready.' She gave Will a little wink and he cringed. She always did that.

It was almost as if she could read his mind and see what he was really thinking.

Business. That was what this was. And if he kept that in his head he'd do fine. Weddings. He tried to stop the shiver going down his spine at the mere thought of it. He could write a list. That was what he'd do. He'd change his shirt, then write a list for Rose of the things she'd need to plan.

Anything to keep him on track.

* * *

Rose was used to luxury. Their family home certainly didn't scrimp on anything. Hawksley Castle had been something else entirely. But this place—Gideon Hall—added a whole new dimension.

It wasn't quite as big as Huntingdon Hall but it had more land—more space. And Will's taste was surprisingly good. The furnishings were comfortable but stylish. It had a show-home look about it, while still giving that you-could-actually-live-here feel.

She finished drying her hair and opened her suitcase to find some more clothes. It didn't take long. Clean underwear and a bright blue knee-length jersey dress. Even though the sun wasn't quite so high in the sky it was still hot outside and the last thing she wanted to do round about Will Carter was feel hot and bothered.

She gave a quick squirt of perfume, spent two minutes putting on some make-up and stuck on some flat, comfortable gold sandals. Done.

By the time she walked down the main staircase at Gideon Hall she was feeling like a new woman. It was amazing what a shower and change of clothes could do for a girl. Will was standing at the door to the huge kitchen. 'Rose, come and meet Judy. She's made dinner for us.'

Rose came into the kitchen and held her hand out towards Judy. 'It's a pleasure to meet you. I hope you haven't gone to too much trouble for us.'

Judy beamed and shook her hand swiftly. 'You're so much like your sister. It's amazing. Do you ever get mistaken for each other?'

Will could see the tiniest flicker of something in Rose's face. She'd probably heard this for the best part of her twenty-seven years. And from most of the pictures he'd seen of Violet and Rose they normally tried to look a bit different—a bit more individual.

Rose touched her long, straight hair. 'We look alike more by default than anything deliberate. I've been in the States for the last few years. Violet and I always tried something different. I would be shorter, she would be longer. I would go lighter, she'd go darker. I'd be curls, she'd be straight. You get the picture.' She shrugged her shoulders. She fingered a lock of her blonde hair. 'I'll really need to do something with this.'

'Don't you dare.' The words were out before he knew it and both heads turned towards him with startled expressions on their faces. He gulped and let out his best attempt at a laugh. 'Oh, I was just joking. Will we have some wine? What would you prefer—white or red?'

'White, sparkling if you have any.' Both women exchanged an amused glance as Will felt himself bluster around the kitchen. Where was the darn sparkling wine when he needed it?

Judy pulled the chicken from the oven and the smell of bubbling chicken stock, tomatoes and spicy peppers swamped the kitchen. 'That smells great,' said Rose. 'Is there anything I can do to help?'

Judy waved her hand. 'Not at all. Give me two minutes and I'll plate up for you, then you can take it outside. The cutlery and napkins are already there.'

He finally managed to find a chilled bottle of wine and popped the cork before grabbing a couple of glasses. Rose stood waiting with two plates of piping hot food in her hands. 'Lead the way, Mr Carter, and I hope you're prepared for this business meeting we're about to have.'

He couldn't help but smile as he led her through the house and out through the wide open doors at the dining room. The table was positioned on the patio overlooking the gardens and lake. It only took a few moments to pour the wine and he sat across from her and raised his glass.

'To interesting bed companions.'

She grinned and clinked his glass. 'To things that go bump in the morning.'

This was such a bad idea. She knew it from the second they clinked glasses and she let the cold sparkling wine slide down her throat. How many times had he done this before? Had a woman sit with him overlooking the gardens for dinner? The house was spectacular. Judy's cooking was brilliant. And Will was looking at her with that twinkle in his eyes…

He pulled out a piece of paper from his back pocket. 'Here. I've made you a list.'

'A list of what?' She spun the paper around and looked at the printed list with the bold heading of Wedding Arrangements. She bit the inside of her cheek to stop herself from laughing. 'What? You have a ready-made template just sitting, waiting for use?'

His brow wrinkled and he waved his fork at her. 'Enough. If you want my help, you're going to have to stop with all the wedding jokes. I thought you might want it for that black planner of yours.'

She tilted her head to one side as she lifted her glass towards him. 'You're such a spoilsport.'

He lifted his hand to his head and feigned a flinch. 'I think I've already suffered quite enough at your hands.'

'How long are you going to keep this up?'

He couldn't hide his smirk. 'Let's see. Stitches come out in seven days—at least that long.'

'If I find another vase, I'm hitting you again.'

He leaned across the table towards her and hit her with his million-watt grin. 'Oh, go on, Rose, play fair.'

She couldn't help but laugh. Even when he was annoying, Will Carter was still alarmingly cute. And handsome. And sexy.

She took a final bite of the chicken and glanced down at the list. 'Why do some of these have ticks?'

Will leaned back in his chair and started counting off on his fingers. 'Rose, you've no idea how easy you've got it. The biggest thing—the venue. Your parents have already said they want to do it at Huntingdon Hall. Easy.' He gave a little shrug. 'You really need to check numbers though. You'll need to ensure you get a big enough marquee for the grounds.'

She gulped. A marquee. Where on earth was she going to find one of those, big enough to accommodate wedding guests and available in less than four weeks just as they were coming into summer? She lifted her glass. 'I think I'm going to need some more wine. What else?'

He kept counting on his fingers. 'Wedding photographer you've got. Why would you use anyone but Daisy?'

She nodded. 'But what about the pics we want Daisy to be in?'

'Doesn't she have an assistant?'

Rose racked her brain. 'I'm not sure. I'll need to ask.'

Will continued. 'As for the flowers, it goes without saying that Violet will do them. Even if it does mean getting up to go to some flower market at three a.m.'

Rose nodded. Violet would be able to conjure up whatever concoction her mother wanted for the day. Sherry had a tendency to like beautiful, bright and exotic flowers rather than the quiet-style flowers she'd named her daughters after.

'So what does that leave?'

Will took a sip of wine. 'Band, celebrant—or whoever they want to say their vows to—caterers, décor, wedding favours, drinks and bar.' He wrinkled his nose. 'Will you need a children's entertainer? Or a nanny for the guests' kids? Cars?' He waved his hand. 'No, they're getting married at home.'

Rose felt her stomach start to lurch. He was saying this was easy, but it sounded anything but. 'I have a horrible feeling that both Mum and Dad will want to make an entrance. They'll probably leave by the back door and come back up the drive for the wedding in front of the guests.'

'So you will need cars?'

She picked up the pen sitting on the table and drew a thick black line through the word *Cars*. 'Absolutely not. With what I know is sitting in Dad's garages? Between what Mum knows about, and what she doesn't, there will definitely be enough for her to pick something she likes to come up the driveway in. Surely it's not that big a deal?'

Will let out a laugh. 'Oh, you've got so much to learn in so little time.' His hand came casually across the table and touched hers. 'Are you really ready for this?'

In an instant her tongue was sticking to the roof of her mouth, the inside so dry a camel could be marching through it. A dozen little centipedes had just invaded her body and were racing their way up the inside of her arm and directly to her fluttering heart. It was a warm evening. She wasn't the least bit cold. But the heat currently shooting up her arm could light up this whole mansion house.

What on earth was wrong with her? She'd been on lots of dates. She'd had a few relationships. But she'd never felt any of the old thunderbolts and lightning. She'd always thought that was nonsense.

But it seemed as if her body was trying to tell her something else entirely.

When she'd got ready earlier she hadn't really been that concerned about what she was wearing or how she looked.

But all of a sudden it felt as if her dress might be a little too clingy, a little too revealing. She could sense his eyes on her curves, following the slope of her hips and swell of her breasts. She sat up a little straighter.

Her brain kept trying to temper her body's responses. *Runaway Groom. He's the Runaway Groom. He's absolutely, definitely* not *for you.*

Was she ready for all this? Not a chance.

Will wasn't quite sure what was happening. He'd virtually face-planted himself into his last four relationships and engagements. He'd been swept along with the early joy and the passion.

But this was something else entirely.

All he wanted to do was reach across the table and grab her and kiss her. It didn't help that the world was plotting against him and the sun had started to dip slightly in the sky, silhouetting her figure and perfect blonde hair on her shoulders. Or, more importantly, highlighting her silky skin and waiting-to-be-kissed lips.

It was automatic. The thought made him lick his lips and he could swear he could still taste her from earlier. He pulled his hands back from hers and lifted the wine glass to his lips. Empty. Darn it. It seemed as if both of them had inexplicably dry mouths.

He made an attempt to focus on the list. *Out of bounds.* He had to keep saying it over and over in his head.

His eyes scanned down the list of wedding items. There. That would stop him. Nothing like a list of wedding to-dos to temper his libido.

'What about catering? Do you have anyone in mind?'

Rose visibly jerked in her chair. It was as if her brain had been circling in the same clouds as his. At least that was what he was hoping.

She groaned. 'Oh, no. That will be a nightmare. Mum and Dad are so fussy about food.'

'You can't pull any special favours?'

She shook her head. 'I've already pulled special favours for the tour. And that was only to cater for five members of the band. We don't even know how many people they're inviting yet but I can guarantee you—it won't be five.'

Will frowned. 'It's such short notice. I hate to say it but you might need to take what you can get.'

'Oh, don't say that.' Rose put her head on the table, her blonde hair flicking up dramatically behind her. He smiled. She might appear calm on the surface but when the moment occurred it appeared that Rose could do drama.

He frowned. 'There's a conference on Monday at the Newbridge Auditorium. It's for businesses but there are always lots of caterers in attendance, trying to tout for business at events.'

She lifted her head just a little from the table. He could only see one eye beneath the long locks. 'Catering for a business event isn't even in the same league as catering for a wedding.'

He arched his eyebrow at her. 'You'd be surprised. Some of these events have cordon bleu chefs. Again—numbers might be an issue. And you'll need to have some idea of a menu. Do you know what they like?'

'That's easy. Mum likes chicken and Dad will want steak with all the trimmings. But it has to taste just right.'

'Like mother, like daughter?'

She straightened in her chair. 'Yeah, I guess so. Though in most things I'm most like my dad.' She picked up a pencil. 'Dessert will need to be something chocolate for Mum—usually with orange—and anything with straw-berries or raspberries for Dad.'

She screwed up her nose as she studied the list. 'Balloons, seat covers, wedding gifts, evening favours, wedding cake, hors d'oeuvres, and a bar.' Her head thumped back on the table. 'I can't do all this!'

Will reached over and grabbed her hand, this time propelling her from her chair and pulling her towards him. She barely had time to think about it before he plunked her down on his knee and wrapped his arm around her waist. 'I'm helping you. That's what the deal is. By Monday night we will have a caterer. By Tuesday we'll have sorted the chair covers, balloons and favours. If you pay enough you can pretty much get what you want.'

He stood up and turned her around in his arms, reaching up to touch her cheek, trying not to drink in the feel of her. 'Rose, stop worrying. I've already told you—the biggest things are sorted.' Her hands had moved automatically to his waist, her fingers gently pressing through his shirt. He wanted them to move. He wanted to feel them stroke across the expanse of his back and shoulders. He wanted to feel them running up the planes of his chest and wrap around his neck. If they could just move a little closer...

She was staring up at him with those big blue eyes. It made his breath catch in his throat. She'd never looked so beautiful. And for a second he was sure she was looking at him exactly the way that he was looking at her.

But then she blinked. And it was as if something had just flicked on in her brain. 'Yes, because you know all about this stuff, don't you?' Her hands fell from his sides and she took a step back.

What had just happened?

He gave himself an internal shake. 'Okay. Sit down. I'll go and get some of Judy's pavlova for us and some coffee. Then you can tell me all about your PR ideas for my homeless charity. Fair's fair.'

He picked up the plates and gave her a smile as he headed back inside. It only took a few minutes to be out of her sight and he stopped and pressed his head against the cool corridor wall. What was he thinking?

He was going to have to put a No Touching sign on her head.

Because if he didn't—he'd get himself into a whole load of trouble.

The pavlova looked magnificent, with lots of layers of gooey meringue, lashings of fresh cream and oodles of strawberries, raspberries and kiwi fruit. A girl might think she was in heaven. That, followed by the smell of rich coffee, was making her already full stomach think it might have to squeeze a little more inside.

She was ready. She was prepared. She'd taken the few moments of Will's absence to gather herself. A quick dash to the bathroom and a splash of water on her face and wrists had cooled her down. Technically speaking. It hadn't stopped that crazy irregular pattern inside her chest that she was trying to ignore.

Now, she was in control. And Will was back to his amiable, joking self. No more hot looks of what might be. No lingering glances or widening pupils.

'So what's the plan for PR?'

His voice sounded so calm, so laid-back. Now was the time to find out if he really was.

She savoured the last mouthful of pavlova and set down her fork. Her words were simple and she said them as if they were the most obvious thing in the world. 'The plan, Will—is you.'

He wrinkled his nose. 'What?'

She waved her hand. 'I didn't know you were associated with that homeless charity until you told me. And then I asked myself why. Because you've had more than enough media coverage in your time.'

He gave a shake of his head. 'But that was all the wedding stuff. It was all personal. It doesn't really count.'

She shook her head and leaned towards him. He really didn't get it. 'But that's just it, Will. *You're* the story. *You're* the person people want to read about. People love you. Your reputation as the Runaway Groom precedes you and it's time to use it to your advantage.'

The frown seemed to be spreading across his face. 'No. I don't agree. I hate all that stuff. How on earth can being known as the Runaway Groom help a homeless charity?'

She took a deep breath. It was obvious he was going to take some persuading. 'You've seen all the TV shows with phone-in voting?'

He nodded warily. 'Yes, all the wannabe pop-star stuff?'

'Exactly. They often have the same things in newspapers. Vote for your favourite TV soap star. Vote for your favourite model.'

He was nodding slowly. 'I still don't get it. What does that have to do with me?'

She gave him her best PR smile. 'We're going to do something similar with you.'

He was shaking his head again. 'Why on earth would anyone vote for me?'

Rose sucked in a deep breath and talked quickly. 'People love the fact you were the Runaway Groom. Imagine we had a number of trials or dares for you to do. All hideous. All things that people would cringe at. We can ask the public to vote on which of them you should do for the homeless charity—earning money and raising awareness along the way.'

'But why on earth would people be interested in that?'

This was it. This was when she finally revealed her master stroke.

'Because there'll be four separate possibilities. All set by each of your jilted brides.'

'What?'

Rose jumped in quickly before he had too much time to think about it. 'Just think about it. I bet some of them still want revenge on you. They'll probably take great pleasure in making a hideous suggestion for a dare. And I can spin it. From what you've told me, each one of your brides-to-be were interested in being in the media. If I pitch it to them as an opportunity to take a bit of revenge on you—plus the fact the money will be going to charity *and* you'll have to do whatever the winning dare is—I'm sure they'll take part. What's more the press will eat it up.'

Will's head had been shaking from the second she started speaking. His face wasn't pale as if he were shocked—it was starting to go red as if she'd made him angry. 'You have got to be joking. *This?* This is your plan?'

She shifted in her chair. 'If you'll just take a minute to consider it…'

He stood up sharply and his chair flew backwards. 'Take a minute? Take a minute to consider humiliating myself in front of millions? Have people talk about me instead of the charity? I'd be a laughing stock.'

Rose stayed as cool as she could. She lifted her coffee cup and took a sip as if guys shouting at her happened every day. In New York it wasn't that unusual and she was made of sterner stuff.

'Yes, you would,' she said simply. 'But people would be interested to know why you were doing it. Why the world's most eligible bachelor would put himself through it. That would lead them to the homeless charity.'

His fists were clenched and pressing down on the table.

She could see the flicker of an angry tic in his jaw. But after a few moments his breathing seemed to ease and the flush in his face died down. Rose sat quietly, sipping her coffee and looking out over the view.

This was the perfect solution to his PR problems. It had come to her earlier on and she'd known he wouldn't like it. But if he was as committed to the charity as he claimed to be, he'd realise just how much this could work.

He glanced behind him and grimaced as he picked up the chair. After a few seconds he sat back down and put his head in his hands.

Patience. Men had to be left to think things through. In a few days Will Carter would probably be claiming the idea was his own. Or maybe not.

He lifted his head slightly, his deep blue eyes locking on hers. 'You really think this could work?'

She nodded slowly. 'I think it's a darn sight better idea than dealing with El Creepo footballer. You know he's a recipe for disaster.'

Will groaned and leaned back in the chair. 'I know he is. But people like him. Even if he is a prat.'

She smiled at him. 'No, Will. People like *you*.' She let the words hang in the air for a second or two.

He was still looking sceptical. 'Do you honestly think you could persuade my exes to take part?'

She bit her lip. 'If I pitch it right they will be jumping all over this. There's nothing like a woman scorned.'

He grimaced. 'But I never wanted to hurt any of them. And this will just bring all those bad feelings to the surface again.'

'And some of those bad feelings are exactly what we need. Those bad feelings will probably give us some spectacular dares that the public will be willing to pick up the phone and vote for.'

She hated that it sounded so mercenary. It wasn't really Rose's nature but the reality was, if Will really wanted publicity for his charity in a short space of time this was exactly the way to do it.

He started pacing. She could almost see his brain ticking over all the pros and cons.

'I'm still worried. Two of my exes will probably be fine. They've moved on. They've got married. Both of them have told me they were glad things didn't work out between us.' He waved his hand and gave a rueful smile. 'They know we just weren't right for each other. And they've got their happy ever after with someone else.' He frowned. 'Another has got into the media spotlight. The extra publicity will probably suit her. Looking back, I'm sure that's why she dated me in the first place. But the fourth? I just don't know...'

'Is this the one you actually left at the altar?'

He nodded and shook his head. 'Melissa was fiancée number two. I still feel terrible. She didn't take things well and she still hates me.'

'Might this be a little redemption for her? A way to draw a line under things?'

'I just don't know.' He pulled out his phone.

'What are you doing?'

'I'm going to talk to Violet.'

For the weirdest reason her heart plummeted. 'You are?' How ridiculous. Violet was his best friend. Of course he wanted to talk to her. It was only natural.

But it made her stomach curl up in the strangest way.

A way she'd never felt before.

She'd never once been jealous of her sister. They were close. They always supported each other. They'd never had a serious falling-out. Only the usual sisterly spats. But all of a sudden she was feeling strangely jealous of the relationship between Violet and Will. He trusted her. He valued her opinion. And it was almost as if he were second-guessing her advice.

The call lasted only a minute and there was nothing secret about it. She could hear Violet's shrieks of laughter at the other end of the phone. 'It's perfect. The press will love it. I told you my sister was a genius!'

Guilt flooded through her, heat rushing to her cheeks. Violet always had her back, always—even in the worst of circumstances.

Will glanced at her, uncertainty still lacing his eyes. She held her tongue. There was nothing she could say at this point to persuade him. He had to think it through for himself. There was only one natural conclusion he could come to.

She stood up and held out her hand. 'Thank you for a lovely evening, Will. I'm feeling tired. I think I'll go to bed. I take it you've got no ill effects from your headache and I'll be free to go home tomorrow?'

He stared at her outstretched hand for a few seconds. Maybe it was the strange formality between two people who'd kissed a little earlier? But he took a few steps and walked over and shook her hand.

Darn it. There it was again. The little shot straight up her arm, tingling all the way. No matter how many times she tried to ignore it, it wasn't a figment of her imagination. His hand was warm and firm.

It was the first time she'd been around Will and he looked anything less than confident and sure of himself. Her suggestions for publicity had obviously unsettled him.

'Thank you, Rose,' he said distractedly.

She turned away to head back in the house. It was odd. The strangest feeling. She'd much preferred it when the atmosphere between them had been light and flirty. This horrible unsettled feeling was uncomfortable. As much as she didn't want to admit it, being around Will Carter was a lot more interesting than she'd first expected.

Her head told her one thing, and every female hormone in her body told her a whole other. It was exhausting.

But she was curious to see where it would take her.

'Rose?' She turned at the sound of his voice, her heart giving a little leap in her chest.

'Remember Monday—the business conference. We'll find you a caterer.'

'Sure.' She nodded, hoping to not let the disappointment show. 'Thanks.'

She turned back and lengthened her strides back into the house.

Monday had never felt so far away.

CHAPTER FIVE

Violet and Rose waited impatiently on the chaise longue. Their mother was doing her usual—making them wait. 'Do you have your phone to text Daisy?' Violet asked.

'No pictures,' yelled their mother from the other room. 'I don't want there to be any possibility of a leak to the press.'

The girls rolled their eyes at each other. Sherry had already tried on eleven dresses from various designer friends ranging from barely there to tulle princess. None of them had really suited. 'Has she given you any instructions on the flowers yet?' Rose whispered.

Violet nodded. 'And I'm sworn to secrecy. I've not to say a word.'

'But you can tell me.'

Violet shook her head. 'Not even you.'

Rose felt the indignation rise in her chest. 'You've got to be joking. After everything that's been dumped on me—you're not allowed to tell me about the flowers?'

Violet shrugged. She was entirely used to their mother's little quibbles and obviously didn't think it was worth getting tied in a knot about.

She shot Rose a look. That kind of look. 'So how's things with you and my best friend?'

Rose could feel the hackles rise at the back of her neck. She was instantly on the defensive. 'What do you mean?'

'Have you kissed him yet?'

'What? Why on earth did you ask me that?'

Violet counted off on her fingers. 'Because he's Will Carter. He's charming. He's lovable. And everyone loves him.' She lifted her eyebrows. 'And you two haven't met before. And don't think I didn't notice the little buzz of chemistry yesterday. What's going on?'

Rose was annoyed. 'Chemistry? There was no chemistry. The guy climbed into my bed and I cracked him over the head with a vase. How is that chemistry?'

'But you spent all day yesterday with him *and* you spent the night at his place.'

If only she knew that Rose had spent the whole night tossing and turning in the bed at Gideon Hall wondering— even for a second—if Will might appear. Useless thoughts. Ridiculous thoughts. And thoughts that had made her even angrier and made her feel even more foolish as the dark hours of night had turned into the early hours of morning.

'Nothing happened. Absolutely nothing. You know exactly why I had to stay there—because *you* wouldn't help me.'

Violet gave a few tuts. 'Wow. I think the girl protests too much,' she joked. 'Watch out. He'll sucker you in.'

Rose sucked in a deep breath, ready to erupt at her sister but she didn't get that far.

'What about this one?' Their mother's voice cracked a little as they turned to face her.

Sherry Huntingdon had never lost her model figure or her mane of golden locks. She easily looked fifteen years younger than she actually was.

Rose gasped and lifted her hand to her mouth. 'Oh, Mum, that's it. That's the one. It's perfect.'

Violet was on her feet, walking over to touch the ruched fabric scattered with tiny jewels. The dress was a showstopper. It hugged every curve of her frame, fitting like a glove in satin covered in tiny sparkling jewels with a huge fishtail.

'You think?' Yes, her voice was definitely breaking. It was all getting too much for her. It was the perfect dress for the perfect wedding.

'I love it, Mum,' said Rose with pride. Her mother had never looked quite so stunning as she did today.

'Veil or no veil?'

'No veil.' Both girls spoke in unison, then turned to each other and laughed.

Their mum hesitated a second. 'I've picked a dress for all three of you. You just need to pick a colour each.' She held up a bright blue dress on a hanger. It had sheer shoulders, a fitted bodice with a jewel clasp gathered just under the breasts and a loose full-length skirt. 'Do you think it will suit Daisy? I didn't want to pick something that made her pregnancy so obvious.'

Rose nodded. 'I think it looks great.' She held the layers of material in the skirt and swished it from side to side. 'What colour do you want, Violet?'

'Either red or dark purple. What about you?'

'I like this bright blue. Will we wear jewel colours? Do you think Daisy would wear emerald green?'

'I don't see why not.' She nodded. 'Bright colours would be nice.' Violet exchanged a glance with her mother. It was obvious thoughts were spinning through her brain. Rose was curious. What were they thinking about?

'We'll talk colours later,' Sherry said quickly before spinning around. 'Now, will someone unzip me so we can talk headpieces?'

Rose was exhausted. Her mother's dress was picked. Their dresses were more or less agreed on, and they'd tried on

an endless amount of jewellery and headpieces yesterday.
And that was only the dresses.

She'd emailed a number of caterers and not had one
single response. Marquee companies were being equally
silent and it was all starting to make her panic. Hopefully
things would be better with Will today.

He'd assured her that as long as they were willing to pay
a premium price they'd be able to find someone suitable.

She shifted nervously on her feet and fiddled with an
earring while she waited for him to arrive. Two minutes
later she could hear the purr of a car coming down the
driveway. Will pulled up in a car identical to her father's
vintage Rolls-Royce only this time in silver. She raised
her eyebrows in surprise as he climbed out and walked
around to open her door for her.

'What?' He grinned. 'Did you think only your dad had
one of these?'

She climbed in. 'I thought you would have wanted
something more modern—more environmentally friendly.'
It was a nice touch—a man opening a door for her.

He slid into the seat next to her. 'Quality and class. I
spent a number of years waiting to buy this car. Now I've
got it, I fully intend to drive it.'

She squinted at the row of stitches on his head. The
swelling had definitely gone down now and she could see
the edges pulled tightly together. 'How's your head? Does
it hurt?'

'Is that concern after what—two days?' He was mock-
ing her, trying to get a rise out of her. He leaned a little
closer conspiratorially. 'It's itchy. I thought I was going to
have to put a set of gloves on last night to stop me scratching it in my sleep.'

'Ouch. Isn't there a cream or something you can put on
it to stop it itching?'

He shook his head as the car sped along the winding country roads and headed towards the motorway. 'I'm not to touch it at all. So scratching is definitely not allowed!'

There it was again. That annoying little flutter in her stomach that let her know this was her fault.

'Do you really think we'll find a caterer today? I'm getting worried. I've contacted a few and heard nothing.'

He nodded as they turned towards the motorway. 'I think we'll find someone. I hope you're hungry.'

'Why?'

'Because they'll all have workstations and they'll be cooking so all the businesses can sample their food. Catering an event is a really big deal. It pays big bucks. They go all out at these events.'

'Really? We'll get to eat the food?'

He smiled. 'Really. I guarantee you. You won't be able to eat for a week after this.'

She sighed and leaned back into the comfortable leather seat as they started to hit the traffic. 'It's just a pity we can't clone Judy and get her to make all the food. That chicken the other night was great.'

He smiled in appreciation. 'She's great. And no. You can't have her. She's my secret weapon.'

She shuffled in the seat. 'Have you given any more thought to the publicity?' Great. She could see his knuckles tighten on the steering wheel and start to blanch.

'Let's talk about it later.' He leaned over and turned on the radio. The conversation was obviously over. Rose turned and looked out of the window. She was still ticking off things in her head. She'd have to talk to Will about marquees; they were proving a real problem. If she could get the caterer sorted out today that would be at least one more thing off her list. Then it would be into the murky world of wedding favours and table decorations.

Will signalled and pulled off the motorway towards the conference centre. The car park was already jam-packed but he moved straight to the valet parking at the front and jumped out. Rose didn't even want to consider how much this was costing.

The conference centre was full of people in designer-cut suits and Italian leather shoes. She looked down at her simple fitted beige trousers and white loose shirt with a variety of beads. 'You should have warned me I'm under-dressed,' she hissed. 'I could have changed.'

His brow wrinkled as he walked forward. 'You look perfect. What are you worrying about?' He glanced at the map in his hands. 'Here, Hall C is where all the caterers are. Let's head there.'

He nodded and said hello to a few folk as they wove their way through the crowds. There really wasn't much need for the map. The smells emanating from Hall C would have led them in the right direction.

It was definitely the busiest part. Will didn't hesitate. He made his way straight over to the first booth and picked up a disposable plate and fork. 'Come on,' he whispered. 'Have a quick taste. If you don't like it we'll move on.'

The aroma of spicy chicken and beef was wafting around her, making her ravenous. She took a spoonful and grabbed a taste just as Will did. Her eyes watered and she turned to face him, trying not to laugh.

Within a few seconds he had a similar expression on his face. He gestured towards a nearby table stocked with iced water and glasses. 'Water?' The word squeaked out and she had to put a hand in front of her mouth. She nodded and followed quickly to the table, grabbing the glass of iced water that he poured. She swallowed swiftly and allowed the cool water to ease her scorching throat.

'Wow. I think they overdid the chillies.' She could almost feel a tear in her eye.

Will gulped down a second glass of water. 'Well, that was a wake-up call.' He grabbed her hand. 'Here, let's go somewhere things will be more soothing.'

He pulled her over towards an Italian stand where lasagne, spaghetti bolognaise and chicken *arrabiata* were all waiting to be sampled. They both played safe, taking a small sample of lasagne and spaghetti. It was good. Meaty, creamy with just the right amount of herbs. 'It's lovely,' Rose sighed. 'But it wouldn't do for Mum and Dad's wedding.'

Will nodded. 'Let's try some more.' Half an hour later they'd tried some Chinese food, some sushi, some Indian food and lots of traditional English dishes. Rose was no closer to finding something she really liked. She was pushing some food around her plate. 'Oh, no. This chicken looks a bit pink. I'm not eating that.'

Will whipped the plate out of her hand and dumped it in the rubbish bin. 'Wait. There's someone I know. His food is good. Let's try him.'

He walked with confidence, his hand encircling hers just as it had all day. It sent nice little impulses up her arm and gave her a strange sense of belonging. England had always been her home. She'd lived at Huntingdon Hall since she'd been a little girl. But spending most of her time in New York these last three years had given her a bit of space and distance.

Being around Will was making her think hard about her choices. Her father had already mentioned she would need to be back here for the band's European tour. But as much as she loved New York and her friends, it was beginning to lose its shine. Seeing her younger sister Daisy get married had made her feel a little flutter of homesickness.

Knowing that Daisy would have a baby soon and wanting to be around her new niece or nephew definitely made her want to stay close to home.

Will steered her over towards a new stand. 'Hi, Frank. This is my friend Rose Huntingdon-Cross. We're hoping to get an event catered soon.'

Frank put his hand out and shook Rose's hand warmly. 'Pleasure to meet you. Tell me what you want to taste. Any friend of Will's is a friend of mine.'

Rose smiled. The first stall that seemed promising. 'My parents' tastes are simple. My mother likes chicken. My father steak. They just like them to taste exquisite. What you do with them is up to you.'

'Chicken and steak. My two favourite English dishes. Give me a second.'

He knelt behind the counter and put up a range of plates. 'Okay, steak. Here's a plain sirloin. I can give you gravy, pepper sauce or whisky and mushroom sauce. Here's my version of steak stroganoff, and another steak traditional stew. For chicken I have chicken with cider, apples, mushroom and cream, a chicken stew with tomatoes and pepper and a traditional Balmoral chicken with haggis and pepper sauce.'

The plates appeared one after another with a variety of cutlery. Will smiled broadly. This guy could be perfect. As Rose worked her way along the row each dish tasted every bit as good as the one before. She sighed as she reached the end.

Frank was standing with his arms crossed. 'What's your dessert wish list?'

She turned to face Will, who was finishing off the sirloin steak with some mushroom sauce. 'Really? You knew this guy and didn't phone him straight away?'

Will smiled. 'He's my secret weapon. Everyone's tastes are different. Frank's always my number one choice.'

She looked up at Frank. 'Dessert would be something chocolate and orange for my mother and something strawberry or raspberry for my father.'

'No problem.' He disappeared again and started thumping plates up onto the deck. 'Chocolate and orange torte, raspberry pavlova, strawberry cheesecake, chocolate and cherry gateau and chocolate and raspberry roulade.'

Rose felt her eyes widen. 'I've just died and gone to heaven.' She lifted a fork and worked her way along the dishes, reaching the end as her taste buds exploded. 'All of them. I want all of them.'

Frank's smile reached from one ear to the other. He pulled out a diary. 'When's your event? Next year? Two years away?'

Rose gulped and glanced at Will for help. 'Eh, just under four weeks.'

'What?' Frank's voice echoed around the surrounding area.

Will moved swiftly behind the counter, putting his arm around Frank's shoulders. 'This is a very big event, Frank. And if I tell you money is no object, would it help?' He pointed towards Rose. 'Her mum and dad are renewing their wedding vows. They have a massive kitchen that you will be able to have full run of. You might have heard of them: rock star Rick Cross and ex-model Sherry Huntingdon. It's pretty much going to be the celebrity wedding renewal of the year. Everyone will be talking about who catered it.'

Frank's face had initially paled but as Will kept talking she could see the pieces falling into place in his brain. 'I have reservations for the next two years. Taking something on like this would be no mean feat. I'd have to hire other staff and make alternative arrangements for my other booking without scrimping on quality.'

Rose's stomach was currently tied up in knots. His food was perfect. His food was *better* than perfect and would suit her mum and dad and their exacting needs far more than anything else she'd seen today.

'Please, Frank. Can you have a look at your diary and see if you can make this work? Your food is fantastic. Mum and Dad would love your menu.'

He hesitated as he flicked through an appointment book in front of him. 'That date is for a corporate event—not another wedding. I'd be able to let my second-in-command take charge. But I'd need extra staff.' He stared off into the distance as if his brain was mulling things over. 'I'd also need to see the kitchen before I make a final decision.'

Rose found herself nodding automatically. She was sure the kitchen would meet his standards and if there was anything else he needed—she'd find it. 'Any time, Frank. Any time you want to see the kitchens would be fine with me. Just say the word.'

He glanced between Will and Rose once again. 'This will be expensive. You realise that, don't you?'

Rose answered quickly as she pulled out one of her business cards and handed it to him. 'I've tasted your food. You're worth it. Don't worry about the costs. Do you need a deposit?' She pulled out the corporate credit card she usually used for all the band expenses. It had the biggest credit limit.

He waggled his finger. 'I haven't seen the kitchen yet.' Then he laughed and turned to Will. 'Where did you find this one? She's your best yet—by an absolute mile.'

Rose felt her cheeks flush with colour. 'No, I mean… we're not… There's nothing going on between us.'

Frank winked. 'That's what they all say.'

Will tried to break the awkwardness, but his immediate reaction was to slide his arm around her shoulders and pull her closer. 'Rose and I are just good friends. I'm helping her out with the wedding stuff for her parents and she's helping me out with some publicity for the homeless charity.'

Frank looked at her again. This time she could see a flicker of respect behind his glance. He held out his fist towards Will's and they bumped them together. 'See you Wednesday night at the soup kitchen?' He waved the card. 'I'll call you later today and arrange to come and see the kitchens, okay?'

'Absolutely. That's great. Thanks very much.'

Will steered her away and over towards an ice-cream stand. The warmth from his arm was seeping through her shoulders. She should object to him holding her so closely—particularly when there was no reason. But something felt right about this. It was almost as if she were a good fit.

She gave him a nudge. 'I forgot to tell you. There's a wedding fair on Saturday in one of the nearby hotels. Will you come with me to try and sort out some of the other arrangements?'

He groaned. 'I can't think of anything worse. I hate wedding fairs with a passion. I've been at more than I could count.'

She grinned. 'Good. Then it won't be a problem. I'll come for you at ten o'clock.'

He raised his eyebrows. 'You'll come for me?'

She nodded. 'I'll try and drive something inconspicuous. The sooner we get in, the sooner we get out.'

'Okay, I can live with that.'

'You never told me you volunteered at the shelter, too.'

He looked down at her. 'Didn't I? I just thought you

would know. Violet's come along a few times to help when numbers have been short. I go there once a week. It helps me try and connect with the people I'm trying to help. Some of their stories would break your heart.' He stopped walking and turned her to face him, placing his hands on her shoulders. 'I'm completely serious about this.'

'I know that. I get that.' She could see the worry and concern on his face.

'That's why I'm so hesitant to do what you suggested. I get that it's a good idea. But I don't want this to be about me. I want it to be about *them*.'

She lifted her hand up to his arm and gave it a squeeze. 'I understand. I really do. But our world doesn't always work the way we want it to, Will. If it did—none of those people would be homeless in the first place. I can't give you a long-term fix here. What I can give you is a way to get people talking about the charity—because that will happen. But first, we need an angle.'

He sighed. 'And the angle is me.'

The guy standing in front of her now wasn't the Runaway Groom. He wasn't a guy that had made a host of headlines in all the tabloids. He was sincere. He was committed to his charity. And he wanted to do the best he could for it. There was a whole other side to Will Carter that no one else knew about. If she'd thought he was charming before, she hadn't counted on how much a little glimpse into the real Will could actually impact on her heart.

She nodded. 'Are you worried about the trials your exes might suggest?'

He shook his head and gave a rueful smile. 'I probably should be, but that's actually the last thing I'm worried about.' He reached over and tucked a wayward lock of blonde hair behind her ear. It was the simplest movement. But the feel of his finger against her cheek sent her back to the church on the island. Back to the feel of his lips on hers. Back to the surge of hormones that had swept her body and done crazy things to her brain.

If she stood on her tiptoes right now their noses would brush together and their lips could touch again.

She needed a reality check soon.

And there was only one way to get it.

She gave his arm another squeeze. 'Then let's get this done. You need to give me details on who they are—and how to contact them. Leave it to me. I can deal with them.'

There. Nothing like a bucket of cold water over the two of them to break the mood.

His arms dropped from her shoulders. 'Sure. Let's see what I can do.'

He walked away in front of her, heading towards the exit. She waited a second. Letting her heart rate come back to normal and trying not to fixate on his backside.

Her stomach gave a little flutter. Nothing like hearing about all Will's bad points from his multitude of fiancées to give her a little perspective.

CHAPTER SIX

WILL WOKE UP with his head thumping. A wedding fair was the last thing he needed. Helium balloons and tiny bottles of whisky were not filling him with joy.

He threw on his running gear and went for a run in the grounds, circling the house and gardens a few times, then pounding around the lake. Running was always therapeutic for Will. It helped him clear away the cobwebs and get some clarity on things.

But the cobwebs this morning were Rose shaped. And they didn't plan on moving no matter what he did.

The last thing he wanted to do was let her down. So, no matter how much he hated it, he would spend the day talking about wedding favours, chair covers and balloons.

Everything about this should be making him run for the hills. But the promise of being around Rose again was just far too enticing. He pounded harder on the driveway. No matter how hard he tried, Rose Huntingdon-Cross was finding a way under his skin. It didn't matter the messages that his brain was sending. The messages from his body were a whole other matter. And they were definitely leading the charge.

He rounded back to the main front door just as his phone beeped. A text. From Violet.

What you doing today?

His stomach dropped with a surge of guilt. He texted quickly before he changed his mind.

Helping Rose with wedding arrangements.

He waited. Expecting Violet to send something back. But she didn't. And it made him feel even worse. It had only been a few days but he was neglecting her. Any day she'd call him on it and ask him what was going on.

Then he'd be in trouble.

He strode through the hallway and up the stairs, hitting the shower in his room. He automatically pulled a suit from his cupboard, then stared at it, and put it back. This wasn't a suit kind of day. Hell, the last thing he wanted was to be mistaken for a groom.

He pulled on a short-sleeved shirt and a pair of army trousers before driving to the local surgery and getting the nurse to remove his stitches. The scar was still angry and red but she assured him it would fade over time and he arrived back just as Rose was pulling up outside the house. She gave him a hard stare as he climbed into the tiny Mini.

'You got your stitches out?'

He nodded. 'It's official. I'm now Harry Potter and I'll get all the girls.' He looked around. 'What's up?' She had her black planner sitting on her lap.

Rose was perfect as always. She was wearing a pink and white fifties-style dress. It was demure and gave nothing away. But he'd already seen and touched what lay beneath those clothes. His fingers started to tingle.

'Is this the casual look?' she asked stiffly.

'What—you wanted me to wear a suit and pretend to

be a groom? You think I haven't had enough practice at that?'

She frowned. 'Well, it could have been part of our disguise. I'm not sure I want to tell people today that I'm organising a wedding renewal for my parents. The news isn't exactly out yet.'

'Haven't you contacted their friends with the date?'

He didn't want to appear critical. But he could only imagine that most of Rick and Sherry's guest list would already have bulging diaries.

Rose was concentrating on the road. She was cute when she was driving, glasses perched at the end of her nose.

'I have. But there's always a few I can't get hold of.' She rolled her eyes without diverting them from the road. 'And you know, they're the ones that have a monster-size tantrum if they hear the news from anyone else.'

'Tell them to get over it.'

'What?' She seemed shocked by his abrupt tone.

'These people are adults. If they want information they should check their emails or answering machines. I hate the way some of these celebrities want to be spoon-fed. They act like a bunch of toddlers.'

He heard her suck in a breath as if she were thinking what to say. Had he just offended her? Violet was so normal he just assumed that Sherry and Rick didn't behave like other celebrities. Rose was biting her lip.

He couldn't help himself. He couldn't wait. 'Are you mad?'

She shook her head. 'No. I'm not mad. And I guess you're right. It's just I get used to dealing with these kinds of people.' She wrinkled her nose. 'And it starts to all seem normal to me instead of outrageous.'

She turned the car towards a country estate. The road

was already backed up with cars and Will sank lower in his seat. 'I've got a bad feeling about this.'

She laughed and gave him a slap. 'Oh, come on. How bad can it be?'

'You've never met a bunch of Bridezillas, have you?'

She pulled over. The car park was jammed and the traffic was virtually at a standstill.

'You're parking here? On the driveway?'

She nodded and smiled. 'Why not? In the next five minutes everyone else will, too. Let's go.'

She climbed out into the morning sun and waited for Will to join her. Everywhere they looked there were people. The doorway was crowded, so they walked around the large mansion house and went in another entrance at the back. Will pulled out some cash to pay their entrance fee and picked up a leaflet with a floor plan.

Rose had an amused smile on her face. 'These things have a floor plan?'

He laughed and put an arm around her shoulders. 'Let me introduce you to the world of crazy brides. If we hang out here all day I guarantee at some point we'll see two brides scrapping over a date somewhere.'

'No way.'

He nodded solemnly. 'Way.' He glanced at the plan. 'What first?'

She screwed up her nose and leaned against him, her scent reaching up around him. It was light and floral, like a summer day. Just exactly the way a girl called Rose should smell. 'We don't need to wait for the fashion show of the bridal dresses. That's all sorted. Let's hit the favours. I'm still not really sure what we should get.'

Will guided her through the large mansion rooms. 'Lots of people just go for the traditional—miniature bottles of whisky for guys and some kind of trinket or chocolates for the women. Lottery tickets are popular, too.'

Rose shook her head. 'I don't think my mother would be happy if I gave her wedding guests a lottery ticket. It has to be something more personal than that.'

'More personal for around two hundred people?'

He could see her bite the inside of her cheek. 'More like three hundred.'

The room was already crowded and they walked around. Some things were cute. Some things were practical. And some things were just quirky.

Rose held up flip-flops in different colours. 'What are these for?'

The girl behind the counter smiled. 'It's our most popular item right now. Flip-flops for the women who've been wearing their stiletto heels all day and want to spend the night dancing.'

Rose nodded. 'Good idea.' She moved on to the next stall, which had personalised notebooks with pictures of the bride and the groom on the front. Little heart-shaped glass pendants. Handkerchiefs with the bride and groom's name and date of wedding stitched on them.

He could see her visibly wince at some of the more cringeworthy items. She turned and sighed. 'I don't see anything I love.'

Will breathed in deeply and caught the whiff of something sweet. In the far corner there was a glass counter from one of the most well-known stores in London. 'How about chocolates?'

She walked over next to him. 'Isn't that a little boring? A few chocolates in an individual box for the guests?'

'How about you try and personalise it? Strawberry, orange, blackcurrant, limes—you could find out people's favourites. In fact,' he bent forward and whispered in her ear, 'if you speak very nicely to that man behind the counter and showed him your guest list I bet you he already knows some of the favourites of the people on it.'

Will bent over and picked up a triangular bag of popcorn. 'Some of the guys might prefer this. They've got shortbread, too. They even do mini-doughnuts.' He shrugged. 'Everybody eats. Everybody likes food. If you personalise it as much as you can it could be a hit.'

She was beginning to look a little more relaxed. The room was starting to get crowded. She shot him a smile. 'Give me five minutes to see what I can do.'

She disappeared across the room in a flash and within two minutes was behind the counter charming the white-gloved chocolatier. She pulled out a list and the two conferred over it for a few minutes before the chocolatier carefully folded it and put it in his pocket. Rose pulled out her chequebook and quickly scribbled a cheque, leaving her card.

She came rushing back over with a small basket of chocolate creams in her hand.

'Success?'

She was beaming. 'Better than success. He's even going to come to the wedding and set up the counter for the day.'

'As well as do all the favours?'

She picked up a chocolate and popped it in her mouth. 'Mmm…strawberry, delicious.' She held out the basket. 'Do you want one?'

'I'm not sure—is it safe? If I didn't know any better I'd say you were guarding them with your life.' He was laughing. Even though she'd offered a chocolate she'd automatically pulled the basket back to her chest as if she were daring anyone to try and take one.

She looked down at the basket and reluctantly pushed it forward again. He waved his hand. 'Forget it. I know when there's a line in the sand.' He leaned forward. 'Are you going to tell me how much all this is going to cost?'

Rose smiled and popped another chocolate in her mouth. 'Absolutely not. Now, let's look over here. The chocolatier just gave me the best idea in the world.'

They walked towards a smaller stand at the back of the hall. It was covered in jewellery and different mementos, a lot of them encrusted in crystals. She picked up the nearest one and shot the guy behind the table her biggest smile.

'I think you're about to hate me, but Paul, the chocolatier, sent me over.'

The guy smiled and rolled his eyes as Rose let out a gasp and picked up a little jewelled guitar. 'Oh, this is it. This is so perfect.' She spun to face Will. 'How perfect is it? A jewelled guitar for Rick and Sherry's wedding renewal?' She could feel the excitement building in her chest. Trouble was, the workmanship of the guitar set with jewelled stones was beautiful. How long did it take to make?

She took a deep breath. 'What would you say if I asked for three hundred of these in three weeks' time?'

The guy's jaw bounced off the floor. 'I'd say, "Do you know how much that would cost?"'

She nodded. 'I think I have a pretty good idea.'

He held out his hand towards her and walked around the table. 'John Taylor.' He wrinkled his nose. 'Rick and Sherry? Are you talking about Rick Cross?'

She nodded. 'He's my father. My parents are renewing their vows. I'd really love it if we could have some of the mini-jewelled guitars as favours.'

She could see him bite his lip. 'I'm a huge fan.' He sighed. 'The guitars are ready. The stones just need to be glued in place. They're semi-precious crystals. It takes a bit of time. But…' he paused '…for Rick Cross? I think I could pull out all the stops.'

'You could?' Rose let out a squeal and flung her arms around the guy. Will's face creased into a frown but she was too busy pulling out her credit card and setting up the order to pay too much attention.

After a few minutes she glanced around, placing her hand on Will's arm. 'Now help me find, accost and probably blackmail some company into hiring me a marquee for the day.'

He rolled his eyes. 'You'll need an even bigger chequebook for that.'

But Rose was getting lost in the atmosphere of the place. 'I think I want ones that have those fairy lights at night—you know, so it looks all magical?'

Her hair tickled his nose as he bent forward. 'Watch out, you're in danger of turning into one of the Bridezillas. I think you've been bitten by the bug.'

She stopped walking abruptly and turned around. 'Oh, no. Don't be fooled. Not for a second. This is my mother's dream wedding. Not mine.'

'And it was pretty much Daisy's, too.'

She nodded. 'I know. But I don't want any of this.'

He wasn't convinced—not for a second. 'Doesn't every girl want a dream wedding and to feel like a princess on the day they marry?'

But Rose's face was deadly serious. 'Absolutely not. Seeing all the chaos with Daisy getting married just made me even more convinced. The only part of that wedding that mattered was the two people standing at the front and looking at each other as if they couldn't wait to say they'd love each other for ever.' A Bridezilla pushed her from behind as she hurried past, and Rose almost faceplanted into his chest.

He pulled her close and put a protective arm around her waist. She sighed. 'I definitely don't want all this. I want me and my Mr For Ever alone—just the two of us— saying our vows without any of the kerfuffle.'

He smiled at her choice of word. 'Kerfuffle? I don't think I've heard that in years.'

She raised her hands to the bedlam around them and lifted her head towards his. 'Well, isn't that the most accurate description? Who needs it? Not me.'

Something soothing and warm was washing over him. Four fiancées. And not one of them had ever wanted this. He'd known all along how different Rose was. He'd known she was sneaking under his defences in every which way. He just hadn't realised how much. And it was the way she'd said those words. *Me and my Mr For Ever alone.* The words *Mr For Ever* should have terrified him. But for the first time in his life they didn't.

'Really? You really don't want all this?' He knew she'd loved the church on the island and remarked how perfect it was. But he hadn't been entirely sure that wasn't just saying she didn't want a big wedding. But the one thing Rose couldn't hide was the sincerity in her eyes. His head was crammed full of thoughts of the palavers over wedding plans with the four previous fiancées. Not one of them would have agreed to walk away from the dream and just have the husband.

Today was totally different. Today he didn't want to run from the room in the start of a mild panic. That could be easily explained. This wasn't his wedding and Rose wasn't his fiancée. But everything about this felt different. And it felt different because of Rose.

Her face was just inches from his. Her pale blue eyes unblinking. 'I really don't want any of this,' she whispered.

The buzz around him was fading away. All he could concentrate on was the face in front of him. All similarities to her sister had vanished in the mist. This was Rose.

This was only Rose. The woman who was having more of an effect on him than he could even begin to comprehend.

Any minute now a white charger would appear in the room and he'd just pick her up and sweep her off somewhere.

But being Rose, she would probably object.

She lifted a hand up and placed it on his chest. The warmth from her palm flooded through his fine shirt and their gazes locked and held for a second.

Was she really having the same kind of thoughts that he was?

Then it happened. A wayward thought he could never have dreamed of. He could actually imagine doing all this kind of stuff with Rose.

Was it because her vision of a wedding was close to his? Because the funny thing was, even if she changed her mind, he could see himself doing all this planning with Rose. Rose felt right. Rose felt like a part of him.

For Will it was like a revelation. Fireworks were going off in his head. His brain was spinning and his mouth resembled the Sahara desert. Was this it? Was this what it felt like for other people? Was this what it felt like for Rick and Sherry?

Her eyes twinkled and a grin appeared on her face. 'Come on, wedding guy. There were three things on the list today. Favours—done. But you promised me marquees and balloons—you better deliver.'

The spark in her eyes broke the increasing tension between them and brought him back to reality. He had to be sure. He had to be *more* than sure. The last thing he wanted to do was hurt Rose.

He nodded and grabbed her hand. 'Let's see how quickly we can do this. There's a bridal show about to start. Everyone will disappear to watch that.' All he really wanted to do was get out of here and get Rose all to himself.

It didn't take long. It just took an exceptional amount of money. But they finally found someone who could supply a marquee—complete with twinkling fairy lights—on the date they needed. Once they heard the magic words *Rick Cross and Sherry Huntingdon* the deal was done.

The balloons were another matter. One side of the hall had a whole range of displays and colours, from table decorations with a few helium balloons to archways covering the whole top table.

'Do you know what colour scheme your mum will want?'

'Yep, jewel colours. Bright and bold. Red, green and blue.' She wandered between all the stands touching all the metallic bobbing balloons, some held down by balloon weights and some tied to walls and chair backs.

'What's the story?' he asked. 'Were you the kid that never got bought a balloon?'

She smiled and tipped her head to the side. 'I just like them, that's all. Don't get me wrong—if you ever tried to get me in a big balloon—up in the sky—I'd run in the opposite direction. But these…' she jiggled her hand amongst an array of bobbing balloons '…I just love.' She pointed ahead. 'See those ones, all heart-shaped and just the colours I need? I'd love a really big display like that in all four corners of the marquees.'

Will stared at the bobbing balloons. They made him nauseous. He couldn't understand the attraction. The heat in the mansion house was starting to rise. The number of people surrounding them seemed to be growing and growing. He couldn't wait to get out of there. He had a one-track mind—get Rose away from all these people and just to himself.

The double doors in the large room they were in opened out onto the wide gardens. But the air was hardly circulating around them.

Rose took a few moments to place her order and pay by cheque. She walked over smiling. 'I love those. I think they'll be perfect.'

'Good. Can we get out of here now?'

She pivoted on her heels, her dress bouncing out around her. He could see several eyes in the room on her. She really didn't have any idea just how pretty she was, or what a statement her older-style dress made. It was like having Doris Day in the room with them. He couldn't help the smile that spread from one ear to the other.

It was official. This was the Rose effect.

'What about cakes? We haven't looked at cakes yet...' Her voice drifted off as her hand trailed against silver and pink heart balloons in a wide arch next to her.

The bridal show must have just finished as people started to surge through the entrance towards them. Rose stumbled on her square-heeled shoes and fell into the display balloons, dislodging them and making them drift free from their anchor and rise up all around her.

For an instant the whole room held its breath as two hundred balloons escaped their tethers and started floating and bobbing free. Will could see the horror on her face and grabbed her hand as he stifled a laugh and pulled her towards one of the open garden doors.

It was infectious. Rose started laughing too as they burst from the doors, out into the grounds as several balloons escaped around them.

Behind them there were squeals and bedlam. But Will couldn't have cared less. The fresh air of freedom was just too much as they ran across the grass together to where the cars were parked.

The last thing he saw was a pink and silver balloon floating in front of them as they dashed to the car.

CHAPTER SEVEN

ROSE WAITED NERVOUSLY as the phone rang. She was regretting her suggestion big time right now. 'Hello?'

The voice was sharp at the end of the phone.

'Hi, there. This is Rose Huntingdon-Cross. I'm looking for Melissa Kirkwood.'

'Violet's sister? What on earth do you want?'

She cringed at the instant recognition. Melissa was the bride who had been jilted at the altar. She was always going to be the most difficult.

'I'm phoning you because I'm doing some charity work for Will Carter and his homeless charity.'

There was a hiss at the end of the phone. 'Don't even say his name to me!'

It came out with such venom that she was actually taken aback. Although her brain was telling her to stay calm, her tongue just went into overdrive. 'I'm sorry to upset you. It's just—I thought you might be interested in this. We're contacting all of Will Carter's ex-fiancées to see if they would be willing to participate in a charity event. All you'd be required to do is put forward some kind of trial or dare that you'd like Will to do, and it will go to a public vote with all proceeds going to the charity.' Her mouth was gaining momentum like a steam train. 'You can be as horrible as you like with the dare or trial. Pick something you know he would hate to do.'

Oh, no. Had she actually just said that out loud? It was too late. Her PR head had gone into salvage mode. She couldn't take it back now.

There was silence at the end of the phone and a deep intake of breath. Rose's heart thudded in her chest. Part of her wanted Melissa to refuse, the other needed her to say yes. 'We've already negotiated a deal and coverage with the national press—and there will be television interviews, too. So you'll be able to show the world how you've moved on.'

Please let her have moved on, prayed Rose. Will had described some of his exes as a little fame hungry and eager to be in the spotlight. Hopefully the temptation would be too much.

'Just how hideous can I make his dare?' The voice had developed a calculating edge.

'As hideous as you like. At the end of the week's voting he will have to carry out the one with the most public votes.'

She could almost hear Melissa's brain ticking at the end of the phone. 'I need a day to think of something suitable.'

'Absolutely no problem at all. How about I call you back on Tuesday and set up an interview with the press for you then, too?'

Best to kill two birds with one stone. She really didn't want to have prolonged conversations with any of Will's exes. No matter how curious she was about the collection of women. Once she'd made the initial phone calls she was backing out of the limelight and letting the momentum carry the whole thing forward. The newspaper editor had loved it, and one of her favourite morning TV presenters had already agreed to interview all the women on TV.

The tone in Melissa's voice had changed. It was almost as if her brain was currently contemplating exactly what she could plot. 'Tuesday will be fine.' The phone went down with a click and Rose gulped.

She made a mark on the list in front of her. One down. Three to go.

'Rose? Rose, are you there?'

Will's voice echoed down the corridor and his head appeared around the corner of her bedroom door. He was clutching something in his hand and looking a little wary.

By the time she'd finished the phone calls she was exhausted and had adopted the starfish position on her bed. She hadn't moved for the last twenty minutes and didn't have any intention of moving any time soon.

She turned her head. 'If you ever get engaged to a crazy woman again you and I are never talking.'

He winced. 'You've done it? You've called them all?'

He didn't wait to be invited in. He just crossed her room in long strides and sat down at the edge of her bed.

Her head flopped back. 'I've called them all and you owe me—*big time.*' She turned on her side and rested her head on her hand. 'Where on earth did you find them?'

He frowned. 'Don't be like that. All of them have good points. I'm just not their favourite person.'

Rose laughed. 'Oh, you can say that again. Just wait till we find out what the trials are on Tuesday. I have the feeling that some of these ladies will spend the next two days plotting.'

He rolled his eyes. 'Not some. Just one of them.' His fingers drifted over and touched the edge of her trousers. 'I didn't mean to hurt any of them. Things just got out of hand.'

Rose pushed herself up the bed. 'Once or twice I might

let you off with. But four times. Do you never learn your lesson?'

'Looks like I'm about to.' There was something about the way he said the words. He was pretending to be flippant. But the atmosphere had changed quickly around them. She might be relaxed around Will, but it didn't deplete the buzz of electricity she felt whenever he walked in the same room as her.

She sighed. 'What's that?' She pointed to the curled-up newspaper in his hand and flopped back onto the bed.

'Yeah, about that.' Will flopped back onto the bed next to her.

The corners of her lips turned upwards. 'We've been in this position before.'

He smiled, too. 'I know. I remember. I even have the scar to prove it. I'm just hoping I'm not about to earn another one.'

She wrinkled her brow. 'Why would you do that?' It was disconcerting having those dark blue eyes just inches from hers. This was exactly what waking up next to Will Carter would feel like. All six feet four of him just inches away. That rogue thought was doing strange things to her stomach.

He moved a little bit closer. She could see the tiny freckles on his nose, feel his warm breath on her cheek and certainly smell his fresh aftershave. Her senses were scrambled. Was he about to kiss her?

'I think your PR campaign has just taken off in an unexpected way,' he whispered as he unfurled the newspaper.

She was muddled for a sec. The kiss wasn't coming. Her eyes tried to fixate on the coloured picture on the front of the red-top newspaper.

The effect was instantaneous. She sat bolt upright just as the text sounded on her phone.

The photo looked staged. It was just too perfect. Rose with her Doris Day–style dress and blonde hair streaming behind her and Will in his casual shirt and trousers. But it was the expressions on their faces that gave everything away—they were laughing and the elements of pure joy shone from their faces, in perfect unison with the pink and silver heart-shaped balloons escaping into the sky behind them.

If Rose worked in PR for the movies, she would have paid a fortune for a shot like this.

But it was the headline that took her breath away. *Has the Runaway Groom finally found his bride?*

'What?' She snatched the paper from his hands. 'What on earth is this?'

Will opened his mouth to speak but nothing sensible came out. 'I'm not sure… It's just a picture… It will blow over in a couple of days.'

The paper was crumpling beneath her fingers. Rose worked in PR. She knew exactly how big this was. She also hated the fact it was her face staring back at her from the front of the newspapers. It brought back horrible memories of a few years ago when she'd made every front page. She'd hated every second of that and never wanted to repeat it again. 'How many, Will? How many calls have you had this morning?'

He flinched. 'About a dozen.'

'A dozen!' She was shrieking and she couldn't help it. If it was any other girl—any other girl in the world right now photographed with Will—she'd be doing a happy dance. This would be a great kick-start for the publicity for the homeless charity.

But it wasn't any other girl. It was her. And she hated the fact this could blow out of proportion. Hated the fact it was her in the headlines. How ironic. She hated the media but had learned how to use them to her advantage. Maybe this was a wake-up call for her? Maybe she'd started to get a little complacent?

Something twisted inside her. 'Violet,' she breathed.

Will's cool hand touched her arm. 'I called her. She laughed. And warned me off again.'

'She laughed?' Rose could feel the waves of panic washing over her. She hadn't even hinted to Violet the thoughts that were clamouring through her head about Will. How on earth could she? She couldn't make sense of them herself. The last thing she wanted to do was tell her sister she was falling for the Runaway Groom.

'All those calls I made this morning. Just wait until your exes see this. They'll think I'm next on your hit list. They'll think I'm just doing this because you've sucked me in.'

'Sucked me in how?' His voice was low and tinged with anger. He reached over and grabbed the newspaper from her hands. 'You know what they say about this—today's news, tomorrow's chip paper. It's a photo snapped by someone at the wedding exhibition yesterday. There's nothing we can do about it.' He shrugged his shoulders. 'If you go to a public place there's always a danger you'll get papped. You must be used to it.'

He had no idea. No idea what had happened a few years ago and how it had changed everything for her. Changed how she felt about herself. Changed how she thought her parents felt about her.

She took a deep breath and tried to think logically.

He was making sense but she couldn't even acknowledge it. 'But this is a disaster. What happens when I phone those women back? What if they refuse to participate because of this?' She pointed at the paper again. She hadn't even read the whole article. 'I mean, it's all rubbish.'

'No. It isn't.'

She turned quickly to his voice. Will was still lying on the bed. He reached up his hand and pulled her back down next to him.

'What are you talking about?' She couldn't help the tremble in her voice. They were back in their original position. Lying on the bed next to each other with only a few inches between their faces.

'Rose, stop pretending that nothing is happening between us. We both know that it is.' He lifted his finger and touched the side of her cheek, oh, so gently. She shivered. She couldn't believe he'd actually just said it. Acknowledged it out loud.

She wasn't going crazy. She wasn't imagining things. He felt it, too.

But he'd felt it four times before. History proved that. She didn't want to be number five.

This was the one and only time she'd felt like this.

Part of it was horrible. Last time she'd felt this vulnerable was after her friend's death when she'd been splashed all over the media.

Rose had learned quickly it was better to be the person to try and control the PR, than the person *in* the PR.

And the more her feelings grew for this guy, the more she questioned herself and her ability to trust her instincts. What had happened three years ago had affected her more than she'd ever realised. She would always regret leaving her friend. She would always regret the fact she hadn't hung around when there was even a possibility that Autumn could have put herself in harm's way. She'd spent the last three years playing the *if only* game.

And she couldn't afford to do that any more. She had to live in the real world.

And only her parents really knew that she'd been aware

of Autumn's drug-taking. What would Will think of her if he knew the truth? If she revealed all her flaws to him?

'Why couldn't you just be an ordinary guy?' she whispered.

Will smiled. He was so much more laid-back about this. He didn't seem to have a single problem trusting his instincts—and that was probably part of the problem. What was more he didn't have a shadow of doubt in his eyes. Not like the clenched hand she currently felt protecting her heart.

'Why couldn't you just be an ordinary girl?'

He leaned forward and brushed his lips against hers. She was scared to move at first. Acknowledging it was one thing. Seeing where it might take them was entirely another.

But everything he did was completely natural. From edging closer so their bodies were touching, to his hands wandering through her hair and around her face and neck. Each kiss was designed to lead on to the next. To make her want more. And she did. *So* much more.

All the sensations in her body were on fire. As if Will had more than one set of hands and they were currently skimming her erogenous zones as if he were reaching out and kissing and caressing each one in turn.

Rose pulled back sharply.

'What's wrong?' Little creases appeared around his eyes.

'I don't know. I'm just nervous. I'm not sure about any of this.'

'What part are you not sure about?'

Her hand was resting on his bicep. She could feel the heat of his skin through her palm. Every sense in her wanted to run her hand up under the short sleeve of his shirt and feel more.

'I'm not a spotlight kind of girl, Will. I agreed to help you with the PR but I don't want PR for myself.'

She felt him suck in a deep breath. 'I'm afraid with me it might be part of the package. We could release a statement about your parents' renewal. That would explain why we were there. They may well leave you alone after that.'

Forget about it. Forget about everything. Act on impulse, Rose, and just kiss him the way you really want to.

But she couldn't. For Rose this was all about control. Since her friend's death she'd become a control freak. It was why she did the job so well for the band. Nothing left to chance.

Now people were taking pictures of her she didn't know about. Pictures of her that told the whole world exactly how she felt about Will.

And the whole world exactly how he felt about her.

It was like a jolt—and probably just as well she was already lying down.

Her silence had obviously worried him. 'Am I overstepping the mark, Rose? Do you want me to leave you alone?'

'No.' It was the first concrete thought in her head.

She was so confused right now. She didn't want to be the next girl to be swept along in the flurry of love that surrounded Will Carter.

She wanted a chance to be normal. To be just Rose and just Will. Two people that were attracted to each other. The electricity sparking between them was everywhere. But while this was all new to her, every precautionary bone in her body kept reminding her it wasn't for Will.

And no matter which way she looked at it—it hurt.

'I can't be number five.' Her words came out solidly. Definitely.

Will looked sad as he shook his head. 'You're not number anything. You're Rose.' His hand touched her cheek again. 'Can't we see where this relationship takes us?'

'But that's just it, Will. You don't have relationships. You have engagements, wedding plans and then nothing. You're a commitment-phobe—even though you can't see it for yourself. I can't set myself up for that. I don't want to start a relationship that won't ever go anywhere.'

'That won't happen, Rose.' She'd expected him to say something different. She'd expected him to crack a joke about her being way too keen and these things being years away. He couldn't possibly know the surge of terrifying emotions in her chest.

She could see him trying to find the words and the thought he was trying to placate her made her wish the ground would open up and swallow her. Even saying those few words had been too much. She should have known better. She shouldn't even have acknowledged anything between them.

'This is different.' His words were unexpected. But she just couldn't let herself believe them—no matter how much she wanted to.

'I bet you've said that before.'

The wave of hurt on his face was obvious. And even though she should probably want to take the words back, she just didn't. It had to be said. Will's reputation had gone before him. It didn't matter that her own experience of him felt entirely different. For all she knew, all the other girls had thought that, too.

Will sat up on the bed as her phone beeped again. 'I don't know how to show you this is different, Rose. I don't know how to explain.'

She sat up and pulled out her phone. It was from her father.

Can you come and see me? There's something special I want you to do for me.

'It's my dad. I'd better go.'

Will nodded reluctantly. 'Rose?'

She'd already started towards the door. She hated the way she spun around, desperate to hang onto his words.

'Let's just see. Let's just see where this takes us.'

She couldn't speak. She couldn't even explain to herself why she felt so hurt. She just gave a reluctant nod before she disappeared out of the door and the hot tears started to snake down her cheeks.

Her dad was waiting for her in the kitchen, sketching with deep concentration on a bit of paper.

'Hi, Dad, what's up?'

His eyes narrowed for a second when he lifted his head. He'd always been able to read her like a book. She could see him think about asking her what was wrong, but the paper in front of him was a definite distraction.

He hesitated, then pushed it towards her. 'What do you think?'

It was a pencil drawing of a bangle with little scribbles next to each part. Three strands of gold in different colours pleated together with a little flower intersecting the pleat at each third of the bangle—a rose, a daisy and a violet.

'It's beautiful, Dad. What's this for?'

His well-worn face sagged in relief. 'It's for your mother. It's her gift for her wedding day. I wanted to give her something special. You will make it for me, won't you? And you'll be able to get the yellow, white and rose gold?'

Something surged inside her. Even though alarm bells were sounding all around her head about the amount of time the bangle would take to make, and the intricate details, there was just no way she could ever say no to her father.

The thing that struck her most was the absolute love she could recognise on his face. The fact that he'd spent a lot of time and effort on this design was obvious. But what was even more evident was just how much he loved her mum. After all these years he still wanted to do something to make her heart sing.

That was what she wanted. That was the kind of relationship she wanted. That was the kind of love she wanted. One that would last for ever.

She felt a tear spring to her eye again as her dad put his arm around her shoulder. 'Don't worry, Dad, I've got the three kinds of gold. It will be perfect. Mum will love it.'

But now that he'd sorted out his wedding gift her father's attentions had shifted immediately. Rick Cross was no fool. Particularly when it came to Rose.

'So what's wrong? What's going on with you and that Will Carter? Violet's moping around like a lost cause.'

'She is?'

'Of course she is. You've stolen her favourite pet.'

A tear slid down her cheek as everything just threatened to spill out. 'But I haven't. I was helping him—and he was helping me with the wedding arrangements. It's just that we've been spending so much time together. I didn't mean to leave Violet out. I'll phone her—no, I'll go and see her.' She was babbling and she just couldn't help it. Wasn't it Will that normally did this?

Her father shook his head. 'Rose? What's wrong? I was only joking. Violet can take care of herself. I just wondered if there was something I should know. My daughters seem to be getting married in short order these days.'

Rose felt her breath catch in her throat and her father noticed immediately. She'd just had that awkward conversation with Will. A conversation nobody should be having after such a ridiculously short amount of time. It was almost as if her father could read her mind—and heaven knew what he could find in there!

But Rick Cross was cooler than your average dad. 'I like that fella. Always knew nothing would happen between Violet and him. But you?' He gave a little shrug of his shoulders. 'I guess that depends how you feel.'

He left the words hanging in the air. It was awful. She wasn't ready to have that kind of conversation with her dad. He was still her *dad*. Then again, she wasn't ready to have that conversation with anyone.

She focused back on the drawing. 'Leave this with me. This will be fine.' Where she would find the hours from she had no idea. But if this was what her father wanted— this was what he would get.

If he noticed the abrupt subject change he didn't say anything. She picked up her bag. 'Oh, I forgot to tell you— the guy you wanted to write your biography, Tom Buckley from New York? He emailed today to agree the terms and conditions. He'll have full access to the band tour backstage. I'm just arranging flights for him now.'

A huge smile broke across her dad's face. This was something that was really important to him and he'd been quite insistent about who he wanted to do the job. Just as well Rose had worked with Tom in the past and could use her maximum persuasion skills—along with a hefty salary—to persuade him to write the biography in the timeframe her dad needed. One more ticked box and another thing off her plate. She felt a little surge of pride. Her dad was happy with her.

Her dad gave her a hug and a kiss. 'That's great, honey.

Thanks for doing that. Now, if there's anything you need to talk about, come and see me. Or pick up the phone and I'm there.'

Her heart gave a little squeeze. He wouldn't pry. He wouldn't interrogate her. Just as well, as she didn't know what to say. But it was her dad's way of letting her know that he'd noticed. He'd noticed something was wrong. Dads didn't come much better than Rick Cross. When the whole press thing had blown up when Autumn had overdosed he'd been her biggest ally—her best spokesperson. And he'd done exactly the same for Violet when her sex-tape scandal had hit the press. Rick Cross didn't take kindly to people trying to hurt his family.

He'd taken Rose in the car to see her friend's parents. He'd spent hours talking to them and comforting them—but in no way letting them blame Rose for their daughter's actions. And when the press had started to get nasty a few days later he'd made lightning-fast arrangements and got her out of there. She was lucky that her family were so supportive.

It gave her a little strength. A little fortitude. Maybe it was time to look at herself again. Maybe it was time to start trusting her instincts?

Her father had just told her he liked Will Carter. Will had been Violet's best friend for the last three years. And the man she knew in person didn't measure up to what she'd read in the press.

She reached over and gave her dad a quick hug. 'This bangle will be perfect. I'll make sure of it. Don't worry, Dad. You can trust me.'

He brushed a kiss against her cheek and gave her a curious look. 'Always, Rose.' Before he walked across the kitchen he paused in the doorway. 'Rose?' She looked up again and he gave her a rueful smile. 'When you know—you just know,' and then he turned and walked away, leaving her with the drawing clutched in her hands.

CHAPTER EIGHT

FOUR HUNDRED AND sixty emails. That was how many he had to read. Will groaned and put his head in his hands. This was getting out of control.

He couldn't concentrate. He couldn't focus. Because his head was so full of Rose.

The sensation he'd felt the other day at the wedding fair with Rose had swamped him. The words Rick Cross had said at their first meeting were echoing around his brain. *When you know, you just know.* But it was more than that. It was the way Rick had looked at Sherry, too. The zing between them. He'd never had that before. But he had it with Rose.

Trouble was, he didn't know what to do next. How on earth could he convince Rose that everything about this just felt different—just felt right?

He didn't blame her. He really didn't. How would he feel if Rose had been engaged before? He was lucky she would even stay in the same room as him.

But he just couldn't help how he felt about her. It was taking over every waking minute of his life. He looked at the calendar, then walked over to the window. The island was right in front of him and from this view he could see the roof of the church. Something curled inside him.

A tiny seed of an idea. A wild idea. A crazy idea.

If he told Violet she'd probably dunk him in a bath of ice. If he told Rose she would run screaming for the hills...

For the first time ever Will felt as if he could see himself grow old with someone. It should be terrifying. But instead a warm feeling spread across his chest.

And something about this idea was taking shape in his head. He only had to do one thing. One thing that he hoped no one would find out about.

And it could make all the difference to his life.

Rose put the phone down and laid her head on the desk.

'Was it that bad?' Violet was standing laughing at the door with her arms folded.

Rose didn't even lift her head. 'Worse,' she sighed.

Violet walked over and lifted up the piece of paper on Rose's desk. First it was a gasp of shock, then it was a snort, then it was just a peal of laughter. By the time Rose lifted her head Violet was wiping a tear from her eye.

'I came up to tell you Will's just pulled into the car park. I bet you can't wait to tell him what all his dares are.' She shook her head as she kept looking at the list. 'I can't wait to see his face.'

'Really?' She half hoped Violet wasn't joking. 'Then you can tell him.'

She raised her eyebrows. 'Oh, no, girl. That's your job.' She gave Rose a nod of her head and walked back to the door with her shoulders shaking.

Rose heard the murmur of words down the corridor as she obviously met Will. A few minutes later he appeared at the door, face pale. 'Oh, no. What have they suggested?'

Rose gestured towards the seat opposite her. 'You better sit down.'

For once Will did exactly as he was told.

She started carefully. 'The good thing is that these will definitely generate media interest.'

'And the bad news?'

She gulped as she passed over the piece of paper. 'You might not like some of them.' She bit her lip. 'The thing is, the newspaper already knows about all the dares. So we can't get anyone to change them.'

His brow wrinkled. 'Why would they need to be changed? Are any of them going to kill me?'

She shook her head swiftly. 'No. No. That was one of the conditions they were given—nothing fatal.'

'Please tell me that you're joking.'

She shook her head again and gave him a half-smile. 'Eh, no.'

'Dangling from Tower Bridge and getting dunked in the Thames?'

Rose tried not to smile. There was no doubt the press would have a field day with these. To say nothing of all the TV and media interviews she'd arranged for the ex-fiancées. This could end up being one of the most successful PR campaigns she'd ever been involved in.

Will had been right. Three out of four of his exes had been fine. And even Melissa had started to come round. She was gearing herself up for TV interviews and appeared to be quite happy at the prospect.

'Dress for a day as a gladiator/warrior and parade around Piccadilly Circus? Wear a thong and work in a women's underwear department for the day?' His voice was getting more incredulous as he continued to read.

Rose couldn't help but start laughing. 'Those last two came from Angie and Marta. They were definitely going more for the laughs than the cold, hard revenge.'

Two of Will's ex-fiancées were now married with children. They were happy to help the charity auction and had obviously had fun thinking up what he should do. Both of them had seemed very nice and very happy with their lives.

The third, Esther, had looked on it as good publicity for her new TV-presenting career. She'd been quite mercenary about it. She wasn't that interested in the charity but she was certainly interested in raising her profile.

Will slumped further down the chair as he finished reading. 'A full body wax on live TV?' The paper was now crumpled in his hand. 'Which do you think will win?' he said resignedly.

Rose tried to be rational. 'I think it's a toss-up between a dunking in the Thames and the man thong.' She held a scrap of luminous green material with her pen. 'Look. Marta tried to be really helpful. She even sent the thong.'

Will's eyes nearly popped out of his head as he reached forward and snatched the tiny item. 'You have got to be joking. There's absolutely no way on this earth I'm ever putting that on. Or dressing like a blooming gladiator.'

But Rose was on her feet in an instant. 'Oh, no, you don't. You agreed to this. This isn't about you. This is about the charity. Think how much money will be raised by people phoning in to vote on this stuff. I bet you'll be able to employ some new workers. Don't start being a wuss on me now.'

He groaned and sagged down again, staring at the thong in his hand. 'But people won't be talking about the charity. People will be talking about me and my utter humiliation.'

'So what?' She was feeling annoyed now. This had taken time, effort and persuasive skills she hadn't even known she had. 'It will also raise the profile of your charity—which, if you remember, was exactly the brief you gave me.'

His eyes fixed on hers. For a second it seemed he was

assessing her. If he found her wanting she would find the nearest vase and whack him over the head again.

He stood up. His imposing figure in front of hers. His broad chest filling her vision. His voice had a determined edge to it. 'It has to be about more than this. It has to be something else.'

'What? What else do you want from me, Will?' she shouted, all patience finally lost. 'What else can I do?'

'I want a night.'

'What?' She was losing the plot. None of this made sense to her any more. She had too much going on. Too much to think about. Sisters, fathers, mothers, weddings, band tours, bangles, promotion, interviews, Will, Will and more Will.

Any minute now she would spontaneously combust.

But Will was on a roll. 'I want a night. I want to show people what this is really about. I want to spend a night on the streets the way my friend had to when he was homeless —when he didn't know where to turn. I want people to understand how terrifying and dangerous it can be. I want to give them a real feel for the vulnerability—and the stories—of the people I want to help.'

Her brain started spinning. It was genius. It was perfect. It would complement the other publicity perfectly. People might have fun voting, but if they watched something like that it would really bring the message home. But when he'd said the words 'I want a night' it wasn't quite what she'd hoped to hear. And now she was annoyed with herself for even imagining he might have meant something else.

Will was still mumbling. 'And I want you to do it with me.'

The words clicked into place in her brain. 'Me?'

'Yes. You.'

She was baffled. 'But why?' Could her head really get any more confused?

'Because you're the perfect person to do it with. People know who you are. A famous couple's daughter? They'll love it. They'll think it's something that a girl like you, and—' he pointed to himself '—a guy like me would never do. Let's show them how hard it is. Let's show them just how difficult it is. Let's tell them some of the stories of the people out there.'

Boy, when he wanted it, his charm just came out in spades. And it was rational, businesslike sense. It put another edge to the publicity. She kind of wished she'd thought of it herself. But she kind of wished he wanted to do it with someone else. Could she really put herself in the spotlight again?

His hands rested gently on her shoulders. She could smell him. His scent was invading her senses. It was like a magic potion winding its way around her. She could almost see its tendrils wrapping around her body and throwing all rational thoughts out of the window.

'I need you, Rose. I need to do this. And I need to do it with you. Do you understand that?'

There it was again. That way he made her stomach twist and turn. He knew just how to speak to her. Just how to reach in and touch the little parts of her that couldn't say no to him. Part of this terrified her.

She wasn't in a situation where she couldn't say no. She just didn't want to. And even though this was completely different from years ago, a tiny little bit of her still remembered feeling so distracted by a man she'd forgotten about everything else. The guilt still consumed her. She didn't ever want to be that way again.

It didn't matter this was Will. It didn't matter there was no element of danger. This wasn't about him. This was about *her*. And her ability to trust. She still hadn't completely learned to trust her instincts. And a guy with Will's history? He didn't really have trust stamped all over him.

Still, she couldn't ignore what was happening between them. She couldn't ignore the way her body reacted every time he was near. She'd never felt this way about a guy before. Was this what love felt like? Or was this just infatuation?

'Rose, are you okay? Do you need some time to think this over? Please tell me you'll think about it. I really want to do this with you.'

She took a deep breath. Was she prepared to do this for a charity? No matter how uncomfortable and scary it was? Of course she was. She was lucky. She'd had a privileged life. Her parents had always drummed into her and her sisters how lucky they were. They made a point of supporting their favourite charities and the work her mother did was never-ending. Of course she could spend one night on the streets.

She took a deep breath. This seemed like so much more. It seemed like a partnership. It seemed like a way of cementing things between them—to see if their paths could truly connect or not.

'I'll do it.' There. She said the words before she had too much time to think any more. To mull things over.

And Will did the thing she'd longed for. He sealed it with a kiss.

The interviews were set. The voting lines would be announced tomorrow. With so much publicity for the homeless charity and the papers filled with all his ex-fiancées everyone seemed to have forgotten about the picture of him and Rose in the press. Everyone but him.

For the first time in his life he'd cut a picture from the

press. He'd even saved it and printed it from one of the press Internet sites.

He loved it. He loved the way they were captured in it. Daisy was the photographer in Rose's family and he'd heard her talk with passion about her pictures and what she wanted to capture in them. But he'd never really got *it* before.

Not before now.

Not before he could see the look on both his and Rose's faces. Captured for an eternity. And he loved it. He was actually going to frame it.

But it made him nervous. Now, everything else paled in comparison to how he felt about Rose. He could see it now. He could see the infatuation. But he'd never felt the love. Not like this.

How would she be when he told her what he'd done? If she felt the same way he did, everything should work out fine. If she didn't?

He'd need to learn to live with having a runaway bride.

CHAPTER NINE

PAUL SCHOLAND WAS her favourite ever TV presenter. With his bright, sparkling blue eyes and prematurely grey hair the female audience just loved him. He had all the exes eating out of the palm of his hand and had got the mixture of personal and publicity just right. Rose's tightly tied-up stomach was finally starting to relax. Particularly when she got a text about the sudden upsurge in voting. Things were going better than she could ever have imagined.

Will had spent most of the morning pacing around the room; Violet had come in every now and then to howl with laughter at some of the comments and then left again. Will's segment had been pre-recorded and when his face filled the screen Rose took in a deep breath.

The camera loved him. She'd always known it, but she'd never really appreciated it before. His eyes were even more remarkable than Paul's, his dark hair framing his face, with tiny lived-in lines around his eyes enhancing his good looks. But better than everything was his easy, laid-back attitude. The whole world was falling in love with him right now—her included—and Rose was feeling sparks of jealousy.

This was her Will. Hers. She didn't want to share him.

'Is it over yet?' He was watching from beneath his fingers. She nodded. 'Just about.' She turned her phone towards him. 'Look how things have gone.'

His eyes widened and he dropped his hands. 'How much?'

She smiled. 'Yeah, that much. And it's only the first day. You were on the front page of one of the red tops today, too. People are talking about this—talking about your charity.'

He looked a little doubtful. 'I'm being made a laughing stock on national TV.'

Rose stood up and walked towards him. 'Paul handled those interviews really well. In the meantime, money is being raised for your charity. You've got another interview on the main news channel tomorrow. That will give you an opportunity to speak about your friend and why you're doing this. You'll be able to talk about the night on the street, too. It will all balance out, Will. This is a good thing that you're doing.'

He stood up next to her. 'I know. I just wonder what I'm going to end up doing.' He shook his head. 'It could be a disaster.'

'It will be fine. No matter what it is at the end of the day, it'll be worth it.'

He nodded slowly. 'You're right. Of course you're right.' He lifted his hand and twisted his finger through a lock of her hair. 'So where are we with your list?'

For a second her thoughts were jumbled, then her woolly brain came into focus. 'The wedding list, yes.' She turned and walked over to the table and picked up her black planner. 'Okay, venue, marquees, food, band all sorted.'

'Is your dad playing at his own wedding?'

She sighed. 'Of course he is. But not till later. Their support band is playing for most of the main event. But there's no show without punch. At some point my dad and the guys will want to get up there and rock out.'

She ran her finger down the rest of the list. 'Violet's doing the flowers—apparently my mother's already given her instructions. Mum's got her dress and we've all picked ours. Daisy is doing some of the wedding pics and her assistant is doing some others.'

'What about everything else?'

'Well, the wedding favours and chocolates are sorted, as are the chair covers and balloons. I've just got to sort out a wedding cake and to choose wine and a drinks list for the bar.'

'When do you need to do that?'

She wrinkled her nose. 'In around an hour. I was kind of hoping you would come with me and help me choose the last few things.'

Will shrugged. 'I can choose wedding cake and the wine is already sorted. Sounds like every guy's dream date.'

She opened her mouth to stop him, to tell him it wasn't a date, and then stopped. She was almost glad he was thinking like that. It felt kind of nice.

She took a few minutes to finish up with emails and phone calls, finalising the flight arrangements for the reporter flying in from New York to write her father's book. She'd worked with Tom Buckley on numerous occasions and he was great. The only hiccup this time was the scheduling. Tom was on another job and the soonest he could get here was the same day as her mother and father's wedding renewal. She'd have to leave at night to pick him up from the airport. It couldn't be helped.

Will finished on his phone around the same time she did. 'Ready?'

She nodded and they walked outside to his car. 'Do you have an address?'

She bit the inside of her cheek and turned her phone

around to show him. He blinked. Twice. 'Really? What on earth…?'

'Yeah, I know. When I phoned Angie to ask her to take part in setting a dare she asked me how things were. Before I knew it, I'd told her about my parents' wedding renewal and how difficult it was to find everyone at short notice. She said her sister would be delighted to make the wedding cake.'

'Does she know I'm coming along?'

Rose looked at him nervously. 'It might be a little awkward but I'm sure it will be fine.'

'I sure hope so. Otherwise we're both in trouble. You won't get any cake and I'll probably end up wearing some.'

She laughed. 'I'm sure it won't end up like that. Angie was great on the phone. She couldn't have been nicer. She seems really happy now she's married with a baby of her own.'

He looked thoughtful as they continued along the road. 'Angie is nice. She's great, in fact.'

The words did strange things to her insides. She liked Angie. She really did. She just didn't want to think about the history between her and Will. She couldn't even bear to think about it.

'She just wasn't right for me—like I wasn't right for her.'

It was like a wave of relief washing over her. And it was almost as if Will realised her apprehension because one of his hands left the wheel and squeezed her leg through her dress as he glanced sideways at her.

'You're right. I'm sure it will be fine.' He put his hand back on the steering wheel and they continued along the road until they eventually reached the address.

Angie's sister Deb was the ultimate professional. Small and petite with a bright red bob, she had a whole portfolio of cake photos to show Rose along with lots of samples of her baking.

They were all laid out before her. 'Here are the sponges—try a bit of each. If there's a special request I can make it. I have traditional fruit cake, carrot cake, chocolate cake, strawberry and white chocolate, dark chocolate and orange, coconut and vanilla sponge, lemon sponge and coffee sponge.' Each one was more delicious than the last.

'Do you like them?'

'I love them all.' Rose kept flicking through the cake book. It was difficult to know which style and what kind of decorations to choose. She turned the book towards Will. 'What do you think? A traditional tiered cake or something more novelty?'

'What do your parents like best?'

'That's just it. I don't know. For birthdays we quite often have novelty cakes. But I'm not sure if they'd want that for their wedding.'

'How many tiers do you want? Do you know how many guests are coming?' Angie's sister had her order book poised.

Rose groaned. 'It could be three hundred.'

Deb blinked twice. 'Do you want some advice?'

Rose nodded. 'Gladly. I know nothing about this kind of stuff. I just don't have a clue.'

Deb flicked through her portfolio. 'Keep it simple— or as simple as you can with that amount of guests. How about an eight-tier cake with one of every kind of sponge? That way your guests will be able to find something they like. I can cover it in royal icing with some pale ribbons and you could get your florist to do a display for the top that matches your mum's flowers.'

Rose nodded quickly. She was happy to take any suggestion right now that made things a little easier. Deb pointed to the cakes in front of her. 'I'll go and make you some tea. Just pick which sponge for each layer.' She handed over a diagram. 'Remember sponge one will be the biggest and sponge eight the smallest so all you need to do is decide the order. I'll give you some space because this can take a little bit of time.'

She left Rose and Will together in the room. Will had barely said a word since they got there. 'Are you okay?'

He gave the tiniest nod. 'It's just weird, that's all. She hasn't even mentioned the dares or the press stuff.'

'She probably doesn't want to.' Rose pointed to all the sponges. 'This is her business and doing Mum and Dad's cake will be good publicity for her portfolio. I'm expecting her to charge a lot more because of the short notice but I'm just so relieved to have someone.'

Will frowned. 'This wedding is costing a lot of money.'

Rose nodded.

'But doesn't that kind of go against your mum and dad's principles?'

She wrinkled her nose. 'I know what you mean. To be honest they probably give away the same amount of money that they spend.' She shrugged. 'From a strictly PR perspective the wedding will look ostentatious. It will feed the public image that they're successful and doing well. But it also means that they can continue to give to all the charitable causes they want to—with or without publicity.'

Will nodded. He looked thoughtful and picked up a piece of one of the sponges. 'Which is your favourite?'

'I can't decide. They're all delicious.'

'What would you pick for your wedding cake?' It was a simple enough question. 'If it was up to me I'd have the whole thing chocolate.'

'Oh, no.' She waved her hand. 'I wouldn't want a wedding cake anyway.'

'You wouldn't?' He was surprised. He knew she'd said she didn't want a big wedding. But just how small did she actually mean?

Rose shook her head and waved her hand. 'I don't want any of it. Any of it at all.'

A horrible feeling crept over him. 'Do you mean the wedding?'

She tilted her head to the side. 'No, but that's all I want. The wedding. A dress and a bunch of flowers for my hands.'

He raised his eyebrows. 'And presumably a groom?'

She threw back her head and laughed. 'Well, hopefully that's part of the package and not an optional extra.'

Relief started to flood through him. It was odd. He hadn't actually realised that when Rose said small, she actually meant minimal. It wasn't quite what he'd imagined. But the more he got to know her, the more he understood.

Rose lifted a little piece of carrot cake and nibbled. 'This one is delicious.' She sighed and lifted up the strawberry and white chocolate. 'But I like this one, too.' It crumbled as she bit into it and Will reached over and put his hand under her chin. She spluttered as he caught the crumbs. 'Never thought of you as a messy eater.' His eyes twinkled as he lifted some of the chocolate cake. 'Here, try my favourite.'

She hesitated. There was something so intimate about being fed by someone else. Even if it was in the middle of the day in someone else's house. Her eyes darted to the door. Deb was nowhere in sight.

She opened her mouth as he positioned the light, moist sponge at her mouth. The chocolate frosting was perfect, sending little explosions around her mouth, to say nothing of the ones as his fingers contacted her lips.

His thumb smudged across the edges. 'You've got a little bit stuck,' he whispered.

'Where?' She looked around for a napkin.

'I'll get it,' he offered as he bent forward to kiss her. His lips touched hers, lightly at first, delicately, before he eased her lips apart and joined their mouths together. His hand slid around the nape of her neck and through her hair, making her want to beg for more. This was it. This was what he did to her. Gave her a little taste that left her begging for more.

The voices started in her head. She was getting in too deep. Every kiss took her a step closer to never wanting to go back. *Angie's sister's house* floated around her head. There was a thought to chill her heated blood. She pulled back and made a grab for a napkin. It was perfect timing as Deb appeared with the tea, her bright smile still firmly in place.

Rose picked up the diagram and quickly numbered each tier of the cake with the sponge she wanted. 'Thank you so much, Deb, for doing this. Let me know how much I owe you.'

Deb hesitated but shook her head. 'It's fine, but I'd be really grateful if you could get a photo with your mum and dad and the cake for my portfolio.'

'Of course. Of course. No problem at all.'

Deb gave a hopeful smile. 'Thanks.'

It only took them a few minutes to get in the car and leave. Rose was feeling happy. All the things on her wedding list were finally ticked off. For once, she could relax. All she needed to focus on now was making the bangle for her mum.

Then there was the horrible sinking realisation that she really had no reason to spend time with Will any more. All of a sudden his proposition about being on the streets one night didn't seem quite so scary.

Will seemed laid-back. 'So, are you ready for your night on the tiles with me?'

'When a guy invites a girl for a night on the tiles he doesn't usually mean it literally.'

Will glanced over at her. 'I like to do things a little differently. Anyway it will take my mind off those hideous dares. Have you heard any more about them?'

She nodded and smiled. 'It's a definite split vote between the gladiator, the thong and the total body waxing.' She shrugged. 'Personally I thought people might be more inclined to go for the more venomous one—the dunking in the Thames. But no, it seems it's humiliation all the way.'

'Does the total-body hair wax include the hair on my head?'

'Absolutely.'

He shuddered. 'It just doesn't seem that appropriate for a homeless charity.'

'But dressing in a thong and working in a lingerie department does?'

His eyes were fixed on the road but his lips turned upwards. 'No, that's definitely pure humiliation all the way.'

He was taking it really well. The whole dare thing didn't seem to bother him or annoy him. He was prepared to take it on the chin.

It was just another reason to like him all the more. Somehow she knew spending a night out on the streets with Will wasn't going to be the best idea in the world. He was already ticking so many boxes for her. Was she really prepared to let him tick the last few?

'What will I need?'

'Warm clothes, especially a jacket and shoes. It can be really cold at night.'

'Do you think we'll get any sleep at all?'

'I have no idea. I guess we'll find out. Is one of the reporters from the paper coming along?'

She screwed up her face. 'He'll do a cover story. It took quite a bit of persuading. But I don't think he'll stay all night.'

Will's phone sounded and he lifted his hip slightly. 'Can you pull that out for me?'

She stretched over and slid her hand into his pocket. The skin next to the thin cotton lining of the pocket was warm. She tried not to focus on that as she made a grab for the phone. She pulled it out and glanced at the screen.

'It's Violet. She wants you to phone her.' Her stomach did a little flip. This was her sister. Will was Vi's best friend. She had no reason to feel jealous.

Will gave a slight nod of his head but said nothing. It just made her feel worse.

'Just drop me back at home,' she said abruptly. 'I need to spend some time on my mother's bangle.'

'Okay.' They drove in silence until he reached her parents' house and she jumped out of the car as quickly as she could. 'Thanks. I'll text you about Saturday night.' She slammed the door quickly as she strode inside, passing Violet in the corridor. 'Is Will outside? I need to talk to him.'

Violet wandered past her and outside as Rose made her way to her workshop. She needed to get a hold of herself. She needed to get things into perspective. Her mind was playing tricks on her these days. Making her think irrational thoughts. Was this what it felt like to be in love? Because if it was—it wasn't good. All of a sudden she felt sick to her stomach.

There was no getting away from it. Saturday night on the streets was going to be make or break for her and Will. He knew it. And she knew it.

CHAPTER TEN

IT WAS THE final dress fitting. Daisy was back now with her ever expanding tiny bump. The green dress covered it to perfection and standing side by side the three sisters in their green, blue and purple dresses made a striking picture.

Sherry clapped her hands. 'Oh, my beautiful girls. You all look perfect.'

Rose tugged at her hair. 'Do we need a tiara or a fascinator or something?'

Sherry exchanged a look with Violet. 'We've got that all under control. You'll have a fresh flower for your hair.'

Daisy was distracted. She sat down and eyed her jewelled sandals suspiciously. 'Can I wear Converse instead?'

'No,' Sherry said swiftly. She held up an alternative pair of flat jewelled sandals. 'I've got you flatties for the night. You only need to wear the heels for the renewal vows.'

Sherry turned to Rose. 'Everything is ready? Everything is done?'

Rose nodded and started to reel everything off. 'Marquees will be set up the day before. Violet's taking care of the flowers, Daisy the photographs. Dad's backup band is organised. The chairs and tables come the day before. The favours and cake are organised—along with the menu. Everything will be perfect, Mum, you don't need to worry about a thing.'

Sherry enveloped her in a hug. 'That's why we trust you with everything, honey. You're just so good at organising. I don't know what we'd do without you.'

Rose beamed; she didn't even know about the bangle yet. Her mother would be delighted. But Violet didn't look delighted. Violet looked mad. As if her mother's words had just irked her.

Rose had no idea what was going on. But she'd too much to think about right now.

And most of her thoughts were around a runaway groom...

He could hardly even see her face. The hood of her parka came right down over her nose. He stuck his face inside. 'Is anyone alive in here?'

'You said it would be cold. I'm just trying to make sure I'll be warm.'

He slid his arm around her shoulders. 'It will be cold. But I'll do my best to keep you warm.'

She glanced around. There were a number of people in the homeless shelter drinking tea and soup. 'What time does this place close?'

'Eleven.'

'And where does everyone go then?' She was looking around at the array of figures in the room. Most weren't dressed very well; all of them were in layers. He saw her look down and knew exactly what she'd see. Lots of the people who slept on the streets had shoes that were mis-matched and falling apart. Once they found a pair of shoes that fitted they wore them until they literally fell off their feet.

'That's just the point. I guess we'll find out.'

Rose inched a little closer to him. Will was used to coming here. He often came and helped out in the food kitchen. He wasn't fazed by the sometimes unkempt people that used it. This place was a safe haven. Somewhere they could be fed and get a few hours' warmth. It was staffed completely by volunteers and Will would like nothing more than for it to be open for longer.

As the staff in the kitchen started to clean and tidy up Will moved forward to help. Rose was right by his side, washing dishes and cleaning worktops. It was all hands on deck here.

By the time they locked the front doors darkness had fallen. Rose was glancing around at the people gathered in small clumps around the door. Few words were exchanged. Most were trying to decide where to stay safe for the night.

'I had no idea so many people stayed on the streets,' she whispered. 'Can't they get emergency accommodation from the council?'

Will shook his head. 'Some of these people have been through the system—some haven't. A few have addiction problems and weren't able to manage a tenancy even though the council had found one for them. Managing money is a skill that some people find really difficult. There's just not enough support out there.'

A thin, wiry teenage boy walked past, head down and hands in his pockets. Rose sucked in a breath. 'Will,' she whispered, 'he doesn't even look sixteen.'

Will's heart squeezed. 'That's Alfie. And he's seventeen. He's been on the streets for the last two years and he won't let me help him. I've tried.'

Rose looked horrified. 'Why on earth would a kid that age end up on the streets?'

Will shook his head. 'That's just it. He won't say. And he's one of about twenty kids I know that really shouldn't be here.' He nudged her with his elbow and pointed across the road. 'That's Danny, one of the voluntary workers.

He'll spend most of the night keeping watch over the young ones to try and keep them safe. He's a real godsend.'

Rose's brow was wrinkled and she turned to face him. 'I don't get it. Why don't these kids want to be under a roof and sleeping in a bed?'

'Because not all homes are like yours and mine. Not all homes are safe. I suspect some of these kids have come through the care system and slipped through the net. Others are escaping abuse. Some have mental health disorders that make it difficult for them to cope.' He looked around and pointed towards a group of middle-aged men. 'And it's not just the young ones. Last year they estimated around three thousand people slept rough in London, people who just don't have family or friends to help them. Lots of them ended up homeless because of redundancy or domestic abuse. There's a whole host of different reasons people end up like this.'

Rose slipped her hand into his. 'Your friend. How is he?'

Will felt himself bristle. It was the whole reason he was here but it was still a sore point. He still felt as if he'd let his friend down. 'He's getting there. It took a long time before he'd let anyone help him. That's just it. I could stand here in the street and announce I'd give everyone somewhere safe to sleep for the night but most of them wouldn't believe me—wouldn't trust me. They wouldn't come.' His voice was tinged with sadness as Rose's fingers curled around his own. He couldn't imagine being here with anyone else. He couldn't ever have imagined any of his previous girlfriends agreeing to do this with him—he wouldn't have wanted them to.

But this was different. This was important to him. And if the decision he'd made about Rose was right, this was the kind of thing he needed to share with her—he needed her to understand.

He pointed to the dark streets. 'Are you sure you're okay with this?' She looked nervous, even though she was obviously trying her best not to.

'I'm fine,' she said quietly before adding, 'I'm with you.'

He nodded and took a few steps down the street. 'Then let's go. Let's see how you survive on the streets at night.'

This London was completely different from the London that Rose knew. She wasn't naïve. She knew people slept rough and there were homeless hostels all over London but, while she'd taken part in a lot of charity work with her parents, she'd never worked in any of these places.

London at night for Rose and her sisters had involved trendy streets and clubs. Coming out late at night, clamouring into a cab and grabbing some food from an eatery on the way home. The streets they were walking down now were unfamiliar to Rose. Dark, damp, creepy.

Will took her down alleyways, stopping by rubbish bins to speak to people hidden in the shadows. Handing out biscuits and cards with addresses for assistance. As the cold crept around them and the night became even darker they kept going. Tramping unfamiliar streets without fear. Occasionally they met other workers, voluntary organisations and a few cops on the beat. Will seemed to recognise most of them, stopping to compare notes and talk about trouble spots. A few made jokes about his press coverage, though all thanked him for trying to raise the issue.

Fatigue started to settle in. Her muscles were tiring. The cold was creeping down to her very bones. Will steered her towards one of the bridges spanning the Thames. 'This is a hotspot,' he murmured. 'Lots of people sleep under this bridge at night. Stay close. Fights sometimes break out.'

The rain had started to fall. Thick, heavy drops that soaked straight through her jacket. They hurried under the bridge. There was no lighting under here. It was almost completely black with only a flicker from the occasional match somewhere.

At the other side there was a fight starting over some cardboard boxes. Rose drew close to Will, wrapping her arms around his waist and shielding her face away. The fight ended as quickly as it had started, with the victor claiming his spoils and arranging his cardboard box on the ground.

'They were fighting over a cardboard box?' Rose whispered.

Will nodded. 'You've no idea what has value on the street. Especially on a night like this. Here.' He pulled her over to the wall under the bridge and pulled her down next to him. The cold concrete quickly wound its way through her clothes and she shifted on the ground. Will still had his arm around her shoulders and she snuggled closer to get some body heat. 'Are we going to stay here?'

It all seemed so alien to her. So cold. So uncomfortable. So unsafe.

He nodded. 'This is it. This is where a lot of the people on the streets spend the night. How long do you think you could actually sleep for?'

'I don't think I can sleep at all,' she whispered, not wanting to offend any of the huddled figures around her.

'I know. But we have to try. We have to understand what it is these people go through every night. That's the message I want to get out there.'

Something struck her. 'What happened to the reporter?'

Will sighed. 'He got waylaid with something else. He interviewed me earlier and I've got a little camera attached to the pocket of my jacket. He should pick up some things from that.'

Rose put her hand on the freezing ground. 'But he won't

pick up this. He won't pick up how cold it is out here. He won't get how the wind whistles under the bridge and the raindrops still reach you even though you're in the middle.'

Will smiled. 'But you do.'

Something fleeted across her face. 'Yeah, but I don't like it, Will. I'd be terrified if I was here myself. I can't stand the thought of living every night like this.'

He looked out over the darkness of the still water of the Thames. 'This is where Arral used to sleep at night.'

'Your friend?'

He nodded. 'I still can't fathom how it happened. How a guy who did so well at university, got his first job and flat just ended up on a downward spiral that ended up with him stabbed and in hospital.' He shook his head as he looked at the bodies huddled around them. 'Arral was married. But when he lost his job and his home, his wife just upped and left. She didn't take her vows seriously. The whole for better or worse part just seemed to pass her by. I've thought about it for the last few years. How marriage was about good and bad.' He squeezed his eyes shut for a second. 'It always made me second-guess things. It always made me scrutinise my relationships. Would this person still want to grow old with me if I didn't have the fancy house, jobs and cars? It made me question my abilities to choose wisely.'

She frowned. 'But I've met all four of them. Marta and Angie seemed nice. Both of them weren't bitter. They knew they weren't destined to be with you. Esther is focused on her media career. And Melissa?' She shrugged. 'She seems to have her own demons. I doubt very much you can do anything about them.'

She squeezed his hand. 'This place gives you a whole new perspective on life, doesn't it?' She was looking around. Looking at the array of faces, some hidden beneath hoods or cardboard boxes. There was a real mixture of people here. Mainly young and middle-aged. There were around forty people under this bridge, but only two she would have termed elderly.

'Are you okay?'

She shivered and huddled a little closer. 'Yes. I'm just remembering, I guess.'

'Remembering what?'

'My friend, Autumn,' she said sadly. 'She died from a drug overdose at a party one night. We were both there, but I made bad choices that night. We both did.' Her voice started to shake. 'No one knows, Will. But I knew that Autumn had dabbled with drugs before. I knew and I still left her alone that night to go off with some guy. I wasn't a silly teenager. I was a twenty-four-year-old woman and I left my friend behind. I let her down. I let myself down. And I let my parents down. They had to deal with the fallout of my actions. They had to deal with my bad choices.' She was ashamed to say those words out loud. What would Will think of her now he knew all about her flaws? 'I wonder how many of these people didn't even get to make a choice to end up here?' she murmured. 'It seems so unfair.'

Will nodded. She couldn't really tell him how horrible she found this.

'I had family. I had a really strong family. My dad took over. He came with me to speak to Autumn's parents. He was there for hours.' She glanced up at Will. 'People just don't realise what my dad is made of. "Rock star" doesn't equate with supportive parent.' Will gave her shoulder a squeeze. 'But after the funeral was over I just couldn't take it. I couldn't take the bad press. I'm not a good person, Will. I'm the most flawed person you could meet.' She was shaking her head in disbelief.

'I went to New York to escape. To start again.' She held up her hand as the tears formed in her eyes. 'But now I feel a thoroughly pathetic human being. I didn't feel strong enough to cope—so I left. But what if you don't have the means to leave?' Her voice was starting to waver. 'Or what if the means to leave makes you end up on the street?' Being out here was scary. Having this as your reality must be terrifying for some of these people. 'I wasn't strong enough. I couldn't take what the press said about me. I hated having my picture in the paper. I couldn't take the lies. I didn't trust my judgement any more and I hated the fact that I felt as if I'd let my parents down. But I still had my family. I still had them around me. Is this what happens when you don't have family to support you?'

He tilted her chin up to face him. 'Rose, you and Violet are two of the strongest people I've ever met. The press has had a field day with you both. You, with your friend's death and Violet, with her leaked sex tape. But it hasn't dragged either of you down. If anything, it's made you both stronger. You didn't run away. You regrouped. You've spent the last few years working hard for your dad. You haven't hid away. And you've found something else. You've found something that you love—your jewellery making. And you've worked hard at that, too. How does that make you weak? How does that make you a failure? We've all got to take what life throws at us and deal with it the best we can.'

He stroked a finger down her face. 'Is this it, Rose? Is this what you're so afraid of? The press putting things you can't control about you in the papers? Letting your parents down? Trusting your judgement?'

He gave a gentle laugh. 'Have faith, Rose. Have faith in yourself. Because I have faith in you, and so does every member of your family. You've organised your parents'

renewal vows in record time. *They* trusted *you* to do that.'
He emphasised the words by pressing his palm against her
chest. 'They trusted your judgement—even if you don't.'
He leaned closer. 'And I trust your judgement, Rose, more
than you can ever know.'

His face nuzzled against hers, his cold nose sending little delicious waves down her chilled bones. 'Do you think
I would have brought anyone else here? Do you think any
of my previous girlfriends would even have made an attempt to understand this?' She could hear the conviction
in his voice. He really believed in what he was saying. 'It
could only ever have been you, Rose. Just you. You're the
only person I could share this with.'

He straightened a little. 'I told you about Arral and his
wife leaving. I told you that in the lead-up to my weddings
I started to have doubts. Doubts about whether I could
see myself growing old with that person.' He touched her
cheek. 'I don't have any doubts about you, Rose. I can
see myself growing old with you. You've got to give us a
chance. You've got to know that this is real between us.'

There they were. The words she'd thought she wanted
to hear. Every ounce of him believed what he was saying.
How could she tell him that even though he was sure, she
was the one with doubts?

Realisation was seeping through her with the cold concrete beneath her. This wasn't really about him. This was
about her.

Will might well be the Runaway Groom. It was a label
that was never going to disappear. Every instinct told her
to trust him. Every instinct told her to believe what he
was saying.

But she hadn't learned to trust her instincts again yet.
It was the one thing that was holding her back. The wary
part of her brain said he was in the first flush of romance

again. That in a few months none of this would be real. How well could you possibly know someone after a few weeks?

But then there was Daisy. She'd had one night with Seb and returned weeks later to give him baby news. They'd married in the space of a few weeks, and, while there might have been a few initial doubts, on their wedding day their faces hadn't lied. It was two people, totally in love with each other, who'd said those vows. If it worked for Daisy—why not for her?

It was so easy to get sucked in. Will was gorgeous. Will was charming. And even on a wet, rainy, cold night he made her feel like the most special person in the universe.

'Once we get through this, let's go someplace else. Let's go someplace it's just the two of us. I didn't want to share this with anyone else, Rose. And I don't want to share you either.' His lips were hovering just above her own. His warm breath heating her skin.

All she could see in this dim light was the dark blue rim around his eyes. The thing that she'd first noticed about him. The thing that had drawn her in and made her heart do that first little flip-flop.

There were no alarm bells ringing. No 'do this and you'll regret it' voices screaming in her head. Maybe, for the first time ever, she was really ready to take a chance on love?

His lips made contact with hers. It was the briefest of kisses. The warmest of kisses. Telling her everything she wanted to know and sending signals that her body was screaming for.

She couldn't walk away from Will right now if she tried.

So she stayed there, with Will's broad arms wrapped around her, sending a little heat into her numb bum and chilled bones. It felt right. It felt secure. It felt as if this was the place she was supposed to be.

Part of her brain kept ticking. She'd need to come clean with Violet. And Daisy. She'd need to tell her sisters how she really felt. All of this wasn't true until she'd done that. Her family were so important to her. But she would wait. She would wait until after the whole PR announcement tomorrow and the wedding renewal.

It would give her a little time—a little space to have confidence to trust her instincts once again.

Nothing would happen before that—surely?

CHAPTER ELEVEN

HER EYES FLICKERED OPEN. She could hear Will's breathing next to her, feel the rise and fall of his chest against her back. His arm was curled around her. Waking up next to Will this time was an entirely different sensation.

Her eyes wandered to the clock and widened in shock. It was nearly midday. Will had booked them into a boutique hotel in the West End of London. When they'd finished their night on the street she'd been utterly exhausted. The journalist had been waiting for Will and he'd done a short interview without letting go of her hand. Then he'd brought her to this hotel and done a whole lot more before they'd finally fallen asleep.

Her heart started thudding against her chest. There was a host of further interviews later today, then the TV show tonight with the reveal of the winning dare. She'd promised she'd be there. But right now she had to get home and do some work on her mother's bangle. Time was running out. She didn't just have commitments to Will to fulfil—she'd commitments to her family.

Especially now. Especially after what had just happened between them. She needed to talk to Violet sooner rather than later.

In a familiar motion she slipped out from under the covers. Her clothes were lying across the floor and she picked them up and slipped them back on. She should wake him. She really should. But he'd been every bit as exhausted as she'd been. She could let him sleep and order him breakfast in an hour or so. That way she'd have time to get across London and put in a few hours' work on the bangle before she had to get back for the TV show. If she woke him now he might try and distract her. And it was likely that she wouldn't say no.

She grabbed her phone. Out of charge and she'd forgotten to bring her charger—typical. She bent over the bed and laid a gentle kiss on his forehead. He didn't even flicker. Just kept breathing deeply. So she smiled and slipped out of the door, remembering exactly what had happened earlier that morning on her trip back across London.

Something wasn't right. The space in the bed next to him wasn't filled with a warm, comfortable body. There was just a little divot in the bed where that warm body should be.

Will's eyes flickered open, first to the space beside him, then to the bathroom door. Every part of his body was coiled up right now, hoping that any second there would be a flush, a sound of running water and Rose would walk out of the door. But everything was silent.

The knock at the door nearly gave him heart failure and sent him bolt upright in bed. The door opened with a member of the staff carrying a tray that he set next to the bed. 'Breakfast for you, Mr Carter.'

'I didn't order breakfast.' His stomach grumbled loudly as if it were part of the bad joke.

The staff member gave a nervous smile. 'The young lady ordered it for you.'

Will flung the cover back and went to stand up—right until he realised he wasn't wearing anything. The poor guy was already walking backwards to the door. He covered himself quickly. 'The young lady? Where is she?'

The guy couldn't get out of the room quickly enough. 'I think she left, sir,' he said as he pulled the door closed behind him. The smell of bacon, eggs and coffee filled the room as Will sagged back on the bed.

She'd left? Why on earth would she leave after the morning they'd had together? Will's stomach curled. Had he misread the signals? Had he misread Rose completely?

He grabbed his phone and dialled her number. Straight to voicemail. He sent a text. Delivered. He held the phone in his hand for a few minutes, willing her to reply. Nothing.

This couldn't be happening. Why on earth would Rose send him up breakfast but leave without saying goodbye— or, worse, without leaving a message? He looked around for pen and paper. But there was nothing obvious.

He pushed the breakfast tray away. He couldn't stomach anything right now. Not while everything he'd wished for was hanging in the air. His phone beeped and he jumped. But it wasn't a message. It was a reminder that the TV studio car would be picking him up in an hour. He wasn't on until six that night but they wanted to rehearse and since the whole show was about him and his charity he could hardly let them down.

Clothes. He needed new clothes. His fingers were still clenched around his phone, rapidly turning white. Rose would have to wait until later.

She was out of breath and cursing herself like mad.

'What's the name?' The guy at the front desk looked distinctly uninterested.

'Rose Huntingdon-Cross.'

He gave a cursory glance at the list and shook his head. 'Not on it.'

'What do you mean I'm not on it? I'm the one that arranged the interview.'

The guy almost sneered. 'You're not on the list.'

She could feel the pressure building in her chest and resisted the urge to grab the guy by the nape of the neck and drag him across the desk. She'd never use the 'Do you know who I am?' card but she hated ineptitude.

She folded her arms across her chest. 'I'm here for Paul Scholand's interview with Will Carter—you know, the Runaway Groom? I can give you the name of each and every one of his fiancées that must have checked in with you by now.'

The guy didn't even blink. 'Not on the list,' he said again. It was almost like a challenge.

She took a deep breath. 'Why don't you check under Cross? People often list my surname wrongly.'

His eyes went reluctantly to the page again and he blinked. 'Hmm. Cross by name, cross by nature?' he said in a sing-song voice. She really could pull him across the desk and thump him.

'You bet,' was her reply.

He gestured with his hand, waving her in, and she strode past without a second glance.

Once she was through she found the studio no problem. Paul Scholand had been interviewing out of the same studio for the last five years and Rose had been there on a number of occasions with the band—in fact, she was due back in another month.

But today was a bit different. The studio was normally always slick and smooth but with four extra women, who for reasons unknown to Rose seemed to be being kept apart, along with Will—who seemed to be being kept apart from *everyone*—the studio runners and assistants seemed harassed to death.

This thing had just taken root and sprouted into a complete forest. One she wasn't even sure she wanted to enter. She gulped. If this was how she was feeling—how on earth must Will be feeling?

She reached into her pocket. Nothing. Then remembered she hadn't even charged her phone from this morning. Darn it. Things had got a bit fraught when she was in her workshop. There had been problems with one of the kinds of gold. She was going to have to get more and it would take more than a day to arrive. All cutting into her time to work and make the bangle on time. It was her own fault. She'd been distracted when she'd started work and not totally focused on the job. Under normal circumstances she would have noticed a problem with the gold straight away. But no. She was too busy dreaming of the feel of Will's hands on her skin and his lips coming into contact with that sensitive area at the bottom of her neck.

Her hand automatically lifted to the area. Whenever she thought of him her skin tingled.

She looked around, trying to see him through the crowded studio. Her eyes locked on another set that was watching her carefully. Angie—one of Will's ex-fiancées.

Her feet hesitated for a second before she put a smile on her face and walked over, holding her hand out. 'Angie, it's so nice to meet you. Thank you for doing this. The phone lines are doing brilliantly. We're raising lots of money for the charity.'

Angie gave a controlled nod of her head. She was in the middle of getting her hair and make-up done. 'That's really good to know. I'm glad it's going well.'

Rose felt something creep up her spine. Angie was being very reserved. Had she done something to offend her?

'And thank you so much for putting me in touch with

Deb. Her cakes are to die for. It was a real weight off my mind.'

As if on cue Angie pushed forward a plastic tub towards Rose. 'Deb sent something else for you to try. This is chocolate and hazelnut sponge. She wondered if you wanted some extra cupcakes for later?'

Rose picked up the tub straight away. She couldn't wait to try it. 'Oh, thank you, this is great. I'll give her a call later.'

Angie glanced sideways, as if to check to make sure no one else was listening. 'Be careful,' she said in a low voice. 'You've got that glow about you, Rose. Believe me, it can fade quickly. You're a nice girl.'

Rose opened her mouth to deny everything but the studio hairdresser had appeared again and was fussing around Angie. She walked away with her mouth hanging open. *Angie could tell just by looking at her?* How was that even possible? Nothing had happened until this morning. Up until then it had only been a few kisses. Nothing of any significance. And if she kept saying that she might actually believe it.

Will was at the other side of the studio with Paul Scholand. She lifted her hand to give him a wave and he wrinkled his brow, as if he was trying to work out who it was. She was forgetting. The studio lights were directly in his eyes.

She wandered closer. Round the back of the cameras and right round to the other side of the studio.

'You,' came the voice behind her. She spun on her heels and pulled the plastic tub a little closer, as if it were some kind of shield. Melissa Kirkwood had that kind of effect on people. This was a woman that certainly hadn't got over the Runaway Groom. She was the one who'd suggested dunking Will in the Thames.

'What can I do for you, Melissa?' Rose tried her sweetest voice. She'd no intention of doing anything for Melissa; she already couldn't wait to get away from her.

Melissa folded her arms across her ample chest. She was wearing a bright pink dress with a slash right down the front. One of the studio hairdressers was behind her, teasing her hair into waves. Melissa had obviously decided there was no need to be as discreet as Angie.

'So are you floating on a cloud right now? Thinking that Will could never look at another woman the way he looks at you? Has he told you that he loves you yet?' she sneered. 'Because we've all been there, honey. Don't think you're special.'

It was like having someone tip a whole bucket of ice over your head.

What was it with these women? Did she have a neon sign above her head?

'I have no idea what you're talking about,' she said quickly.

'Sure, honey, that's what they all say before the engagement ring appears, then your groom races down the aisle like he's being chased by killer zombies. It's written all over your face. You're just the next sucker in line.'

She could feel the colour rush up into her cheeks. Two ex-fiancées in almost the same number of minutes accusing her of the same thing. Was there a camera in the hotel room this morning? Last thing she wanted was to end up part of a sex-tape scandal like her sister.

She turned and walked away from Melissa. She'd already heard enough.

Will was standing at the edge of the set now while one of the make-up girls dusted some powder on his face. She was batting her eyelids and talking incessantly, but his gaze came into direct contact with Rose's.

It only took two strides to cross the space. 'Where did you go? I called you. Why didn't you call me back?'

Rose hesitated; her cheeks were still flushed from the comments from Angie and Melissa. She hated that people seemed to be able to read her so easily—particularly when she hadn't even had a chance to speak to her sisters. Was she really ready for this?

Her hesitation caused something to sweep over Will's face. He looked hurt. Even a little angry.

Paul Scholand was on his feet. 'Are you ready, Will? It's time for the countdown.'

Will nodded. 'Wait here,' he said quickly to her, shooting her a glance that made her insides curl up.

Everything about her felt in flux. She wanted to tell him the truth. She was confused. She needed time to think. She needed time to talk to her family. Last night and this morning had been great. She'd almost been convinced that he meant everything that he'd said.

But being here, in amongst the women he'd 'loved' before, was overwhelming. Words that he'd never said to her. She felt crowded—swamped. She felt as if there weren't enough room in the building for her own feelings while there was a huge rush of female hormones everywhere else. How on earth could she know how Will really felt about her here and now? This had disaster written all over it.

Will could feel the claustrophobia in the room. None of this was good. Paul kept looking at him reassuringly and patting him on the knee. He must sense that Will really just wanted to bolt from the studio.

The cameraman gave the signal and the theme tune started reverberating around the studio. On the other side of the studio, his four exes were being lined up on a curved sofa. He winced. Some of them had exchanged words in the past. He just hoped the studio had prepared for this adequately.

No matter how much he squinted at the spotlights he couldn't see Rose. All he'd felt from her was an overwhelming sense of panic. She'd left this morning as if she'd had second thoughts. She hadn't responded to any of his messages. And for the first time ever Will felt as if the shoe was on the other foot. He wanted Rose to feel the same as he did. He *needed* Rose to feel the same way he did.

Otherwise all his plans would be for nothing and he was about to make an even bigger fool of himself than normal.

Paul was talking now, playing the audience a clip showing each of his ex-fiancées talking about choosing their dare for him.

He looked at the four women. At one point he'd loved every one of them. At least he'd thought he had. He recognised it now as infatuation.

Nothing like what he felt for Rose. She was his first thought in the morning and his last thought at night. He'd seen her vulnerability last night. He'd wanted to do everything he could to protect the woman that he loved.

He wasn't running scared from Rose. Just the opposite. He was running towards her so quickly he was afraid he'd scare her off.

What if he'd misjudged the situation completely and she really didn't want to take things that far? All he knew was it was so important to him to show her that she was different. That she was *The One*. To show her he wasn't the Runaway Groom any more.

Paul touched his arm. 'Are you ready for the final figure?'

Will blinked. He hadn't been paying the slightest bit of attention.

Paul was still smiling his perfect TV smile. 'Would you

like to give the audience a little insight into why this charity is so important to you?'

Focus. Will nodded. This was the important bit. 'The charity is so important to me because I've had a friend affected by homelessness. There are a lot of misconceptions about people who live on the streets. Not all are drug addicts or alcoholics. Not all have been in trouble with the police. My friend hadn't done anything wrong, but because of the economic downturn his company went out of business. As a result he lost his home. He couldn't apply for jobs because he didn't have a permanent address. He didn't have family to turn to. He was embarrassed to tell his friends. I only found out after he was stabbed on the streets one night and the police contacted me because they found my card amongst his things. I want people to understand that there are a whole host of reasons people end up on the streets and there are lots of things we can do to help prevent it. Find out where your nearest shelter is. See what you can do to help. It doesn't have to be a lot. It can be donating clothes, donating food. It can be helping out in the kitchen. It can be helping people learn new skills.'

Paul nodded solemnly and turned to the camera. 'The votes have now closed. We're just about to find out how much money has been raised for charity. Ladies, are you ready?'

The camera panned along the four women with smiles on their faces. This was so not Will's idea of a good time. But if it got the message across he really didn't care.

'Is there any particular dare you'd like to avoid, Will?'

He shook his head. 'Paul, I'm willing to do whatever the public voted on no matter how humiliating it is. I just want to thank each and every person who picked up the phone and voted, contributing to the fund.' He put his hand on his chest. 'Thank you all from the bottom of my heart.'

Paul waited for the drum roll. It seemed to last for ever. Dramatic TV seemed to be his forte.

'Voting on the dares has finished. Will Carter, the total amount of money raised for your homeless charity is…one point one million pounds!'

Will's legs took on a life of their own and he shot upright with the wildest yell, punching the air. 'Yes!' His brain was jammed full of all the things the charity could do with the money. All the things that would make a difference for the people on the street. Staff. Housing. Employment. Rose was a genius. He could kiss her. He would kiss her.

Paul was still talking as Will pushed his way through the buzzing studio. He'd stopped listening to Paul. He'd stopped worrying about the cameras. All he wanted to do was find Rose.

Rose. There was a stunned smile on her face as he elbowed people out of the way to get to her. He picked her up in his arms and spun her around. 'Way to go, Rose! Have you any idea what this means?'

He didn't wait for an answer, just lowered her down and planted a kiss square on her lips, reaching his hands up to either side of her face. She tasted of strawberries. Sweet, juicy strawberries.

But she wasn't kissing back. Not as she usually did.

The buzz in the studio seemed to have died down a little. Will felt a tap on the shoulder. Paul, with a camera and light at his side. 'Will, who is this? Is this someone that we all should meet? Could this be your newest fiancée?'

He felt her bristle under his touch, every muscle in her body tensing. She pulled her lips away from his.

Panic. That was all he could see in her eyes. He'd misjudged this so badly. The one thing he didn't want to do. He'd just been swept away by the momentum of the event, and the memories of this morning. He hadn't even asked Rose if she was ready to go public and now, he'd just kissed her on national television in front of all his ex-fiancées. Could he get this any more wrong?

'Rose. Don't panic. This will be fine. Let me handle this,' he whispered.

But she looked horrified. Her hands fell from his sides. 'I'm not ready for this, Will.' Her words were cold. Definite.

Will stepped back as if stung. She looked hurt. She looked confused. *He'd* done this to her.

Will was used to women falling in love with him. He wasn't used to them stepping away. But Rose was different. And he'd known it from the start. It was why he loved her.

He turned to Paul. Right now, he could cheerfully punch him. Paul knew exactly who Rose was—he'd worked with her often enough.

'Rose is just a friend,' he said quickly before turning and beaming at the camera. 'I don't think I'm quite ready for another fiancée, do you?' He gestured towards the four sitting women. 'Let's find out what dare I will be doing.'

Paul led him back over towards the TV sofas as his head spun round and round. How was he going to get this back? How was he going to sort this?

He glanced behind him. But the spot that Rose had been standing in was empty. She was gone.

Rose had never walked so quickly. Hot tears were spilling down her cheeks. *I don't think I'm quite ready for another fiancée, do you?*

How much more of a wake-up call did she need? Fiancées. He collected them like some kids collected dolls, or rubbers, or cars. Will Carter made promises he couldn't keep. He never saw things through to the main event.

That wasn't for her. It never would be. Rose was a traditionalist. She wanted what her mum and dad had. Love to last a lifetime. Nothing less would do. She wouldn't, *couldn't* settle for anything else.

She waited until she burst from the studio doors and the cool fresh air hit her before she finally released all the pent-up sobs. Home. She needed to go home. She needed to see her sisters.

Because at a time like this—only sisters would do.

CHAPTER TWELVE

WILL'S PHONE SOUNDED and he bolted across the room, knocking over a chair and leaping over his bed to reach it.

'Rose?' he answered breathlessly.

'Violet,' came the snarky reply. 'And I'm going to kill you with my bare hands, Will Carter.'

He sagged onto the bed. 'I thought it was Rose. I've left her a dozen messages and sent about a hundred texts.'

'I know. I've read them all. I'm in charge of Rose's phone now.'

He winced. The messages were private. They weren't really for family viewing.

'Please, just let me talk to her.'

'You did my sister, Will.' The blunt words cut through him. 'Of all the women in the world, you had to break my sister's heart.'

'No,' he cut in quickly. 'That's the last thing I want to do.'

'Well, it's too late.' He'd never heard Violet like this. They'd been good friends for years with never a cross word.

'Violet, how long have you known me?'

There was a pause. 'Three years.'

'Have I ever lied to you?'

The pause stretched on and on. 'Well…no.'

'Violet, I love Rose with all my heart. I've even done

something really crazy to prove it to her. But it's a bit hard to tell her about it if she won't even talk to me. I need your help.'

He could almost hear Violet's brain ticking over at the end of the phone. 'Violet, please. This is it for me. *Rose* is it for me. There won't ever be anyone else. Help me prove it to her.'

There was a loud sigh at the end of the phone. 'This better be good, Will.'

The relief was immense. 'It's better than good, Vi. I promise you. Here's what I need you to do…'

She hadn't had a minute. The last week had been frantic. Finalising every detail of her parents' wedding renewal. Trying to make sure that Daisy wasn't doing too much in her current condition and avoiding the messages from Will.

She'd had flowers every single day. Followed by balloons and cupcakes and the chocolates she'd loved at the wedding fair. It was nice. It was charming. But it was a token from a guy who was good at giving tokens, just not good at giving his whole heart.

Violet initially had been mad. Daisy had been sympathetic. But for the last few days both sisters had been surprisingly quiet. Maybe they were as caught up in the arrangements as she was.

But at last everything was ready—or least it should be.

The marquees were finally in place and their corners filled with metallic heart-shaped balloons. The flower arches and covered chairs for the outside ceremony were complete. The weather had even decided to let the sun shine for the day.

People had been arriving at Huntingdon Hall since this

morning. One celebrity friend after another with their little lists of demands. Rose had ignored every one of them. They were big enough to sort themselves out. She had her mother to deal with.

Daisy was lying across the chaise longue in her green gown, her hair in curls around her shoulders. 'Do you think I'm getting kankles?' she moaned.

'What on earth are kankles?' asked Violet. Her purple gown fitted perfectly and the beautiful exotic flowers that their mother had picked were the perfect explosion of colour against the rich jewel-toned gowns.

'Puffy ankles. Pregnant woman ankles. Do you think I'm getting them?'

Violet gave a cursory glance at Daisy's perfectly normal ankles in her flat jewelled sandals. 'Oh, belt up, Daisy.'

Rose winced. That was sharp—even for Violet, but she seemed a little on edge today.

'Well, girls, what do you think? Am I ready to face the world?'

Sherry Huntingdon looked magnificent. Her cream lace fishtail gown hugged every inch of her perfect body. All three girls were around her in an instant. Group hug. It was something they'd done since early childhood.

'You look spectacular, Mum,' said Rose quickly, trying to bat back the tears from her eyes. 'Dad won't be able to take his eyes off you.'

Daisy gave a little nod. 'Let's go to the staircase and get some pictures of that gown on the stairs. It will be gorgeous.' She was already thinking like the professional.

But Rose couldn't relax and be happy for the family portraits—even though she wanted to. Her stomach was wound like a tightly coiled spring. She should be able to relax. Everything was coming together. All the hours she'd spent working on the plans were finally coming to fruition.

The endless nights she'd spent in her workshop working on the gold bangle for her mother would be worth it. She was sure of it. So why didn't she feel good?

Everything was perfect. Everything was hitch free. Three hundred people attended the wedding renewal ceremony. Amongst them, somewhere, would be Will—but she hadn't seen him yet.

After the renewal ceremony there were more photos, cake cutting, hors d'oeuvres and lots of wine. Then it was time for the sit-down meal.

Her father stood up to make a speech and she felt her breath hitch in her throat. He raised his glass. 'I want to thank you all for coming today, to see the wedding that my beautiful wife always deserved.' He gave a little laugh. 'Even if I am twenty-eight years too late. Most of you know that Sherry and I got married on a whim in Vegas. We hardly knew each other at all. But—' he raised his glass and looked at his wife '—when you know—you just know.' There was no hiding the love and devotion in his eyes. 'I want you all to know that every day that has been filled with Sherry has been perfect. We've fought. We've argued. There has been the odd occasion that we haven't spoken. But there hasn't been a single day I haven't wanted to be part of this partnership—part of this family with our three wonderful, if challenging, daughters.'

He picked up a box from the table. 'Lots of people buy new wedding rings for a renewal ceremony. But Sherry and I didn't want to do that. We've had these rings for twenty-eight years and they've seen us through the good, the bad and the beautiful. They're sort of our lucky charms. So...' he gave a little nod to Rose '...with the help of one of our fabulously talented daughters, I got her something else.'

He handed over the box to Sherry, who opened it with

shaking hands. She took out the bangle, the three twisted strands of gold intersected with a rose, a violet and a daisy. The recognition was instant and she leapt to her feet and wrapped her hands around Rick's neck. 'It couldn't be more perfect,' she declared.

The waiters were standing behind everyone, ready to put down the perfectly made first courses. But Rose's stomach was done. She couldn't even try a mouthful.

She'd always known it. It had played along in the background all along. This was what she wanted. This. The perfect part of knowing that every day, no matter what, there was one person you wanted by your side.

'Excuse me,' she said quickly to the person sitting next to her. 'I have to powder my nose.'

Her footsteps covered the gardens quickly, taking her back to the sanctity of the house. The quiet of the house, the coolness of the house.

She took a deep breath, closed her eyes and leaned against the cool wall. Hold it together. Stop being so pathetic. This is your parents' wedding renewal. All you need to do is get through the day. This isn't about you. This isn't about Will. This is about them.

The voices circulated in her head, but they did nothing to stop the tears pooling behind her eyelids. There was a small thud beside her, the sound of another pair of shoulders hitting the wall right next to her. Violet. Then a hand slid into hers. A broad, thick hand, its fingers interlocking with her own. Not Violet.

Her eyes flew open. 'Will.' She didn't want him to see her like this. She wanted him to see her when she was sure of herself, when she knew exactly how to react around him.

He let go of her hand and stepped in front of her, placing one hand above each shoulder, fencing her against the wall.

'Rose,' he said matter-of-factly. 'No phones, no messages.' He gave a wry smile. 'No flowers, no balloons, no cupcakes. Just you. And me.'

Her breath was caught somewhere in her throat. Halfway up and halfway down and not being of any use at all.

'I… I…' She couldn't find any suitable words.

He shook his head. 'Not I. Not you. Not me. Us. We need to talk about us, Rose.'

'There is no us.' The words rushed out.

'But there should be.' His reply was equally quick.

Her brain was working on overdrive. She had so many things she wanted to say. 'I'm sorry. I couldn't handle that day at the studio. When I saw all your exes lined up and looking at me I just felt as if I were the next lamb to the slaughter.'

He blinked. It wasn't her best choice of words. But her brain wasn't treading carefully right now.

'It was too much, Will. It was too soon. After what we'd just done and then Angie said something, then Melissa… and then you kissed me and Paul cracked that joke.'

He lifted a finger to her lips. 'Stop, Rose. Just stop.'

She stopped babbling and tried to think straight. He lifted his finger gently from her lips and placed it over his heart.

'Angie, Melissa, Paul.' He shook his head. 'You are the person that matters to me, Rose. All those women were my past. None of them matter. You're what matters, Rose. You are my future.'

She opened her mouth again and he shook his head to silence her. 'I should have known how you would feel in the studio. I didn't want to be there—why on earth would you? It was claustrophobic. They hadn't spent the night we just had. They hadn't seen what we'd just seen, or shared what we'd just shared. When Paul told me how much money we'd raised the first person I wanted to see, the first person I wanted to share that with, was you, Rose. Nobody else. You were the person I wanted to celebrate with.'

He raised his eyebrows and his mouth quirked. 'And I want to thank you for not coming to that department store and helping me sell women's lingerie all day dressed in nothing but a thong.'

She couldn't help but smile. The pictures of Will's butt had probably sold a million newspapers. The store had never had such good sales and had pledged part of them to the homeless charity.

She sighed. 'I just couldn't, Will. I needed some time. I needed some space.'

He reached up and wound his finger through one of her blonde curls. 'I get that. I do. But I've missed you. I've missed you every single day, Rose. I don't want to spend a single day without you.'

The lump in her throat was growing by the second. He was good. He was really good. And he was being sincere. But she still had the horrible doubts that she wasn't the only woman to hear those words and it was breaking her heart.

He touched her cheek. 'I love you, Rose. I don't want to be without you. I don't want to be without you ever.'

A tear slid down her cheek. She should be singing with joy and while part of her wanted to, she couldn't face the heartache that being left at the altar might bring. Not when she loved him with her whole heart.

It was just the two of them in the corridor. She had a clear, unblinking view of the dark rim around his eyes. Something she could spend the rest of her life looking at.

'And I can prove it.' He reached inside his jacket and her heart lurched.

No. Not this. Anything but this.

'I don't want to be your next fiancée,' she cried. The words just blurted out.

'And I don't want you to be my next fiancée,' he replied coolly. His hand came out slowly from his jacket pocket. It wasn't a ring box. It wasn't anything remotely like jewellery he was holding. It was a piece of paper. No matter what she'd said before, her heart gave a little sag.

He handed it to her silently and took his other hand down from the wall next to her head.

Her hands were trembling as she unfolded the paper. She stared at it for a few seconds. Blinking at the words. She couldn't make sense of it at all because she'd never seen anything like this before.

'What is it?' Her voice was shaking.

'It's our wedding banns. For tonight, for a wedding in the church on the island. I don't want you to be my fiancée, Rose. I want you to be my wife. I didn't know how else to prove it to you.'

'But...but...how did you do this?' Her hands were still trembling as she looked at the date. Sixteen days before. Now she really couldn't breathe. Her legs felt like jelly beneath her. 'You knew then?'

He nodded. 'I knew then, Rose. I didn't doubt it. The only person I had to convince was you.'

'You want us to get married today?'

He smiled and knelt down. 'This is how I'm supposed to do it, isn't it? I guess I just was scared you wouldn't let me get this far.'

He reached up and took both her hands. 'Rose Huntingdon-Cross. I love you with my whole heart and I want you to be the person I wake up next to every morning. And I don't care what continent we do that on. If you want to go back to New York and work, I'll come with you. If you want to keep designing wedding jewellery—I'll build you a whole workshop. Whatever you want, Rose, I'll do it.'

He bent forward and kissed the tips of her fingers, one after the other. 'I've listened to every single thing you've told me. You don't want a big wedding. Check. You loved the church on the island. Check. You don't want a runaway groom. Check. You want things to be simple. Check. All you want is a dress, flowers and I've taken a gamble on a string of fairy lights. Check. You want someone who loves you with their whole heart. Check. You want the kind of love that your parents have—' he winked at her '—Violet let me in on that secret. Check. So, will you do me the honour of becoming my wife tonight? I love you, Rose. I'll never love anyone like you, and I'm hoping you feel the same way. Because I want that kind of love too, Rose. The kind that your parents have—the kind that lasts for ever.'

She couldn't believe it. She couldn't believe her ears. 'You really want to do this now—tonight? You planned this two weeks ago?'

'I planned this two weeks ago.'

'But how could you possibly have known?' She couldn't wipe the smile from her face.

He tilted his head. 'Because when you know, Rose, you just know. Remind you of anyone we know?'

The words flooded over her. He'd used her father's expression and it had never seemed so apt. It was time. It was time to let go and trust her instincts. She'd grown more than she could ever have predicted in the last three years. It was time to throw off the seeds of doubt. Will was standing in front of her declaring his love. He'd done all this for *her*. He'd done all this because he loved *her*. And she loved him with her whole heart.

She smiled. In her head she could see them already. Sitting on a little wooden bench with grey hair growing old together—of that, she had no doubt.

He stood up and put his hands on her hips. 'Ready to visit our island?'

She grinned. 'Our island. I like the sound of that…'

CHAPTER THIRTEEN

WHEN HER STOMACH flipped over now it was with pure excitement. They pulled up straight next to where the boat was moored. Even from here she could see multicoloured fairy lights strung across the thick trees on the island.

'What about witnesses?' It was the first time she'd given it any thought. The drive here had just been a blur.

Will touched her face. 'I spoke to Violet. If we'd tried to sneak your sisters away from the renewal it might have attracted some attention. They'll be waiting for us when we get back. Our witnesses—as long as you're happy—will be Judy and my friend, Arral. I invited him along specially.' She smiled and nodded as tears pooled in her eyes. He'd thought of everything.

She fingered the fine material of her blue dress. It wasn't quite what she'd imagined herself getting married in, but then again, this was how she'd always wanted to do it—just as her parents had—no fuss, just two people who loved each other saying their vows.

The journey to the island was smooth as silk. He helped her out of the boat at the other side and pointed her towards the cottage. 'There's a surprise for you in there. I'll give you a few minutes.'

She nodded as she walked into the cottage. It was just as beautiful as she remembered. But the ambience had changed. Last time it had been full of pent-up emotion and surging hormones. This time it was balanced. This time it was full of hope, promise and love.

She caught her breath. A full-length dress was hanging part way from the ceiling, just within her reach. It was a real-life wedding dress. Cream embroidery at the top with an embroidered tulle straight skirt, it was exactly what she would have picked for herself.

It only took a few minutes to slip out of the blue dress and into the cream one. On a table at the side were a few lemon roses tied with lemon and cream ribbons. All the while she'd thought Will was helping her plan her parents' renewal he'd actually been planning their own wedding.

There was a knock at the door. 'Rose? Is everything okay? Are you ready?' He sounded a little nervous.

She walked over and opened the door. He'd changed into a grey suit with a matching lemon rose buttonhole. Her husband-to-be couldn't have looked more perfect.

She slid her hand into his. 'I can't wait.'

They walked hand in hand to the church. Will smiled as he opened the door and a wave of heart-shaped foil balloons burst from the doors and floated into the sky above. Then he led her down the aisle where their witnesses and celebrant stood waiting.

It was perfect. It was magical. The room was lit with fairy lights and candles. The evening light behind the stained-glass windows sent beautiful shards of rainbow reflections over the white walls.

She walked over and gave both Judy and Arral a kiss on the cheek. 'Thank you for coming,' she whispered. 'Thank you for sharing this with me and Will.'

The celebrant nodded. 'Can we begin?'

Rose took a deep breath and nodded, looking into the

eyes of the man she loved. No Runaway Groom. No waiting. Will was about to become her husband.

They repeated their names and made their declarations. For a second Rose expected the church to be invaded by a wave of angry objecting ex-fiancées, but everything was silent.

Will turned to face his bride, holding up a plain yellow band. 'This was the one thing I couldn't plan. I could hardly ask my wife to make her own wedding band without letting her in on the secret. So, I decided we'd make do for now because she'll have the rest of her life to change them if she wishes.'

Rose nodded. 'These will be perfect.'

Will held the ring poised at her finger. 'Rose Huntingdon-Cross. I love you more than I ever thought possible. I've shared things with you that I could never share with another living soul. You complete me. You are my world. I want to spend the rest of my life getting to know you more and promise to love you more each day until the end of my life.' He smiled at her. 'Because when you know— you just know.'

She let out a nervous laugh and picked up his wedding ring, her fingers trembling as she slid it onto his finger. 'Will Carter, you burst into my life in the most unpredictable way and will probably bear the scar for the rest of our lives. I love you, Will Carter, even though I was afraid to. You've taught me that after three years it's okay to trust my instincts again. You've taught me that people aren't always what we presume they are. You've taught me that there's a whole world out there that I knew nothing about. I want to spend the rest of my life working side by side with my husband and helping those who want to be helped. I want to grow with you, Will. I want to love you more each day.

And you'll never be my runaway groom, you'll always be my husband, the man who has captured my heart.'

She leaned forward and they kissed. His hands sliding down her back and cupping her backside, pressing her against him. She wound her hands around his neck. She couldn't have planned anything more perfect. This was all she'd ever wanted from a wedding. Her and her husband saying their vows at a beautiful setting. Two people who loved each other for ever.

'Do we get to have our honeymoon in the cottage?' she whispered.

He shook his head. 'Oh, no. The honeymoon is a complete surprise. We'll be gone for three weeks.'

She pulled back. 'Three weeks? But what about the tour and the charity concert?' She put her hand to her mouth. 'Oh, no. I'm supposed to pick up that reporter from the airport in a few hours.'

Will laughed and shook his head. 'Oh, no, you don't. That's all under control. For the next three weeks Violet is in charge. I've given her your black planner and she's picking up Tom Buckley at the airport. She's even packed your case. All we need to do is go back and tell your parents and Daisy that we're married.'

'Really?' He'd thought of everything.

He held out his hand towards her and she slid her fingers into her husband's. 'Really.'

By the time they arrived back her father had just finished rocking out on the stage with his band. His hair was damp with sweat and his jacket and tie had been flung aside.

Daisy and Violet were pacing. It was obvious Violet hadn't been able to keep things to herself.

She rushed over straight away. There was no mistaking the look on her face; she was genuinely delighted. She grabbed hold of Rose's left hand. 'Have you done it? Are you genuinely Mrs Carter?'

Rose gave the tiniest nod; she couldn't hide the grin that spread from one ear to the other as she looked at her brand-new husband. 'Mrs Carter, wow.' She hadn't actually said the words out loud and they seemed unreal.

But that didn't stop Violet. 'Wheeeee!' She let out a yell and jumped on Will, sending him flat out onto the grass. 'Finally!'

Will couldn't stop laughing. 'I take it you approve.'

Violet bent forward and kissed him on the forehead. 'Finally, I stop having to pretend to like all your fiancées.' She winked at Rose. 'This one, I love!'

'Rose!' Her mother's voice cut through the crowd of people.

Will stood up from the grass, dusted himself off and slid his hand into hers.

Sherry was gorgeous as ever. Her eyes widened slightly as she noticed the change in Rose's dress. She wrapped her arms around her daughter's shoulder. 'You look beautiful, darling.'

She reached her hand over to touch Will's cheek. 'I take it you have something to tell me, Mr Carter?'

Rick appeared at Sherry's side, sliding his arm around her waist. Rose was holding her breath, well aware that both her sisters were doing the same thing. But Rick Cross grinned and held out his hand towards Will. 'I take it she said yes?'

Will shook his hand. 'You've no idea the relief I felt.'

Sherry's eyebrows rose. 'You knew?'

Rick laughed. 'Of course I knew. Will's a traditionalist. He asked me a few weeks ago.'

Sherry shook her head. 'And you kept it a secret from me?'

Rick rolled his eyes. 'You and secrets, Sherry? Oh, no. I wasn't getting myself in that much trouble.'

'I've got something to tell you, too, Dad.' Rose's heart was thudding in her chest. She'd never been so sure of anything.

'What is it, honey?'

She intertwined her fingers with Will's. 'When I come back from my honeymoon I'll help with the final plans for the tour and then I'll be resigning.' She shot Will a smile. 'I'm going to be working on my jewellery collection full-time.'

Her father gave a little nod of his head. It was almost as if he'd been expecting it.

He leaned over and kissed Rose's cheek. 'I take it you got the wedding you always wanted, beautiful?'

She breathed in deeply. Her parents were happy for her. Her sisters were happy for her.

And she had a husband she loved and trusted with her whole heart.

She leaned up and whispered in his ear. 'Can the honeymoon start now?'

Will slid his hands around her waist as his blue eyes twinkled. 'Absolutely.'

* * * * *

MEET THE FORTUNES!

Fortune of the Month: Brodie Fortune Hayes

Age: 33

Vital Statistics: Six feet of maddeningly adorable British charm. He tastes of champagne and mint and… challenge.

Claim to Fame: The mastermind of Hayes Consulting, Brodie can make business troubles disappear. He is also known for stealing hearts.

Romantic Prospects: "Brodie the Brit" has no interest in getting serious. Work is his mistress, the lady love of his life.

"Alden Moore hired me to fix his Cowboy Country theme park. What he neglected to mention was that he put his daughter in charge of the project. I cannot work with Caitlyn Moore! I suppose her daddy had no way of knowing what, ahem, previously transpired between us. Success in business depends on keeping a clear head and a closed heart. And Caitlyn is simply too warm, too sensitive and too...much. Between her and all my newfound Fortune relatives, I am being bombarded by good intentions. How is a man supposed to get any work done?"

The Fortunes Of Texas: Cowboy Country
Lassoing hearts from across the pond!

MY FAIR FORTUNE

BY
NANCY ROBARDS THOMPSON

Published in Great Britain 2015
by Mills & Boon, an imprint of Harlequin (UK) Limited,
Eton House, 18-24 Paradise Road, Richmond, Surrey, TW9 1SR

© 2015 Harlequin Books S.A.

Special thanks and acknowledgement to Nancy Robards Thompson for her contribution to the Fortunes of Texas: Cowboy Country series.

ISBN: 978-0-263-25133-3

23-0515

Harlequin (UK) Limited's policy is to use papers that are natural, renewable and recyclable products and made from wood grown in sustainable forests. The logging and manufacturing processes conform to the legal environmental regulations of the country of origin.

Printed and bound in Spain
by CPI, Barcelona

National bestselling author **Nancy Robards Thompson** holds a degree in journalism. She worked as a newspaper reporter until she realized reporting "just the facts" bored her silly. Much more content to report to her muse, Nancy loves writing women's fiction and romance full-time. Critics have deemed her work "funny, smart and observant." She resides in Florida with her husband and daughter.

You can reach her at
www.nancyrobardsthompson.com and
facebook.com/nancyrobardsthompsonbooks.

This book is dedicated to all the Fortune fans and
to Susan and Marcia for making it happen.

Chapter One

February

"Brides or grooms?" the tall, handsome guy asked.

He had a British accent.

Caitlyn Moore had locked eyes with the tall hunk of gorgeousness only a moment before he'd moved across the room to stand next to her. The accent was the icing on top of an already delicious-looking bit of eye candy.

Too bad eye candy wasn't on her diet.

"I beg your pardon?" she said.

"Are you here in support of a friend or relative of one of the brides or one of the grooms? Or, perhaps, you're acquainted with all of them?"

When he'd said *all of them*, he wasn't kidding. There were four of each—this *was* the soon-to-be-famous

Grand Fortune wedding—and Caitlyn didn't know a single one of them personally. From what she'd heard, the Fortunes always did everything in a big way.

"None of the above," she said.

"So you're a wedding crasher, then?" Twin dimples winked at her when he smiled.

"No, of course not."

Dressed in an expensive-looking dark suit and crisp white shirt, the Brit had a cocksure James Bond air about him. He probably didn't have to work very hard at getting women to engage. Still, Caitlyn didn't feel like explaining that she hated weddings and wouldn't be here unless it was absolutely necessary. She'd come in place of her parents, who had received the invitation to Horseback Hollow's social event of the decade…in a town this small, it might even be the wedding of the century.

Tonight not one, but four Fortunes had gotten married on their parents' sprawling ranch. They'd exchanged vows on a huge outdoor stage that had been constructed for the ceremony. She'd overheard someone talking about how the large red barn on the property had been renovated especially for tonight's reception. The place looked like a magical wonderland lit by thousands of candles and twinkle lights. There were so many flowers she shuddered to think of the bottom line on the florist's bill. It might even surpass the catering bill for the sumptuous-looking buffet dinner, which she was going to miss because her objective was to sign the guest book and leave. No one would miss her if she left a little early, especially since she was there on a mission that might best be described as *keep your friends close, but keep your enemies closer.*

In this case, the Fortunes—all fifty jillion of them—were the enemy.

It still baffled her that the Fortunes, who had gone to such lengths to get the locals all riled up, making everyone believe that her family's venture, Cowboy Country USA, a Western-themed amusement park, was the root of all evil and would be the demise of Horseback Hollow, would invite her family to the wedding.

Her parents had regretted missing out, but her father had fallen ill this morning, and her mother had stayed home to care for him. Caitlyn had come to the wedding on their behalf, to represent the Moore family and Cowboy Country. She wasn't here to glad-hand and win people over, of course. She'd simply signed the guest book *Alden Moore and family*, a subtle reminder that Moore Entertainment was not the enemy. On the contrary. They wanted to be the good neighbor, getting along with the residents of Horseback Hollow, every one of whom, it seemed, had been invited to the wedding.

She looked at the Brit, who wasn't acting shy about eyeing her.

And that part of the saying that talked about keeping your friends close? Yeah. It definitely applied to this new friend.

A moment ago, she was sure her work here was done, and all she needed to do was wait for the brides and grooms to finish their first dance before she made a discreet exit; except now the hot guy with the cool accent was smiling at her like he found her utterly fascinating.

"All right, then, love," he purred. "What is your story?"

He pinned her with the most spectacular pair of blue eyes she'd ever seen before arching his right brow a fraction of an inch in a manner that suggested he was waiting for her to elaborate. And then there was that accent. Why had she always been a sucker for an accent? It was her libido's Achilles' heel.

"What?" she said. "Are you the bouncer here to throw me out?"

He crossed his arms and appraised her in a less than subtle way that had her insides going all warm and melty. She needed to stop *that* right now. Mirroring his stance, she crossed her arms and tilted her chin up, hoping for some self-preservation, but her warm and melty insides offered no structure. Her resolve started to slowly crumble under the heat.

"If you must know," she said. "I'm here by proxy."

"I didn't realize wedding invitations were transferable," he said. "Don't worry, I won't land you in it, because—" he leaned in and whispered in her ear "—really, I don't belong here, either."

I won't land you in it. He was so maddeningly, adorably British it was almost too much, and he was standing so close that she could smell his cologne—something that was probably expensive. Something vaguely green and woodsy—maybe sandalwood…and some cedar—and oh, so manly and delicious.

"So *you're* the one who doesn't belong here?" she countered. "How do you know I'm not the wedding police, ready to bounce *you*?"

His eyes glistened as his gaze made an even bolder

perusal of her body, meandering down the length of her and back up again. Her heart beat with the pulse of the music, and she reveled in this irresistible, magnetic physical awareness.

"Not in that dress, love."

His breath held a faint hint of peppermint.

"What's wrong with my dress?"

"Not a bloody thing."

He flashed a smile that showcased perfect white teeth, and there were those dimples again.

Oh, God, just take me now.

A thrill the likes of which Caitlyn had never experienced skittered down her spine, waking up places that had been sleeping for far too long. This was…fun. A lot more fun than she'd dreamed she'd have tonight.

As a waiter passed by with a tray of champagne, he grabbed two flutes and handed one to her.

"Thank you." She raised her glass to him, and he followed suit, clinking his to hers before they sipped.

She'd purchased the red dress and strappy heels on the fly this morning. Since she'd only planned on visiting her parents for a few days, she'd packed light and casual. She hadn't brought along anything that was appropriate for an elaborate Valentine's Day wedding. She'd been pleasantly surprised to find the flirty little dress in a boutique in Lubbock. With his eyes on her, it felt a whole lot sexier than it had when she'd tried it on and decided it would do. She hadn't really been excited about the dress or the thought of attending the wedding of four couples she didn't know. It had barely been a year since she'd called off her own engagement.

The only reason she'd agreed to come tonight was because it had seemed so important to her father. He'd asked her to represent the family because he thought it would be a sign of solidarity for the good folks of Horseback Hollow, or possibly considered a slight if no one from the Moore family bothered to attend. As if anyone would even notice in such a crowd.

Who knew she'd meet someone so fun to play with. Maybe she wasn't in quite as big a hurry to leave after all. Then again, if she knew what was good for her, she'd leave right now before she gave this Brit a chance to charm her new red dress right off her.

"What's your name?" he asked.

"Cait—" She always went by Caitlyn, but tonight it felt more fun to simply be Cait.

"Ah, as in *Kiss Me, Kate*?"

"Oh, are you a fan of musical theater?"

"Not particularly. I simply wanted to say that." Their gazes locked. "Kiss me…Cait."

For the life of her, she didn't know what came over her, because the next thing she knew, she was leaning in and claiming his lips.

She didn't even know his name, but she adored the taste of him—champagne and mint…and something else she couldn't name, something that made her lose herself a little bit and lean in a little closer. His kiss sang through her veins, sent spirals of longing coursing through her, causing the fire deep in her most personal places to rage.

It had been a long time since she'd kissed a man. Since Eric— No, she wouldn't think about him. Eric would not ruin this moment…or this night, which was becoming better and better with each passing second.

The sound of the bandleader inviting the wedding guests to join the happy couples on the dance floor edged out the interloping thoughts of her ex. When she pulled back, the reality of what she'd just done washed away any lingering residue of Eric.

She'd kissed a man she'd known for less than ten minutes.

And she wanted to kiss him again.

Bloody hell.

Those were the only words echoing in Brodie Fortune Hayes's mind as he locked lips with *Cait.* And he meant those words in the best, most reverent way possible. Just when he thought he'd seen everything, life threw him a curvy surprise wrapped in a sexy red dress. He was obviously finding it difficult to express exactly how much he liked this shapely little package. All he knew was what had started out as a night of familial obligation was turning out to be rather mind-blowing.

Cait pulled back just enough to gaze up at him through thick, dark lashes. She had the loveliest green eyes he'd ever seen. "By the way, what's *your* name?"

"Brodie," he heard himself murmur.

"Brodie the Brit," she said. "Nice to meet you. I'm Cait from Chicago. I'd shake your hand, but…" She leaned in and dusted his lips with a featherlight kiss.

Then she smiled up at him, looking rather pleased with herself.

"Charming to meet you, Cait from Chicago."

The band shifted from an up-tempo tune into a slow, sultry number just as he decided to lean in for another taste of those lips, but Cait pulled away.

"Listen," she said. "This has been fun, but I really should go now."

"What? But we just got here. Well, we just got *here*."

He reached out and ran the pad of his thumb over her bottom lip. "I'm quite eager to see where we'll go next."

She opened her mouth as if she were about to say something, hesitated then pressed her lips together, drawing her bottom lip between her teeth in a way that nearly drove him mad.

"Dance with me?" he said.

Of course, he wouldn't force her to do anything she didn't want to do, but he'd try his best to convince her.

"Just one dance," he said. "If you want to go after that, I won't argue."

He took her hand, fully prepared to let go if she protested. But she didn't.

As he led her onto the dance floor, he noticed his brother Oliver dancing with Shannon Singleton, the pretty brunette they'd sat with during the ceremony. Oliver seemed to be lost in the moment as he gazed into Shannon's eyes. But when Cait sank into Brodie's arms and he pulled her closer, his body responded, and then it was as if they were the only two people in the entire world.

They swayed to the strains of "Unforgettable" and

kept dancing close through a couple of fast songs, until the band decided to mix things up with a country-rock medley, and an overzealous guest, who was dancing with a beer in his hand, tried to demonstrate his John Travolta moves and upended it on the dance floor.

"Okay, what do you say we take a break?" Brodie suggested. "How about if I get us something to drink?"

"Actually, I could use some fresh air," Cait said. "It's a little stuffy in here."

With the number of people dancing and drinking in the confines of the renovated barn, it was a bit close. It was unseasonably warm for February. In fact, he'd heard his mum and aunt Jeanne Marie say it was as if spring had graced them with an early visit, which was undoubtedly fortuitous for the four couples who had said their vows.

"That sounds like a great idea," he said. "Wait right here. I'll get us some refreshments to go."

He tipped the bartender fifty dollars and was rewarded with a chilled, unopened bottle of champagne and two flutes. On his way back to Cait, he plucked a long-stemmed red rose out of one of the many freestanding floral arrangements.

He took the bounty back to where he'd left her, but she wasn't there. As he made a three-hundred-sixty-degree turn, it dawned on him that it probably hadn't been a brilliant move to leave her alone. He hadn't been gone that long, but if she really had wanted to leave, this would've presented the perfect opportunity for her to make her getaway. His gut tightened at the thought, but then he sobered. Really, if she had decided to go, it was for the best. He was set to return to London in two days. True, Cait of the magical lips had an unnerving ability to knock him void of all common sense, but really, what would they do two days from now when he boarded the plane to go home? The likelihood of him traveling to Chicago anytime soon was slim. Business was booming at his company, Hayes Consulting, the management consulting firm for which he'd sacrificed everything. It had been a struggle even to find time to come for the wedding. If truth be told, he wasn't happy about taking time off for four cousins he barely knew. It had only been a couple of years since his mother had discovered that she was adopted and had three siblings who had so many grown children that it seemed to be necessary to marry them off in bulk. Still, it had been important to his mother that he attend this affair. She was the one woman in the world for whom he'd drop everything. Plus, it was a chance to catch up with his brother Oliver.

All the negativity drained away when he turned and saw Cait with her wrap and handbag, making her way toward him in the crowd. She was still here, and suddenly nothing else mattered.

He handed her the rose.

"This is beautiful," she said, bringing the flower to her nose. "How romantic, sir."

Her eyes glinted and at that moment, Brodie was sure she was the most beautiful woman he'd ever had the privilege to set eyes on.

"And what else do you have there?"

"A spot of champagne. What do you say we get out of here? There's something I'd like to show you."

He started to offer her his arm, but his hands were full with the two glasses and the bottle.

"I'm intrigued." She laughed. "May I carry something?"

"I've got this." He set down the bottle and tucked each of the champagne flutes into his suit coat pockets.

"Let's try that again." He offered her his arm.

She accepted, and he led her out of the noisy reception.

Once they were outside, it was quiet, except for the faint sound of the party going on in the barn behind them. A few people milled about. A line of golf carts, which were there to drive the guests back to their vehicles after the festivities ended, waited at the ready several feet in front of the barn. The cart attendants sat at tables, playing cards as they waited.

Brodie and Caitlyn walked from the barn toward the pond on the east side of the property. The night was unseasonably warm for February, but despite the mid-fifty-degree temperatures, he thought he felt Cait shiver. She'd put her coat on over that fabulous red dress.

Still, priding himself on being a gentleman, he said, "Is it too cold out here? We can go back inside…or I'm happy to give you my jacket. You could drape it about your shoulders."

She shook her head. "Thanks, but no. Actually, the cool air feels great after being inside. With everyone dancing and all that romantic energy in there, it was a little bit warm. Besides, I wouldn't want to take a chance on breaking one of those glasses that you worked so hard to steal for us."

"I didn't steal them. The bartender graciously gifted them to us. He thought we looked like such a lovely couple."

"Oh, really?"

"That's what he said." Brodie winked and took a great deal of pleasure watching the color spike in her ivory cheeks.

"So you're an honest guy?" she said. "Does that mean I can trust you to lead me out into the darkness? You're not some deranged serial killer, are you?"

Brodie stopped, unsure for a moment if she was serious. "Well…no. Of course not."

But really, could he blame her? They didn't know each other.

She assessed him for what felt like an eternity.

"Where are we going?" she asked. "What is it that you wanted to show me?"

"There's a meteor shower tonight. Out here, away from the city lights, the waning crescent moon coupled with the clear sky provides excellent viewing conditions."

Her brows knit together, and she cocked her head to the side as if she didn't understand.

"A meteor shower," he repeated. "You know, shooting stars? I thought it would be…romantic." He rocked back on his heels.

"I know what a meteor shower is." She smiled. "What I didn't realize was that you're an astronomy nerd."

The light from the tiki torches that lined the path caught the teasing sparkle in her green eyes, turning them an alluring shade of jade, and it took everything Brodie had to keep from leaning in and kissing her again.

"I've been accused of being a lot of things in my life, but I must say tonight is the first time anyone has called me a nerd...or a serial killer. However, if you like nerds, that's exactly what I'll be tonight. Just for you."

"Just for me? What about serial killer?"

He narrowed his eyes. "Sorry, that's not in my repertoire."

"Good to know," she said. "Call me crazy, but for some reason, I believe you."

Suddenly, she looked away and pointed toward the sky. "I think I just saw one. Was that a meteor?"

"Indeed."

"What are we waiting for?" she said. "Let's go where we can see better."

She grabbed his hand, and he led her toward the open field by the pond.

When they stopped, they turned their attention up to the sky.

"This is a rather slow shower," he said. "There may only be four or five meteors per hour."

"What should we do to entertain ourselves in the meantime?" Her voice was low and raspy. There was something in her tone that made him want to suggest all kinds of inappropriate things. She seemed to read his thoughts because she reached out and ran her thumb over his bottom lip. He was still holding the champagne bottle and the glasses when she leaned in and brushed a kiss over his lips.

"If you want to do something like this," she said, "I wouldn't object."

Before he could stop himself, he caught her bottom lip between his teeth and teased it with his tongue.

"How about something like that?" he asked, his mouth a breath away from hers.

"That? Oh, yes, definitely *that*. And more, I hope. But first I'll need a glass of champagne."

He spread his jacket on the ground, and they sat down on it. He popped the cork and poured them each a glass of bubbly. They clinked glasses and settled into the silence of the first sip. He reached out and brushed a strand of long, dark hair off her shoulder.

She inhaled a quick breath and seemed suddenly shy. Even though he was dying to kiss her again…and again and again, he knew he'd be smart to slow things down until he was sure she was comfortable.

He gazed up at the sky for a moment, searching, until he found what he was looking for.

"See those three stars in a row that are close together?"

He leaned in so that she could follow where he was pointing.

She didn't pull away.

"That's Orion's belt. Do you know the legend of Orion and Merope?"

She shook her head.

"Orion, the great hunter, fell in love with Merope. He made a business deal with her father. In exchange for clearing the land of all the savage beasts, Orion would have Merope's hand in marriage, but Merope's dad reneged and wouldn't let Orion marry his daughter."

"Poor Orion," she said.

"Yes, the poor guy was stricken with such sadness. He couldn't get the girl off his mind. He wasn't watching where he was going and stepped on a scorpion and died."

She slanted him a dubious glance. "It that really how the story goes? I thought there was more to it."

"I thought you didn't know the story," he said.

"I wanted to hear your version," she said, leaning into him. "I was hoping you'd make it a love story."

"Oh, it is." He clamped his mouth shut before he could add something stupid like *this is a real-life love story, sweetheart. Love hurts.*

Instead, he continued. "The gods took pity, and they immortalized him and his dogs up in the sky as constellations."

He outlined the stars with his finger.

"They put all of the animals he hunted up there near him—like the rabbit and the bull. But they put the scorpion all the way on the opposite side of the sky so Orion would never be hurt again."

"What about Merope? What happened to her?"

"She's still there. She's a star that rides the shoulders of the bull. So he can always see her."

"You have a romantic heart," she said.

"Funny, others have claimed I don't have a heart."

"Well, they were mistaken, my romantic astronomy nerd."

She rested her head on his shoulder. Her hair smelled so good he breathed in trying to identify the fragrance… it was something floral…and sweet. The combination was intoxicating. He thought he could live happily here.

Just the two of them sitting close, sipping champagne under the inky starlit sky.

He slid his arm around her shoulder, ran his hand down the length of her arm. She tilted her head up and leaned in closer, tempting him. His lips found hers, and this time the kiss wasn't quite so gentle. She responded, her body pressing against his. The way they fit together might have brought to mind tired clichés like puzzle pieces or bugs in a rug, but he was too caught up in *her* to give it much thought.

All he could focus on was the feel of her…the taste of her…the all-consuming thought of what it would be like to make love to her…their bodies even closer than they were right now. Him buried deep inside her. Them moving to their own private rhythm.

He heard a sound—a low, guttural rumble—and realized he was the one making the noise. As if the force was driving him, he deepened the kiss. He couldn't get enough of her. She tasted like the champagne they'd shared. But there was something else… something uniquely her. And it was threatening to drive him crazy.

His hands slid from her hair down her shoulders, and he closed his arms around her, pulling her closer. He memorized the feel of her as he lowered her back, onto the ground.

"Are you okay?" he asked in a brief moment of clarity. He would never force her to do anything that made her uncomfortable. "Is this…okay?"

"I've never been better." She smiled up at him. "I

have a feeling I'm going to be even better very soon. So please don't stop now."

He held her gaze for a moment, until little pinpricks of longing injected him with a need so powerful it had him seeing stars. When he reclaimed her lips, it lifted him off the ground and into the heavens of lusty bliss. When was the last time he'd wanted a woman so badly that it bordered on greed?

On need…

He unbuttoned her coat and slipped his hands inside, savoring every inch of her—her tiny waist, her sexy hips. That red dress was all that stood between him and that glorious body. He slid his hands back up her torso, around her rib cage and paused underneath her breasts, giving her one more chance to slow things down, if she wanted.

God, he hoped she wouldn't.

When she deepened the kiss and pulled him closer, stretching one long leg out, crossing it over his, he knew she wasn't going anywhere without him tonight.

That's when what little control he had left shattered.

He eased her down onto his jacket, taking care that his touch wasn't as rough and desperate as he felt. When he covered her with his body, the only thing he was aware of was how her lips and tongue were doing amazing things to his mouth. When his hand slipped under the neckline of her dress and his fingers found their way to her breast beneath her bra, she moaned, a muffled sound under his lips.

"You okay?" he said, resting his forehead on hers. "If you want, we can stop."

* * *

She appreciated his concern. He was a gentleman, but she didn't want to talk.

She didn't want to stop, and she didn't want to talk about it.

Because if they started talking, she might try to explain herself.

She was *so tired* of explaining herself.

It was her body. Her choice to have him… Just because she chose to make love to a virtual stranger, it didn't make her any less of a human being. Men did it all the time…had one-night stands…even when they were engaged…with the church booked and the catering ordered…the white dress hanging in the bride-to-be's closet and the wedding two weeks away.

But she wasn't going to think about men like that tonight. She was going to prove to herself exactly how liberated she was. She was going to take back her power by enjoying this fine, hot guy. Her *wedding favor.* Actually, he was more like a gift…but not a wedding gift. She'd sent all those back after she'd thrown the ring in Eric's face.

She needed to *stop* thinking about Eric. He'd already ruined her life once.

There was no room for him—especially not tonight.

To drown out the incessant chatter in her head, Caitlyn deepened their kiss. Brodie groaned and nudged her thighs apart with his knee, nesting his lower body into hers. When she felt his arousal, thick and hard against her, she grabbed his backside and pulled him even closer, just to make sure there was no doubt about exactly how okay she was with their closeness.

His murmured answer was muddled and unintelligible against her lips; he seemed to understand. His intention was clear in the way he smoothed his hand up her bare leg. When his fingers reached her upper thigh and he deftly eased her out of her panties, his actions told her everything she needed to know.

When they were naked and ready, she held on tight as he unleashed himself up on her body.

Later, when they lay spent and sated in each other's arms, she wasn't sure if hours or days had passed. It was as if they'd been lifted out of space and time into a world where only the two of them existed.

But no… It couldn't have been days because it was still dark outside, and she had to go home before the sun came up. She was staying with her parents while she was here. They'd send out the National Guard if she didn't come home. She snuggled into the warmth of him for one more luxurious moment, breathing in the scent of him…of them…before she gently wriggled out from under his protective arm.

He stirred. "Where are you going?"

"I have to go home."

"Chicago? Tonight? Don't do that. Stay with me. Some of the best meteors happen just before dawn."

It was already late, but she could see her mother's face if she came in doing the walk of shame, with the sun on her back. Caitlyn may have been twenty-nine years old and living on her own since she'd gone off to college, but when she came home to visit the folks, she was twelve years old again.

"No, I'm sorry. I really do have to go."

As she straightened her clothes and smoothed her hair into place, she watched Brodie lying there, propped up on one elbow, watching her. He really was a beautiful man. That face…and that body. Oh, what he could do with that body. It was one of the best experiences she'd ever had. Not that she'd had that many. She'd certainly never done this before. Brodie the Brit had been nothing short of amazing. It was a shame that she'd never see him again. What had started out to be an evening of obligation had turned into a night she would never forget.

Never forget and definitely not regret.

"Will you walk me to my car?" she asked.

"Of course." Once he'd righted himself and brushed off the dirt from his jacket, they were walking arm in arm back to the parking lot.

"I'm sorry about your coat," she said.

"Don't give it a second thought. In fact, I might just have it framed and hang it on my wall to remember tonight."

The temperature had dropped a good ten degrees, and by the time they made it back around to the lot, most of the cars were gone. The courtesy golf carts and their drivers were nowhere to be found. It was *that* late.

As she fumbled in her purse for her keys, she checked her phone for the time.

Three forty-five in the morning.

Irrational panic ceased her. She should've been home hours ago.

She didn't want to ruin everything with awkward goodbyes, but she had to get out of there.

"Brodie the Brit," she said. They were standing maybe five inches apart. "This has been such a wonderful evening. Look, if you're ever in Chicago…"

She realized how that sounded, *a shot of needy with a chaser of desperate.*

"Goodbye, Brodie."

She kissed him one last time before she drove off.

When she did, she forced herself to not watch his fading image in her rearview mirror. Or to think about how tonight was not only her first one-night stand, it was also probably the best sex she'd ever had in her life.

The faster she drove, the louder doubt rattled behind her like a string of tin cans tied to a wedding car.

She was never going to see him again. She didn't even know his last name.

It was best that way.

Wasn't it?

Chapter Two

May

Couldn't *anything* be simple? Caitlyn Moore silently lamented.

Just once?

Apparently not, she affirmed as she listened to Jason Hallowell, head electrical engineer for Moore Entertainment, drone on about the problem.

"If Clark Ball leaves early, we will not get the work done in time to pass the electrical inspection. I'm sure I don't need to remind you, ma'am, that this will be the second time we've failed it."

No. He didn't need to remind her. The reality was an albatross, constantly following her. They were racing against the clock, and if they failed the inspection again, it would probably mean that they'd have to delay the Memorial Day soft opening of Moore Entertainment's newest theme park, Cowboy Country USA.

Caitlyn would rather eat dirt than delay the opening. She had to prove to her father that she was capable. She could pull this off despite his doubts and worries.

Even more important than proving herself, this was the one thing she could do to help her father get well. He'd suffered a massive heart attack earlier in the week, and he was under strict doctors' orders to avoid stress so that his body could heal. Caitlyn had dropped everything and flown into Lubbock from Chicago the moment she'd gotten word that he was ill. But she soon realized that sitting at his bedside wringing her hands wasn't helping anyone. That's when she decided the proactive approach would be to take a hold of the reins at Cowboy Country and make sure that the park opened as planned.

When her father heard of the plan, he'd balked and blustered—even through the tubes and the admonitions of nurses who sedated him when he wouldn't calm down. So Caitlyn did what any loving daughter would do. She told her dad that she loved him, but she wasn't coming back to see him until he promised that he could remain calm.

"Dad, I'm your best chance for making this project successful," she'd said.

"Well, that's not very good news," he'd said. "You're a beautiful girl, and I'm sure you're good at all that animal research you do, but Caitlyn, this is the real world."

"Dad, I'm not a girl. I'm twenty-nine years old, and

I'm more than capable of handling this. I mean, everything is in place. The park is practically ready to open its doors. I can do this. You have to trust me."

By that time the sedative was kicking in. Through heavy eyes that were threatening to close, he said, "We'll see. Make sure you keep the appointment with Hayes Consulting. They can help you. They're expensive and hard to land an appointment with. So whatever you do, keep that appointment. Janie will tell you when it is. And listen to this Hayes guy, Caitlyn. He knows what he's talking about."

With that, he drifted off to sleep. Her mother had smiled at her through watery eyes. Validation that she was doing the right thing, the only thing in her power that would allow her to take some of the pressure off her father so that he could focus on healing.

Little did she know what she was actually getting herself into. To the uninformed eye, the park may have looked like it was ready to open, but the reality was, things were a mess. As of now they hadn't passed the necessary inspections and they didn't have the permits needed to open their doors. If they didn't make the grade on this latest inspection, there was no way they'd open on time.

It was little things like this episode with Clark Ball that kept threatening to set them back.

"Jason, I'm sorry. I told Clark he could leave early today. I ran into him yesterday when I was making my rounds and he asked. I believe his wife is having medical issues. He said he needed to be there for her."

"Ms. Moore, ma'am, I'm very sorry if his wife is

sick. Truly I am. But he's been cutting out early at least once a week for the past three months. Besides, he may have asked you yesterday, but he asked me on Monday, and I told him he could not leave early today. He knows it's all hands on deck this week if we are going to get the work done."

"Are you sure there's no other way?" she asked, immediately regretting the question.

Heavy silence hung on the other end of the line. "I wouldn't be making this call if there was another way. I don't have time for this. None of us do if we're going to meet these deadlines. However, I have to say I'm disappointed that you seem to be missing the point that by asking you after I told him no, Clark has deliberately defied my authority. That's insubordination."

"I understand that, Jason, and no, it's not right. I will speak to Clark. We will come to some kind of understanding. I'm sure he will be reasonable once he understands the situation."

Again, her words were met with silence before Jason murmured a stiff, "Thank you, ma'am."

Somehow, Jason always seemed a little disappointed when he talked to her. She could offer him a fifty percent raise, and she was certain he'd greet the news with the same stony stoicism followed by and unemotional, *thank you, ma'am*.

He wasn't the only one. The crew leaders did their jobs well, but they all had a way of making Caitlyn feel as if they were simply tolerating her, as if they could see right through her bravado. Maybe she needed to give them more credit, because she wasn't at all sure that Clark Ball would be reasonable and eager to work things out. Jason had been too polite to call her bluff.

She squared her shoulders. She was the boss. Her number one objective was to make sure Cowboy Country passed all necessary inspections so they could open the park as scheduled on Memorial Day.

"Where can I find Clark right now?" she asked.

"He's supposed to be working on the wiring over at the Twin Rattlers Roller Coaster. I don't mean to tell you what to do, ma'am. But if you plan on talking to him, I wouldn't wait much longer because he says he's leaving at noon."

"Thanks, Jason. I'll head over there now. I'll let you know once I've talked to him."

"Thank you, ma'am. I'd appreciate it."

She hung up the phone and sat back in her chair for a moment. She hated being the bad guy. She really did. That's why she preferred working in the lab, doing research and development for Moore Entertainment. She was a zoologist by training, and she'd been perfectly prepared for the low entry-level salary that came with most R&D positions, but her father had hired her just out of college. Despite his reputation for being a hard-nosed, take-no-prisoners kind of businessman, he'd brought her on board. His version of the story was that he fully intended to make her fall in love with the family business. Despite her zoology degree, he intended to put her through the Alden Moore school of business, which included several years of courses like Hard Knocks and Trial by Fire.

Her father was doggedly determined that she would fall in love with the business and someday take over.

What her dear old dad didn't understand was that the research and study of animals wasn't just a passing fancy. She wanted to make it her life's work. When she graduated, she'd been hard-pressed to find a job. So when Alden offered her the job as vice president of research and development for Moore Entertainment along with a healthy salary and benefits, she'd been tempted, sure, but it was the bonus that had sealed the deal: he offered her the chance to make her dream come true. If she stayed on and helped make Cowboy Country USA a success, then there was a chance they could develop a second phase of the park, a zoo park featuring animals indigenous to Northwest Texas.

But then her father had gotten sick, and all thoughts of zoo parks and resentment for his herding her into the family business gave way to what was really important: her dad's health.

When he'd suffered a nearly fatal heart attack, she'd stepped in to make sure her father's dream didn't founder while he was fighting for his life. She'd felt so helpless when she saw him lying there in that hospital bed hooked up to all those machines. This man, who'd always been larger than life and twice as fierce, was facing a challenge that might best him. Rather than sit by his bedside wringing her hands, she vowed to step up and see Cowboy Country through the way he'd want so he could focus all his energy on getting better.

Well, in a perfect world that's what he would do, but the other side of the coin was that he had little choice but to have faith that she could pull it off. Relinquishing control would be difficult. Believing that Caitlyn was capable to lead the park through a successful opening was another matter altogether.

This was her chance to prove her worth to her father, and she intended to succeed.

She knew the longer she put off talking to Clark, the more difficult it would be. She gathered herself mentally, sat forward in her desk chair and buzzed her assistant, who was really her father's assistant. "Janie, I'm going into the park to take care of something."

"Ms. Moore, before you head out, I wanted to let you know that Mr. Hayes of Hayes Consulting is here to see you."

Oh, that's right...Hayes Consulting.

Caitlyn glanced at her watch. He was twenty minutes early. She decided to go out and greet him and then ask Janie to show him around while she put out the most recent fire. She'd only be gone thirty minutes, tops. Then she'd come back and get Mr. Hayes whatever he needed to get started with whatever it was he did to work his magic.

If she had a dime for every time her father had reinforced how important working with Hayes Consulting was to Cowboy Country, she could retire a wealthy woman. Apparently, the firm was very good at fixing the images of businesses that had managed to do something to sully their reputation. Or, as in Cowboy Country's case, had simply gotten off to a bad start in the community.

Her father had a lot of faith that this Hayes guy could

fix things. He'd underscored how expensive and difficult it was to book time with this outfit. Keeping this
meeting had been one of the few mandates her father
had given her.

"Please tell Mr. Hayes I'll be right out."

She stood and slid on her navy jacket because it was
one of the few pieces of business attire that she owned
that made her feel professional and pulled together. *Fake
it until you make it*, she told herself and strode out into
the reception area. All the blood drained from her head
when she saw Brodie the Brit—that guy from the qua-
druple Fortune wedding—standing in the middle of
the room.

"What in the world are you doing here?" She immediately regretted her tone and the words. Good grief.
Way to finesse it, Caitlyn. Or Cait. He'd only known her
as Cait. And he'd never called. So how on earth did he
find her here, two and a half months later?

For a moment, he looked as surprised to see her as
she felt, but then his handsome features hardened into a
mask so different from the way he'd looked *that night*.
His eyes were cold and guarded. Wait a minute, neither
one of them should be cold and guarded because they
were adults and they both had known what they were
getting themselves into.

"Hello, Cait," he said, offering her a hand to shake.
A hand. What was it they'd said that night at the wedding? That they were way past shaking hands. And that
was *before* they'd left the reception.

She looked at his outstretched hand but didn't shake
it. She was tempted to tell him to put that thing away,

but she should've thought of that two and a half months ago. Now she had more important things to worry about—like an employee who was about to cost them the inspection they desperately needed to open and a costly consultant who was… Speaking of… Where was he? She glanced around the waiting room. Restroom, perhaps?

His absence was a stroke of luck. She'd have time to get rid of Brodie before the situation became sticky.

"Walk with me," she said to him.

"I'd love to. However, I have an appointment."

"What a coincidence. So do I. Could you please tell me why you're here?"

He narrowed his gaze at her. "Do you work here?"

She quirked a brow at him. "You might say that. I'm not usually in this office, but my father is ill, and I'm filling in for him. Who is your appointment with?"

She watched the color drain from Brodie's formerly tanned face. "You wouldn't happen to be Cait Moore? Er…*Caitlyn* Moore?"

"The one and only."

"Fancy that. I'm Brodie Hayes, Hayes Consulting."

Caitlyn opened her mouth to say something and then closed it, because what was there to say? Nothing. Or at least nothing they could say out loud or discuss out here in the open, with Janie's eyes on them, mentally recording everything they said and did.

"Can we please go into your office?" Brodie asked.

"Not right now. I have a situation I need to take care of. You can wait for me in there, though. Make yourself comfortable, and I'll be right back. Janie, please show Mr. Hayes into my office."

"A situation?" Brodie asked.

Caitlyn glanced at her watch. She needed to hurry; she didn't want to end up chasing Clark Ball down in the parking lot. "Yes, a situation. So you'll have to excuse me."

Brodie's large body blocked her path, and when she looked up at him to send the *you need to move* message, she remembered how that body felt moving on top of her that night nearly three months ago. Heat started in her cleavage, which was modestly covered up today— as it should've been that night—and crept up her neck, spreading to her cheeks.

He crossed his arms. The body language was so defensive that she couldn't help but glance up at his face, which was stone cold and lacking any hint that he might be glad to see her.

She groaned inwardly, silently admonishing herself.

Of course he wasn't glad to see her. This wasn't a date. This was…awkward.

For God's sake, how was it that the one and only one-night stand she'd ever had in her life would turn up again—not because he'd been so smitten that he'd tracked her down. Oh, she could've handled that. But this…having him show up right now, right here. In the last place in the entire world she wanted to be reminded of her indiscretion.

"If there's a problem, I should come with you." His voice was all business. "You can brief me on the way."

She bristled, but before she demanded for a second

time that he go into her office and wait for her, she re-membered he father saying Hayes Consulting was ex-pensive and in demand. Even if he had arrived early, she had him for one afternoon, and she intended to get Moore Entertainment's money's worth.

"Okay, Brodie Hayes, if you're willing to hit the ground running. Prepare to show me what you've got."

He smirked.

Oh, God. He could take that a couple of different ways. She imagined him thinking, *honey, you've al-ready seen everything I've got*. But that was inappropri-ate, and she wasn't about to let him know his appearance here today was fazing her in the least.

She turned to Janie. "Mr. Hayes and I are going out into the park. I have my cell phone if you need to get in touch with me."

Caitlyn kept walking toward the door without look-ing back to make sure Brodie was following her. He could keep up on his own. Plus, there was the problem that every time she looked at him, all she could think of was how he'd made love to her so thoroughly that night. There went the heat bomb, exploding in her lower parts and raising the temperature in her entire body.

Damn him.

Damn *her* for not having more self-control.

He was walking beside her now. She would not say another word about *that night*. Not on company time.

"Since I only have you for an afternoon, I'll start bringing you up to speed with all that's happening."

She dared a glance at him, if for no other reason than

to prove that she was a professional…and immune to those broad shoulders.

Stop it.

Stop thinking about shoulders.

He was looking at her as if she had two heads. It knocked any wayward thoughts of broad shoulders and meteor showers right out of her head.

"What do you mean you only have me for an afternoon? Alden Moore booked me for the entire month of May."

Bloody hell.

How could he have been so stupid to not realize what he was walking into?

Brodie prided himself on never being surprised. How had he not known his client—the client he'd worked so hard to land—the client whose business could make or break the Tokyo deal—had a daughter.

He would've never slept with her if he'd known Cait from Chicago was even remotely related to Alden Moore, much less his daughter.

Way to get off to a rocking start.

He needed to get a hold of this situation and fast, before it blew up in his face.

He drew in a deep breath to steady himself. How was he to know Cait from the wedding was *Caitlyn Moore*?

They hadn't exchanged last names. In the moment, it had seemed sexy and edgy. One night of bliss with no strings attached. Or so they'd agreed.

A few days ago, after he'd learned that Alden Moore had fallen ill and his daughter would be standing in, he'd done a cursory internet search of Caitlyn Moore, and all he'd turned up was a very private Facebook page with a profile picture of a very large dog—or maybe it was a pony?—and a dated photo with Alden Moore and a little girl who looked to be five or six. The photo looked like it was taken in the early 1990s. Nothing that would've cued him in to the fact that Cait from Chicago was not only Alden Moore's daughter, but also the executive in charge at Cowboy Country.

Still, what was done was done. His only choice now was to regroup and move past this unexpected turn of events. After all, that was how he made his living, helping people spin bad into good.

"We seem to have a miscommunication here," he said to Caitlyn as they left the office. "Your father had contracted me to work with Moore Entertainment until Cowboy Country opens successfully."

She was speed walking slightly ahead of him.

"Wonderful," she said. "Just wonderful."

"Hey, will you please stop for a moment and talk to me?"

She stopped walking so fast, he nearly ran into her. When she turned, she looked him square in the eyes. It was almost as if she were looking through him.

"Look, I need to be on the other side of the park in about five minutes to deal with a personnel issue. I don't have time to talk about what happened between us. Frankly, this isn't the time or the place. If you're going to be here for a month, I say we just move on and forget the Fortune wedding. Okay?"

The last thing he wanted to do was talk about *them*.

"That's perfectly fine with me," he said. "I give you my word of honor that I won't speak of it. Actually, what I had in mind was your briefing me on this urgent personnel issue so that I understand the situation before we arrive."

"Of course." She smiled, but it didn't reach her eyes.

As they resumed walking, past various pavilions, cowboy-themed gift shops and refreshment stands, she filled him in on Clark Ball, the employee in question.

"He deliberately defied his supervisor when he asked you for the time off," Brodie said, wanting to make sure that he understood the situation correctly.

"That's right."

"Since he's made a habit of leaving work early, has he been formally counseled about the unacceptable behavior?"

"Yes, his supervisor told me he wrote him up last week. In fact, there he is." Caitlyn nodded toward a tall, thin guy who looked to be in his early twenties. He had his keys in his hand and his cell phone pressed against his ear.

"I'll handle this, okay?"

He nodded, hanging back to watch her take care of the situation. As he watched her walk over to Ball, he couldn't help but notice the way her sensible navy blue suit hugged her in all the right places. Just like the red dress that she'd worn to the wedding. Of course, her business suit was much more conservative, but still no less tempting. He pressed his lips together, as if doing that might extinguish the attraction simmering inside him. It was the same magnetic pull that had drawn him to her the night of the wedding. The same force that had drawn him away from the twin blondes he'd been talking to before he'd glimpsed her across the room and excused himself to meet her.

Of course, everything was different now. For the next month she would be his boss, for all intents and purposes. He'd advise her on how to pull the park together in every department from staffing and personnel issues to community relations.

He watched as she stood in front of Ball, who was still talking on the phone. When Caitlyn gestured that she needed to talk to Ball, the guy turned his back on her. Something that might've qualified as primal stirred inside him. That was no way to treat a lady. It was definitely no way to treat his superior. But Brodie swallowed the urge to step in and tell the guy to get off his phone and show her some respect.

Caitlyn was being entirely too nice. He made a mental note that they'd need to talk about that. She was probably good at her job; otherwise, Alden Moore wouldn't have put her in charge while he was out. Despite the way she'd laid down the law with him a few moments ago, observing her now, he got a very strong sense that Caitlyn didn't like being the bad guy—and that her employees knew it, too.

Finally, Caitlyn tapped Ball on the shoulder. He looked a little annoyed, but he put his hand over his phone and said, "Listen, I can't talk to you now. I need to run. Remember, you told me I could leave. I'll stop into the office tomorrow and chat. How's that?"

"No, Clark, it's not all right. I said you could leave if you had your supervisor's permission."

Clark gave an oh-well shrug. "I have to pick up my brother over in Lubbock in twenty minutes. I'll be lucky to get there in half an hour. I still have to clock out and get to my car."

"You haven't clocked out and you're on a personal call?" she asked.

"Yeah, so I'll come in five minutes early tomorrow." The guy rolled his eyes as he bent to place something in his toolbox.

"Clark, when you asked for the time off, you said you needed to take your wife to an appointment. Now you're taking your brother somewhere."

This time he ignored her as he turned to walk away.

"You don't have my permission to leave," Caitlyn called out after him.

"Sorry," he called back, not even turning around. "I'll make up the time. We'll talk about it tomorrow."

Brodie had let her have a go at it; clearly it was time to step in and help her.

"Mr. Ball," he said. "I think what Ms. Moore is trying to say is if you leave, don't come back. Because you will no longer have a job here."

Chapter Three

"How dare you put words in my mouth?" Caitlyn said through gritted teeth once they were out of earshot of Clark and others who might overhear.

"I'm sorry you took it that way," Brodie said. But he didn't look one bit sorry. "Obviously, your softer approach wasn't getting through to him."

"Excuse me? What exactly do you mean by *softer approach*?" The sun was high in the sky, and she felt heat prickle the back of her neck. "Just because I didn't steamroll right over him doesn't mean I wasn't effectively handling the situation. You butted in."

"The guy was walking out the door, and you were letting him."

"*I was handling it.*" She purposely lowered her voice.

"Look, we are not going to talk about this here. Meet me in my office."

She turned and walked away without him, but he managed to catch up with her. They walked in stony silence as they made their way down Cowboy Country's Main Street, past the Foaming Barrel Root Beer Stand and Gus's General Store, to the rough-hewn wooden gate that separated the nineteenth-century cowboy town from the stark, modern Moore Entertainment executive offices.

Of course, after Brodie's sudden-death ultimatum, Clark had sullenly taken himself back to the job site. Brodie should've stayed out of it and let her do her job, rather than jumping in with both feet and a sledgehammer. She hadn't even had a chance to brief him on… anything. He didn't know what was going on or that she was completely capable of turning that situation around. She would've helped Clark see the light. He would've done the right thing in the end. She had faith in him

Apparently, Hayes Consulting was good enough to inspire her father to contract them for a month…*an entire month*. However, the Brodie Hayes of Hayes Consulting was *not* Brodie the Brit.

Was this man really the same guy who'd swept her off her feet? Because aside from his good looks and that maddeningly delicious British accent, the guy who'd presented himself today didn't resemble Brodie the Brit at all.

This guy…

Ugggh…

This guy was cocky and smug, not at all like *anyone* she'd allow to seduce her. She would never hire this guy, much less spend the better part of the night in a field, watching meteor showers and letting him put his hands all over her body…and putting her hands all over his.

The memory made her shudder…and, much to her dismay, not in a bad way. She needed to stop that right now.

She didn't slant him a glance.

From a purely objective, woman's point of view, Brodie Hayes was a handsome man, there was no debating that. But why did he have to be so disagreeable? He certainly seemed to take pleasure in pushing her buttons. Caitlyn knew his type: all flash and no substance.

A womanizer, no doubt.

But she couldn't blame him for the Valentine's Day love and dash. That was on her as much as it was on him.

Quickening her step as she approached the office, she reached out and opened the door herself, holding it for Brodie and gesturing for him to step inside first. She was no expert at office posturing and body language, but holding the door for him felt like she was putting herself back in the position of power.

Exactly where she needed to be now that everything had changed so drastically.

"Hello, Janie, we're back," she said. "Please hold calls. Oh, unless it's about my father. We're awaiting word on the latest round of tests."

Of course, her mother would probably call Caitlyn's

cell with any updates, but she just wanted to be clear…
just in case.

When Caitlyn turned around to head back into her
office, Brodie was staring at her with that same im-
passive mask he'd donned the moment they'd figured
out who was who and the mess they'd created thanks
to *that night*.

Who was this icy stoic sitting across from her? If
Brodie Hayes had acted like this, she would've left that
wedding when she should've.

"Heavy-handed threats are no way to inspire people and build a team," Caitlyn said. "Even if the team
needs some refining, they are all Cowboy Country has
right now. Electricians aren't exactly standing around
in herds. Bottom line is, that's not how we operate here.
Do you understand?"

He sat back in his chair, staring down at his hands,
which were steepled at chest level. For a moment she
thought he might apologize.

"It wasn't an easy decision for your father to hire
Hayes Consulting. Alden Moore is extremely good at
what he does. He's the amusement-park king. Hiring
me for Cowboy Country was him admitting he may
have been in a little over his head. Your dad is damn
good at what he does, but this park is a departure from
his wheelhouse. When your father hired me, one of the
first things he asked me was, 'Hayes, are you afraid to
fire people?' I assured him I wasn't."

"So what? You decided to walk in here and prove
yourself first thing, even before I could bring you up to
speed on how things work around here?"

"I didn't need to be briefed to see what that guy was about," Brodie said. "Your father has already given me my marching orders. Did he not brief you? I thought you were his second-in-command."

No, she was not his second-in-command. That would've been Bob Page. Bob had left unexpectedly after suffering critical injuries in a horseback riding accident. This happened about a week before her father's heart attack. Based on the catastrophes of Cowboy Country's number one and number two honchos, if Caitlyn didn't know better, she might've worried that this project was cursed.

She was too much of a realist for that, and she was dead set on proving to her dad that she could deliver.

"I actually work out of the research offices in Chicago."

She paused to see if he'd make any Cait from Chicago cracks.

He didn't.

She may or may not have been a little disappointed. Her rational side was relieved, but her traitorous heart, the place where she stored the snow globe memory of that night, still held out hope for some wayward spark to leap out, revealing the dashing romantic she'd met that night in February.

It didn't.

"I transferred to Horseback Hollow to take the reins while my dad is recovering."

"Yet, you don't have a copy of the briefing your dad gave me." He held up the papers.

He was so smug. She didn't know what she wanted

more: to smack that smirk off him or to walk up and kiss him to see if he could still turn her inside out.

"That's easy to fix."

Caitlyn pressed the intercom that connected her to her assistant.

"Janie, please come in here. I need you to make some copies for me."

Five minutes later, the woman was standing in front of Caitlyn with the papers.

She scanned them quickly, reading on the first page that Alden had, in fact, instructed Brodie to "slice and dice," as Alden had put it.

Slice and dice.

Get rid of anyone who didn't do the job past expectations.

She looked up. "This is how my father works. However, since he's not here, and I'm the Moore Entertainment executive in charge, you're reporting to me now. And I'm telling you, we will be making some adjustments to this plan, because it doesn't work for me. The first rule is, you don't fire anyone until you talk to me. Do you understand me?"

"Every single employee on this team needs to be *all in*. One hundred percent. If not, we won't meet our goal."

"I agree," Caitlyn said. "That also goes for the two of us working as a team and not against each other. Do you think we can do that?"

He was quiet for a moment. Their gazes were locked, but he seemed to be looking right through her.

"Of course," he said. "What's done is done. Let's put everything behind us and move forward."

For a moment she wasn't sure if he was talking about the Clark Ball incident or their Fortune wedding after-party. She certainly wasn't going to ask or let him think he could intimidate her with innuendo.

"Why don't we go walk the park? It's the best way for me to bring you up to speed. Then we can come back and figure out how we need to revise that plan, while making sure we open on time."

Brodie considered himself a go-with-the-flow kind of guy. However, when it came to business, he had one hard, fast rule: do not sleep with the clients.

It complicated matters.

He was living the reality of that truth today, and it was throwing him off his game.

He'd been blissfully unaware the night he'd met Caitlyn and had given himself over to the lure of their attraction. How could he resist? How could he have known that their worlds would collide in the most jarring way? In the years since he'd been in business, he'd never found himself in a situation like this.

After dealing with other peoples' *complicated matters* on the job all day, every day, he did his best to keep his personal life as unencumbered and hassle-free as possible. Of course, things didn't always go smoothly. He'd faced the occasional sticky wicket of finding it necessary to extract himself from the casual fling that clung too tightly. And there were uncomfortable cases when he was out with a beauty only to run into the previous evening's delight. But he prided himself on being up-front with the women in his life. Those who played by his rules stuck around for the fun of it. Those who fancied a different level of commitment usually ran out of patience and moved on.

He couldn't blame them.

In his circles, everyone knew that Brodie Fortune Hayes wasn't interested in getting serious. Work was his mistress, his lady love. He had no reserves or residual to give of himself.

As he stepped inside the Hollows Cantina, he had to ask himself if somehow he'd been able to glimpse the future and known that *Cait from Chicago* would be the person to whom he'd report at Moore Entertainment, would the night of the wedding—Valentine's Day— have taken a decidedly different turn?

His head—the place he relied on, the one voice that he always knew wouldn't steer him wrong—trumpeted a resounding *yes*. But another part of him, a place that was foreign and uncomfortable, begged to differ.

Well, then, that was easy. He was going with his head. It was the only sensible thing to do. Especially since the workday wasn't over yet.

After he and Caitlyn had wrapped the disastrous day at Cowboy Country, they'd agreed to meet for dinner at The Hollows Cantina, where they would iron out the details of their *united front* plan.

When he took the job, he'd known good and well that Alden Moore would be difficult to please. The man had a formidable reputation. Little did he know that working with Moore's daughter would prove to be even more challenging!

It went deeper than the fact that they'd seen each other naked. This woman was different from anyone he'd ever worked with. She was trying to manage a group of hostile employees with warm, fuzzy Kumbaya nonsense. She didn't seem to realize that people were walking all over her. He was willing to bet that Clark Ball wouldn't have pulled that bit of insubordinate baloney on her father. If Caitlyn Moore would simply get down from her high horse and listen to him tonight, he just might be able to help her save Cowboy Country.

First, Caitlyn had to run an errand. For that, Brodie was grateful. Her side trip took a bit of the pressure off, since that meant they were driving separately and meeting at the restaurant. Even though their dinner most definitely was not a date, taking separate cars gave them each a little breathing room to process what had transpired…*er*…on the job.

As far as he was concerned, he was putting their night under the stars behind him. In his head, *Cait from Chicago* was a different person from Caitlyn Moore, daughter of Alden Moore, the man who could make or break his chance to land the Japanese theme park account.

Brodie was used to flying solo, especially when it came to business. The companies that hired Hayes Consulting trusted him and tended to not interfere. Most had gotten themselves into messes of one kind or another, or their public profiles needed a boost. They hired him to pull them out of the bad and into a better standing in the community.

This job wasn't difficult.

Even if one might label the circumstances he dealt with...*complicated*.

He was *this close* to landing the Japanese account, and that would secure Hayes Consulting's position in the Asian market. Brodie liked to joke that the Japanese account would put him one continent closer to world domination.

It was a pretty serious joke.

When he walked into the restaurant, the hostess, a woman with long, dark hair greeted him with a bright smile.

"Good evening." Her lilting voice was bright and solicitous. "Welcome to the Hollows Cantina. How many in *your* party?"

"There will be two of us." He glanced at his watch. "I'm a little early. I'll wait in the bar until my dinner partner arrives."

"Have you dined with us before?" she asked.

"I have, but it's been a while. Since February."

"I thought you looked familiar."

Her comment gave him pause, and that's when he realized that she was looking up at him through long, dark lashes. She was an attractive woman, no doubt, but he wasn't even tempted to flirt with her. Flirting was one of his favorite sports. But he had enough sense to know that Horseback Hollow and London were worlds apart. The last thing he needed was to get himself into another romantic conundrum.

"I'll just—" He pointed toward the bar area to the left of the hostess stand and started to walk away.

"There's about a twenty-minute wait for a table," the woman said. "What's your name? I'll add it to my list."

Really? How strange, he wasn't even tempted.

Even stranger, he was relieved when Caitlyn chose that moment to enter the restaurant.

"There you are," Brodie said, realizing a little too late that he'd infused way more enthusiasm into his voice than he would have liked.

"Hello." Caitlyn cocked a brow. "Did you miss me?"

And that was another thing about her. She was cheeky. She had just enough sass to keep him from labeling her a total pushover. Probably because that sass was mostly directed at him.

The woman was a delightfully aggravating dichotomy. Just when he thought he had her figured out she pulled a U-turn and took off in the opposite direction.

"There's a bit of a wait for a table," Brodie said. "Why don't we have a drink in the bar in the meantime?"

As they turned to go, the hostess said, "If you want a table, I need a name." She tapped her list with her pen.

"Fortune Hayes," he said. "Brodie Fortune Hayes."

Caitlyn stopped. "What? You're a Fortune?"

Chapter Four

Never mind that she'd met Brodie at a Fortune wedding and that they'd skipped the last names and jumped right to the sex. Finding out this way that he was part of the illustrious Fortune clan felt like she'd discovered an enemy who'd infiltrated her family's camp.

The Fortunes were vehemently opposed to Cowboy Country because they were afraid that the park would bring in too many outsiders to Horseback Hollow and ruin the idyllic small town. Since the park meant so much to her father, Caitlyn couldn't help but take their scorn personally. Now here she was sitting at the bar with Brodie, while he perused the wine list as if the revelation of who he really was hadn't made things strange and different and even more *wrong*.

"Does my father know you're a Fortune?"

It took him a minute to look up from the leather-bound listing.

In that time, she thought about calling her dad. But then reality set in. If he didn't know, the shock would upset him. After his heart attack, he was supposed to remain as stress-free as possible. That was the whole reason she'd moved to Horseback Hollow, to steer Cowboy Country to a successful opening.

"Of course he does." He looked at her as if she'd suggested they order orange soda rather than the bottle of wine, which, given his upper-crust airs, was sure to be the best the restaurant had to offer. "Why does my being a Fortune bother you?"

Why did it bother her?

He'd done nothing to indicate he'd taken the job for nefarious reasons—to spy and report back…to whoever he'd report back to… Umm, okay, so that sounded far-fetched. But wait! What if he'd come on board to wreak sabotage to keep them from opening?

The moment the thought formed, it seemed equally ridiculous. After all, he had been the one who'd exercised tough love on Clark Ball, sending him back to work rather than letting him take the afternoon off. If Brodie wanted to sabotage them, he could've simply let the electrician walk off the job. They wouldn't have met the deadline to fix the electrical problems, and Cowboy Country would've failed the inspection.

Why *did it* bother her?

"Because it feels like you haven't been honest with me."

That seemed to wipe the smug smirk right off his face.

For about two seconds.

"*I* haven't been honest with *you*?"

She let his words hang in the air, knowing where he was going with this.

"I suppose I could say the same about you, *Cait from Chicago*."

She refused to let his words faze her. Until he said, "Do you see how bloody ridiculous this is?"

She sighed. "Oh, my God. I do. As hard as we've tried to skirt the issue, we're going to have to talk about what happened that night."

"Well, I don't know if we have to go *that* far."

"Brodie, we do. Because if we talk about it—or at least acknowledge it—then we can move past it and get to work."

"Fair enough. We had sex and it was quite wonderful, if you must know."

She felt her face flush. "Well, I really wasn't thinking we should editorialize, but thank you."

Dammit, it had been good. One night of pure pleasure that would've been pretty darn-near close to perfect if he hadn't reappeared in her life and reignited that longing she felt every time she looked at him…or caught him looking at her…like he was doing right now.

But if this—this partnership—was going to work…

"It can't happen again."

"I know."

Even though it went against everything she knew was right, the thought of not touching him, of him not touching her, made her heart hurt.

But why? For what?

"We have to be a team, Brodie. A platonic team."

He nodded, but the way he was looking at her sort of canceled out the word *platonic*, and she wished she could recant that part. But she couldn't. They had work to do. She couldn't let her father down because her mind was occupied with a man who had one-night stands and was perfectly content—no, he wasn't just content, he preferred to not see the woman again.

Until him, she'd never done that before. She'd had one serious relationship, and she would've married the guy if he hadn't cheated.

No, she and Brodie Fortune Hayes were too different. Clearly, they approached business and love from two opposing perspectives.

"We have to be on the same page."

He nodded again.

Stop looking at me like that.

"Absolutely," he agreed. "Why don't we start by picking out a bottle of wine and then we can talk specifics."

The wine helped. It loosened them up enough so they could start talking plans and strategies. It probably helped to talk about the ten-ton elephant that had been standing between them, Caitlyn thought as she walked with Brodie down Main Street later that week, looking at all the crafts and food booths set up for the inaugural Horseback Hollow Arts and Crafts Festival, an event created by the Fortune Foundation to reinforce Horseback Hollow's sense of community. It was clear that the two of them had very different ideas of how to turn Cowboy Country around in the weeks before the soft opening.

She knew he was a professional and darn good at what he did. He'd have to be for her father to hire him. But she couldn't help her gut feeling that his slice-and-dice approach—one that utilized fear and an iron fist to push people into place—just wasn't right.

Most of the workers were Horseback Hollow locals who needed the jobs Cowboy Country USA was providing. Clearly, some of them were torn, possibly feeling like traitors to the community. Caitlyn had reminded Brodie more than once that this unrest was due in large part to his relatives taking such a negative stand against the amusement park.

"How can they do that when they don't really know us?" she'd asked after they'd been seated for dinner at a table upstairs on the Cantina's open-air terrace.

He'd maintained that she couldn't manage by gut feelings. That his tactics had a track record and were proven to work. Just when she started to consider the evening a stalemate, he finally hit on something that allowed them to climb to middle ground.

"You said the folks of Horseback Hollow don't know Cowboy Country and what you're all about," he said. "Have you gotten out into the community to meet people?"

She'd blinked at him.

"I've been here less than a week, Brodie, and part of that time was spent at the hospital in Lubbock with my father."

"That sounds like an excuse to me." He said the words with such a straight face she searched his gaze to see if he was kidding. As usual, she couldn't tell.

"Are you kidding? Because if not, that's really harsh. That's exactly the kind of attitude I'm having a difficult time with."

He'd reached out and put his hand on her arm and darned if her traitorous body didn't zing all the way down to her toes, and some very private places perked up at the memory of his touch.

"I'm sorry," he said. "I don't mean to come across as heartless—"

She pulled her hand away, reclaiming her space and willing the humming in her body to go away. "Well, then stop saying heartless things. And if you tell me that you don't have a heart—again—I just might have to spill my wine in your lap."

He held up his hand as if to fend her off. "I'm very sorry your dad is ill, but the reality is the clock doesn't stop. Time is ticking whether or not you have good reasons for not doing everything in your power every single day to fix what's wrong with Cowboy Country. I'm here to help you, but you're going to have to let me help you."

"I appreciate your expertise," she said. "However, I can't stand by your philosophy of coming in and firing the locals. That's not going to win us many friends. Except maybe to the staffing agency we'll have to use to ensure we have enough warm bodies for opening day. How loyal do you think temps will be? Then if you start importing people from Lubbock, that'll simply compound the town's resentment. Not only have we fired the locals, we've given those jobs to people from out of town."

They'd studied the menus in silence for a long time before Brodie finally said, "I have an idea. When I was downtown, I saw a poster that said the Horseback Hollow Arts and Crafts Festival starts on Friday. Let's go have a look. That would be one of the best ways to get out in the town and get a feel for who you're dealing with. Maybe even meet some people who can give you some perspective."

It was the first idea he'd offered that she could get on board with. So here they were in the middle of Main Street. She felt as anonymous as she had at the wedding. At least the town was large enough that she wasn't conspicuous.

They strolled along together, and Caitlyn tried to ignore how they probably looked like a couple walking by booth after booth—a stand of bright watercolors; another one offering gorgeous quilts; others proudly displaying hand-thrown pottery, free-form sculpture and delicate orchids that were apparently crafted out of clay and looked more alive than the real deal.

Just as they passed the clay flowers, Caitlyn had the feeling someone was watching her. She looked across the street and locked eyes with a lady standing at the cotton-candy vendor. The stylish woman, who looked to be in her late fifties, maybe her early sixties, had silver hair cut into a smart, chic bob. Even at a glance, she had an air of class and elegance.

The woman held Caitlyn's gaze a little longer than what might be considered a casual coincidence. Just as Caitlyn began to fear that she'd somehow recognized her as part of the Cowboy Country crew, the woman ducked into the crowd and disappeared.

She was so put together, Caitlyn hated to admit that she seemed a bit more stylish than the typical woman of Horseback Hollow… Oh, that wasn't fair. Who was she to judge?

The woman was probably one of the artists. Maybe she'd seen her in one of the booths they'd passed earlier.

Then again, maybe she was a local who'd gone to rally her neighbors with their torches and pitchforks. And that was the craziest thought yet. If she was going to get to know the locals, she'd inevitably have to have that first uncomfortable moment when they discovered who she was. But then she'd be on the right track to showing them she and Moore Entertainment fully intended to be good neighbors.

She didn't say anything to Brodie, who seemed to be unaware as the two of them walked, talking and taking in the lay of the land, getting a sense of the cute little town and people who'd come to display their wares. Each booth sported a tag with the artist's name, art medium and hometown. Caitlyn was surprised to see how many of them were not local.

"So I'm guessing the good folks of Horseback Hollow support the arts and crafts festival because it's not permanent?" Caitlyn asked. "I'm intrigued that so many of the artists are from places other than here."

Brodie nodded. "Well, you have to consider that it's a small town, and there's a relatively small number of artists. Or at least ones who are good enough to win a place in the festival. From what I understand, this show is by invitation only, and it's quite an honor to be selected to participate. In other words, Horseback Hollow doesn't discriminate when it comes to discriminating."

Hmm… Obviously.

Finally, a booth manned by a local caught Caitlyn's eye: Susie's Silverworks.

"Wait," Caitlyn said. "I want to go in here."

Brodie scanned the booth, and she saw his eyes virtually glaze over.

"While you're having a look," he said, "if you'll excuse me, I'm going to go return a phone call. It shouldn't take long. Shall I meet you here when I'm done? That way you won't have to rush."

"I take it sterling-silver jewelry isn't your thing?" Caitlyn teased.

"No, I'm more of a chunky golden chain kind of guy, myself." He gave her that sexy half smile, and suddenly she was picturing him with his shirt open—not in a smarmy 1970s lounge lizard way. In fact, gold chains didn't even figure in her mind's picture.

And she needed to stop that—

"You are the golden boy, aren't you?"

He shot her a look that implied she didn't know what she was talking about. "I'll see you in a few minutes."

Caitlyn waited until two browsers had finished looking and moved over so she could take their spot. Then she could see that Susie offered a gorgeous array of handcrafted jewelry—rings, earrings, necklaces and free-form charms. But it was the tray of hammered silver cuff bracelets that caught her eye.

"Are you Susie?"

The woman nodded. "I am. These are my creations."

"They're beautiful."

"Thank you." Susie beamed at her. "Please, try on anything you'd like."

"Oh, I love this one." Caitlyn pointed to a concave hammered silver cuff with beveled edges. Susie picked it up and polished it with a velvety black cloth before she offered it to Caitlyn.

"May I?" Susie nodded toward Caitlyn's wrist.

"Please." She held out her arm and allowed the artist to slip on the bracelet.

"What do you think?"

"I think I'm in love," Caitlyn said.

Out of the corner of her eye, she glimpsed that silver-haired woman again. The one she'd caught staring at her and Brodie as they'd wound their way through the crowd down Main Street. This time there was no doubt. The woman was watching her from the next booth. In fact, she was craning her neck.

Caitlyn smiled at her. The woman smiled back. But a knot of people meandered through their line of vision, and by the time they'd moved on, the woman was gone.

At least she'd smiled, which was a good indication that she hadn't summoned the angry mobs. But the woman's attention did make Caitlyn squirm a little bit. Probably because she spent so much time alone in her research. In a city the size of Chicago, it was easy to be alone in a crowd. She saw some of the same faces on her walk to and from her office, but she never connected with any of them. Maybe it was the city girl in her that made her feel suspicious of a smile. When she thought of it that way, suspicion didn't feel right, either.

"Try this one." Susie held up another cuff bracelet. This one was smooth and shiny and about half the width of the other one. Caitlyn removed the first bracelet from her wrist and put on the one Susie offered in its place.

"This one is beautiful, too."

"If you want something a little less dressy, I have these."

She placed five silver bangles on a black velvet pad she'd set atop the glass case. Some of them had inlaid stones; others were plain.

"And here are the matching earrings."

Caitlyn sighed. "It's all so pretty, but I think I prefer the cuff bracelets. Now, for the difficult decision. Which one?"

"Try them both on," Susie urged.

Caitlyn slipped one onto each wrist and held out her arms to admire and compare the two pieces of jewelry.

"I vote for the hammered silver," said a female voice behind Caitlyn.

When she turned around, she saw the woman with the silver hair. She held up her own arm, showing off a cuff similar to the one Caitlyn was partial to, but it was just different enough to make each piece unique.

"She has good taste," the woman said to Susie.

"She certainly does," Susie agreed. "How are you, Jeanne Marie? I was wondering when you were going to stop by and see me."

Susie turned to Caitlyn. "Jeanne Marie is one of my best customers."

"Please don't tell that to my husband," she said.

She turned to Caitlyn. "Have we met? You look very familiar."

So that was the reason the woman had been staring. Of course. It made Caitlyn feel better knowing she was simply trying to place her.

"I don't believe we have. I'm Caitlyn Moore."

Caitlyn offered her hand. The woman accepted it.

"Nice to meet you, Ms. Moore. Are you a Horseback Hollow resident, or are you just here for the art festival?"

"I recently moved to the area," Caitlyn said.

"Is that so? What brought you here?"

Caitlyn took a deep breath. Her mission today was to reach out to the people in the community. Jeanne Marie seemed like a great person to start with.

"My job brought me here. I'm with Cowboy Country USA. I've come to town to help open the park."

In a split second the air seemed to change, to chill. Jeanne Marie and Susie glanced at each other and then back at Caitlyn. Jeanne Marie raised her chin and tilted her head to the right as she conjured a polite smile that didn't reach her eyes.

Caitlyn removed the cuffs from her wrists and set them on the piece of velvet.

"Susie, I'll take the hammered silver bracelet." She pulled her wallet out of her purse.

"That's a good choice," Jeanne Marie said, her voice proper and chilly.

Caitlyn tried to think of something clever to say or some way to spin this situation—where was Brodie when she needed him?—but only the truth felt right. It was all she had to offer.

"Jeanne Marie, I haven't been in Horseback Hollow very long, but I already love this town. I love the way everyone here looks out for their neighbors. They only want what is best for the community. I understand why people might be a bit skeptical about a place like Cowboy Country USA. You're probably afraid that it won't fit into the fabric of your close-knit community. But if you'll just give us a chance, I assure you, we want to be good neighbors."

Jeanne Marie's polite smile didn't waver, but it wasn't any warmer, either. Obviously, she wasn't convinced.

"I appreciate you saying that. You seem very sincere. However, I'm more interested in hearing how you are acquainted with my nephew, Brodie Fortune Hayes."

It took Brodie a little longer than he'd intended to take care of his phone call. He was half expecting Caitlyn to have moved on from the jewelry tent where he'd promised to meet her. But there she was.

Even in the midst of a crowd, his eyes picked her out, the same way he had at the wedding. With her long, dark hair and ivory skin, the woman was a stunner. Her warm heart and ready smile made her even more beautiful. What man in his right mind wouldn't find her attractive?

However, his appreciation was derailed when he realized she was talking to his aunt Jeanne Marie.

Uttering a choice word under his breath, he quickened his pace. This was not good. Not good at all.

"Hello, Auntie." He planted a kiss on the woman's cheek. "It's a lovely day for an art festival, right? I see you've met my friend, Caitlyn."

"Yes, I have, dear." Jeanne Marie's lips thinned as she secured Brodie with her gaze. "I understand congratulations are in order. Ms. Moore was telling me that the two of you are working together. I didn't realize you had landed the Cowboy Country account. In fact, I'd wager that our entire family will be just as surprised as I."

Surprised being the operative word. It was clear that she wasn't happy for him. He should have told her that was the reason he'd come back to Horseback Hollow. Or he should've at least confided in his mother or his brother Oliver. Of course, his mother would have, no doubt, shared the news with the rest of the family.

Bloody hell, now he'd stepped in it deep.

He'd been busy, and frankly, he knew how his family felt about Cowboy Country USA, and didn't want them to deliberate on the merit of his client. In the past, they had never taken an interest in his client list. Why should they get involved now?

He knew this spelled trouble. He needed to fix it. And fast.

"Ah, well, Caitlyn, dear, you spoiled my big announcement."

Caitlyn shot him a don't-you-dare-try-to-blame-this-on-me look. His only defense was to redirect and redouble his efforts toward his aunt.

"I was going to tell everyone at the barbecue tomorrow night. May I trust you to keep my secret? It would be such a shame to spoil the surprise for everyone else."

Jeanne Marie sighed and shook her head.

He turned back to Caitlyn. "My aunt Jeanne Marie and uncle Deke throw the best barbecues you've ever seen in your life. No one does authentic Texas barbecue the way they do. The best you've *ever* seen."

He was speaking the truth, even if he was laying it on a little thick.

"Auntie, I was serious when I said I wanted to tell everyone at the barbecue tomorrow. Will you please keep this revelation between us until I have a chance to make my announcement?"

The woman didn't suffer fools lightly. She knew when she was being played, even if that wasn't his intention. She had backed him into a corner. It was his only available move.

Jeanne Marie put her hands on her slim hips. "I'll tell you what, Brodie. I will let you break the news to the family on one condition."

"Sure, what would that be?"

"I would like for you to bring Caitlyn to the barbecue. I think she might do a better job of helping you win the family over for Cowboy Country USA than you will explaining yourself on your own."

Chapter Five

Caitlyn Moore was better at charming his family than he was, Brodie thought as he pulled open the door to the rehabilitation center in Lubbock where Alden Moore was convalescing.

It shouldn't come as a surprise. She was passionate about Cowboy Country, well-spoken and beautiful. Oh, yes, she was a beauty, Caitlyn Moore—with her long, dark hair, green eyes and that flawless face of fine-boned porcelain.

She was the type of woman who haunted a man's dreams, the type who inspired a guy to cross the room to meet her. Once he got there, he realized she was so much more than a pretty face.

That *so much more* was the reason her mixing with his family was a problem.

He'd been ruminating on it for the past two days since his aunt Jeanne Marie had invited Caitlyn to the family barbecue. Brodie knew winning over the locals was crucial to improving Cowboy Country's profile, but accomplishing this through his family wasn't the route he wanted to take. He needed to keep work and family separate.

While he'd been blessed with this new group of close-knit relations, beneath the surface, everything was not as bright and shiny and perfect as it appeared.

Make no mistake, he adored his mother. He had nothing but the deepest respect for his late stepfather, Sir Simon Chesterfield. After all, the man had raised him as one of his own. In fact, he was the only father figure in Brodie's life. He and his natural brother, Oliver, understood each other because they were cut from the same cloth—literally. Oliver and Brodie were spawns of their mother's first marriage to Rhys Henry Hayes, an abominable man who was best forgotten. A man who abandoned his wife and turned his back on his children because he didn't deserve the energy that it would take to hold a grudge.

Then there was the matter of the Fortunes. His relationship with his extended family was complicated.

A couple of years ago, his mother had discovered she had been adopted when she was very young—too young to even remember—and was reunited with her American siblings, one of whom was none other than James Marshall Fortune, the American business tycoon. All of a sudden she had a branch of American family. Actually, the Fortune side of the family was more like an entire forest than a branch due to the vast number of them. There seemed to be a Fortune on every corner in Horseback Hollow.

His mother had enthusiastically embraced her new family, and she had expected her children to follow suit. Out of respect to Josephine, Brodie had taken the Fortune name when his mother had asked her children to do so.

Sometimes when Brodie Fortune Hayes was alone with his deepest, darkest thoughts, he mused that bearing the surnames of a man who had made it perfectly clear he did not want to be a father and a clan he really didn't even know, was it any wonder he didn't feel as if he had a genuine place in this world?

When he felt himself sliding down that slippery slope, he redoubled his focus on work and his determination to succeed. He was a self-made man, after all. He had built Hayes Consulting from the ground up, with no help from anyone.

That was his place, his identity, his armor.

Even though he cared deeply for his family, sometimes their enthusiasm only complicated things.

They were human. Humans were fickle and self-serving. In this dog-eat-dog world, when it came down to it, wasn't everyone out for himself?

For what other reason would salt-of-the-earth Jeanne Marie mean to interfere in his business? He didn't need to ask her permission. That's why he wasn't keen to elaborate on the reason that had brought him to Horseback Hollow.

Family could get inside your head, under your skin

and cause you to second-guess yourself. They could change everything, and they didn't always have your best interest at heart. He'd let that happen once. *Once*. Now he subscribed to the theory *Fool me once shame on you, fool me twice—* Well, that would simply make him a jackass.

Businessmen like Alden Moore didn't hire jackasses.

The rehabilitation center was nicer than some private clubs Brodie had visited. An attractive young woman greeted him from a polished dark wood desk in the center of the marble entryway.

"Good morning, sir, how may I help you?"

"I'm here to see Alden Moore. He's expecting me."

The woman typed something into a computer and then picked up the telephone.

"Your name, sir?"

"Hayes. Brodie Fortune Hayes."

It still felt odd including Fortune in his name, but if there was any place in the world that he could get mileage out of it, surely it was in Texas. He might as well take advantage of it.

As the woman murmured something into the telephone receiver, Brodie glanced around the posh surroundings. The place looked new, with its high ceilings lined with crown molding and large windows that let in just enough light to show off the Persian rugs and expensive-looking furniture. Not that he'd had the occasion to visit many rehab centers, but this one seemed more like a luxury hotel. It also allowed him to glimpse the type of service Alden Moore expected. He would get nothing less from Hayes Consulting.

"Mr. Moore is expecting you. You may go on back. He's in room 222. Take the elevator up to the second floor and follow the posted signs."

The luxury didn't stop at the reception desk. The elevator also had marble floors. It carried him to the second level where tasteful artwork adorned walls with wainscoting. Alden Moore's room was at the very end of the hall. The door was shut, just slightly ajar, as if someone had just left. Brodie knocked and pushed it open a hair.

"Brodie Hayes, my man," said Moore. "Come in, please."

The last time Brodie saw Alden, the man had been the picture of robust health. It was shocking to see him lying in a hospital bed hooked up to tubes and machines. He knew Alden wouldn't want his pity, so he made sure to keep his face neutral.

An elegant older woman with dark hair pulled back away from her face and beautiful green eyes sat in a leather chair at his bedside. Brodie had a vision of what Caitlyn might look like in about twenty-five years. Something flared in his chest for the briefest second, before he got a hold of himself.

Alden Moore introduced his wife, Barbara. After a moment of polite small talk, Barbara excused herself.

"It's nice to meet you, Mr. Hayes. I'll leave you and Alden alone to talk business. I'm trusting that you will keep things light and short. My husband is still recovering. He's not supposed to get upset about anything."

She smiled at Brodie, and he understood where Caitlyn got her quiet strength.

"Of course," he said. "I've simply come to update him on the progress Caitlyn and I have made. No upsetting news to share."

Unless you counted the fact that three months ago he'd had a one-night stand with their daughter. Brodie did not kiss and tell, so that was not even on the agenda. However, it struck him hard… He had slept with the man's *daughter*, and it just didn't feel right.

Well, actually, it had felt right. It had felt better and more natural than just about any other sexual experience he'd had. He and Caitlyn had been two consenting adults who had entered into their night of passion willingly—enthusiastically—but standing here in front of her father, it felt wrong. Until this very moment he hadn't given much thought to having a family. However, if someday he had a daughter like Caitlyn, any guy who disrespected her in any way would have a hefty price to pay.

"How is everything? What have you and that daughter of mine been up to?"

Reflexively, Brodie wanted to say, *nothing*. But he knew that was simply his guilty conscience speaking. Brodie knew Alden was speaking in terms of business.

"What progress have you made?" Moore continued.

"We are working together well."

"I'm sorry I didn't have a chance to brief you on my situation before you arrived." Moore gestured to his chest. "This was a bit unexpected, as you can imagine. I appreciate you being so flexible and willing to work with Caitlyn."

"It's not a problem, sir. In fact, we make a good team

because she sees things from a different perspective than I do."

Alden surprised Brodie by waving off his words. "I'll be honest with you. Caitlyn is at Cowboy Country because it's where she feels like she's doing the most good. There wasn't enough room for two women to sit by my bedside wringing their hands. So when she came up with the idea of working at the park while I recovered, frankly, I was in no physical condition to protest. As long as she's not in the way—not keeping you from getting the job done—just work around her."

Brodie didn't know what to say. He and Caitlyn certainly didn't see eye to eye, but she did have some good ideas. He was sincere when he said they balanced each other.

"Or if you feel you can work better without her there, I'll have her mother talk her into going back to Chicago," Alden continued. "Obviously, I'm out of danger. There's no sense in her hanging around. She'd probably be happier going back to her animal research."

Brodie was weighing his words, looking for the right response when he looked up and saw Caitlyn standing in the doorway holding a large vase of flowers.

"Excuse me?" Caitlyn said. She'd always heard the expression *seeing red*, but this was the first time she'd experienced it. She took a deep breath before she said anything else, because she knew her father's condition was serious, and fighting was the last thing he needed—even if he'd just marginalized her and hurt her as she'd never been hurt in her life. Not even when she was in college and he'd tried to talk her out of majoring in zo-ology. Not even when he'd told her it was a worthless degree and she'd be wasting her time and his money. Not even when he'd created the research position for her and she'd had to endure his barbs about that job being the only place she would be able to earn a decent wage.

Now he was telling Brodie Fortune Hayes that she was extraneous? That she could simply be shipped off and put back in her office in Chicago if she were *in the way*?

"Ahh, there she is," her father said, as if she'd walked in and overheard them singing her praises.

She pinned Brodie with a pointed look.

But she looked at her father—really looked at him. He looked much smaller, almost frail, lying there in that hospital bed with all those tubes stuck in his body and all the blinking and beeping machines registering his vitals. Dear God, he'd suffered a massive heart attack. He'd undergone major surgery not even two weeks ago.

He could've died.

That was the tipping point. The reality.

When it came down to it, family was the only thing that mattered.

The best way to prove that she wasn't simply his lit-tle princess who could be dismissed and kept *out of the way* was to prove that she was strong enough to handle even the toughest situations.

Situations like this.

She let the hurtful words roll off her and mustered her bravest smile. "I'm so sorry I'm late for the meeting. Maybe next time you'll let me know. How are you feeling, Dad? These are for you."

She placed the vase on his nightstand and leaned down to kiss him on the forehead.

"I'm fine. Just fine. In fact, as soon as I can get the nurses to unhook me from these contraptions, I'll go start training for a triathlon. Can you think of a better way to test the improvements being made to my old ticker?"

He laughed, but it sounded so hollow and sad to Caitlyn.

"Are you behaving yourself for the nurses?" she asked.

He waved her off. "What fun would that be? But Caitlyn, Brodie and I were just talking about Cowboy Country. Since I am on the mend, there's really no reason for you to stay in Horseback Hollow. It sounds like Brodie has everything under control. If you want to go back to Chicago, he can work with the staff we have in place to get the park up and running. That way you won't have to be inconvenienced."

"Inconvenienced? Is that what you think? Because it couldn't be further from the truth. I really want to stay."

Caitlyn took extra care to keep her tone light yet businesslike. She wasn't going to spar with him, even though verbal jousting sometimes seemed like their language of love.

And she refused to look at Brodie, even though she could feel his gaze on her—staring right through her, boring a hole with those maddeningly blue eyes.

It wasn't fair that one man could be so attractive and

such a double-crossing rat fink. Stronger words came to mind, actually. But she refused to lose control.

He was good at that—making her lose control—but she wasn't going to think about that right now. If she knew what was good for her she wouldn't think about it ever again.

"I thought you would be eager to get back to your research," her father said.

"Sir, if you don't mind my saying so, I could use Caitlyn's help. We're a good team."

She did a double take to make sure she was hearing him right.

She had. Apparently.

What was he up to? He even had the audacity to look sincere.

She had to bite her tongue to keep from telling her father the reason she didn't want to leave was because if Brodie were left to his own devices, they wouldn't be able to open because he would probably fire the entire Cowboy Country workforce.

How would he explain that to his Fortune family? Better yet, how would the Fortunes explain to the community that it was one of their own who had taken jobs away from the locals and given them to people from Lubbock or God only knew where else?

But she doubted her father would have much sympathy for a guy like Clark Ball.

It dawned on her that Brodie and her father were cut from a similar cloth. She was the lone wolf here. But she would stand her ground.

Her gut told her she could prove to the citizens of

Horseback Hollow that Cowboy Country USA and Moore Entertainment would be good neighbors.

She would start proving that at the Fortune barbecue on Friday night.

"Dad, Brodie and I do bring different strengths to the table. So don't worry about Cowboy Country. We have it under control. We will open the park on time. I promise."

Her dad didn't argue. That, more than anything, worried her. As he lay there in a hospital bed, he didn't seem to have any fight in him.

"Okay," he said. "I will leave it to the two of you."

The door opened. "Caitlyn, darling, I didn't realize you were here."

Her mother walked over and enfolded her in a hug.

"Hi, Mom. Have you met Brodie?"

Her mother smiled her gracious smile. "Yes. We met a few moments ago. As happy as I am to see you, I am afraid the two of you will have to leave because your father needs his rest."

When Caitlyn glanced back at her dad, he was lying there with his eyes closed.

Barbara walked Brodie and Caitlyn to the door and ushered them out into the hallway. She pulled the door closed, but took care so that it didn't make noise.

"May I bring you anything, Mom?"

Her mother had been practically living at the rehabilitation center since Caitlyn's father had been released from the hospital. She hadn't felt up to the task of caring for her husband on her own in these critical postsurgical days, but that didn't mean she wasn't attentive.

She spent every waking moment with him, only going home to sleep. And those brief breaks had only come after she was sure he was stable.

"No, thank you, sweetheart. It's so nice of you to offer, but I have everything I need right here. They bring me a dinner tray when they bring your father's. The food here is delicious. I know, who would've thought? But that was one of the criteria on your father's list before he would agree to come here. You know how he is about his food. I'm just glad he has agreed to change some of his ways so that the triple bypass will take. The doctor warned him that surgery alone would not be enough. He needed to make some major lifestyle adjustments."

Tears welled her mother's green eyes, and Caitlyn reached out and took her hand. Brodie was uncharacteristically quiet, standing there observing.

"Are you taking care of yourself, Mom? That's important."

She waved away Caitlyn's words with the flutter of her manicured hand and swiped at her tears. "Oh, I'm sorry for being so silly. Look at me. Well, actually, no, don't look at me." She laughed and Caitlyn did, too. Brodie maintained his stony silence.

"I'm sure the two of you have better things to do," she said sweetly. "You two go ahead and get out of here. Go get some lunch or go take care of business. Whatever it is, thank you both for taking the worry off Alden. It's such a blessing to have the two of you to count on."

Caitlyn hugged her mother.

"I love you, sweetheart," she said. She pulled away

then turned to Brodie and took his hand. "I just met you, but clearly Alden trusts you to run the business—and with Caitlyn, of course. And if Caitlyn thinks enough of you to work with you, you must be a fine young man."

"Thank you for saying that, Mrs. Moore. We make a good team."

They said their goodbyes. The two of them were quiet as they waited for the elevator.

It was slowly sinking in that Brodie had not only stood up for her, but he had also admitted that they each brought qualities to the job that complemented each other.

She had a flashback of the night they met and how they had complemented each other as they lay together under the stars. The memory was visceral, and she felt it all the way down to her toes.

When the elevator dinged and the doors opened, she realized that night was in the past. If she knew what was good for her, good for Cowboy Country, she would leave it there and leave those feelings alone.

She stole a glance at Brodie, remembering how good he had been to her father. In fact, the demeanor of the man she glimpsed talking to her father was closer to the Brodie who'd swept her off her feet the night of the wedding.

Which Brodie was real? The Brodie of that night or the one who had burst onto the scene at Cowboy Country? Or did it really matter?

Somewhere along the way someone had persuaded him he didn't have a heart. Despite his bravado, her instincts told her that wasn't true. Who had hurt him? Who had convinced him he was heartless?

She intended to find out and help Brodie see that holding a grudge didn't change the past, it simply clouded the future.

Chapter Six

The following Friday, Brodie arrived at Jeanne Marie and Deke's ranch a few minutes before people were due to start showing up at the barbecue. He had assured Caitlyn it was okay if she wanted to bow out of the dinner. He would've bowed out if it wouldn't have created an international incident.

With or without Caitlyn in attendance this evening, Brodie planned on telling the family Cowboy Country USA was his newest client and the reason he'd come back to Horseback Hollow.

In his line of work, he'd learned that it was all in the presentation. He wasn't there to ask their permission, because it certainly wasn't up for discussion. So he was simply going to mention it in a matter-of-fact way and remind everyone about the economic benefits that Cowboy Country could offer this tiny Texas town.

After all, his sister-in-law-to-be, Amber Rogers, was set to star in the park's Wild West Show, and Horseback Hollow wasn't the first small town to coexist with an outfit like Cowboy Country. Their presence certainly didn't spell imminent demise.

He didn't want to get that heavy-handed, and he hoped they wouldn't make it come to that, but he was prepared, just in case. Best-case scenario would be that he mentioned it, and the party went on as usual. He would certainly steer the conversation that way. He would remain in control of the situation, and everything would work out fine.

He parked his rented BMW next to a line of three pickup trucks and a large SUV. Noting his brother Oliver's car among the bunch, he grimaced, wishing he'd just confided in Oliver before breaking the news to the family as a whole. For moral support, if nothing else.

Ah, well. He was used to dealing with greater setbacks—if you could even call that a setback. Poor planning was his own fault.

Brodie grabbed the bottle of red wine and bouquet of spring flowers he had picked up at the superette on the way through town. His mother had taught him that one should never show up to a dinner party empty-handed. He supposed a backyard barbecue counted as a dinner party. Better to be safe than rude.

When he got out of the car, the first thing that hit him was the delicious smell of barbecue. His stomach rumbled, and he realized he was starving. He had to admit one of the things he had grown genuinely fond of in the United States was Texas barbecue.

As if his heart had a mind of its own, it wanted to add Caitlyn Moore to that best-loved list, too. Perhaps he was feeling more protective than fond… But were those feelings mutual?

Blinking away the thought, he let himself in the front door.

He still felt funny about not knocking, but the first time he had announced himself rather than just walking in, he'd had to endure a lecture about *family never closing their doors to family*. He was sternly reminded he was family and he was to simply let himself in, no matter what.

As if that made him feel more welcome.

They really didn't understand, did they? While his mum and stepfather, Simon, had been very good to him and his siblings, they had grown up in boarding schools and had spent many of their holidays away from their relations. This *one-big-happy-family, what's-mine-is-yours, no walls—or doors—*mentality was hard for him to digest even if his mum had adopted it wholeheartedly. For that matter, his half sister, Amelia, had come to Horseback Hollow for another Fortune wedding about a year ago, and had fallen in love with and married Quinn Drummond, a real-life cowboy. And of course, his brother Oliver was married to Shannon Singleton, a local woman he'd hired as nanny for his toddler son.

It was frightening. His family seemed to be taking to Horseback Hollow like rodeo riders to bulls. And then he inhaled more delicious smells coming from the kitchen and forgot everything except that he was famished, and the food for this dinner party—er, barbecue—smelled divine.

He followed his nose and the voices coming from the kitchen, where the unmistakable lilt of his mother's British accent contrasted with the gentle, down-home twang of his aunt's Texas drawl.

"Hello," he said as he stepped through the kitchen door.

"Brodie!" The two women greeted him with such enthusiasm it brought a smile to his lips. His aunt showed no signs of animosity or hints that she had spilled the beans about his association with Cowboy Country. He had to admit that his aunt was a good woman who could be trusted to keep her word. A twinge of remorse bit at him for doubting her.

"These are for you." He held out the wine and flowers.

"How sweet of you, darling," Jeanne Marie said. "Thank you."

As she took a large crystal vase down from one of the cupboards, she said over her shoulder, "Where is your *friend* Caitlyn?"

Her emphasis on the word *friend* didn't escape him. Neither did the glance that his aunt and his mother shared. Obviously, they had talked. Maybe he'd given Jeanne Marie too much credit too soon.

"Who is this Caitlyn?" His mother's blue eyes shone brightly. "I understand she's very pretty."

So they *had* talked.

Perhaps rather than waiting to tell the family as a

whole, it was better to nip this in the bud. Besides, whether or not Jeanne Marie had realized it, she'd just presented the perfect opportunity for him to casually talk about his association with Cowboy Country.

"It sounds like you already know quite a bit about her." Brodie cast a pointed look at his aunt. "Yes, she is exceptionally pretty."

"Why didn't you pick her up, like a gentleman would?" His mom frowned at him down her perfect aquiline nose.

"As I was trying to say, this is not a date. Caitlyn and I are purely platonic, Mum. We're work associates. Caitlyn Moore's family owns Cowboy Country USA, that amusement park they're building over off Buchanan Highway. Moore Entertainment hired Hayes Consulting to help with the opening because it seems that the majority of the people of Horseback Hollow have preconceived notions and have already made up their minds that pumping dollars into the local economy is a bad thing. I don't understand that kind of thinking, and I am happy to help them get off on a better foot."

The two women stared at him as if he had just slapped them. He supposed in a way he had. His words had come out harsher than he had intended, but sometimes it took a verbal slap to dislodge preconceived notions.

Still, he hated the thought of hurting either of them. Perhaps he had come on a little too strong. He knew Caitlyn would have certainly thought so.

Since she would be arriving shortly, he didn't want

to have poisoned the two matriarchs of the Fortune family against her.

"That sounded a little strong, and I apologize. If anyone was able to keep an open mind and consider the good that Moore Entertainment is bringing to Horseback Hollow, I know it would be the two of you. Auntie, you met Caitlyn. You spoke with her. You liked her well enough to invite her into your home even after you knew she was with Cowboy Country."

He paused to let his words sink in, and was relieved when he saw his aunt's demeanor soften.

"That's true," said Jeanne Marie. "I was impressed with Caitlyn's warmth and openness. She seems genuine. I think she will be willing to consider our opinions and suggestions."

"Exactly," Brodie said. "The harsh reality is Cowboy Country is a done deal. The county zoning board approved it, and the park is going to open whether you like it or not. Isn't it nice to know someone like Caitlyn Moore could be an ally?"

His mother stiffened.

As if her triplet sensed her discomfort, Jeanne Marie put a gentle hand on her sister's arm.

"He's right," Jeanne Marie said. "There's a lot of things I don't like about big business moving into Horseback Hollow. Those of us who oppose it are afraid it will change life as we know it. I've lived here all my life, and my hometown has always been my safe haven. It scares the ever-living daylights out of me to think that I might lose my sanctuary. And I know I speak for the majority of those who have opposed this park.

However, I suppose it's very old-fashioned and maybe even a little backward to think you can freeze a place in time. We fought the good fight to keep Moore Entertainment from moving in, but we lost. Amber is looking forward to being in the Wild West Show. We need to support her. Don't you think it's time that we look for proactive ways to coexist with them?"

"You're family, Brodie. I trust that you would not advocate for a business that didn't have our best interest at heart. I believe in you, and I believe you would never do anything to harm your family."

Now it was his turn to feel as if he'd been slapped, but it wasn't an angry, nasty blow. It was the strangest feeling. She believed in him. She trusted him. The weight and responsibility of the emotions that she had invested in him were heavy.

In his mind, as he backed away from the public spin he had just exercised on his aunt, he was left with a sinking feeling. For the first time in all the years that he had been in business, he really had to examine what he was promising. Because this time when he finished the job and moved on to the next assignment, his work would have lasting effects on the people he...cared about.

He felt like a fraud sitting there—and he wondered if his aunt might be subtly calling his bluff—because he knew he could go into Cowboy Country and make their persona look pretty, but Alden Moore was a businessman. All that good-neighbor hoo-ha amounted to a bunch of smoke and mirrors. Moore hadn't succeeded with his theme park empire by playing nice. Like any businessman worth his salt, he was all about the bottom line and what best benefited Moore Entertainment.

When he'd taken this job, he hadn't realized exactly how close to home the cyclone created by his spin would hit.

He had to do what he had to do. It was his motto. But this time it chafed.

"Besides," Jeanne Marie continued. She was smiling at her sister now. It was that look that Brodie had come to realize meant she was up to something. "There seems to be a charge in the atmosphere when Brodie and Caitlyn are together. I was watching you two at the art festival last weekend. He may claim they're simply platonic, but watch them together once she gets here. You'll see what I mean."

The barbecue took place in the spacious backyard of Jeanne Marie and Deke's home. It was a lovely space, behind the house, separate from the large area where the stage and barn were located for the wedding and reception.

While the barn had been newly renovated for the wedding, this part of the property radiated a lived-in family love. Strands of globe lights illuminated the generous patio area, casting a warm glow over twin trestle tables that seated twenty-six people each. Both tables were full, loaded with food, friends and family—brothers and sisters and nieces and nephews.

This shindig was a fraction of the size of the wedding she'd attended in February—and much more personal. She met Brodie's cousins, Jeanne Marie and Deke's children Stacey and her husband, rancher Colton Foster; Jude and his wife, Gabriella Mendoza; Liam and Julia, who worked at the Hollows Cantina; and Christopher and Kinsley, who worked for the Fortune Foundation. They were the couples who had gotten married at the wedding in February. It was also good to see Amber Rogers, who worked for Cowboy Country and was engaged to Brodie's half brother Jensen.

There were so many Fortunes, it was difficult to keep track of everyone.

She was both relieved and a little terrified when Jeanne Marie directed her and Brodie to sit across from each other at the table, at the same end as Josephine, Deke and herself.

This feast looked like something out of a magazine —one that exemplified family living at its best. There were barbecued ribs and sliced brisket, fresh corn on the cob, green beans, sliced tomatoes, fresh potato salad, coleslaw, baked beans and cornbread. And that was all Caitlyn could fit on her plate. There were other dishes, too, but she didn't want to look like a glutton. She was nervous enough as it was.

When she'd arrived and parked her car in front of the house amidst at least twenty other vehicles, it occurred to her that she wasn't completely sure she was walking into friendly territory. It was common knowledge that the Fortunes were opposed to Cowboy Country. Yet, here she was, accepting the invitation to their family dinner. For all she knew, she might be walking into the angry mob with its torches and pitchforks. But her gut told her that probably wasn't the case. Jeanne Marie seemed levelheaded. Actually, she seemed lovely. And Brodie was family.

She and Brodie worked together. Business was business, but family was sacred.

So this seemed more personal.

Still, she knew she'd be kidding herself to believe that her invitation didn't stem from a little bit of curiosity on their part. The Fortunes had proven that they could be civil when they had invited her parents to the wedding. A family wedding seemed like a much bigger deal than a dinner.

The wedding.

Her stomach flip-flopped at the memory of it. This was the place where it all began.

And, if she was perfectly honest with herself, the place where both she and Brodie had intended for it to end. What happened under the stars stayed under the stars.

She would be doing herself a big favor to remember that once he was done with this project and they had successfully opened the park, he would be on his way back to London or wherever his next conquest led him. Caitlyn's heart tightened at the thought, but she dismissed it.

Tonight's visit was a means to an end—to help Cowboy Country get off on a more secure footing; to get the job done. She was ready and willing to be questioned. Checking her posture, she walked up to the door and took the plunge.

After the whirlwind of introductions, here she sat enjoying the most delicious barbecued brisket she'd ever tasted in her life. She waited for one of the Fortunes to turn the talk to Cowboy Country.

It happened as soon as there was a lull in conversation.

"I was sorry to hear that your daddy had a heart attack," said Jeanne Marie. "How is he doing?"

Caitlyn set down her fork and wiped the corners of her mouth with her napkin. "Thank you for asking. The surgery went well, and he is on the road to recovery. It takes a long time to heal after open-heart surgery."

Everyone at her end of the table nodded solemnly.

"What does that mean for the opening of Cowboy Country?" Deke asked. "Will you push it back?"

Okay. There it is. Here we go.

She glanced at Brodie, who must've taken it as his assignment to answer the question.

"We will absolutely open the park on time," he said unapologetically. There was a little bit of an edge to his voice.

Caitlyn was afraid they might mistake his stance for hostility—or a challenge.

"I'm not sure how well you know my father, but he has several roller-coaster-based theme parks throughout the United States. While he loves his roller coasters, this park is special to him. It's personal. He's always been a big John Wayne fan and a cowboy at heart. Cowboy Country is a bucket list item for him. He almost died when he had that heart attack, and I want to make sure that he sees his dream come true."

The elder Fortunes exchanged glances.

"If you'd rather not talk about this at the dinner

table," Caitlyn said, "I completely understand. However, if you don't mind, I would love to know if you have any questions about the park or if you wouldn't mind sharing what it is that you're opposed to."

For a moment the group at their end of the table didn't say anything. Caitlyn held her breath as she listened to the buzz of cicadas and the murmur of other conversation going on around them. The rest of the dinner party was blissfully oblivious to the serious turn of their conversation.

Deke cleared his throat and sat forward in his chair, but Jeanne Marie placed a gentle hand on his and said, "Horseback Hollow is my family's home. It's the only home I've ever known. It's a safe place where just about everyone knows everyone else. I suppose objections around town have stemmed from fear, from people not wanting Horseback Hollow to change or to be swallowed up by a large conglomerate."

Okay, it was out on the table.

"We understand and respect your concerns," Brodie said. "All I'm asking is that you keep an open mind to the good Moore Entertainment and Cowboy Country can bring to Horseback Hollow. Think about the economic upturn, the money that it stands to pump into the local economy. This really is a win-win situation."

"Moore Entertainment has prided itself on giving back to the community. We host school programs, scholarships and family-friendly work-sharing opportunities. As a matter of fact, for the past several years, Moore Entertainment has been named on *Forbes Magazine*'s top twenty-five family-friendly list for work and life balance. We really do pride ourselves on being good neighbors in the community. And Cowboy Country could be my father's reason to live."

Caitlyn clamped her lips shut. She hadn't meant to say that last part out loud, even if it was the truth. It wasn't a very businesslike thing to say. She was opening her mouth to apologize when the looks on the Fortunes' faces registered. She saw something new.

Empathy and understanding.

If it took everything she had she would make sure Moore Entertainment held up its end of the bargain. Cowboy Country *would* be a good neighbor.

Jeanne Marie nodded, and Caitlyn understood that this part of the conversation was over.

"Could I tempt you with another piece of cornbread, Caitlyn?" She smiled, and Caitlyn smiled back.

"Yes, please. It's delicious."

"Be sure you save some room for dessert," said Josephine. "My sister makes the best red-velvet cake you've ever tasted. I have put on nearly ten pounds since I moved here."

She was so grateful for the life her parents had given her. She'd never wanted for anything—except for a sibling or five, like Brodie had.

And cousins? He had so many cousins she couldn't keep track. No wonder the wedding's guest list had been so long. Inviting the family would've made for a lively, full house, but then when you included everyone in the community and you managed to make room for your adversaries…

Adversaries. It was such an ugly word. Caitlyn was so happy the Fortunes and the Moores were on the road to being allies, but if she had anything to do with it, they would call each other friends. Because tonight, the only torches burning were the ones that lined the patio's perimeter.

Now that dinner was done, Caitlyn was surprised by how little conversation there had been about Moore Entertainment and Cowboy Country. In fact, all that had come up was that Brodie and Caitlyn were working together to open the park. There had been no gasps or digs or declarations about how unwelcome Moore Entertainment and its associates were.

Instead, this big, boisterous Texas family had so much to say about everything else that each one had a hard time getting a word in edgewise. They laughed and talked over each other and enjoyed the meal and each other's company in a way that made Caitlyn feel humbled to be a guest at their table.

Now, as she was helping clear the table, she kept stealing glances at Brodie, who was standing across the patio talking to his brother Oliver and his wife, Shannon. Brodie's gaze snared hers, and he smiled at her from across the way.

There it was again, that attraction that was so powerful it threatened to consume her. Her heart hammered against her breastbone as she smiled back.

"You two are adorable." The voice caught her by surprise, and she accidentally knocked over a glass of water as she whirled around to see who was talking to her. It was Amelia Fortune Chesterfield Drummond. Brodie's sister.

"If you don't mind me saying as much, the two of you could be exceptionally good for each other."

Caitlyn felt heat blossom from the neckline of her scoop-neck dress and climb its way up her neck to her cheeks.

Caitlyn chuckled. "Your brother and I are just friends. And work associates. Really, that's all we are."

Protesting too much, Caitlyn?

She ducked her head as she grabbed a napkin off the table to mop up the spilled water.

"If you say so," Amelia said, not sounding the least bit convinced. "I say just give it time. I know he's not easy to deal with sometimes. He puts up such a hard exterior, but please believe me—deep down he has a heart of gold."

Obviously, it hadn't been Amelia who had convinced him he didn't have a heart.

She seemed to have a pretty good read on her brother.

"He's just been through some…*stuff* in his life," she said. "Circumstances have made him that way."

And she seemed to think she had a pretty good read on Brodie and her as a couple. Caitlyn's heart turned over at the thought. Drawing in a quick breath, she straightened and followed Amelia's gaze to where Brodie was laughing with Oliver and Shannon. It was the most relaxed she'd ever seen him.

What had happened to that beautiful man to make him wear such heavy emotional armor? Was it a woman?

Had he given his heart to someone who treated it so carelessly that he'd closed himself off?

Caitlyn knew how that felt. She'd almost married the guy.

But what was worse, she realized as she stood there feeling alive for the first time in what seemed like years, not only had she allowed the guy to crush her heart, she had allowed him to sweep away all the broken bits and pieces, too. For the longest time, she'd been left with only an empty hole. But Eric had missed some of the pieces, and slowly, they were beginning to grow back together and fill that spot in which she thought she'd never feel again.

If a woman had hurt Brodie, she hoped he wouldn't allow her to continue to rob him of one of life's best pleasures…falling in love.

Amelia knew what had happened to him. And it took every ounce of strength Caitlyn possessed to keep from asking her for details. Because if she did, Amelia would know she'd hit upon something. That Caitlyn and Brodie *could* be good together. Caitlyn had already experienced that live in person, that very first night, before names were exchanged and they knew they'd play a much bigger role in each other's lives.

Brodie glanced her way again, and the smoldering flame she saw in his eyes—as if Amelia weren't standing right there taking it all in—startled her and stoked a gently growing fire deep inside her.

"I hope you'll be patient with him, because I can see that the two of you have a very strong connection."

Amelia must have sensed that Caitlyn didn't know

what to say. After all, what does one say when her head knows good and well she should keep things all business, but her heart and other more vulnerable parts of her body are aching for something completely different—things that should be completely taboo?

"It was the same way with my husband, Quinn. I can assure you, a love like that is worth the time and patience."

Amelia's words made Caitlyn's senses spin. To steady herself, she began stacking plates on the tray.

"You are our guest tonight. You shouldn't be clearing dishes. Go enjoy yourself, please."

Amelia gave an anything but settled glance in Brodie's direction. In fact, it was almost a nod.

"After enjoying that delicious dinner, I can't leave all the work to someone else," said Caitlyn. "I insist on helping."

"Well, in that case, I'll help, too." Amelia laughed. "Otherwise you're going to make me look bad."

As the two of them headed toward the kitchen, Caitlyn wondered if Amelia had any idea of the ringing impact her words had made.

"Married life does seem to be agreeing with you," Brodie said to Oliver and Shannon.

The couple looked at each other with such adoration he had to look away. He glanced over at the table where Caitlyn had been talking to Amelia.

They weren't there anymore.

His gaze combed the area, and he glimpsed the two of them as they disappeared inside the back door that led to the kitchen, each of them holding a tray loaded with dishes. Brodie took a step in that direction as the door banged shut behind them. He wished he would've noticed sooner, and he would've been there to help.

"We've never been happier," Oliver said. "I highly recommend it."

"Caitlyn is so nice." Shannon hitched little Ollie up on her hip.

"Yes, she is," he said. He knew what she meant, and he knew he should clarify that they were strictly platonic—or at least they were now.

His cousin, Galen Fortune Jones, must've overheard Oliver and Shannon's less than subtle verbal nudging.

"She may be nice, but some men just aren't cut out for the husband thing."

Oliver and Shannon made protesting noises.

"Those men obviously haven't met the right women," said Shannon. "Or they are not attracted to women. But hey, I'm not judging. I'm all for live and let live."

Galen frowned. "Believe me, I am attracted to women. That's exactly my point. I'm attracted to *women*. Lots of women. I see no reason to limit myself to just one. And I know Brodie feels the same way. Hence the Enduring Bachelorhood Club of Horseback Hollow. Welcome to the club, cousin."

Galen guffawed and held out his fist for a bump. Brodie complied, but his heart wasn't really in it.

There was a time when he might've been president of an Enduring Bachelorhood Club, but tonight it seemed like the last place he wanted to be. It just seemed…sad.

Someone put some music on, and several people

started dancing. Oliver took Shannon's hand and pulled her a few steps away from Brodie and Galen.

"We will leave you two enduring bachelors alone," he said. "My wife and I have better things to do."

He pulled Shannon into his arms, and the two of them began swaying to the music, lost in their own little world.

He wasn't really in the mood to stay and discuss enduring bachelorhood with his cousin. "I'm going to go into the kitchen and get something to drink. May I bring you something?"

Galen held up the beer in his hand. "Nah, I'm good, thanks. I'll catch you later, bro."

In the kitchen, Caitlyn was helping Amelia scoop leftovers into plastic containers. His mother was washing dishes, and Jeanne Marie was drying them.

The buzz of conversation—something about the secret ingredient in Jeanne Marie's red-velvet-cake recipe—stopped when he entered the room.

"I suppose the ingredient is not a secret any longer if you tell everyone," he said.

"Look who's come to help us," said his mother.

"I have a feeling he didn't come in here to help us," said Amelia, a knowing smile spreading across her face.

"She's right," said Brodie. "I've come to rescue Caitlyn from a life of servitude."

"Run," said Amelia, taking the serving spoon out of Caitlyn's hand. "Run while you can. Save yourself."

"Absolutely," said Jeanne Marie. She shook her head. "Where are my manners? I was so enjoying talking to you that I kept you in the kitchen far too long. You two run along and have some fun. Go on now. Skedaddle."

"It was such a lovely meal," Caitlyn said. "I hate to leave you with the mess."

"We won't hear of it," said Josephine. "You've already done more than your share. More than I can say for some people."

She arched a brow at Brodie.

"We'll go find Galen and send him right in," said Brodie. "I understand he's looking for something to do."

In a stage whisper he said to Caitlyn, "We'd better make a run for it while we can."

He offered her his arm, and she took it, a strange smile on her face.

Once they were back outside, a slow country song came on.

"Dance with me?"

He didn't give her a chance to refuse. He simply wrapped his arms around her, and they joined the others who had turned the patio into an after-dinner dance floor and began swaying to the music.

"Your family is wonderful," she whispered. "Not nearly as scary as I thought they'd be."

"You're brave," he said, inhaling deeply as she leaned in close. Her scent and the feel of her in his arms took him back to that first night. His body responded and the base, most primal part of him wanted to ask her if she wanted to take a stroll down meteor lane. But there wasn't a meteor shower tonight, and holding her like this felt more intimate than taking her back to the field by the pond and peeling off her denim jacket and that sexy green sundress and claiming the prize underneath. "Most of the time they still scare me."

Not that he didn't want to claim that prize.

Holding her like this felt like ten giant leaps forward. Especially when she looked up at him. For a moment he could've sworn he glimpsed forever in her eyes. He pulled her closer so that it wouldn't slip away.

All he had to do was lower his head a few inches, and his lips would be on hers, but she said, "I need to go. Will you walk me to my car?"

The distance and perspective he gained while she was getting her handbag and saying thank-you and good-night to his family was a godsend.

He'd almost kissed her. Right there on the patio in front of anyone who might've been paying attention, which was probably more people than would've owned up to it.

He'd gotten lost in the moment. Lost in a wonderful evening where she had been magnificent with his family. She'd won them over with her grace and ease.

This wasn't a personal victory; this was about getting the job done. It was a victory for Cowboy Country. Now that they were on the right track, he needed to keep his mind on the job and his hands off his boss's daughter.

As he walked Caitlyn to her car, she must've sensed the shift in him.

"Why does intimacy scare you, Brodie?"

"Intimacy doesn't scare me." He crossed his arms.

"What happened to you to make you put up such a wall?"

Nobody had ever asked him the question. He knew

the answer, but he couldn't talk about it. Because that would mean he'd have to return to dark, emotional places he swore he'd never visit again.

"What's in the past can't be changed," he said. "There's no sense in rehashing it."

She opened her car door and slid behind the wheel.

"Sometimes the only way to exorcise your demons is to face them."

"They're not demons unless you allow them to get the best of you."

She shook her head, and there was so much pity in her eyes, he had to look away.

"Suit yourself," she said as she started the car.

What could he say to that?

Nothing.

Instead, he opted for watching the taillights of Caitlyn's car grow dimmer as she drove away.

Chapter Seven

All week long Brodie had been furious with himself. What the bloody hell was the matter with him?

At the barbecue Friday night, he'd gotten swept up in the moment.

All weekend long he had tried to tell himself he'd simply been jazzed because Caitlyn had won over his family so easily and naturally. But a nagging little bugger of a voice deep inside kept insisting that was wrong. That he wasn't being honest with himself. That he was terminally attracted to Caitlyn Moore.

Brodie tried to remind himself of his A-number-one rule: *do not sleep with the clients*. Now amended to include: *do not kiss the clients*.

Before, that had always been a given, along with *do not mix business with pleasure*.

He would've been wise to have talked Caitlyn out of attending the barbecue, but he usually didn't associate family gatherings with pleasure. This woman had a way of inserting herself into places in his life that made him…uncomfortable. And now she was asking questions—personal questions. Questions about what made him tick, what made him so damn defensive.

Personal relationships made him defensive. If she was so bloody intuitive, why couldn't she figure that out without grilling him?

What was it about Caitlyn Moore that had his self-control puddling in a pool at his feet?

And then, even against his best judgment, he found himself stepping over that pool like a madman, possessed with the need to get closer to her.

Brodie simply wasn't cut out to fall in love. And Caitlyn…she was so family-oriented.

This had the potential to be one hell of a bloody mess, didn't it?

Granted, she was a beautiful woman, but he'd worked with plenty of pretty women before, and he'd never had this much trouble keeping his mind on the job.

It was just about sex. Nothing more. It was some crazy chemical reaction—what did they call it? Pheromones? Whatever it was, it was making him lose control. And there was nothing Brodie Fortune Hayes loathed more than being out of control.

Logic told him the sooner he could get back to London, the better off everyone would be. But the part of his brain that was still working reminded him that his contract dictated that he still had more than two weeks here in Horseback Hollow.

Really, if he thought about it—and kept his mind on the job—it wasn't a lot of time to get done what he needed to do to get this park up and running to Alden Moore's satisfaction and secure the recommendation for the Tokyo project.

It really was quite simple. He needed to quit thinking about Caitlyn in any terms other than business. Because doing that was making things harder on him than the job needed to be.

In that vein, this morning he had gotten up extra early—well, if truth be told he hadn't been able to sleep—and got into the office early enough to avoid Monday-morning office coffee chat. He'd brought in his own coffee in his stainless-steel travel mug. It was his own brew from his French press, and it was head and shoulders over the dirty dishwater from the coffee machine in the break room. It would also buy him a little more time and give him that extra caffeinated edge he needed to see Caitlyn this morning.

He wasn't kidding himself; he wasn't pretending he could avoid her all day. He would have to see her eventually. Avoiding her would be unprofessional and downright juvenile.

That's what he was thinking when Caitlyn burst into his office, all smiles and electric energy.

"I've finally figured out how to fix the park," she said, those green eyes so bright and lovely it hurt him to look at them.

"You figured it out?" His voice sounded as exhausted as he felt. "Please enlighten me."

"Yes, I have. What's wrong with you? You're scowling."

He sat back in his chair. "Nothing's wrong with me, thank you. I was in the middle of something, and you interrupted."

She frowned at him. "I'm sorry. Should I come back later? Although really, this can't wait."

He crossed his arms and put his palms in the air. "I'm waiting."

He wasn't sure if she rolled her eyes at him or simply shrugged off his sarcasm—probably both—but it was obvious she was not allowing him to bring her down.

"What Cowboy Country needs is the perspective of genuine cowboys. It needs the heart of folks like the Fortunes—your family. And we need to draft a solid plan of how we intend to give back to the community. Once that's done, I want to present it to the community at the next town hall meeting. If we can get on the meeting agenda, we can have an open forum and encourage an exchange with the citizens of Horseback Hollow. I want your mother and aunt to use their influence to get us on the agenda. I almost called you this weekend to tell you about this, but I didn't. Maybe I should have, because obviously you didn't have a very good weekend."

Maybe she should have? Did she realize what she was suggesting?

No. Because she probably wasn't suggesting what he had in mind. The thought took his dark mood down another notch.

He dragged his hands down his face, trying to scrub some of the bad out of his mood. How could she be so chipper on a Monday morning? On *this* Monday morning, after *that* Friday night?

Obviously, she hadn't taken the dance or the near-miss kiss to heart the way he had.

That was sobering.

And a little bit liberating.

"I'm sorry," he said. "I had a rough night. I didn't sleep very well."

She studied him for a moment, and he would've given his BMW if he could've known what she was thinking.

"Everything okay?" Her expression changed from upbeat to concern. "Your family didn't change their mind about Cowboy Country, did they? I thought everything went so well."

"No. No worries. My family loves you. How about we start over? Or at least let me start with talking to Jeanne Marie about getting us on the next town-meeting agenda. If we do get to address the citizens, it will put us one step closer to recruiting the genuine cowboys. But let's tackle the town meeting first."

Caitlyn was onto something. She could feel it in her bones.

If the Fortunes were willing to come around, then the rest of the town couldn't be too hard to win over. Maybe it was optimism, but Caitlyn was sure that they could do it. Especially after Jeanne Marie had agreed to help them get a place on the town meeting agenda.

She'd also shared a nugget of information that had the potential to be golden: apparently the on-property hotel her father had planned to build—the Cowboy Condos—was one of the biggest sticking points with some of the staunchest adversaries. Jeanne Marie couldn't tell them why, but with a little bit of internal digging, she was able to find the name of an investor who had pulled out of the deal—Hank Harvey, a venture capitalist from Dallas. He was going to be in Lubbock on Wednesday and had agreed to drive to Horseback Hollow to meet Caitlyn and Brodie at the stalled jobsite to talk about what went wrong.

According to Brodie, who had talked to him, Mr. Harvey was prepared to give them an earful.

Caitlyn hated to jump to snap judgments, but Hank Harvey rubbed her the wrong way from the moment he'd opened his mouth. It was eight o'clock in the morning, and his breath reeked of alcohol, and that wasn't even the worst of it.

Strike one: when she introduced herself and offered her hand for him to shake, this textbook Texas good ol' boy raked his gaze down her body as he gave her fingertips a lackluster press.

"Ma'am." Now his gaze veered somewhere over her right shoulder. She wanted to turn around to see who he was looking at. Before she could, he turned and vigorously pumped Brodie's hand with a solid man-grip and slapped him on the back.

"Brodie Fortune Hayes. Good to meet ya, man. Are you kin to *that* bunch of Fortunes?"

"Guilty as charged," Brodie said.

As the *boys* exchanged pleasantries, Caitlyn glanced around the empty construction site. Located on the east side of the property, the parcel was far enough away from the park so it would not interfere with business as usual. The two ventures were separate, but the original intent had been for them to feed each other. Out-of-town guests coming to the park would stay at the hotel, and exhausted revelers, tired out after a long day of Cowboy Country fun—or those wanting to extend their visit— could book a room and stay right on the property.

After the construction had come to a halt, the work-site, which had sat untouched for several weeks, had been secured with chain-link fencing. The leveled ground was mottled by the elements and littered with trash; weeds grew amidst the infrastructure, which the workers had begun to build before the investors had pulled out. The sky was overcast, and it was a lit-tle cooler today than it had been recently. The clouds seemed to cast everything around them in gloomy shades of gray. As it stood, this part of the property looked like a razed ghost town.

It was a little sad and eerie.

"So you're from London, are ya now?" Hank asked, hitching the waistband of his blue jeans over his ample belly. "The wife keeps pushing for me to take her there, but Vegas is more my style. No offense to you and your queen and all. I'm tellin' you, if ya know the right peo-ple you can get in on some pretty sweet gambling jun-kets in Vegas. Let me know if you're interested. I can hook ya up."

Okay... Let's stay on topic.

"Mr. Harvey," Caitlyn said. "We really appreciate you meeting us out here today. I know you have a plane to catch in a couple of hours. So we won't keep you long. We are looking into the possibility of resuming construction on the Cowboy Condos. Apparently, there was a problem that caused you and the other investors to withdraw support? Brodie and I are trying to piece together what happened."

Hank pulled his cell phone out of his back pocket and looked at something displayed on the screen. He didn't answer her.

Maybe she needed to be more specific.

"Would you mind telling us the reason you withdrew your support from the project?"

He typed something on his phone with his fat thumbs.

"Uh, yeah. It wasn't a..." he muttered as he typed.

When he looked up—strike two: his gaze landed and stayed on her breasts.

"Uh, yeah. It just wasn't a..." His voice trailed off. "Wasn't a good investment. Didn't work for me."

Caitlyn crossed her arms over her chest, shielding herself from his invasion of privacy. Brodie must've noticed, because he stepped slightly in front of her and diverted the creep's attention.

"What didn't work for you, exactly?" he asked.

"All kinds of things," Hank murmured. "So now, do you actually live in London? I hear it's one of the most expensive cities in the world."

"Yes, I own a flat in Notting Hill. Mr. Harvey, would

you mind being more specific? Why did the project not work for you? What about it caused you to pull your investment? We need to know so that we can make corrections going forward."

"Hank. Please call me Hank. Mr. Harvey is my dad. I'm Hank."

"Fair enough. Hank it is." Caitlyn could see Brodie's profile. He smiled at Hank's nonsense.

Caitlyn wanted to stomp on Harvey's toe. Why was he being so chummy with Brodie when he was having a difficult time answering her questions with complete sentences?

Then came the coup de grâce.

Strike three: misogynistic creep not only turned his back on her, he actually clapped Brodie on the back and motioned with his fat head for Brodie to walk with him.

And Brodie did. Giving him the benefit of the doubt, he cast a remorseful glance back at Caitlyn. From that glance she read, *Bear with me. This might be the only way to get the info out of the guy.*

Caitlyn should've stomped his foot when she'd had the chance.

"Shoddy construction?" Caitlyn asked once she and Brodie were back in the office. "What the heck is that supposed to mean?"

Brodie could tell she was irritated. Personally, he'd wanted to deck the guy when he'd noticed him ogling Caitlyn.

"That's what he said. I'm sorry. Don't shoot the messenger. He said he didn't want his name associated with an inferior product. When Cisco Mendoza withdrew from the project, Harvey said he was done."

She stammered a bit. "Inferior product? How—What was inferior?"

Cisco Mendoza was engaged to his cousin, Jeanne Marie's youngest daughter Delaney Fortune Jones, but Brodie hadn't had the opportunity to get to know him since Cisco had only been in town almost as short a time as Brodie had. From what he understood, Mendoza had been a real-estate developer in Miami, who had been handpicked to head up Cowboy Country's hotel division—to act as a rainmaker of sorts and bring in investors. From where Brodie sat, it seemed Mendoza had done more damage than good. That's one of the reasons Brodie hadn't been keen on talking to him about Cowboy Country. Brodie needed Alden Moore as a client. He wanted to come in and assess the situation with fresh eyes and not be influenced by someone who had left with a bad taste in his mouth.

Apparently, after Cisco left, operations at the park had gone from bad to worse. Shortly after that, his supervisor—a man named Kent Stephens—had thrown in the towel, and then Alden Moore had suffered the heart attack.

It was too soon to pump Alden for more information. It was a sore subject, and Brodie didn't want to bring him any stress. He had been hired to fix things, not tally up the problems and present them to Moore.

In fact, wouldn't it be nice if, in addition to opening the park, he could sort out the issues with the Cowboy Condos and present Alden with a new workable plan?

"I'll talk to Cisco and ask him to level with us," Brodie said.

Caitlyn nodded. "Yes, please. There has to be more to the story than what Harvey Wallbanger is telling us."

Brodie snorted at the name.

The color spiked in Caitlyn's cheeks.

"Not only did the jerk completely marginalize me, but if what he's saying is true, I'm really worried about my father. Brodie, why would a man who has built his name in the theme-park industry settle for something of bad quality? It just doesn't make sense."

Brodie had wondered the same thing himself.

"And did you see him staring at my—" She gestured toward her bodice. "He wouldn't even look me in the eye."

Brodie cleared his throat. "Well, I wasn't going to say anything, but since you brought it up, yes, I did notice, and I wanted to punch the guy."

Her face went soft, and her lips curved up at the corners. "You would've done that for me? Defended my honor?"

He nodded.

"But you do realize I hate violence. So you did the right thing by distracting him instead."

They sat there in silence for a moment. Brodie stared at his clenched fist and then flexed his fingers because she'd just said she didn't like violence. He didn't, either. Yet he'd been perfectly prepared to defend her.

"At least the guy left us with some information to go on," Caitlyn said.

Brodie looked up and fixed his gaze on hers. He

didn't find it difficult to look at those beautiful eyes. They were actually quite mesmerizing.

Through the hazy fog that was addling his brain, he heard himself saying, "Don't worry. I'll talk with Cisco and find out the rest of the story. We'll find a way to make this right."

Chapter Eight

A knock on the frame of her open office door made Caitlyn look up from her computer. When she saw Brodie standing there, her stomach did a low flip that made her breath catch.

"Hi," she said, noticing the rolled-up papers he held. They looked like blueprints.

"Hi, do you have a minute?" He smiled. "I have good news."

She motioned him in. "I'd give you an entire day for some good news. Please, do tell."

"Let's go over here where I can roll out these." With the blueprints, he gestured toward a small conference table set up on the far side of the rectangular room.

"Are these what I hope they are?" she asked.

"If you mean the plans for the Cowboy Condos,

you're spot on." She watched as he began spreading them out on the table.

"Where did you get them?" she asked.

"I made a couple of calls late yesterday and got in touch with Cisco Mendoza. He dropped them off and filled in some of the missing pieces."

She narrowed her eyes and cocked her head. "You met with Mendoza without me?"

Brodie held up his hand. "I did, but don't get upset. He left for business in Red Rock this morning. He's training for his new job with the Fortune Foundation. If I hadn't gotten together with him last night, he wouldn't have been available until next week."

"You should've called me."

"Really? You wanted me to call you after hours?"

Yes, I wish you would.

She could've read so much into his gaze, his tone, that question. Instead, she put her hands in her lap and squeezed them together so tightly that her nails dug into her skin. That touchstone brought her back to her senses.

"Of course, you can always call me…"

But she let the words hang there so he could form his own conclusion.

"Next time I will."

He smiled at her, and there was that instant rush attraction that pulled her right in. She could've sworn he felt it, too.

She smiled and looked away. "I'm surprised Mendoza was willing to meet with you on such short notice. Because from what I understand, he didn't leave here a very happy man."

"Obviously, you don't know that Cisco is engaged to my cousin Delaney," he said.

Caitlyn laughed. "Why am I not surprised? Is anyone in this town not related to the Fortunes?"

Brodie considered the question. "Not many people."

"Wait," Caitlyn said. "Cisco and Delaney were not at the barbecue, were they?"

"No. They were in Miami packing up Cisco's apartment. He's moving to Horseback Hollow permanently. They just got back, and Cisco left for Red Rock this morning. That's why last night's meeting was more like a hand-off of the blueprints than an actual meeting. He brought me the blueprints and told me his side of the story. Really, there wasn't much to tell."

Caitlyn blinked at him, reality eclipsing the attraction she'd felt just seconds ago.

"I thought you said you had good news."

"Sometimes good news comes in small packages. Mendoza didn't have much to say, but what he said was important. He didn't back out because of shoddy construction. It had nothing to do with the quality of the hotel. It was the style that had everyone in an uproar. Apparently, the architect your father hired had designed something very kitschy—buildings shaped like cowboy hats with cowboy-boot-shaped windows, that sort of thing."

Brodie raised his eyebrows for emphasis, and Caitlyn cringed.

"That sounds dreadful."

She crossed her arms and thought about it for a moment.

"However, I hate to admit that my dad may have

gotten a little bit carried away. You have no idea how this cowboy obsession of his can take over his better judgment. Never in a business sense, but sometimes the kitschy-tacky knows no bounds."

Brodie laughed. "Well, it's good to know that even the master can get it wrong once or twice."

"Yeah, he'd never admit that. I'm sure he would give his eyeteeth to stay in a cowboy-hat-shaped hotel."

Looking past Brodie's good humor, she saw true reverence in his eyes. He really did respect her dad. For some reason she found it a little curious given his tendency to keep his own family at arm's length.

She remembered what Amelia had said and had the urge to ask him about it. But he changed the subject, and the moment was lost.

"Apparently, Cisco Mendoza left because of creative differences. He knew one of the main reasons the locals were opposed to the park was because of the kitsch factor. He'd had a whole new set of plans drawn up, but his supervisor, Kent Stephens, refused to take the plans to the next level. Mendoza seems to believe that Stephens was in bed with the original architect, and that's why he put up roadblocks to keep Mendoza's plans from your father. The investors left when Mendoza pulled out. Stephens left about a week later, and then that's when things happened with your father."

"It all makes sense," Caitlyn said. "You said he had the plans drawn up?"

Brodie nodded.

"Did he happen to mention the name of the architect?" she asked.

"He did one better."

Brodie lifted the cowboy hat blueprints to reveal another set underneath.

"Take a look at this. This design is much earthier, a better complement to the feel of Horseback Hollow. Cisco ran it by some of the locals, and they were much more amenable to something like this that better fit into the landscape. In fact, if landscaped properly, it would probably almost disappear rather than sitting out like a dozen giant cowboy hats that somebody forgot to put away."

"This makes me so happy," she said. "Having the blueprints already drawn up and basically endorsed by the town puts us so much further ahead than I ever dreamed possible at this point."

"Glad I could help," he said.

They were standing so close to each other *looking at the blueprint* that their arms were touching. She stood there for a moment reveling in the nearness of him. She knew this was dangerous; she knew pushing this defied all logic.

Yet she moved just a fraction of an inch closer so she could feel the heat of him against her.

"I think we need to celebrate," she said.

If she turned just so to her left and he did the same, they'd be standing face-to-face, close enough for their lips to touch, for their bodies to be flush.

"I vote for that." His voice was deep and raspy, the sound sweet as syrup. "What did you have in mind?"

She knew what she had in mind, and she was fairly certain it was exactly what he had in mind, too.

Her desk phone rang, ruining the moment.

"Are you going to get that?" he asked.

Of course she was.

She moved away from him and felt an almost palpable change of altitude.

"Yes, Janie," she said, trying not to sound annoyed with this woman, who was only doing her job.

"Les Campbell is on the line. May I put him through?"

"Yes, please."

Please don't let this be bad news.

Seconds later, Les said, "Hello, Ms. Moore. The Twin Rattlers coaster is ready for its inaugural run, and we were wondering if you'd like to take a ride?"

Oh, good!

She glanced at Brodie, who had his back to her, leafing through the pages of the blueprints. She wondered idly if he knew how to read the pages beyond the elevation on the first page.

He was a man of so many talents…her gaze followed the line of his broad shoulders. He was wearing a white dress shirt tucked into trousers that did a fine job showcasing his…assets.

Caitlyn tore her gaze away. She was as bad as Hank Harvey.

No, she wasn't. This was different.

Completely different.

"I'd love to, Les. Thanks so much for thinking of me. Oh, and Les, there will be two of us. We will see you in fifteen minutes."

"Sounds good, ma'am."

She wished people would stop calling her *ma'am.*

It made her feel old. But she supposed it was a sign of respect. Besides, Les was one of the nicer members of the crew, and she appreciated how hard he worked and the way he went out of his way to be nice—not just to her, but to others, too.

She hung up the phone.

"Come on," she said to Brodie. "Let's go. I know how we're going to celebrate."

He turned around and arched a brow at her. A dimple winked at her from his cheeks. "And what exactly are we going to do?"

"We're going to ride a roller coaster."

His smile faded, replaced by a *you've got to be kidding me* look.

"Um. No, thank you. You go ahead, though."

"Brodie, it's the inaugural ride of the Twin Rattler. This is the big-ticket ride. The moneymaker that's going to draw in people from all over the country. It's an honor to do the inaugural ride."

His brow knit. "Even better reason to say no. I'd rather not be the rattlers' guinea pig. Sounds like a likely chance of being eaten. Or flung into the next town."

She cocked her head and looked at him. "Are you afraid?"

Brodie shrugged but then shook his head. "No, I'm not afraid. I simply have common sense. That's all."

"You're a chicken."

"You're a bully."

They both burst out laughing.

"What are we? Twelve years old?" she said.

"Apparently so. I never knew you were a mean girl, Caitlyn Moore."

"I'm not. I swear. You don't have to do anything you don't want to do. But I'm not a big chicken. I'm going to ride the Twin Rattlers."

"So you're that confident that this ride is ready to go?"

"Yes, I am. My father is the roller-coaster king. To date, no one has ever died on a single ride in a single one of his theme parks. He handpicked the rides for Cowboy Country, and I highly doubt that he would want to end such a stellar no-injury record at his bucket list park. I have to trust that everything will be fine."

He looked at her for a moment, a look that seemed to reach all the way into her soul.

"You really do see the best in everyone, don't you?"

She shrugged. "I try. There's good in everyone. Sometimes you just have to look past the roadblocks that they throw in your way."

He nodded, and she took it as a nonverbal signal that he knew exactly what…or who…she was talking about.

"With that endorsement, how can I say no? Besides, I don't want to listen to you calling me a chicken, you insufferable bully. But before we go, let me make a phone call. This is a photo op, exactly the kind of fun, positive story we should be getting out there into the community."

Truvy Jennings from the county newspaper, *The Cross Town Crier*, said she would send someone out in fifteen minutes and with that, Caitlyn and Brodie made their way to the Twin Rattlers, which was the park's crowning glory, situated in the very center of the property.

When they got there, Caitlyn was surprised that Les Campbell and his team were the only other people there.

"Where is everyone?" Caitlyn asked.

Les gestured to Caitlyn and Brodie. "Right here. You're all present and accounted for."

"But Les, usually when we do the first run, there's enough people to fill the entire train."

"I'm sorry, ma'am," he said. "We wanted to make this run special for you. We thought you'd like to do this by yourself."

By herself? No, this was about team building.

Les frowned. "I suppose we could delay it for a couple of hours so we could round up others."

"A representative of the newspaper will be here shortly," Brodie interjected. "We need to do this now. A delay might make people think we're having problems."

He glanced at his watch and shifted uncomfortably. There was something he wasn't telling her.

"Les, is everything okay?"

"Ma'am...um...may I speak candidly with you?"

"Of course, Les. Always."

He exhaled. "We tried to round up a crowd, but we had a hard time finding people who were interested."

"No one wanted to do the first run?" Brodie's voice had an edge. Caitlyn feared that what was coming next wasn't going to be pretty. But she saw him take a deep breath and steady himself.

"I suppose it was spur of the moment. I think we need to schedule some participation for later in the week. Everyone in the park should be familiar with the rides and the layout of the park."

Les nodded his agreement, but she could see he was stiff and possibly afraid to do or say anything else.

Brodie turned to Caitlyn. "After we're finished here, let's schedule meetings with the department heads and look at the calendar to plan a mandatory pre-opening orientation for all employees. I want this place to be happier than the happiest place in the universe."

Oh, gosh, he needs to have some fun. He needs to loosen up.

Somehow she was going to have to make him see that he needed to take a gentler approach. They'd have to talk about it later because in the distance, Caitlyn spotted Truvy Jennings from the paper approaching them with her camera in hand. Apparently, she'd decided to cover the story herself.

Great. Just great.

"Here comes Truvy from the paper. I need you to work your magic and convince her that this unceremonious ride for two is exactly what we'd planned. Can you give her your best impersonation of a roller-coaster-lover?"

"I will bring nothing less." He winked at her, back in PR professional mode.

Watching him as he greeted Truvy and had her melting under his charm, no one would ever know just a moment ago he was ready to dismiss everyone who might refuse to ride a roller coaster. Especially when he hadn't been very eager to ride himself.

Then again, he'd changed his tune once she'd co-erced him.

The man was a puzzle who constantly kept her won-dering who he really was deep down: Passionate lover? Stern dictator? Emotional stoic? Public charmer?

But once they were seated in the Twin Rattlers' first car, and he reached out and took her hand, her doubt melted away under his touch.

Then the ride took off, carrying them up, up, up the first huge climb. He never let go of her hand as it spilled down the first drop and curved into the first twist.

They laughed and screamed and held their hands up in the air—his fingers protectively laced through hers. The roller coaster definitely brought out Brodie's un-inhibited side, and Caitlyn loved it. It was the most fun she'd had in a really long time. But it stopped being fun when the train came to a jerking halt, halfway through the ride atop the highest point.

"Are you kidding me?" Brodie said as he searched Caitlyn's face to see if she could offer an explanation for what was happening. "Is this some sort of joke?"

She shook her head. "If it is, I'm not in on it, I as-sure you."

Brodie let go of her hand so he could lean forward, to try and see what was going on below, but the height gave him a pit of vertigo, and he sat back.

"Do you have your cell phone with you?" he asked. "Maybe we can call someone and see what's going on."

"I left mine on my desk because I don't have any pockets."

Brodie raked his hand through his hair, trying to tame his mounting frustration. "I tossed mine onto my desk, too, before I came into your office with the blueprints. I should've grabbed it before we left."

"I'm sure it won't take them very long. Les assured me that all the kinks had been worked out."

Brodie threw his hands up in the air. "And we were gullible enough to believe him. No wonder nobody else wanted to go on this inaugural ride. I'll bet Truvy is getting one hell of a story. This is simply not acceptable—"

He stopped midsentence when he realized Caitlyn was frowning at him.

"Well, it's not."

Caitlyn covered her face with both hands. "Can we not do this up here? Please?"

He could hear the tinges of panic in her voice. Her breath was a little shallow.

"Not everything is controllable," she said. "Things happen. Rides break down. People don't always perform the way you expect them to or want them to. Life is messy. You can't control everything."

She was shaking. He took her hand.

"Hey, I'm sorry. It's okay. It's going to be okay. Really."

He slipped his arm around her and pulled her in close. She took a deep breath and settled into him.

It was a beautiful day. Not too hot, with a pleasant breeze every now and again that ruffled the treetops.

"Really, this is the best view in the house."

He felt her relax a little bit more as he rubbed her shoulder. With his free hand, he pointed. "Look over there. That's Main Street. It looks different from up here, doesn't it?"

She nodded, her breathing growing steadier. "It's pretty. I didn't realize there were so many trees."

He traced where Main Street would have continued under the canopy of oaks to a stretch of open highway. "I believe if you follow that highway on down, that's the road that leads to my aunt Jeanne Marie and uncle Deke's ranch."

"Everything looks so much smaller up here. Down on the ground everything seems so much closer together. I never asked this, but where do you live?"

He gestured behind them.

"I live in the complete opposite direction. About five miles from the Fortune ranch. I am renting a carriage house from my brother's father-in-law. Oliver stayed there before he and Shannon were married. I'm lucky to have it since rental property in Horseback Hollow is hard to come by. If not for the Singleton house, I probably might have been forced to bunk with my extended family. Even the thought of that scares me."

Caitlyn gave him a little nudge with her shoulder. "You have a wonderful family. I don't understand why living with them would be such a horrible thing."

He sighed. "There's such a thing as too much togetherness. My family takes a nice thing and turns it into smothering."

"When I was a little girl I used to wish for a large family. Don't get me wrong, I adore my parents. But my dad has always been a workaholic—"

Brodie smiled. "A man after my own heart."

"I've been wanting to thank you for being so good to my father while he's been ill. I mean, I know he's paying you handsomely—as he should—but you seemed to connect better with him than most people—certainly better than my ex. I saw that when you defended me to him the other day. Granted, he's trying to be a little more relaxed because of his condition, but if you hadn't handled that just right it could've turned pretty ugly. I've seen it happen before."

Brodie shrugged. He liked hearing her open up about her family, her childhood and her past.

"Tell me about your ex," he said. "What happened?"

She tried to wave him off. But then she sighed. "Two weeks before the wedding, I found out that he'd slept with someone else. The worst part was that it was someone he just picked up one night. He was willing to sacrifice everything that we had for one night with a stranger."

"So, was that your motivation for sleeping with me after the wedding?"

Oh, hell. Why had he said that? The look in her eyes made him want to kick himself.

Then she lifted her chin. "What if I said yes? Is it only acceptable for men to pick up women?"

"I'm not judging," said Brody. "But you sound like you're the one who isn't comfortable with the idea of one-night stands."

She shrugged and looked away.

He wondered if they would be sitting here like this right now, getting so personal, if not for that one night in February.

Of course they'd both be here at Cowboy Country, and they'd probably be attracted to each other—this thing between them was magnetic—but he'd bet money that they would both be all business. They might wonder, but if he'd known out of the starting gate that she was Alden Moore's daughter, he probably wouldn't have acted.

As far as he was concerned, that one-night stand in February was one of the best things that had ever happened to him.

"When a guy cheats, when *anybody* cheats," Brodie said, "it's not a reflection on the person who was cheated on. It's a reflection of the cheater's cowardice. There's not a thing in the world wrong with you, Cait. This one's all on him."

She turned back to him. "You sound like you speak from experience."

"In a roundabout way. My father cheated on my mother. He treated her terribly."

"Poor Josephine."

Brody nodded. "She didn't deserve it. No one does."

"As far as I know, my dad has never cheated on my mother. He may be a lot of things, but at least he's always been an honorable man. But despite the fact that I'm twenty-nine years old, in my father's eyes I will forever be twelve. Know what I mean?"

"No. Not really. I mean, I understand what you're saying, but I have not personally experienced that. I never really had a relationship with my natural father."

"But your mother is lovely. She seems to dote on you."

"My mother *is* a lovely person. I've just had a very different upbringing than you."

"Tell me about your childhood. I want to hear everything."

She snuggled in closer to him and right about then she could have persuaded him to talk about anything, especially if it meant that he could hold her like this.

She fit so perfectly next to him.

"Really, it's a rather boring story. I went to boarding schools, and then I went off to university. I started my own company, and here I am."

She nudged him again. "I don't want the Brodie Fortune Hayes bio. I want to hear about the real you."

He held up his free hand in a one-shoulder shrug, keeping his other arm snugly around her.

"I'm sort of a what-you-see-is-what-you-get type of guy—"

"No, you're not. You are much more complicated than that, and I want to know what's made you that way."

He stiffened, but he resisted the urge to squirm. Because anyone who knew anything about body language understood that was one of the first signs that a person was uncomfortable.

"You may ask me five questions," he said. "And I will answer them."

"Really?" She glanced up at him. As he nodded, his gaze focused on those lips of hers. They were so full and kissable…and tempting. His body responded.

"Then I get to ask you five."

"It's a deal," she said. "Tell me about your father."

That was one way to kill the mood. How was he supposed to know she'd zero right in where it hurt?

"That's not a question," he said.

"What is this, *Jeopardy*? You didn't specify that it had to be phrased as an interrogative. That one doesn't count. Let me rephrase it. Will you tell me about your father?"

"No. Next question."

"That is so not fair. You didn't answer my first one."

"Yes, I did. You asked if I would tell you about my father. I answered no. Next question."

"I suppose we could sit here in silence until you answer me."

"I forgot to mention that *open season* expires once the ride starts again."

He felt her tense up again. "Oh, right. Thanks for reminding me. For a moment we were having so much fun, I forgot we were stuck."

Brodie sighed. "My parents were divorced when I was three. I never really knew my natural father. My mother remarried Sir Simon John Chesterfield—he's Amelia's natural father."

"Is he also Oliver's father?"

"Is that your second question?"

"What? No! I was just continuing conversation. That doesn't count."

"Just so you can't say I'm not a nice guy, I'll give you that one since we are a complicated bunch. Oliver is older than I am. We have the same natural father. I have four half siblings: Amelia, Jensen, Charles and Lucie."

"That's amazing. Not only do you have this expansive extended family, your immediate family is like an army, too."

"You have no idea. Next question."

He wanted to steer the conversation away from his family before Caitlyn started digging any deeper. That was all she needed to know, anyway. He'd set himself up for this, left himself wide open when he'd given her free rein. He should've set parameters, but the nearness of her made his senses spin, messed with the equilibrium of his common sense.

"Have you ever had your heart broken?" she asked, stealing a glance at him.

He nodded, and she rested her head on his shoulder.

"What was her name?"

"Nina."

"And?"

"Is that your third question?"

She nudged him with her knee. "Of course it's not my third question. We're still on number two. You can't just give me one-word answers. What happened?"

"That's question number three. She married someone else."

"Oh. I'm sorry. No one should have to go through that."

"Obviously, we weren't meant to be."

Caitlyn was quiet for a moment. "Yeah, that happens sometimes. I suppose it's better to discover it before you marry the person rather than afterward."

Her right hand had found its way onto his thigh. She nearly drove him crazy the way she traced small circles on his leg with her forefinger.

His skin prickled under her touch.

"Is Nina the one who convinced you that you don't have a heart?"

He shrugged and coughed out a laugh. "If I had a pound for every time someone told me I was heartless, I'd be the wealthiest man in the world."

"Don't skirt the question. Did she?"

"She did, as did many others. Does it really matter?"

"Yes, it matters, because they were wrong. You're not as heartless as you would like everyone to believe, Brodie. I've glimpsed that heart of yours when you didn't know I was looking. You don't have to pretend with me."

The heartrending tenderness in her eyes.

His body ached for her.

He wasn't sure who moved first, but they went from zero to sixty in a heartbeat. His lips were on hers, and she gasped a little. The sound she made was nearly silent—more of a shudder than a sound. Brodie wondered if maybe he'd *felt* rather than heard her. But it didn't matter. The important thing was she didn't pull away; she didn't break contact.

They shouldn't be doing this—for so many reasons. But she was kissing him back and he wanted to devour her like a starving man at a sumptuous buffet.

Their kiss sent him reeling back to that first night. It nearly took him over the edge as new spirals of ecstasy unfurled in his body. Heat stirred and pooled in his groin as his body responded. He couldn't remember when he'd needed a woman as badly—as desperately—as he needed Caitlyn Moore.

He had no idea how long the two of them were up there tangled up in each other's arms because for a beautiful while, time vanished, and they were the only people in the universe. The only thing that brought Brodie back to reality was the jolt of a deafening alarm that sliced through the bliss and broke the two of them apart.

Caitlyn blinked at him as if she were gathering her faculties. Then her eyes flew open wide. "Hang on. This thing is about to start again."

He stole one more kiss.

With his lips a hair away from hers, he assured her, "I can guarantee you it already has."

Chapter Nine

It was a hell of a long walk back to the office. They took care to keep a respectable amount of distance between them. Caitlyn was too quiet. So Brodie knew it was up to him to break the ice.

"I hope Truvy left before the malfunction."

"That would be a lucky break," Caitlyn said.

Once they were back on the ground, trying to act normal—as normal as one could after making out atop a stalled roller coaster—the second thing they asked was what time the reporter had left.

The first question was, of course, "What the hell happened?"

Les didn't know what caused the malfunction, but he assured them he would get to the bottom of it in short order. But when it came to info about Truvy, he wasn't so helpful.

"She was here snapping pictures when the ride blasted off, but I couldn't tell you how long she stayed after the thing started malfunctioning."

"Did she realize it broke down?" Caitlyn asked.

Les shrugged. "I couldn't tell you how long she hung around. I was working. But I don't see her around here now. If you'll excuse me, I need to get back to work."

Brodie decided if Truvy had witnessed the malfunction, she would've waited around to ask questions. No need to worry when it probably would turn out to be nothing.

"Right, Les," Brodie said. "Please let us know when you figure out what went wrong with the ride and when you think it will be good to go. We're only a few days away from opening. We need to make sure everything is shipshape."

Les nodded curtly and turned away.

He'd given no indication that he or anyone else on the ground was any wiser to what had been going on high up there on the apex of that final hill. On one hand, he knew behavior like that wasn't professional, but on the other hand Caitlyn was all that mattered.

Since that day when he'd walked into the Cowboy Country USA offices and saw her standing there, he'd been fighting these feelings.

He'd been grasping at any reason to prove that they were not good together.

But *why*?

Ever since Nina he'd buried himself in his work.

With the exception of a few casual relationships, he hadn't allowed himself to look away from work long enough to see what was good or right or true about love.

Or maybe he'd been waiting for the right person to lift him out of his slump.

As they passed Gulch Holler Rapids log flume ride, Brodie stole a glance at Caitlyn.

Is she the right person?

Was she the one or was he telling himself that to make himself feel better about getting involved with Alden Moore's daughter?

He felt himself wanting to backpedal, but he recognized that traditionally, this was where the walls would go up, and he would slip out the side door.

Then he rode it out and after the wave broke, his feelings for her were still standing.

They didn't have to rush things, but he didn't want to delay things, either.

Caitlyn paused outside the entrance to their building.

"Do you really think we're going to be ready to open Memorial Day?" she asked. Even if we have to delay a week or two, don't you think that's better than running the risk of something like this happening with guests in the park?"

"If the Twin Rattlers isn't ready to go, we don't have to run it. But we do have to open the park as promised. It's in my contract."

"I don't have a contract—"

Brodie leaned in and silenced her with a kiss.

"What are we doing?" Worry clouded her eyes.

"Are you talking about business or—" He motioned back and forth between them.

She gave a quick one-shoulder shrug, and he knew exactly what she was talking about.

He smiled at her. "I'd show you, but I don't know if it would set a very good example if someone walked around the corner and saw me ravishing you right here. They might have to fire both of us."

"Yeah, about that. It probably wasn't the smartest idea to make out on a roller coaster in the middle of the park. Although, I must admit, I've always wanted to do that."

Brodie feigned surprise. "What? The Princess of Coaster World has never made out on a roller coaster? I'm your first?"

"Yes. Given that it's the first time I've ever been stuck on a roller coaster. They're not exactly the tunnel of love when they're going at full speed."

"Touché."

She caught her top lip between her teeth and looked up at him, emotion darkening her eyes.

"I'm not cut out for flings," she said. "That woman who ravaged you at the wedding wasn't me. I mean, it was *me*, obviously, but I'm not like that. I've never picked up a stranger before. So I don't want you to have the wrong impression. Although, I guess it's too late for that."

Color rose in her cheeks as she rolled her eyes. He loved how flustered she got sometimes when she tried to explain herself.

Now more than ever he wanted to pull her into his arms.

He opened his mouth to tell her so, but she silenced him by raising her hand.

"I want you to think about it. You don't have to give me an answer right now—right here. This isn't really the time or the place to decide something so personal."

A smile tugged up the corners of his lips. "I agree. So why don't you have dinner with me tonight, and we can talk about it when we have more privacy?"

Janie held out a piece of paper to Caitlyn as she and Brodie made their way back to their offices.

"Ms. Moore, Truvy Jennings from the newspaper called for you. She says she needs more information about the Twin Rattlers for the article she's writing. I told her that you and Mr. Fortune Hayes were still out in the park, and she asked if y'all were still having problems with the ride. Is there a problem?"

Caitlyn and Brodie exchanged an alarmed glance, but Janie's expression was earnest as she looked back and forth between the two of them.

"What did you say to her, Janie?" Caitlyn put on her professional smile and did her best to make sure the panic crawling up the back of her throat didn't croak through in her voice.

"I told her I didn't know. That you and Mr. Fortune Hayes were just out in the park like you always are and I wasn't aware of anything being wrong."

Caitlyn's alarm slipped a couple of notches.

"You did the right thing, Janie, thank you," said Brodie. "This is not a reprimand. It's simply a directive for the future because it's likely we will be receiving more calls from media outlets from all over the world in the next couple of weeks. But it's important that no one speak to the media except for Ms. Moore and myself. In a case like this, when someone starts asking questions, simply tell them that you'd be happy to take a message. Do you understand?"

Janie nodded. "I did take a message, and she wants you to call her back. Her number is on the paper."

As they made their way down the hall, Brodie said, "I'll take care of Truvy."

Caitlyn handed him the number and quirked a brow. "She'd probably rather talk to you, anyway. Work your charm."

Brodie took her proffered paper with Truvy's number. "But before I take care of this, how about if I make us a seven-thirty reservation at the Cantina?"

"That sounds wonderful," she said.

Brodie pulled her inside his office and covered her mouth with a kiss.

When Caitlyn came up for air, she pulled back and looked at him with dreamy eyes.

"We really do have to stop doing that at work. Janie might walk in without knocking."

Brodie narrowed his eyes at her. "I thought Janie usually buzzed you when she needed you."

"Well, yeah, there's that, but you never know when she might surprise us and walk in."

Brodie reached out and picked up a strand of Caitlyn's hair and started twirling it around his finger.

"Go," Caitlyn said. Make our dinner reservation and then make us look good for Truvy. In the meantime, I'm going to finish up the outline for the Red, White and Blue team days."

The workers had been divided into three groups of Red, White and Blue teams, and they would each have a day where they could bring a guest to enjoy themselves in the park. Afterward, each person would come to a debriefing meeting and rate their experience. It was like a soft, soft opening, with a report card, done by the workers out on the front lines. They'd use this exercise to work out the first kinks. The exercise was also designed to make the employees buy into this sense of ownership and experience firsthand the expectations of Moore Entertainment.

Brodie came in to tell her about his call with Truvy, which had been pretty standard—she had seen the roller coaster stall and wanted to know if that would have an impact on the park's opening. He told her absolutely not.

He had other news for Caitlyn, too. His aunt Jeanne Marie called and asked them if they could stop by around five-thirty. She wanted to talk to them about their plan to get on the agenda for next week's town meeting. There was no time to waste and since Brodie's aunt had made time for them, Caitlyn certainly wanted to meet with her while they had the chance. Who knew if she would have time before the meeting?

Besides, their reservation at the Cantina wasn't until later. Of course, meeting with Jeanne Marie meant that Caitlyn wouldn't have time to go home and freshen up before dinner, but hearing what Jeanne Marie had to say was more important.

By five-thirty they were sitting at the trestle table in Jeanne Marie's spacious kitchen.

"Where's Mum and everyone else?" Brodie asked.

Jeanne Marie had brewed a pitcher of fresh sweet tea, which she served to them over ice, with lemon rounds and sprigs of aromatic fresh mint.

"Orlando Mendoza drove your mother to Lubbock because she had some shopping to do." Jeanne Marie lifted a brow. "She seems to have that man wrapped around her little finger these days."

"Yes, I noticed they seemed quite chummy at the barbecue," Brodie said. "What's going on there?"

Caitlyn sipped the cool beverage and realized she was a little nervous. The scent of the lemon and mint was soothing, but it didn't completely cure her jitters. This woman could help smooth the way for them... or not.

Never mind Caitlyn's personal plea about the place being so important to her ailing father, Jeanne Marie's own nephew was working so hard to make sure the park opened to rave reviews. Because of that alone, when Caitlyn had left the barbecue last week, she'd been under the impression that the Fortunes' hardline stance toward Cowboy Country had softened.

Caitlyn hadn't been surprised by their perceived change of heart.

Now she wasn't so sure, but she guessed they were about to find out.

"Who knows what's going on between them—if anything." Jeanne Marie sipped her tea. "Your mother insists they're just friends, but they're texting all the time like a couple of teenagers. It's ridiculous."

The corners of Brodie's eyes slanted Caitlyn a glance.

The left corner of his mouth curved up, and there were those dimples.

Her heart kicked up a little two-step as she remembered the way he'd kissed her senseless in the park today.

Oh, Caitlyn. Stop it. This woman could make or break your chances for time in front of the city council, and here you are lusting over her nephew. So inappropriate.

"But that's not why I asked you to come over here today," the older woman said. "We need to get down to business and talk about this plan of yours to speak to the city council. I have to leave here for my canasta club in a few minutes. I wish I could offer to make you some dinner, but I don't have time."

"That's okay, Auntie. I appreciate the thought, but we're going out to dinner after we leave here."

Jeanne Marie's face brightened. "Are you, really? Together? As in a dinner date?"

Brodie's brows knit together. "Let's stay on topic, shall we? Since you're pressed for time."

Jeanne Marie eyed Caitlyn and Brodie with satisfaction for a moment, before she became all business again. "So tell me, what exactly do you hope to accomplish by doing that?"

"We're tired of being the five-hundred-pound gorilla in the middle of the room that no one wants to talk about," Brodie said.

"Oh, they're all talking about you," Jeanne Marie said. "I'm just not so sure they want to talk *to* you."

Caitlyn's heart sank. "Forgive me if I'm being presumptuous, but I thought you'd changed your mind about Cowboy Country."

Jeanne Marie sighed and traced her fingernail over a grain in the wooden tabletop. "I understand where you're coming from and, if truth be told, I admire how this project is important to you because it's important to your daddy. The Fortunes are all about sticking up for family. However, it's not as simple as my liking it or not. The city council doesn't give a pig's snout about my opinion."

Brodie drummed his fingers on the table. "I don't believe that for one minute. You and Uncle Deke carry a lot of influence in this town. In fact, aren't a couple of the council members related to you…to us, I mean?"

Jeanne Marie nodded. "But they certainly don't come to me for counsel. If your plan is to go to the citizens of Horseback Hollow with your hat in your hand asking them to love you, I don't want you to be under the false assumption that their minds will be as easily changed as the family's."

Caitlyn knew she was grasping at straws, but had Jeanne Marie just admitted that she and the Fortunes— at least those in her immediate family—supported Cowboy Country? That's what she heard, and that's what she decided she was going to focus on…the positive.

"No, we're not going there asking them to love us," Caitlyn assured her. "Everything I said to you about wanting to be a good neighbor is absolutely sincere and true. What Brodie and I hope to accomplish in that meeting is we want to show them how we'll do that, how we can help. Cowboy doesn't want to take anything from Horseback Hollow. We want to give back to the community in the ways that I mentioned last week at dinner and even more."

Jeanne Marie's face gave nothing away as she studied them with blue eyes that were the same shade as Brodie's. Caitlyn idly wondered if triplets ran in Brodie's family.

Not that it mattered.

"I hope you can go in there and convey that same conviction," she said. "Because it's not going to be easy to win over everyone, but if anyone can do it, I believe you two can. So since the mayor has asked to hold this meeting in our barn out back because there are too many people for the Grill in town, I called in a favor. I asked him about the two of you doing a short presentation. He said for you to give his secretary a call and he will put you on the agenda for next Tuesday night."

It felt like another victory, Brodie thought as he drove toward Caitlyn's apartment in Vicker's Corners. He'd stopped at the Wok In Carry Out Chinese restaurant where he'd picked up takeout for them to share for dinner. Before that, he'd picked up a bottle of nice champagne. Because tonight was a night that called for some bubbly.

After they'd left Jeanne Marie's house, they'd decided to celebrate in a more casual atmosphere than the Cantina. When Caitlyn said she'd wanted to change into something more comfortable than the silk blouse and snug skirt she'd worn to work that day, he'd offered to pick up takeout and meet her at her place.

When she answered the door, the sight of her virtually knocked the breath out of him. She wore a pretty pink cotton sundress that even in its casualness hugged her in all the right places.

This thing between them was so new—well, it wasn't *new*; these feelings, this chemistry, hadn't gone away since the moment they'd met—but this renewal was fragile. Before he could overthink it, he decided to take the lead and kiss her hello. Standing there with his hands full of bags and the bottle, he leaned in and claimed her lips.

She wrapped her arms around his neck, and he held the parcels out to allow her to get closer. Blood pooled in the center of his body. Hot. Urgent. His senses screamed in a rush of want and need.

"I've been dying to do that again since we got down off that bloody ride this afternoon. Have I told you how much I love roller coasters?"

She laughed. "I thought you hated them."

His lips still on hers, he said, "I've been cured. The tunnel of love ain't got nothing on the Twin Rattlers."

She gently bit his bottom lip and sucked it before she said, "Come in. I don't want to put on a show for the neighbors."

When he stepped inside, he set the goods down on the wooden coffee table in the apartment's small living room. He pulled her to him again, wanting to feel every inch of her body pressed against his hardness. Needing to bury himself deep inside her.

She felt so right in his arms. All at once, all the uncertainty was replaced by a feeling so right, so profound he knew he had to have her.

All of her.

In Brodie's arms, Caitlyn's senses took flight. Or did they take leave?

She tried to think through the fuzzy haze that had invaded her brain. He smelled divine. That green and woodsy scent was so him. She breathed him in as he trailed kisses down her neck. That's when she gave up trying to make sense of it all and gave in to the rapture.

A moan of pleasure escaped from somewhere deep in her throat. Brodie ran his hands over her back, down the soft cotton of her sundress, until he gently cupped her bottom and pulled the center of her to the rock-hard center of him.

"I want you," he whispered.

The room tipped on end. She wondered if anyone had ever drowned in her own desire for a man.

"Caitlyn?"

"Mmm?"

"Is this okay? I mean, are you hungry?"

She smiled.

She nodded and buried her hands into his thick hair. "Yes, I'm so ravenous I don't even know where to begin. Here—"

She unbuttoned the top button of his shirt.

"Or here—" She slid her hand down his flat stomach and dipped her finger into the waistband of his pants.

"Let me help you with that decision."

He lifted her off the ground, cradling her in his

strong arms, and kissed her as he started walking toward her bedroom.

Her heart beat so wildly she was sure he could feel it.
She couldn't remember a time when she hadn't longed
for this moment because everything before him had
faded away. She searched his eyes and answered him
with a kiss that spoke of all the passion and certainty
she felt.

Just inside the door, he adjusted the dimmer on the
overhead light so that it glowed a warm, subtle glow.
Just enough light to see. Barely.

Gently, he laid her on the bed.

She was going to make love with this gorgeous, sexy
man who would probably leave right after the park
opened and never come back. And yes, she would be
devastated.

But tonight he was all hers. They had this moment.
Right now.

Looming over her, he stripped off his shirt and tossed
it away, onto the floor, then eased down beside her and
propped himself up on one elbow.

From this vantage point he looked huge, all muscled
chest and broad shoulders. She shuddered, needing to
feel his bare skin pressed against her own.

He stroked her cheek and lowered his mouth to meet
hers, his lips closing over hers soft and gentle at first,
then more demanding.

His hand had worked its way up underneath her
dress. His finger deftly slid under her bra and brushed
over her breast. Those thoughts of him leaving that had
plagued her a moment earlier melted away under his

very skilled hands. Desire shot through every inch of her body, pooling in secret, vulnerable spots that had been starving for him for way too long.

He seemed to know precisely how to work the hook on her bra, because before she realized what he was doing, he'd tossed it away. She tried not to think about how many women he must have undressed to be that good at it. She hadn't had many lovers—none since Eric. But she'd hungered for Brodie the past few weeks, and any residual preoccupation left her mind as she focused on how tonight felt as if they were about to make love for the very first time. Well, for the second first time.

His hand on her breast sent tendrils of pleasure spiraling through her body. Brodie might be leaving soon, but she would show him how good they could be together, remind him how right they were for each other. He made her feel alive in a way she hadn't felt in a long time. She wanted to make him feel just as good.

Her finger traced the edge of his pants, where a line of fine hair disappeared into the waistband. She slid her palm down over the bulge just below it. He moaned.

Fumbling with the button on his pants, she finally worked it loose. She hesitated and looked up at him.

He reached down and worked her dress up and over her head and tossed it away.

"You're so beautiful." He looked at her body in a way that was positively reverent. He touched her face and then softly stroked her neck and the cleft between her breasts as he worked his way downward. When his lips sought out her nipple, she was gone. Utterly gone. Incoherent, lost in the feel of him on loving her body.

His kiss found her lips again, and his tongue slid into her mouth, as his knee nudged apart her thighs. When his hand found her center, even through her panties, the sensation made her back arch off the bed.

She freed his hard length from his pants and caressed him. He responded with a shuddered moan and eased his pants and underwear off in one easy motion. Then he straddled her and slid off her panties with equal ease.

She lay naked and vulnerable and ready for him.

He kissed her slow and deep for the longest time and when he finally pulled back, she heard the sound of a foil condom package opening. Impatient for him, desperate for him, she watched as he sheathed himself.

He settled himself on top of her, propping his upper body on his elbows. Stroking her hair, his lips found that tender spot where her neck curved into her ear then trailed kisses down her neck. He was about to drive her insane from the need, which had her body moving under him, straining, trying to get close.

One of his hands dipped between them. He shifted his weight, and she felt him positioning himself against her before he entered her body, filling her with an incredible rush of pleasure.

She gasped as fire burned through her veins to the very center of her womanhood. Arching against him, she grabbed on to his hips and threw her knees out as wide as they could go, needing to feel him all the way to her soul. He was sensuous and weighty, rolling on top of her, inside her, the friction of his body creating a growing heat. He gave her everything he had, pumping into her hard and deep until she cried out his name as waves of pleasure built. Swelled. Until she came completely unraveled and spiraling over the edge.

When she lay spent and pliable under him, his head fell to her shoulder, and his rhythm grew steadier, faster, until his entire body began to tremble. With a growl, he let go of his control and spilled everything he had.

Then there was stillness broken only by the sound of their breathing.

Chapter Ten

She thought making love to Brodie Fortune Hayes—again—would ruin everything she'd worked so hard to establish. But she was wrong.

It had never felt so wonderful to be wrong.

Things weren't awkward or strained. Instead, there was a heightened sense of synergy between them. The only challenge she found was keeping her mind on the job and out of the bedroom. And really, when she thought about it, it wasn't a challenge as much as it was the cherry on top.

They were so good together—both in the bedroom and out. And this intensified closeness helped on the night of the town council meeting.

Since the meeting was taking place in the barn on Deke and Jeanne Marie's property, Caitlyn thought those in attendance would be friendly—or at least open-minded. However, even though the Fortunes did wield some influence, it was clear that the folks of Horseback Hollow had minds of their own and would not be easily swayed.

She was amazed by how many people came clutching the newspaper with Truvy's story of the malfunctioning Twin Rattlers. With a headline reading Cowboy Country USA Off To Uncertain Start—Will Malfunctions Derail Memorial Day Opening?

Oh, Truvy, I thought you were on our side.

The reporter was seated in the front row, jotting notes in her reporter's notebook. She wouldn't make eye contact with Caitlyn. She wasn't sure if it was intentional or not. Everything seemed magnified right now.

Her gaze searched the room for Brodie, who was in the back helping serve the fresh lemonade and cookies that Jeanne Marie had provided. They had agreed that he would man that station, and she would work the other side of the room.

The only thing was that she was suddenly feeling a bit paralyzed and what looked like the entire town of Horseback Hollow filtered into the barn. From the looks of things, the crowd might be as large as it had been for the wedding. These good people took their town seriously.

Well, Caitlyn's convictions about Cowboy Country USA were just as strong and sincere. She wasn't here to mislead anyone. That truth would be the North Star that guided her through the evening.

Brodie was talking and shaking hands and doing

what he did best. He was with Cisco Mendoza and Delaney Fortune Jones. Caitlyn had met both of them when she and Brodie had arrived. Wonderful, warm people. Cisco looked animated and happy to be chatting with Brodie. That had to be a good sign, didn't it?

When Cisco left Cowboy Country everything began to unravel. As part of their strategy, Brodie had asked Cisco to stand up tonight and mention that the only problem he'd had with the project and the reason he'd left was because he felt the design didn't mesh with Horseback Hollow's landscape. The plan was that Brodie would assure the citizens that since then there had been a change in personnel, and that Moore Entertainment was discussing a more harmonious plan for the Cowboy Condos. A design that Cisco Mendoza himself had had a hand in bringing to life.

Of course, the unspoken message was Mendoza might have pulled out—and for good reason—but a Fortune had come on board and was fully endorsing the park. Not only was it good for the small town, but it was also economically beneficial.

Yes, Brodie was in his element. Caitlyn envied his ease, the way he seemed so comfortable in his own skin. Granted, he could be a little aggressive when he'd locked in on something he wanted—loyal employees, an iron-clad opening date, a lover—

Inappropriate. Stop it.

Caitlyn blinked away the thought and refocused on how, for the most part, Brodie Fortune Hayes knew how to win people over to his way of thinking. He was headstrong, and Caitlyn didn't agree with all his tactics, but she believed Brodie Fortune Hayes's heart was in the right place.

Good thing, because she feared she was losing her heart to him.

Stop, Caitlyn. Focus. And quit being a wallflower. Get out there and mingle. Do your job.

She knew she needed to, but it was easier said than done. Being at the center of a new situation wasn't her comfort zone. She liked to stand back and observe, get a read on a situation, absorb the vibe before she dove in. That's how her *gut* worked, and when she abided by it, she usually wasn't wrong.

However, today there wasn't a lot of time to stand back and assess. She would be doing herself a favor by meeting as many people as possible before she and Brodie got up to speak. They were the last on the agenda, and if she was anxious now, she knew her nerves would only get worse as the clock ticked closer and closer to their presentation.

She scanned the room for a friendly face, and her gaze connected with Susie Silverman, who was just entering the barn. Susie smiled back, waved and headed in her direction. Good thing she'd worn the cuff bracelet she'd purchased from Susie at the art festival. It wasn't just for show. She hadn't thought about currying favor when she'd slipped it on her wrist to complement the powder blue dress she'd chosen for the occasion—something soft and feminine, something that didn't scream city slicker, but still hinted that she was a professional and knew what she was doing.

All she knew was she loved the bracelet. It made her feel as if she were wearing a work of art.

"Hi, Caitlyn? Did I remember your name correctly?"

Caitlyn beamed at her. "You did, Susie. It's great to see you again."

"Hey, I *love* that bracelet." Susie reached out and lifted up Caitlyn's wrist. "You have impeccable taste, lady. I just finished making some earrings that would look great with it. Not too matchy-matchy, but close enough to harmonize."

"Save them for me. May I stop by your house next week to pick them up? I've wanted to come in and see you and your studio since the art festival. Life has just been a little crazy."

"I hear you. I understand you've had a full plate working toward the grand opening." Suzie gestured toward a newspaper that an older woman with jet-black hair was using as a fan. "Don't worry, though. People around here can be slow to embrace change, but most of them do eventually come around. I've lived here all my life, and I've seen it with my own two eyes. You'll be fine."

Susie waved at someone across the room. "There's Mary Jane Hardy. She's saved me a seat. Plus, it looks like the meeting is about to start. Knock 'em dead."

Susie would be one friendly face in the audience, in addition to Jeanne Marie and Deke, Josephine, Amelia and Quinn, Christopher Fortune Jones and his wife, Kinsley. Then there was Galen Fortune Jones, who could sometimes be a loose cannon, but surely tonight he would support his cousin or say nothing at all. Right?

She felt a hand on her shoulder and turned around to see Brodie. He handed her a small cup of lemonade and a fresh chocolate chip cookie on a red napkin. Caitlyn wondered if the napkin was left over from the wedding.

"Hungry crowd tonight. I saved these for you. Because until you've had Aunt Jeanne Marie's chocolate-chip cookies, you haven't lived."

"Thank you." As she reached to take the goodies, Brodie managed to squeeze her hand under the napkin. It was a private message that came with a smile that seemed to promise, *Don't worry. We've got this. Easy peasy.*

Although, she couldn't imagine that upright, handsome Brit actually saying *easy peasy.*

It really was a silly phrase. Yet the thought of it passing over those lips…*those lips*…

"What?" Brodie asked.

Caitlyn took a bite of the cookie. When she'd swallowed it, she said, "Delicious. That's what. Let's find our seats."

They sat with his family about midway back. Just far enough away to feel a little anonymous—though being the lone non-Fortune to sit with them probably made her stand out all the more. Still, being that far back allowed her to look around and spot some of the people who worked at the park. There was Janie, who must've slipped in just as they were starting because Caitlyn hadn't seen her earlier. And there was Les Campbell. And a group from food and beverage. But not as many as she would've thought.

Hmm…was that good or bad?

Caitlyn did her best to focus on the speakers, who stood on what looked like a modified version of the wedding stage. Before she knew it, it was time for Brodie and her to get up and deliver their piece. Before she stood, her throat went dry so she drank the last bit of lemonade, grateful for its tart coolness. They'd prepared a PowerPoint presentation, which was good because her mind was threatening to go blank right about now.

But all it took was one reassuring smile from Brodie, one touch of his hand as he helped her up the four wooden steps to the platform, and she caught her breath.

No need to be nervous. This is a win-win proposition.

Brodie went first, introducing her and giving the overview as he tried to get people excited. He worked through his part of the PowerPoint. Cisco stood at the appropriate moment and said the appropriate things. Still, something didn't feel right.

All this talk about designs and money flowing in from the outside through taxes and tourist spending seemed cold and...typical. Just a cordial way of saying, or not saying, like it or not Cowboy Country was here and really, there's nothing you can do about it.

"Now I'll turn the stage over to the lovely Caitlyn Moore, who will tell you about some wonderful incentives you're sure to find very exciting."

She gave Brodie a double take.

Incentives? That wasn't exactly the word she was going to use. Partners in business, maybe—

Brodie had done a good job presenting the facts, exactly as they'd discussed. But hearing it made it sound about as warm as a multilevel marketing plan. Not that there was anything wrong with multilevel marketing, but it wasn't for everyone, and rarely did it instill the warm fuzzies.

Caitlyn stepped up to the podium. Looked around and saw a mixture of emotions out there in the audience. She wasn't expecting to please everyone. So maybe she just needed to do what felt right to her.

"I want to tell you a personal story." Rather than following the PowerPoint, she began to speak from her heart. She told them the story of how her father started Moore Entertainment with one hundred dollars he'd saved from working an early-morning paper route when he was in high school. She told them he has always believed that being part of a community is so important. He learned that on his paper route. He knew the name of every single person on his route.

"He hasn't had a chance to meet all of you yet, because he's been having health problems, but just give him a chance and you'll know him like family."

She told them how he loves John Wayne and that Cowboy Country USA was a dream come true.

"It's not just another amusement park in the Moore Entertainment portfolio. This is personal. And out of all the places in the world, he chose Horseback Hollow. He wants to be part of this community, and he would be the one standing here telling you that if he weren't in a rehabilitation center in Lubbock, recovering. I almost lost my father. I think you can help give him a reason to live."

The air in the room seemed to change. Everyone sat quietly watching her.

"But me telling you the Cowboy Country story is only a fraction of why I'm here. I want to tell you how Moore Entertainment will be good neighbors to you, and I will not leave here until I have answered every one of your questions."

A hand shot up—a guy in the second row who didn't look entirely convinced.

"Okay, I have a question for you. According to the newspaper, you're having trouble getting your rides to work. As far as I'm concerned, the only thing worse than having an amusement park in my backyard is having a broken-down eyesore that doesn't work. I'm afraid we're going to be stuck with a theme-park ghost town if Moore Entertainment can't get its act together then pulls up stakes and leaves town."

Thanks, Truvy.

"What's your name, sir?" Caitlyn asked.

"Rodney Young."

"Mr. Young, I can assure you that Moore Entertainment would never leave you with a broken-down eyesore. We are still a couple of weeks away from opening our doors. We are testing equipment and fine-tuning everything around the park to have it ready and working for opening day. To put your mind at ease, I would like to invite you and your family to be our guest at the park on opening day. Come out and enjoy the park and see for yourself."

A wave of murmurs rippled through the audience.

Caitlyn smiled at him. Rodney Young sat up in his chair and arched his brows in a way that wasn't entirely bad.

"Well, thank you, ma'am. I'll take you up on that offer. How do I get in touch with you?"

"You can call me in the Cowboy Country offices anytime. In fact, that goes for all of you. I want to give every resident of Horseback Hollow a ticket for free park admission on opening day."

The crowd murmured again. Brodie put his hand on Caitlyn's arm. She glanced at him and through his smile he was giving her a *look*. It flashed in his eyes for just a moment—a *what the hell are you doing* look—but she ignored him.

"After that, we will offer you deeply discounted resident passes. All you have to do is show your ID with a Horseback Hollow address, and we will have a special rate."

"Could you please give us that number to the Cowboy Country offices?"

Her gaze picked out Janie in the audience. She looked horrified. But Caitlyn was as good as her word. She gave out the number.

Now Brodie's hand was on her back, and he was subtly moving into the microphone.

"Yes, one free ticket for everyone." He choked on the last word, but he quickly recovered. "For the day of the opening. Right. We will all have a lovely time. But getting back on track, there's more about how we would like to help Horseback Hollow's economy. To that end, Moore Entertainment would like to partner with local businesses who are interested in offering food and goods for sale within the park."

Getting back on track? What?

Granted, she had varied from the PowerPoint, and he didn't seem thrilled about her surprise offer of free admission on opening day, but that wasn't his decision to make. Common sense dictated that if they involved the residents of Horseback Hollow, the residents would see for themselves and soften their stance.

She put her hand on his back to signal that she would take it from here and tried to lean into the microphone to finish her part of the presentation, but he didn't budge.

And he kept talking.

So she did the only thing she could to get his attention without making a scene. She slid her hand down to his backside and pinched him.

"Yah!" he blurted.

Well, he deserved it. Edging me out like that.

Maybe it wasn't the most professional thing to do, but the podium was wide enough that nobody would've been the wiser, and her body blocked the view of those who were seated to the side of the stage—and had she mentioned he deserved it?

Caitlyn was a tolerant woman. But one of the things that pushed her hot button like no other was when a man tried to override her in business, treating her like a senseless little lady.

"Yes, Brodie. I'm excited about being a part of the Horseback Hollow community, too," she said in her cheeriest voice. "To pick up on what Brodie was saying, we will offer competitive compensation and make sure park guests are aware that each partner—vendor—is local by supplying signage and encouragement to visit your shop in the downtown area. Brodie and I will be making our way into different businesses in the down-town area to meet you and see how Cowboy Country can partner with you to promote your business, but if anyone has immediate interest, please feel free to see either of us before we leave tonight."

"What in the bloody world was that?" Brodie asked as soon as they were in the car. Actually, the question covered a litany of *bloody worlds.* He'd wanted to say *bloody hell*, but he'd managed to restrain himself. Because he was in the presence of a lady—even if she had pinched his arse in public and given away opening day of park attendance.

"Yes, I could ask you the same thing. What in the bloody world was that?" she asked. "Why did you butt into my part of the presentation? I was handling it."

Her green eyes looked about as wild as he felt. If he hadn't been so angry he might've noticed how sexy she looked when she was mad. But why the hell was *she* mad? She'd given everything away and gotten away with it.

"I didn't butt in, I simply steered you back on track. I understand you were nervous, but that's why we had the PowerPoint presentation." He softened his voice. "Why in the world did you not just stick to the plan we had agreed on?"

She glared at him for a moment that seemed to last an eternity.

"Because the plan may have worked on paper, but we were losing them. Couldn't you see that? We were coming to them with our hats in our hands, asking them to love us, as Jeanne Marie so aptly put it. We are the ones who are encroaching on their territory, changing the face of their community. It was our place to make a magnanimous gesture, and I stand by the offer. I just can't believe you are so blind you can't see it."

"You're right, I have been blind. I've been blinded by emotions that have no business in the workplace. Caitlyn, I signed a contract agreeing to open a profitable park, and you need to know that's what I intend to do."

Chapter Eleven

It was exactly what Caitlyn had feared would happen.

She and Brodie had been distant for days—since their disagreement after the town meeting.

How had it all snowballed out of control?

She'd thought about broaching the subject, but the way he'd been avoiding her made her feel so vulnerable that she always pulled back when she got the urge to reach out. Reaching out meant tracking him down. Reaching out meant pushing herself on a man who obviously had only been in it for fun—oh, and for business.

Business always took precedence.

She refused to let herself think that she could've loved this man.

No. She wasn't going to think about that.

So they continued to avoid each other in the name of

hard work. They both stayed so busy they didn't have to talk about what happened—or wasn't happening—between them.

Of course, there was so much to do in the time leading up to the park's opening that they hadn't had a moment to spare—or share a meal or kiss, certainly not make love. If things got any colder between them, they'd be at a risk for frostbite.

But there was too much to do right now to worry about that. Today was the start of the Red, White and Blue Extravaganza, an event to celebrate the employees' completion of the training program Brodie had created to get everyone "on the same page."

Caitlyn was busy looking over schedules to make sure all of the areas would be covered during the pre-opening employee event.

The Red, White and Blue Extravaganza was a peer review/fun day for each of the employees. Everyone who worked for Cowboy Country USA had been split into one of three groups—red, white and blue. Over the next three days each group would take turns enjoying the park and reviewing their peers' job performance.

Of course, nothing could just be fun when Brodie had a hand in it. Caitlyn had tried to get him to lay off, to let the workers enjoy a day of pure fun in the park that he so desperately wanted them to love. But the unspoken message seemed to be if they didn't buy into Cowboy Country heart and soul he would fire them.

Each day closer to the Memorial Day opening, Brodie seemed to get more intense, and Caitlyn's sinking feeling of impending disaster was nearly overwhelming. Just to keep the peace, she had decided she needed to choose her battles.

That was why she stepped back from taking the hard line on the setup of the Red, White and Blue Extravaganza. Maybe the peer review process would work. Personally, she thought it was a lot of weight to place on the employees' shoulders. Thank goodness, one thing Brodie had agreed to was that the reviews would be anonymous. The last thing they needed right now was for Carl over at the Runaway Stagecoach ride to find out that Karen over in the General Store had dinged him for lousy service.

Brodie's stance was that good service was good service and bad service was costly. The employees from top to bottom needed to get into the habit of providing good customer service even when they thought no one was looking.

Okay, he had a point. Of course she wanted Cowboy Country to provide the best possible experience for the guests, but there had to be another way to inspire the workers rather than put the fear of hanging in their hearts.

One of the things that she found the most distressing was that she thought she had recovered the Brodie she met that night of the Fortune wedding—her romantic, funny, kind, considerate astronomy nerd. But Brodie the Dictator had materialized again, eclipsing Brodie the Astronomy Nerd.

Did the guy have a split personality? Or an evil twin?

Now Caitlyn understood why it was difficult for couples to work together. The power struggles were killer.

Someone had to be the boss, and someone had to be bossed around.

If this project weren't so important to her father, she would just as soon go back to her office and research in Chicago and leave big business to the cutthroats.

Animals didn't talk back to you. If you respected them, for the most part they respected you. It was the truth, but she found it depressing. She'd been having visions lately of growing old surrounded by a zoo park of animals, but without a husband and family to love her.

That was why she couldn't quit now. She needed to stick with this project and see it through until the end. Maybe it was even more important to prove to herself that she could do it than it was to prove it to her father.

It was hard to keep her thoughts on the schedule. She found herself getting to the bottom of the page and having to admit that she hadn't comprehended what she'd read. Did she need to schedule two or three in the Lazy River Shootout? And was that for the day the White team or the Blue team would be hitting the park?

Ugh, she needed to go back and check. The last thing she needed was to mess this up.

She was scrolling through the computer file with the schedule when her cell phone rang.

She was tempted to let it go to voice mail, but then she saw her father's number displayed on the screen.

"Hi, Dad. Is everything okay?"

"It couldn't be better. I'm in the car right now, and your mother is driving me home from that godforsaken rehab center. I am a free man. Looks like I'll probably be able to attend the opening ceremony on Memorial Day. You have planned a ribbon-cutting, haven't you?"

"Yes, of course we have. This is such wonderful news. When I spoke with Mom yesterday, she didn't tell me you were being released today."

"It wasn't finalized until I saw the doctor today. She didn't want to mention it in case it didn't happen. But I knew it would. Hey, listen—" He must've held the phone away from his mouth because what he said next was a little muffled. It sounded something like, "I need to discuss this with her, Barbara, but I'm not getting upset. See, I'm perfectly calm. I can discuss business and keep a level head."

His voice was clear again. "So what's this I hear about you giving the entire town of Horseback Hollow free admission on opening day?"

Great. Just great. The only way he could have learned about that was through Brodie.

"Dad, it made sense. We don't have many fans in the town— Well, we didn't. But now I think people are starting to come around. We need to be good neighbors, and this was the best way to do it. We had to be the first ones to invite them to our *house*. It's amazing how far a little goodwill will take you."

Her dad made a noise on the other end of the phone that sounded like, *hummm*, before he said, "Well, no skin off my nose. I'll take the revenue loss out of the bonus based on opening day sales that I was going to pay Hayes. That way we should break even. And if your theory holds true, we may even come out on top a little bit."

So that was why Brodie was so mad at her. Giving away tickets meant money out of his own pocket. She shouldn't have been surprised, but she was. He was a business consultant. Business consultants earned a handsome reward for pulling off miracles. Still, the reality of it burned a little.

"I appreciate you being my eyes and ears while I've been laid up. You know, taking time out of your own research to hold down the fort for your old man. Your being there has given me more peace than I've had in weeks. Months, maybe. Since you've made the sacrifice, after everything is up and running at Cowboy Country, we will seriously revisit those plans for that zoo park you've wanted for so long."

Caitlyn blinked. Was this her father speaking? Had those words just come out of his mouth?

"Of course, Dad. It's the least I could do. You needed me."

"Well, I need you to keep working with Hayes. Follow his lead. No more surprises, okay? I need that park to open on Memorial Day. If anyone can pull off this opening, he can."

Ah, okay. There it was.

His words were like a sucker punch.

She was the eyes and ears. Brodie was the brilliant mastermind.

She wanted to ask him, *What about inviting the town to the park?* That was her idea.

Despite the fact that he was a Fortune, *she* was the one who'd made inroads with the locals—well, okay, maybe by virtue of his birth they'd had an easier time getting on the town meeting agenda. But again, *town meeting—her idea.*

But there was no time to sulk or demand credit. What would it get her, anyway? A medal? A bonus? Respect?

Hardly.

In her father's eyes she was the dutiful daughter. That role did not command respect. Love, yes.

Respect, no.

She had a vision of her mother, the epitome of the proper wife, who was always at her husband's side. She made life nice for her husband and for Caitlyn, too—arranging her life around them. It had never dawned on her until now how much of herself her mother had sacrificed.

Was this the way she'd imagined her life would turn out?

More important, was she happy? Or was there something else she was capable of that might have made her so much happier? At this point, she might never know.

Because of the subservient role her mother had always played to her father, it had always been important to Caitlyn to be her own person. To know what she wanted and what she was capable of and to go out and get it. That was why she'd broken the engagement to Eric. He'd cheated. If she'd looked the other way, that wouldn't have just been subservient, that would've been selling herself short, giving him permission to disrespect her. Because she knew she wanted and deserved so much more.

She wasn't going to let anyone bring her down or make her feel less about herself.

So why couldn't she tell her father that she'd played so much more of a role in the park's success than he realized?

Searching for the words, she opened her mouth to tell him, but all she ended up doing was sucking in a breath to fill in the cracks that were starting to form in her bravado.

"Don't worry, Dad."

"I'm not. Because I know that you know that the best medicine you could give me would be a park that's up and running."

And what was she supposed to say to that?

It was exactly what Brodie had feared would happen. Even if they needed to keep things strictly business, he'd hoped that they could at least be friends.

For two weeks, they'd been running at opposite ends, only discussing business matters. Strictly avoiding all things personal.

She'd gone rogue on him.

She'd cost him his bonus.

She'd cost him his mind.

But the thing that scared him the most was when he realized he *had* given up the bonus for her by not overriding her off-the-cuff offer of free admission for the residents of Horseback Hollow.

He could've done it. Alden Moore had assigned him the authority to do whatever it took to get that park open and off to a profitable start.

He could have vetoed her getaway.

The only reason he hadn't disputed Caitlyn was because he hadn't wanted to embarrass her in front of the entire town of Horseback Hollow.

And that meant he was going soft.

He never should have kissed her atop that stalled roller coaster. He certainly never should have made love to her that night and then spent most of the next week with her, but it had felt so right. Obviously, his brain had been addled.

It's just that no matter where he was with Caitlyn, it seemed to feel like home, and here they were the day before the opening, and they were still at odds with each other.

It was probably for the best—as long as it didn't get in the way of business. He would be leaving soon. He'd been away from the London office for far too long. This project had been so demanding there was no way he was going to leave here without another success neatly cataloged for Hayes Consulting.

He realized with a start that he'd neglected to book his plane ticket home. He'd have to ask Janie to do that for him when he got back into the office. Right now he had matters to tend to. He needed to do a final walk-through to make sure everything was in place for tomorrow.

Actually, he and Caitlyn should be doing this walk-through together. Today he'd only caught glimpses of her here and there as she bustled about taking care of the matters that had turned up during the three days of the Red, White and Blue Extravaganza.

He silently congratulated himself for coming up with such an interactive plan that gave the employees reason to take ownership. Of course a few feathers had been ruffled in the process of smoothing things out, but this was no time for the rank-and-file to take things personally. He needed everyone to take things seriously. If that meant losing those who refused to do so, well, so be it.

They'd only lost five employees in the process—three had gotten upset and quit when he'd gone to them with the tickets their peers had filled out detailing gum chewing, slow service and basic incompetence. He'd had to fire two: one woman had taken a two-hour lunch break, but had only clocked out for a half hour; and a guy who'd worked in the General Store had eaten a pound of fudge without paying for it. Caitlyn had taken issue with his decision about letting the guy go. She'd sided with him because he had claimed there was a certain amount of fudge to be given out as samples. No one had told him he could not indulge. So he'd eaten an entire pound over the span of one shift. Right in front of his coworkers.

Apparently, no one told him taking candy without paying for it was stealing.

Caitlyn had argued that they should do a better job at making the rules clear. Since they hadn't communicated properly, she thought the guy should be given a second warning. But Brodie had used his veto power and insisted that they make an example of the guy. It would be a lesson that the entire workforce could learn from.

Caitlyn had looked at him as if he were a monster and simply walked away. But not before she said, "It's your conscience. This one is on you."

Damned if that little dig didn't hit home, because it seemed as if she had delivered it with a double meaning.

She was right, actually, about the personal part. The second time they'd made love *was* on his conscience. He should've known better. He'd broken his own rule of not getting involved with clients.

Now he was paying the price.

Brodie stopped to inspect a stack of T-shirts that had been haphazardly plopped on a four-sided shelving unit at the front of one of the gift shops. He was just about to call one of the shop attendants over so that he could demonstrate the correct way to fold and display merchandise, when Caitlyn walked around the corner and nearly ran into him.

"There you are," she said. "I've been looking for you."

His stomach dropped before he'd had a chance to put up his guard. He had to be careful because the woman had that effect on him.

"You could've called me," he said and immediately regretted it because it sounded so personal. He straightened his shoulders—he certainly hadn't meant it to be personal. Although he did miss talking to her. He missed their banter, the way she challenged him.

Well, actually, he didn't miss being challenged. Not at work. But what little leisure time he'd had over the past two weeks had been quite dull since the two of them had taken a step back.

Of course, he'd been so busy all he'd have time for was to grab food on the go and fall into bed at night, exhausted—and alone.

In his weakest moments he missed holding her, he

missed the way she fit so perfectly into his arms, and he missed her smell. How could he have grown so fond of someone after only a week of intimacy? Well, really this thing had been brewing since the wedding in February. But back then he never thought he'd see her again. Now even the thought of their nights together had him breathing in a little deeper as she stood in front of him.

Today, her long, dark hair was twisted off her neck. She wore a green blouse that skimmed her curves and brought out the emerald shade of her eyes. And apparently she'd just asked him a question, and he had no idea what she'd said.

"Brodie, did you hear me?"

His blank look must've said it all because she frowned and said, "I've been over at the Wild West Show for the past hour, and things are not going well. During rehearsal, the horses weren't cooperating. One keeps raring up and the others just seem spooked. It seems that the horses are not adapting. They're still getting spooked by the gunshot sounds."

"What happened? Everything was going so well. I thought they had all the kinks worked out."

"Well, they don't. Some of the horses are acting very skittish. They might need more time to adjust to the sound of the gunshots in the show. I know you're not going to like this, but since the Twin Rattlers ride is still not operational and now with the kinks in this show—those are two of our biggest attractions. I think we need to delay the opening until we have everything under control. Or at least delay the opening of the Wild

West Show. My gut is telling me we're not even ready for a soft opening."

"Come on, let's walk look over there," Brodie suggested. His sister-in-law-to-be, Amber Rogers, was in the show. If anyone knew horses, it was Amber. She was a professional-level rider. She'd won rodeos, exemplified grace under pressure. If anyone could help them make this work, Amber could do it.

Caitlyn was a bundle of nerves. He could see it in her face, in the absence of her smile, the set of her jaw. The urge to pull her into his arms and kiss away all the tension that was etched in her beautiful face was nearly overpowering.

And it was further proof that he needed to keep his distance.

"I just don't see how we can delay, Caitlyn. We have media from all over the country lined up to tour the park, and we can't postpone at this late date. That in and of itself would guarantee the worst type of publicity. Not to mention, there is the small fact that we have all those comp tickets outstanding. Explain that one to the community."

He couldn't look at her. It was a jerky thing to say—even if it was the truth—and his voice sounded harsher than it should have. He hated himself for it. Yet he couldn't seem to stop pushing her away.

"So under no circumstances will we delay the scheduled opening. The purpose of a *soft* opening is that it's a *dress rehearsal*—a chance to work through the kinks."

"I understand what you're saying," she said. "But in a sense, this will be the *fourth* dress rehearsal since we had three days of practice with the Red, White and Blue teams, and we still don't have our act together. Don't you think the bad publicity derived from opening before we're ready will be worse than if we postpone?"

He shook his head. "We will just have to push through this and not let nerves get the best of us."

She stopped and put her hands on her hips. "So this is what it comes down to? You're the one with all the power? You're the one who makes the final call? I get no say in what happens to my father's business?"

"I am simply abiding by the letter of the contract that I have with your father. My reputation is at stake here, Caitlyn. I have to do what I think is best. I can't manage by my gut—there's no room in business for that. I have to go by facts and figures. I'm sorry."

"Wow. Thanks for that." He could almost see the anger radiating off her in waves. "Let's go see that Wild West show. Maybe you'll be able to pick up some additional tips on other ways to ride roughshod over anyone who gets in your way."

This is why you don't get involved, man.

Maybe if he said that to himself enough, he would be able to apply it to Caitlyn.

Deep inside a voice said, *Nope. Not going to happen.*

He had an idiotic flash of fantasy that maybe after all the madness was over they could talk things out and try to make things work. But then reality came crashing down. He'd go back to Hayes Consulting's headquarters in London, and she would go back to her research in Chicago. Neither one could give up their lives for the other.

"You know, I'm not doing this to hurt you," he said. "This is business, Caitlyn. This is not personal. Your father has certain expectations. And I need his endorsement for a potential project I hope to line up down the road."

"Let's just go watch the show," Caitlyn said, bitterness in her tone. "Don't patronize me."

They walked in silence to the ring that housed the Wild West Show. Even before they got there they could hear the horses whinnying and snorting. And it didn't sound good.

The director, Tom, nodded as he saw Caitlyn and Brodie approach the sidelines.

"Places, everyone," he said to the performers. "Let's take it from the top."

When everybody was on their marks, the director called, "Action!"

Even as the riders began to steer their horses into place, Brodie could see that some of the talent was having difficulty. Some of the animals seemed skittish and uncomfortable.

"Cut! Cut!"

Brodie leaned over and whispered, "Do we have other horses we could try instead of the ones that are so nervous?"

"We do have backups, but don't you think the director and the animal trainers have already thought of that?"

"So basically what you're saying is we're stuck with these animals? We have to make it work?"

"The backup horses might work if we altered the

show, or at least that's what Tom was telling me." Caitlyn motioned toward the director, who was sitting in a chair on the side of the ring. "But even so, it would call for new routine blocking and new rehearsals to get everything down. Brodie, what you don't seem to understand is that these are *animals*. Sometimes they don't follow orders. They are often unpredictable, and sometimes no matter how you try you cannot control them. They have feelings and minds of their own."

Feelings?

The way she was looking at him, tempted him to ask if she was talking about the animals or…them. But then a gunshot blasted, and the big white stallion that Amber was riding reared up onto its back legs, came down hard, lost its balance, throwing Amber.

Demonstrating her experience, Amber Rogers managed to throw her small body in the opposite direction of the giant animal.

"Amber! Are you okay?" Everyone shouted the words at the same time and rushed over to tend to her. But she didn't pay any attention. All she wanted to do was get to her horse and soothe him.

Amber was visibly upset, and Caitlyn hurried over to comfort her.

All Brodie could hear was bits and pieces of what they were saying.

"I know," Caitlyn said. "I told him…" The tones of the conversation drifted lower, and he couldn't hear the rest of what they were saying, but he was certain they weren't saying nice things about him and his decision to open as scheduled with as many full shows running as possible.

Brodie dragged his hand over his face. He was beginning to question his decision—but still believed that opening on schedule was in Moore Entertainment's best interests. And Brodie never failed to do as he promised. Still...

He walked over to Amber and Caitlyn. "Are you okay, Amber?"

"I'm fine, but I'm worried about my horse," Amber said, visibly upset. "Brodie, I have to second what Caitlyn is suggesting about not opening the show tomorrow. We aren't ready and the horses still need to get acclimated—"

"I'll tell you what," Brodie said. "You go ahead and keep rehearsing, and we will see how things are tomorrow."

Amber nodded but didn't look much happier. But Brodie had to commend her for being a team player.

He might be the most unpopular guy in Cowboy Country right now, but they were going to open this park on time. Because he had already bet the good name of Hayes Consulting on it.

Chapter Twelve

With the cut of a giant red ribbon stretched across the Cowboy Country USA gates, the park was officially open for business.

And it had opened on time.

Brodie breathed a giant sigh of relief as he and Caitlyn shook hands with the mayor of Horseback Hollow, the town council and a frail-looking Alden Moore, who had come for the opening ceremony.

"Did you see that crowd gathered outside the gates this morning?" he asked Alden, who had given the opening address, thanking the citizens of Horseback Hollow for making this day possible and, with Caitlyn's help, had done the honor of cutting the ribbon with the giant gold-painted scissors.

"I did," Alden said. "I did, indeed. Hayes, you did a fabulous job. Worth every penny I spent on you."

The older gentleman laughed, but it turned into a wheeze that turned into a coughing fit. He put a hand up to his chest and leaned on his daughter.

"Dad, I know this is a big day," said Caitlyn. "But you really shouldn't overdo it."

Caitlyn slanted a glance at her mother, who looked just as elegant as always, dressed in a feminine spring suit and pearls. Somehow the dressy ensemble didn't seem out of place at a cowboy-themed amusement park. Elegance and refinement seemed to run in the blood of Moore women.

Even Caitlyn, who was dressed in a crisp white button-down blouse tucked into low-slung khakis with a cordovan leather belt that lay just perfectly on her slim hips, looked effortlessly cool and chic.

Ah, hell. Who is he kidding? He had never seen any-one make a white Brooks Brothers button-down look downright sexy. His heart gave a regretful squeeze.

Brodie had to hand it to her. Yesterday she had been nearly overwrought with nerves and trepidation about opening the park today. Looking at her now, you would never know that she had been ready to reschedule ev-erything. But her ability to be a team player and remain calm when it really mattered were two of the things that Brodie admired so much about her.

"Alden, I couldn't have pulled this off without your daughter."

And then the strangest thing happened. If looks could have killed, Caitlyn had pinned him with one meant to take his head off. She didn't say a word. She didn't need to; her expression said it all.

But what?

Why had she taken such offense?

Thank God, Truvy Jennings chose that moment to ask for a group photo. Caitlyn's beautiful features softened into her professional smile as Alden, Barbara, Caitlyn and he posed for the camera.

"Truvy, I'd like to introduce you to Alden Moore and his wife, Barbara. Alden is the founder and CEO of Moore Entertainment."

"Are you the one who ran the story about the Twin Rattlers' malfunction?" Alden asked.

The reporter nodded sheepishly.

"Well, Truvy, you may actually have done us a favor by running that article," Alden said. "Because that meant we had to give you something positive to write about next time. I know you'll do us proud. Won't you?"

"If everything is as fabulous on the inside as it was during the opening ceremony, I'm sure I will have many great things to say," Truvy said.

Brodie spoke into his walkie-talkie, calling for the media specialist he had assigned to accompany her around the park. "I have someone who will make sure you get the VIP treatment today."

The woman laughed and blushed and shook everyone's hand one more time before she disappeared into the park with her guide.

Putty in our hands.

Moments later, Alden and Barbara said their goodbyes—he would come back to the park on another day. In so many words, he admitted that the excitement of the opening ceremonies had pushed him to his limits—at least for today.

Now, armed with walkie-talkies, Brodie and Caitlyn stood face-to-face in the midst of the people milling about, gathering their families, getting their tickets and making plans of how to best see the park.

"Are you okay?" Brodie asked. He reached out to place a hand on her arm, but she flinched and pulled away.

"*Don't*. I'm fine." She raised her chin a notch, as if proving as much. "I will take my post at the back half of the park. You're going to cover the front half, right?"

The edge in her voice was chilly, but her words and demeanor were strictly professional. Two coworkers coming together for a common cause that had nothing to do with anything personal.

As she turned and walked away, regret prickled up Brodie's spine. He reminded himself that he couldn't have it both ways. He was here to do a job, not get tangled up in emotions. And his job he would complete at closing time. After that, an ocean would separate him from Caitlyn Moore.

A muffled voice sounded over the walkie-talkie, "Twenty-four? Come in, twenty-four."

That was his radio call number.

"This is Brodie."

"There are some people here looking for you at the west gate, Mr. Fortune Hayes. It's your family."

He gritted his teeth. He really didn't have time for them. He needed to get to his post inside the park. But he remembered how loving and patient Caitlyn had been with her parents, and he decided to borrow a page from her book. Just this once.

"Tell them I will be right there."

Brodie made his way through the people milling about and saw his mother, who had obviously spotted him first because she was waving them over. Next to her was his aunt Jeanne Marie, uncle Deke and his cousins, Stacey, Jude, Liam, Toby, Galen and Delaney, with her fiancé Cisco Mendoza. His brother Jensen was there, too, no doubt to see Amber perform. They'd left the babies with a sitter, but Toby's kids were very excited to be there.

Oh, and there's Orlando Mendoza standing next to Mum. Looking quite cozy, too. Hmm.

They greeted him enthusiastically. His cousins slapping him on the back and joking with him about how nice it was to have an inside source for free tickets.

"I hate to disappoint you," he said. "But that was a one-time perk."

His family laughed and slapped him on the back.

They think I'm joking.

"You know, the jury here is still out on how we feel about Cowboy Country USA," said Deke. "But we're your family, and we had to show up to support you and let you know how proud we are of you for the inroads you've made as you tried to make this theme park harmonious with our community. Offering the residents free admission was nothing short of genius, my boy. Not that I'm a businessman. But I know when a gesture feels genuine. You did good, son."

Suddenly, he felt like the Memorial Day Scrooge. Not only had his family turned up, but he was also starting to believe he had been too hasty when it came to writing off Caitlyn's idea. Maybe he had been a little too focused on winning and making the opening a success.

Even if he did need to keep emotions in check, perhaps an apology was in order. An acknowledgment that he was wrong, and Caitlyn was right.

Maybe he needed to loosen up just a little bit. The ribbon-cutting had gone off without a hitch. Nobody had been trampled in the crowd of people wanting to be the first guests to step foot into the park. And right now communication over the walkie-talkie indicated it was business as planned. There were no crises. Or at least none that needed his assistance.

You're going to be in the park, anyway. Why not give your family the VIP tour?

Brodie pulled a sheet of paper out of his back pocket—a schedule of the street shows that would be taking place and the various seated shows.

"Let's hurry up and get inside," he said. "The very first Main Street Shootout is about to take place. You won't want to miss it."

Brodie deftly directed them to a place outside the saloon where they would have the best view. They'd barely turned around when two classic cowboys—one wearing a white hat and the other wearing a black hat, both clad in jeans and plaid shirts with gun belts slung low on their hips, tumbled out of the saloon and started making a ruckus.

Guests stopped and stared wide-eyed at the two

actors as the cacophony they were creating accelerated. The casting department had done a wonderful job in choosing the actors. That was something that had been in place long before he had arrived, and one of the things that Moore Entertainment had handled exceptionally well.

That thought was seconded by his family's reactions. They gasped in all the right places; cheered for the cowboy in the white hat and booed the bad guy. After the bad guy had gotten his comeuppance, they'd cheered and clapped.

"That was exceptional," said Josephine. "Well done, son. I wish Amelia were here to see this."

"Yes, where is my sister? I thought she was looking forward to joining you today."

"She was, but the baby didn't sleep very well last night. She said the whole family was up with the child. She's not sure if Clementine is coming down with something, and she didn't want to take a chance of bringing her out in a crowd. Besides, as lovely as this place is, it really is no place for an infant."

His mother was right. Family and children changed your life. You were no longer free to do whatever suited you; you had to think of others before yourself. His mind tried to focus on the struggles he and Caitlyn had experienced as they'd worked toward today and how each of them had compromised in certain areas. The strangest feeling washed over him—he hoped she hadn't felt personally compromised.

"What's next?" asked Jeanne Marie.

As they walked away, a street performer came up

to them and took a hold of Galen's hand. She was an older woman, a little crone-ish, but perfect for her role of Wild West fortune teller. Dressed like a gypsy with a bandanna around her head, a peasant blouse and skirt with jangly coin belts, she was obviously a brave one, approaching his family with her act.

Brodie was delighted she was doing exactly what he had instructed the performers to do. They were to always be in character when they were out among the guests, and they were to engage with as many people as possible. Both factors were key to Cowboy Country's ambience.

The fortune teller turned Galen's hand palm up and traced lines with her finger.

"You're a handsome young man," she said, fluttering eyes adorned with long, glittery false eyelashes. "Would you like me to tell your fortune? I have good news."

She made a show of batting her lashes; Brodie thought it was a little hokey, but he had to give her points for effort.

"Good news?" Galen said. "I'm always up for some good news. Knock yourself out."

"I hope you're single," the woman said.

"Of course I am. Plan to stay that way, too."

"Not for long," the fortune teller said. "You will meet a woman in white and be married within the month."

Galen laughed.

"That's a good one," he said. "Not gonna happen. There's no one in my life right now, and I'm not looking. You've got a better shot at marrying off my cousin

Brodie here than you do me. In fact, I'm surprised he hasn't already proposed. The dude is smitten."

Brodie knew he should set his cousin straight, but how did one explain *complicated*? Especially when he didn't understand it himself?

"Speaking of," said Josephine. "Where is Caitlyn?"

Caitlyn stood in the back of the Wild West Show, watching the guests file in for the inaugural show and reminding herself to breathe.

She hadn't been able to shake the bad feeling that had plagued her since yesterday's near disaster. Good grief, when had she become such a nervous Nelly?

When the stakes had become so high. That's when.

She'd resisted telling her father about her trepidations about opening too soon. And apparently that was a good thing, because her fears seemed to be unfounded. It was approaching eleven o'clock, and everything seemed to be going off without a hitch. They would close the doors on the first day at six o'clock, and so far, everything seemed to be fine.

Just as Brodie had assured her it would be.

The thought made her smirk a bit to herself.

She hoped he would be a gentleman when they reviewed how the day had unfolded.

Of course he would be. If there was one constant thing about Brodie, he always knew how to put the appropriate spin on things.

Except when he didn't, and in that case, he somehow managed to win you over to his side. Whether you wanted to be on his side or not.

And she did want them to be on the same side. In the worst way.

You don't always get what you want.

She was just about to go down to the ring to check on the horses and make sure Amber felt comfortable performing the show, when she looked up and saw Brodie and his family filing into the pavilion.

Her heart gave a little tug. She loved the Fortunes so much. They had embraced her and made her feel like such a part of the family—that big, boisterous family of her dreams. They were so engaging she found it hard to drag her eyes away from them. That's when Josephine caught her staring.

"Caitlyn!" Brodie's mother waved and motioned her over.

Caitlyn kept her eyes fixed on Josephine, but she felt Brodie's gaze locked on her. The intensity was palpable. In fact, it was white-hot.

Dammit. She should have gone down to the ring when she'd had the chance. Now, if she didn't go over and greet them, it would look bad. Really bad.

Just because things hadn't worked out between her and Brodie didn't mean she couldn't remain friends with the Fortunes. She genuinely cared for these people, and she certainly didn't want to slight them today by ignoring them. After all, Caitlyn would be in Horseback Hollow as long as it took for her father to recover.

She summoned her courage and went over to say hello.

"There you are," Jeanne Marie said. "We were just talking about you. We came to the unanimous conclusion that we weren't leaving the park without seeing you."

"Wait, I wasn't involved in that *unanimous* decision." Galen winked at Caitlyn.

"That's because your vote doesn't count." Delaney elbowed her brother. "Besides, if we're going to find you a bride within the month, you're going to have to learn to be nice."

"He is nice," Caitlyn said. "Because of him, I know what it feels like to have a big brother."

"Actually, after you marry Brodie, we'll be cousins."

Caitlyn felt color bloom in her cheeks. She still couldn't bring herself to look at Brodie.

She cleared her throat. "So what is this about finding you a bride within the month?"

"The Wild West fortune teller picked Galen out of the crowd and delivered the message that he would marry a woman wearing white within the month."

The family poked fun at him, and the apparent love filled Caitlyn's heart to overflowing.

"Be sure to invite me to the wedding," Caitlyn said.

"Only if you invite me to yours." Galen cast a glance at Brodie, who was staring at his smartphone a little too intently. "Or if you're going to let a good thing get away, maybe I'll marry Caitlyn. Her blouse is white."

The comment made Brodie look up. His brows were knit together, and his expression suggested that he didn't find humor in Galen's joke.

Why not?

It was just a joke.

Then Brodie's expression neutralized. "We should find our seats."

"Please join us, Caitlyn," said Josephine.

"Oh, well, thank you, but no. I need to go make sure everything is okay for the performance."

"That's what your radio is for." It was the first time Brodie had spoken directly to her since this morning. "They have a stage manager and director. If they need you they can call you on your radio. Join us—please."

A spark of emotion flickered across his face.

Was this a peace offering?

Looking into those blue eyes she couldn't even remember why she was upset with him. Well, she could remember, but suddenly with all those Fortune faces staring at her, eagerly awaiting her answer, suddenly it didn't really matter anymore. Then when the music cued and the actors rode the horses into the ring, Caitlyn didn't have much of a choice.

As they took their seats, she noticed that Brodie stepped between her and Galen, causing his cousin to shift down a seat, putting Brodie right next to her.

Jeanne Marie was on Brodie's left. She leaned across and said, "We're having another barbecue before Brodie goes back to London. You make sure he brings you to the party."

That's right. He would be leaving after the park was successfully opened. She supposed she had been too preoccupied with work to remember that. Still, it didn't stop the dull ache in her heart that began to throb with Jeanne Marie's reminder.

Caitlyn was glad when the others began cheering

for Amber, who had majestically ridden into the ring. With her long, tousled blond hair and athletic build, she looked gorgeous on that horse. Caitlyn focused on how Amber really was the perfect person for the show.

She could see why the Moore Entertainment casting and advertising departments had wanted her to be the face of Cowboy Country USA, but she'd declined the opportunity, wanting to stick to the serious riding.

And that may not have been a bad way to go. Her spirited personality and expert riding skills shone brightly in the ring. A less-skilled rider probably couldn't have handled the horse. Caitlyn had all the confidence in the world in Amber, but she was still nervous for her.

And sad that Brodie would be leaving. He hadn't even told her when. Had he planned to?

As Amber put the horse through the routine, Caitlyn leaned forward in her seat. When she did, her knee bumped Brodie's. Subtly, she shifted her body to allow some space for those long, muscular legs.

Strong legs that made her a little weak in the knees. *Really, Caitlyn?*

She refocused on Amber, who had just performed a rather awe-inspiring move with her horse, dancing it slalom-style through the dozen or so horses performing with her in the ring.

But a moment later, Brodie's knee was back against hers.

She had to fight the urge to nudge him away.

Actually, no, she didn't. A traitorous, idiotic part of her longed to reach out and touch his knee.

Instead, she slanted him a glance, hoping she looked a little disgusted. He gave her a single arched brow, which made her simultaneously thrilled and regretful of the flirtation.

Was this his way of trying to make up?

Damn him.

Damn him right to her bed.

No. Because he was leaving, and her heart was breaking all over again.

She needed to be stronger than to let a little knee bump—physical contact that wasn't really physical contact—lead her back into temptation. In addition to him leaving—abandoning her—he'd acted like such a jerk the past couple of weeks.

She had this strange thought that maybe he'd been trying to distance himself because he knew he was leaving. That the closer they became, the harder it would be to leave. She wanted to tell him that was just ridiculous. Pushing her away wasn't going to work.

She leaned toward him to ask if they could talk later. This alternating silence and arguing was just ridiculous. They were both better than that. They'd proved that by working together and getting to where they were today. But before she could form the words, a cap gun misfired in the ring. Amber's horse reared back on its hind legs. The misstep must've surprised Amber because she lost her grip and fell backward. She landed in front of another show horse, and that scared him, sending him into rearing panic mode.

One of the cowboy actors managed to jump off his horse and scoop up Amber. If he'd been a second longer she would've been trampled. But in doing so he'd had to let go of his horse, and that's when all hell broke loose.

The other horses got spooked, causing them to throw their riders. One of the horses knocked over one of the barrels and some other props in the ring. The noises mixed with the screams and shouting from the audience as guests knocked each other down to run out of the pavilion.

Caitlyn, Brodie and his family sprang to life, jumping over overturned chairs and dodging people, as they tried to make their way to the front of the ring. But they were too late. By the time they'd gotten down front, at least nine horses had broken loose and stampeded out of the ring, running rampant through the park.

"Here, grab some rope," shouted Deke. He tossed some that was used for props to the men. "Let's get out there before those animals manage to kill someone."

Chapter Thirteen

A number of men—a combination of park employees, locals and Fortunes—had managed to wrangle and subdue all nine of the horses before they could hurt anyone else. While the damage to the park and the Wild West Show area was major, the actors' injuries were minor and none of the park guests were hurt.

Still, that didn't even begin to cover the real damage that had been done.

People had captured the mayhem on video cameras and smartphones, and now Cowboy Country's stampeding horses were all over the evening news—and not just locally. The story had hit the wire services and internet and accounts of "Horsegate USA" had gone viral.

Members of the media who had been invited to the grand opening had managed to pick out the mouthiest, most colorful people to interview, and they had lambasted Moore Entertainment for endangering everyone's welfare.

The animal handlers and the Fortunes had secured the horses, and the managerial staff had cleared the park and closed the gates by one o'clock. The minute Caitlyn had gotten back to the executive offices, she was greeted with a stack of nearly one hundred phone messages that Janie had taken from additional media asking for interviews.

Brodie had instructed all of the department heads to round up their staff members and bring them to the all-purpose room in the training facility. He would give each employee strict instructions not to talk to the media. He was the only person who was allowed to say anything about Cowboy Country USA in any capacity to the press.

As far as Caitlyn was concerned, he could shoulder that responsibility on his own.

She took the stack of messages from Janie and deposited them on Brodie's neat desk, barely able to contain the slow simmer of resentment.

They hadn't been ready to open the park.

Caitlyn knew that, too well. She'd tried to warn Brodie, but he'd used his veto power over common sense to rush the opening.

Safety be damned, all in the name of getting in and getting the park opened and impressing her father.

There you go, mastermind. Get us out of this mess.

When she got to her office, Janie was buzzing her.

"If it's someone from the media, please take a message. Mr. Fortune Hayes will be handling all media contact."

"No, I'm sorry, Ms. Moore. Your father is on line one. He said it's urgent."

Crap.

In the midst of everything she tried to call him once, but hadn't had time to call back. As eager as Brodie was to please him, now she thought her father would've been the first person Brodie had contacted. Obviously not.

Oh, wait, Brodie Fortune Hayes only dealt in miracles and glory.

She just hoped this episode hadn't set her father back. He'd been so happy this morning at the ribbon-cutting. How had things spiraled out of control so fast?

She let out a carefully controlled breath, and picked up the phone. "Hi, Dad. Please don't worry. We have everything under control."

She spit the words out in one breath because she knew if she didn't, she wouldn't be able to get a word in edgewise.

"Are you kidding me? Are you *kidding* me? How can you say you have everything under control when we are the laughingstock of the evening news? The international news. I can't believe this. Hayes isn't picking up his phone—"

"He is debriefing the employees right now. He's instructing them not to talk to the media. I'm sorry you're upset. I tried to call you, but I didn't want to leave a message on voice mail."

She'd tried to call him, but he hadn't picked up. Caitlyn figured he was either resting or maybe if he got a second wind on the trip back to Lubbock, he and her mother had stopped to get something to eat.

"It was an emergency. Then we had to take care of business, Dad. Brodie is still debriefing the staff, and I just got back into the office."

"Don't take that tone with me. I should've been the *first* one you called. Instead, I had to hear this on the news."

He was yelling now. Full-out yelling. Caitlyn had to hold the phone away from her ear.

"Dad, you were the first one I called. I couldn't get in touch with you. I was in the midst of an emergency I didn't have time to keep dialing you. Calm down—"

"Don't you dare tell me to calm down. I trusted you, Caitlyn. I put my faith in you, and you let me down. I can't remember a time when I've ever been this disappointed in you."

"Dad—"

"Actually, no. You know what? You let yourself down. This disaster was caused by animals, Caitlyn. *Animals.* You are a zoologist. Animals are your area of expertise. If anyone could have prevented this from happening, it was you. You failed. Now I know. It just doesn't make good business sense for me to invest in this zoo park dream of yours. You might as well pack your bags and go back to your research in Chicago."

Caitlyn was too stunned to respond. Just as well, because after he had said his piece, he hung up.

She sat in her chair staring out the window, holding the receiver, and thinking about calling him back.

But why?

So she could absolve herself of the blame? Tell him

that it was his own blindness and Brodie's pigheaded-ness that created the disaster?

No. Because she knew she was just as much to blame. She'd gone against her instincts when she'd known the animals weren't settled and comfortable enough with their surroundings and there were props in use.

She'd let Brodie steamroll her. And that was no-body's fault but her own.

From here on out, she resolved, she would not allow herself to be crushed. By anyone.

Telling on Brodie wasn't going to fix anything. The damage had already been done.

She turned around to hang up the telephone receiver and saw Brodie standing in her office doorway.

"Was that your father?"

Caitlyn nodded. It felt as if she didn't have any words left. But really, what was she supposed to say?

"I was going to call him after I finished the media counseling. How was he?"

She glared at him. "How do you suppose he was? Did you send everyone home?"

"Everyone except security and the stable managers and staff. They're working with the vet to make sure the animals are okay. I sent the others home with the promise of a full day's pay."

Playing the hero again.

Caitlyn gave herself a mental shake. Being catty wasn't going to solve anything. It certainly wasn't mak-ing her feel better.

"It sounds like you have everything under control. So I'm going to leave."

"Where? Wait—what?" He waved away his words. "It's been a stressful day. I totally understand if you need to get away for a bit. Take the rest of the afternoon. Do what you need to do. I'll see you tomorrow."

She shook her head.

"No, Brodie. I don't think you understand. I'm leaving. I'm going back to Chicago. You don't need me. You can handle everything just fine on your own."

Brodie shook his head. "Caitlyn, I understand what it's like to live with a father you can't please."

She looked up at his non sequitur.

"Nice try, Brodie. But I don't think you fully get it. Sir Simon may have shipped you off to boarding school, but it sounds like he gave you a pretty good life. Look at you. You're confident. You're successful. You're a world-class business consultant. If life at boarding school hurt you, it didn't leave any noticeable scars."

She knew that wasn't altogether true. This man was so emotionally unavailable that something had happened to make him that way, something beyond the woman who broke his heart. But she didn't want to think about that right now, because she was saying goodbye. Someone else could try to save Brodie Fortune Hayes.

She was done.

He stepped inside her office and closed the door.

"When I was thirteen years old, I decided I wanted to go see my birth father. His name was Rhys Henry Hayes. He and my mother divorced when I was three. So I really didn't remember him. Oliver couldn't stand him. He used to just rage on about what a bastard the guy was, but I didn't believe him. You see, Oliver was super protective of our mother. He was seven when our dad left. I always thought his attitude toward our dad was colored by childhood resentment.

"I couldn't take his word for it. I had to find out for myself. So it was Christmas. Just before we were to return home for the holiday, I ran away from that fancy boarding school that you were ribbing me about a moment ago. I bummed a ride from a classmate and made my way to London. I was determined to find my father. He was living in a flat in Chelsea and I thought he was going to be the coolest guy in the world. He was going to put that stuffed shirt of a stepfather of mine to shame. He was my dad. He was my superhero. Or at least that's how I'd built him up in my naive little-boy mind. When he answered the door, he looked at me like I was garbage. He asked me what the bloody hell I was doing there and how dare I show up unannounced.

"Long story short, he told me he wanted nothing to do with me. I was nothing but an inconvenience to him. When I showed my disappointment, he told me I was weak, and my reaction to his words proved I would never amount to anything. He said, 'Your brother Oliver is ten times the man you will ever be and I want nothing to do with him. What makes you think I'd welcome you into my life?' I opened myself up, rendered myself vulnerable to the one person in this world I thought would show me unconditional love, and he spit in my face. Figuratively, of course. But it would have hurt a lot less if he had actually done it."

They were both quiet for a moment. Caitlyn was trying her hardest not to let his heartrending story of rejection break down her armor.

"Just so you understand why I'm telling you the story," he said. "It's not to prove that one of our dads was worse than the other or that one of our struggles was less than the other. Each person's struggle makes them who they are, and in some ways—in many ways—it defines them. I know my experience with my natural father has defined me. But in many ways you have changed me. You have helped me see that it's okay to let people in. That not everybody has bad intentions. I'm sorry if you think that of me. I hope you don't."

After Brodie left her office, Caitlyn sat there thinking for a long time.

Her workaholic father had always been hard and blustery, but she'd never had any doubt that she was his princess.

A princess he'd set on a shelf, out of harm's way—giving her a job instead of making her find a job; indulging her with lip service about her dream of opening a zoo park; patronizing her by letting her take over his office while he was sick, but never really believing that she could make a difference.

But the truth was she'd never doubted his love. The comparison of Brodie's verbally abusive father to her own—well, there was no comparison. She was the one who had been soft all these years. She was the one who had allowed people to walk on her.

That's why she needed to leave and start taking responsibility for herself.

* * *

Brodie had to fix this disaster. He would fix it. Even if it meant driving to Lubbock to talk to Alden Moore face-to-face, which was exactly what he was doing. Everything at the park was secured. They would be closed tomorrow, of course, as they started putting the pieces back together.

In the meantime, he was going to talk to Alden Moore. It seemed like the best way to get on the road to making things right.

This went beyond business and reputations and re-ferrals for Japanese theme parks. His stubbornness had nearly broken *them*. It all became crystal clear as he watched Caitlyn walk away.

Now her words still rang in his ears: *You don't need me. You can handle everything just fine on your own.*

She was wrong.

He did need her.

He'd needed her since the moment he'd first set eyes on her in February. It was rather perverse how it took almost losing someone to snap everything into place. Now he knew that he'd been afraid, he'd been too long on his own, yet the thought of loving and losing again terrified him.

Funny thing, he thought he was trying to protect his heart, and all the while he was setting it up to be bro-ken into tiny pieces. As he drove, he knew that even if it took an entire village to prove how much he needed her, he'd make this right.

He was going to win her back.

His phone rang, and he activated the hands-free device.

"Hello?"

"Brodie? It's your mum. Jeanne Marie, uncle Deke and I are worried about you, love. We want to know how you're doing. Is everything all right?"

It felt odd asking for help. Uncomfortable. Unnatural. When you asked for help, opened yourself up wide, you rendered yourself vulnerable. Ever since his encounter with Rhys Henry Hayes, Brodie had done his damnedest to button himself up and not let people in. That's why he'd become the spin master. When he painted happy pictures for the world, no one was ever the wiser of the thirteen-year-old boy who was still crying inside.

Funny, wasn't it, how he thought he was going to help Caitlyn Moore, but it was she who had made him over from the inside?

"Actually, if I may be honest, I've just about hit rock bottom. But I know what I need to do to fix this. But I'll need the help of my family to make things better."

Chapter Fourteen

Caitlyn had been in such a state yesterday that she'd gone off and left her wallet at the office. She hadn't realized it right away, of course. It was only when she had gone to book her airline ticket back to Chicago that she missed it.

By that time it was late, and she didn't want to drive from Vicker's Corners all the way back to Horseback Hollow to get it. Especially when she wasn't even certain that was where she had left it.

Plus, she didn't want to take a chance of running into Brodie, who most likely would still be at the office even at that hour. She was exhausted and much too vulnerable to risk running into him.

Early the next morning, she'd called Janie and asked

her to check for the wallet. Sure enough, it had fallen out in her desk drawer, the place where she kept her purse.

Hearing Janie's voice made her realize that would've been cowardly to leave without saying goodbye in person. She would've called, of course. She wouldn't have just disappeared without telling Janie where she was going.

But it was much better to do this in person.

More difficult, but better.

She was all packed and ready to go, suitcases in the car. The plan was to grab her wallet, say her goodbyes then hightail it to the airport where she would buy her ticket and board the plane. She would be back in Chicago by late afternoon.

She wasn't the least bit excited about the trip, but it was better than hanging around a place where she was superfluous. Who knew if she would even stay in Chicago? But she would regroup there and figure out what she wanted to do next.

What she wanted to do with the rest of her life.

The thought took her breath away, not in an entirely good way. She needed to stop being afraid of the unknown.

She just hoped she didn't run into Brodie this morning.

He would probably already be out in the park, supervising the cleanup. She hoped she'd miss him this morning.

No, she didn't.

Good grief, Caitlyn. After everything? Don't be an idiot.

She parked in her usual spot, got out of the car like

she had every morning since she'd come to work at Cowboy Country and started to make her way toward the executive offices, but she stopped when she saw a caravan of vehicles pulling into the employee parking lot. There must've been twenty-five or thirty of them—gosh, maybe even thirty-five? She wouldn't have given it much thought, but then people she recognized started piling out—every single one of them was a Fortune or Mendoza or somebody else from Horseback Hollow that she recognized from the wedding or the barbecue or the town council meeting. There was a whole parade of them, arriving with ladders and toolboxes. They all wore blue jeans; some wore plaid shirts, others sported T-shirts and most of them sported cowboy hats.

Caitlyn spied Deke and Galen. They waved at her.

"Good morning, sunshine," said Galen. "I'll bet today's going to be a much better day than yesterday. I see you wore your work clothes." He lifted a questioning brow as he took in her dress and heels. "Here, help Tim Marcus carry in this coil of rope, will you? By the way, Caitlyn, this is Tim. Tim, this is Caitlyn. She's my cousin Brodie's girl."

Caitlyn nearly choked.

Galen winked at her, and his harmless teasing made her heart squeeze. She couldn't bring herself to dispute him and explain that no, in fact she was not Brodie's girl. Never had been. Never would be.

So she changed the subject. "What are you doing? Why are you all here this morning? The park is closed."

Galen cocked his head in mock exasperation. "Well,

obviously we're not here to play. I don't usually bring my toolbox to a day at the amusement park."

"We're here to help clean up the park, to get you guys back up and running again," Deke offered as he walked by, carrying a power saw. "Didn't Brodie tell you? He asked us to come."

"Really? All of you?"

Everyone in Horseback Hollow hated Cowboy Country USA. Why in the world would they do this? Why would they help them?

"Deke, no, Brodie didn't tell me."

"Well, you'll have to take that up with him. I need to get this inside. This is heavy. There's a couple gallons of paint in the bed of my truck. Why don't you toss that rope over your shoulder and grab the paint? We've got a lot of work to do, and we aren't getting anything done by standing around talking."

Caitlyn was speechless. This just didn't add up. She thought these people were ready to run them out of town on a rail. Why would they give their time to help out the place that had essentially been put out of commission?

Then it hit her.

Of course. It was so obvious.

What Cowboy Country had been missing, that something that she just couldn't seem to put her finger on was the influence of *real cowboys.*

Well, here they were today, as if heaven sent.

She put the rope over her shoulder and grabbed the paint buckets. She caught up with Deke just inside the gates. He was talking to Brodie.

Brodie did a double take, and his face brightened.

"Good morning. I'm glad you're here. Even if it does spoil the surprise I had planned for you."

Surprise?

What was he talking about?

"Did you hire all these people to put the park back together?" she asked.

"Heck, no," Deke interjected. "This is what real cowboys are about. Helping each other out in times of trouble. We always put personal differences aside when people are in need. If you'll excuse me, I'm going to get to work. Are you here to work or talk?"

Exactly. Real cowboys.

She couldn't very well walk out now. Not when all of these good people had shown up out of the goodness of their own hearts to help out.

She turned back to Brodie. "Did you round up all these people?"

A grin spread over his face. "I did. I realized since it was my fault for not listening to you that I had better fix everything, and fast. You won't find anyone more reliable than these folks. With everyone pitching in, we can have this place good as new and ready to open by the end of the week."

"Excuse me? Did I hear you right? Did you just admit that you should've listened to me?"

"You're absolutely right. I should've listened."

Was this the first time she was seeing the real Brodie? Because there seemed to be no spin on this. No pretense or sleight-of-hand. This just might be the real deal. The real man.

But she couldn't quite let herself believe.

"Brodie, you're so good at what you do, but sometimes you won't get out of your own way."

"I can't argue that point with you," he said. "Sometimes I am my own worst enemy. But today I want you to know how deeply sorry I am and I want to show you that I can make things right."

"Since you're the man with the plan," she said, "tell me where you want me to jump in."

Brodie eyed her dress. "You can't work out here dressed like that. Don't worry about it. We have plenty of people."

"This is your lucky day. I just happen to have some casual clothes in my car. Let me change and I'll be all yours."

Brodie's eyes softened, and for a moment she saw so much emotion in those incredible blue eyes that her heart nearly overflowed. She wanted to hug him or at least touch him, but she couldn't. She might not make the flight to Chicago that was leaving this morning, but there was another one this evening. She would be on that one.

So she smiled at him, a sad smile full of regret, full of everything she had hoped that they could be, but would never be and she turned to get her clothes.

"Caitlyn?"

She turned back toward him.

"I'm sorry. For everything. I wish we could try—"

Oh, no. She was slipping. She could feel the steel pin of her heart being pulled toward the magnet of his soul.

Then felt him pull away and saw his wall go back up.

What is wrong with him?

"Caitlyn." It was her father's voice. She turned around, and there he was. There was Alden Moore with a hammer in his hand. "Good morning, to both of you."

"Dad? What are you doing here?"

"Well, I'm here to work."

"What do you mean?" She looked to Brodie. "Did you tell him what you were doing today?"

"I did."

"But Dad, I think it's too soon for you to be doing manual labor."

Come to think of it, she couldn't recall a time that she'd ever seen her father doing manual labor. He'd always hired somebody to do the job that needed tending.

"You're probably right. But I've also come to talk to you."

He slanted a glance at Brodie and smiled.

What's going on?

"Someone drove to Lubbock yesterday and paid me a visit. During which I learned that you are actually the brains and the heart behind this operation. And I believe I owe you an apology."

Caitlyn shot an astonished glance at Brodie.

He shrugged.

"Brodie told me you tried to convince him that the park wasn't ready to open. We should've listened to you. I promise I will start doing just that right now. And I'm sorry for doubting you. So that's all. Since the doctor says it's too soon for physical labor, how about if I take this opportunity to walk the park and get a feel for the lay of the land? I need to figure out where that zoo park would be best situated. I'll leave you two alone, because I think you have some things to discuss."

As her father walked away, Caitlyn turned to Brodie.

"You did that? You went and talked to my dad yesterday? And he organized the work crew today?"

Brodie smiled at her, and there were those dimples that melted her heart.

"Guilty as charged. But only on the first count. For the work crew, I simply asked my family if they could pitch in. It seems that if you ask for a couple of Fortunes, you end up with the entire town. That should say something about the going rate of a Fortune these days."

And there was that sense of humor that she couldn't resist.

"I'm overwhelmed," she said. "I don't know what to say except for thank you. Thank you for setting things right with my father. Thank you for bringing all these people here today to help—"

Brodie put a finger up to Caitlyn's lips. "I'm the one who should be thanking you. As I quite ineloquently tried to say yesterday afternoon, since I met you, I have seen you put your heart and soul on the line for the people and things that you love and believe in. You've taken risks and exposed yourself, and through it all you always remain true to yourself. You have taught me how strong vulnerability can make a person. I said yesterday there was one person in the world who had made an impression on me so strong that it changed me—and not in a good way. But I am so fortunate to have met someone who has made a similar lasting impression on me and has changed me for the better. That person is you, Caitlyn Moore."

He reached out and took her hand, tentatively at first. She laced her fingers through his to show him it was okay. "I wanted you to know that I'm ready to have a relationship, to open my heart and be part of something greater than myself." Then he pulled her into his arms and lowered his lips to hers. He kissed her long and slow, and she had no doubt that she was going to miss that flight to Chicago tonight.

He pulled away and cupped her face in his hands. "I love you, Caitlyn."

"I love you, too. Don't you ever let anyone tell you you don't have a heart."

"I don't," he said. "Because now it belongs to you."

* * * * *

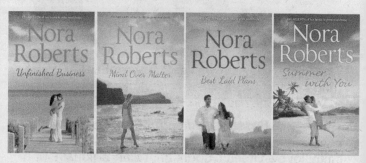

MILLS & BOON®

The Thirty List

* cover in development

At thirty, Rachel has slid down every ladder she has ever climbed. Jobless, broke and ditched by her husband, she has to move in with grumpy Patrick and his four-year-old son.

Patrick is also getting divorced, so to cheer themselves up the two decide to draw up bucket lists. Soon they are learning to tango, abseiling, trying stand-up comedy and more. But, as she gets closer to Patrick, Rachel wonders if their relationship is too good to be true...

**Order yours today at
www.millsandboon.co.uk/Thethirtylist**

MILLS & BOON®

Cherish™

EXPERIENCE THE ULTIMATE RUSH OF FALLING IN LOVE

A sneak peek at next month's titles...

In stores from 15th May 2015:

- **His Unexpected Baby Bombshell** – Soraya Lane *and* **The Instant Family Man** – Shirley Jump

- **Falling for the Bridesmaid** – Sophie Pembroke *and* **Fortune's June Bride** – Allison Leigh

In stores from 5th June 2015:

- **Her Red-Carpet Romance** – Marie Ferrarella *and* **A Millionaire for Cinderella** – Barbara Wallace

- **Falling for the Mum-to-Be** – Lynne Marshall *and* **From Paradise...to Pregnant!** – Kandy Shepherd

---

The World of
MILLS & BOON®

With eight paperback series to choose from, there's a Mills & Boon series perfect for you. So whether you're looking for glamorous seduction, Regency rakes or homespun heroes, we'll give you plenty of inspiration for your next read.

Cherish™

Experience the ultimate rush of falling in love.
12 new stories every month

Romantic Suspense INTRIGUE

A seductive combination of danger and desire
8 new stories every month

Desire™

Passionate and dramatic love stories
6 new stories every month

n o c t u r n e™

An exhilarating underworld of dark desires
2 new stories every month

For exclusive member offers go to
millsandboon.co.uk/subscribe

The World of
MILLS & BOON®

HISTORICAL

*Awaken the romance
of the past*
6 new stories every month

*The ultimate in romantic
medical drama*
6 new stories every month

MODERN™

*Power, passion and
irresistible temptation*
8 new stories every month

By Request

*Relive the romance with the
best of the best*
12 stories every month